Break of Breath:
Angel Syndrome

Book 1

Eden R. Souther

IMPRINTS

Copyright © 2016 by Eden R. Souther

All rights reserved.

ISBN-13: 978-0-9721003-9-7
Crystal Heart Imprints, Springfield, Illinois

Dedication

*To my three wonderful mothers, who gave me the strength to push through.
As well as everyone else who made this possible, through patience and a lot of encouragement.
To you who loved the humor.
To you who encouraged me when I needed it the most.
To you who helped find all the problems.
I couldn't have done it without all of you.
Thank you.*

One

The ever darkening sky painted the foreboding horizon. Rain was imminent. A pressure hung in the air, and the gloomy ominous clouds seemed to be a perfect reflection of his current mood. It almost made him want to laugh. Was nature mimicking him or was he the copycat?

Humidity and the earthy autumn aromas filled his sharp senses. The season was still fresh. This was one of the few places in the world that gave all four seasons equal value. Should the town of Seneal do any less, there could be a revolt by some of the more easily angered citizens. Personally, he didn't care for anything but the warmer months. Although the cooler ones meant that there was ample reason to have another body close to his own.

The unassuming rust-colored building loomed in front of

him. He had been summoned to meet with one of his only allies inside. The business he had with this being took precedence over everything else.

As always, the thick metal entrance was sealed when he arrived. A quick rap of his knuckles on the surface was enough to get the guard's attention. A steel slat slid open just above his eye level. The guardian was not visible from the outside, but Ravin was more than aware of the silent sentinel's presence.

Ravin cast a sour glare at the unseen behemoth and made a short, impatient gesture at the black glossy horns that poked out from his toussled strawberry blonde hair.

With a snap, the slat shot shut. The sound of whirling gears and clicking latches reached his ears. Moments later, the heavy protective hatch swung open, revealing the shadowy interior beyond. It had been days since his last visit, and as always, a thick familiar smell hung in the air. The humming of a priceless antique jukebox mingled with the voices of a midday crowd. Peanut shells crunched beneath his heeled combat boots as he stalked across the bar floor. Holoscreens played, but no one seemed to watch the flashing images.

With a dull sigh, he ordered two drinks from the bartender. One was his gracious host's favorite, and the other was for himself. Disappointment was not an option, or at least that's what he hoped.

There had been enough of that already. He couldn't decide if humans were getting smarter or if he was losing his edge. He was glad that humans weren't typically allowed in as patrons of this particular establishment. It had been awhile since he could say he was happy to not see the squishy creatures within arm's reach. On a busy day, the occasional stray mage found their way in, but for the most part, Sinsation was filled with a more immortal crowd.

"You're late, Raven," purred a velvety voice as a dark haired beauty slid onto the tall stool next to him. Her self-described caramel-sweet skin glowed in the dim light. Thick spiraling midnight horns adorned the top of her head like a crown of obsidian. Her midnight eyes reminded him of a panther stalking its prey. She flicked her long spade tail deliberately, like an agitated cat.

Ravin nodded. "Apologies, my lady. And, it's Rav-in, but you already knew that." He offered her the beverage he had purchased. He forced a quirky smile in an attempt to disguise his unease. It wouldn't make any difference; in a heartbeat she'd see through him. "You had some business to discuss, Sin?"

"Yes." Sin sighed as she accepted his offering. She lifted it to her lips and took a long sip. "I'm sure you're aware that the bounty has gone up again." Her words were airy and light, belying the severity of the situation. He knew that she was testing his resolve. He was also well aware of the fact that she was trying to decide if he was brave or stupid.

Ravin shot her a look.

"So I've heard." He tried to keep his tone as nonchalant as possible. Even though he attempted to maintain a calm outer visage, he knew that Sin saw past his façade. Of course she could sense the turbulent emotions inside of him: the wrath, a hint of pride, and perhaps a healthy dose of fear.

After all, she was the Queen of the Seven Deadlies. Well, at least that's what she claimed.

"I'm going to keep this short, sweet, and to the point, Ravin. I am on your side, but I have other clients as well. Every time the bounty gets higher, I have to stretch my resources just a bit thinner." She paused and let the implications hang in the air. "Bounty goes up, so does my quota. I'm not going to make special arrangements just for you." She stood, her glossy horns sparkling in the neon light of the bar. "Any questions, comments, or concerns? No? Oh, and if you'd like to take a quick survey online, you are eligible to win a free 500 credit gift card." Her lips curled into a grin as she winked at him.

As she spoke, the smile disappeared from Ravin's face. His hand tightened around the beer bottle until the glass began to crack. "I'll start gathering more." His voice was little more than a growl.

"Mirabilé." She ran her nimble fingers across his small horns. "I knew I kept you for a reason." The demon took a final swig of her drink. With a crack of energy and a puff of soot-colored smoke, she disappeared.

It took a few moments for Ravin to repress the shivers caused by her caress. An aggravated sigh left his lips. He knew that with every passing month, the bounty got increasingly higher. His persecutors redoubled their efforts every time he outsmarted them. The first anniversary of the day they posted the reward was fast approaching. He could only imagine what they would have in store for him then.

In a quick motion he finished off his beer then slapped down a few credits to pay for the beverages.

Ravin cast a glance around the bar to see if he could spot any potential prey to use as payment. Much to his dismay, he didn't see a single worthy candidate. His anger spiked.

In a low voice he muttered her name, "Sin," to send the enraged emotions her way. His wrath served as at least some form of payment. What else did one gift to the original embodiment of sin?

After the rage subsided, he left the establishment. He had to find Sin something, and fast. One way or another, even if it meant prowling the streets, he had to oblige. He'd made a vow, and he intended to keep it.

Even though he had not been in the bar for long, the world was dark and bleak. The menacing clouds swirled overhead. Ravin watched as a single bolt of lightning arched and spread across the sky into fingers of light, illuminating the early evening. Trees swayed and danced in the roiling breeze. Moments later, thunder rumbled in the distance. The storm was drawing closer.

Unperturbed, Ravin started off without a clear destination in mind. For the time being, his mistress would get what she wanted. Then he'd figure out what his next move was. At this point, he was going to have to change his game plan.

He didn't want to admit it, but at some point, probably sooner than later, the bounty would be too much for even Sin to handle. The stroke of an ever ticking clock was his enemy. As the reward grew larger, so did the force coming to collect it. Even though Sin was powerful, she could only do so much. Or, *would* only do so much. However, Ravin refused to believe that all his efforts had been in vain.

With a muffled sigh, he skimmed the thoughts of the other

pedestrians. Even with the inclement weather, they were still out, perhaps in greater volume than if it had been a sunny afternoon. The sun was the bane of many of the citizens of the not so quaint town he lived in. Many thrived in the darkness, while others simply preferred the safety that it had to offer.

His tail flicked with impatience. In the surrounding area, nobody was in need of his services. How disappointing and slightly aggravating. That meant he was just wasting his time. Ravin closed his eyes and with just a thought and the slightest exertion of power, he felt the familiar pressure around him. Energy clicked and fizzled against his skin. When he opened his eyes he found, with great satisfaction, that he had appeared in one of the best places for his type of business.

A cemetery.

Already he could sense at least a few possible marks in this place. Loss always made people more desperate. Luckily for him, that seemed to be the case more often than not.

With silent steps, Ravin walked between the headstones. So many souls he had never known unless, of course, they ended up in his neck of the woods. He hadn't been back to his homeland in some years, which was just fine with him. Hell wasn't one of the best neighborhoods. Sure the fire was a nice touch, but the tortured souls got old. 'I want a glass of water,' this and, 'give me just a drop of ice,' that. It was understandable, but it didn't make the broken record any more bearable.

It wasn't long before he spotted his target. A girl, pretty at that. Her head was bowed, and her fragile body shook. The grave in front of her was adorned with fresh bouquets, pictures, and other mementos. Her long mahogany hair covered what Ravin could only imagined were tear-stained cheeks.

This was exactly what he was looking for.

"It's sad, isn't it?" he asked in a gentle, wistful voice and stood beside the girl. "Life is such a fragile thing." His tone was genuine and full of understanding. Ravin's eyes glanced over the tombstone. He was not sure if this had been family, a friend, or perhaps a lover. It didn't honestly matter too much in the long run; as long as it was a deceased loved one and there was a desperate soul crying out for solace. His every word was honey-sweet bait, and the girl took it. They always did. She was waiting for someone to come along and offer the kind of help that Ravin had to offer. First things first, he had to figure out what their relationship had been.

The female sniffed and nodded. Her eyes didn't move from the engraved name upon the stone slab. "It was too soon." Her voice was broken and laden with sadness. "I miss him so much." She held her face as the tears surged back with a vengeance.

He knelt down and offered her a silken handkerchief from his pocket. When her face emerged from the safety of her hands once again, Ravin patted a tear from her heated cheek. "Would you do anything to bring him back?" His tone was smooth, and his eyes gentle. "It is tragic how your love can no longer be by your side." With his free hand he rubbed her back. He let the air settle to silence, disturbed only by the distant thunder.

Her body visibly relaxed. She looked up at Ravin with wide misty eyes. "He was my world."

Ravin could all but see the memories being replayed in her mind. Bittersweet images rolled by on ocean tides. Deep love pooled in the clouds of her eyes and rained out as tears.

"What if I told you that you could see him again?" Ravin whispered as he reached out and brushed the tombstone with his fingertips. "What if I told you, I could help you?" He could hear her sharp intake of breath, and feel the hope beat in her heart. Her misty eyes fixed onto him, they were full of soundless surprise.

"How?" She asked in a breathless tone. There was a flare of pure desperation. Ravin had caught her hook, line and sinker. If only all his dealings were as easy as this. Finally, something was going right after a day of disappointment.

A smile crossed his lips. "'I'd love to help you out, dear one," he whispered to her. "All I ask is for two small things in return." Ravin shrugged. "It's barely noticeable." He added to draw her further into his snare.

She gripped his arm tight, her determination hit him in a delicious wave. With a newfound strength in her voice, the woman vowed, "I'll do anything."

Triumph flashed in his heart. That was exactly what he had wanted to hear. "I will return to collect in the future, you need not worry about that. In fact, you may never even see me again." He would most likely have his mistress come to collect. Sin would gain all the benefits from this deal.

His willing victim nodded with renewed vigor.

"And," Ravin held up a finger. "When you feel that *need*," he emphasized to ensure she knew precisely what he meant. "You are to speak the name Sin, and devote the emotions involved to her."

"If it brings him back, I'll do it!" Her grip on him grew tighter. She didn't quite understand and she didn't care. There was no price too steep to have the one she loved back, and Ravin knew that. Humans were such incautious creatures. Then again, with their short lifespan, they only had a hundred years or so to waste on Eartha.

It took all he had to hold back a laugh of pure delight. "If you agree to these terms, all that's left is to seal the deal," he purred, and held out his hand.

With a confused look, the woman stared at his palm. Slowly and a bit unsure, she reached out and placed her hand on his. The deal was the most important part of the transaction. It was a simple process. Deals were paid in heart and soul.

Using one of his fingernails, he drew a line across the heel of her palm. Bright red blood bubbled to the surface. The demon traced a simple symbol on her petal soft skin. Energy concentrated in his palm. Before she could stop him, Ravin pulled their lips together. He savored the feeling that flowed between them.

Together, the energies of heart and soul twisted in his grasp, and the deal was sealed. The woman had been bound. She would have time to enjoy the love she brought back into the world, but down the road...

He released the girl after a few moments. "He will return soon. Go home and await him."

"Bless you," the woman breathed. Without a backwards glance, she sprinted from the graveyard.

Once he was alone, Ravin threw back his head and let out a bittersweet laugh. If only it was always so easy to get people to sell their souls. Who knew it cost so many lives to save a single one?

Two

Confident he had made a decent dent in the effort to hold off bounty hunters, Ravin started towards home. "Home" was a loose word, but it suited its purpose. In truth it was more akin to a bachelor pad. A rose by any other name, right? Right.

By this time, his roomie would be back for the night, cleaning the mess that Ravin had left for him. Ravin let out a pained groan as he thought about his roommate. Kazun, the reason he was up to his neck in debt, the reason he had to watch his back every time he went out. This kid had cost him a lot. Yet, Ravin couldn't say he regretted it.

In the moment between his inhale and the exhale, he was outside the massive institute that he attended. Being a demon made some things easier. Teleporting was not only a quick way to travel, but it was also eco-friendly.

He admired the academy before him for a few moments. It was one of the most prestigious in the entire world. The school, like the town it was located in, was rather unique even in the day and age that he lived in. To the normal passersby, the city seemed no different than any other. But it was special.

That was why he was in this particular town: it was a modern day melting pot. They welcomed beings such as him, as well as almost all species on the planet, from Angels to Demons, Vampires to Elves, and even Humans. Everyone could feel welcome in a place where estranged races could live in relative harmony. It wasn't perfect, but then again, no place really was. The university he attended schooled the races on the ways of the world. No matter how old, any student was welcomed.

The academy was named after the town it was founded in, Seneal.

Near the university there were schools for the younger students, an exploratory school for young ones so they could pinpoint their interests with hands on learning in fields such as cooking, sewing, and other basic knowledge classes. A Focus school for honing student's particular skills in the field of their choice. There were daycares for the monstrous tots. Most of the students were the children of people who had attended the university and had decided to stay in the area. It wasn't an unnatural occurrence for former students to start lives in the town. Seneal was a safe haven for everyone. If he was the settling type, this was the kind of place he would select.

Not that he would ever settle down.

Ravin wasn't that kind of person.

As he walked through the grand double doors, Ravin admired the ancient architecture. The headmasters had founded the school at the turn of Equilibrium.

Equilibrium had occurred millennia ago. It was said that two planes of existence had been brought together. There weren't many who remembered a time before Equilibrium, some even passed the event off as a mere story. The single most important event in all of history was something of a mystery.

How had Terra and Earth become one and formed Eartha? Only a few knew the real answer. The rest was left to speculation. However, it had come about, it had brought a strange stability. Thousands of years had passed and Eartha stayed relatively the same. There was little technological breakthrough. It was as if perfection had been reached.

Ravin had been working for Sin when it was said to have happened. Nothing had really stuck in his head well those first few years after they'd met. Truth be told, he couldn't remember much from back then. There was nothing left from his life before Sin had found him. Those memories were gone. Sin had said it was as if someone had ripped them from his mind. Not that he really cared. None of it mattered anymore. Who he was before the memory gap was no longer relevant. He was a demon, and he would do his job, steal souls, and cause general havoc.

Ravin excelled at his work. He didn't have a choice.

As if a gift from above, he heard angry voices from around the corner. Without hesitation, he took off towards the source of the commotion. A quick glance gave him the layout of the situation.

It was too perfect. Another deal was waiting for him. This must be his lucky day.

Four rather burly fellows had cornered a female who, much to Ravin's surprise, didn't look scared at all. Yet, her energy read as human.

How did she manage to look so damn brave against monsters that could crush her with a flick of their wrists? Ravin had to give her credit for that. He was going to intervene if her life was put in danger, if only for the purpose of making a deal with her.

"Alright, Sticks and Scales," the girl huffed, putting her hands on her hips and narrowing her bright blue eyes. "I'm going to make a bargain with you. Stop being so stupid, and I will stop outsmarting you." She grinned in a confident manner, even if her peanut gallery grew enraged.

One let out a thick, rumbling growl. The dragon was not happy this squishy little human was pushing its luck. This was unheard of. Who did this girl think she was?

"How cute." Smoke puffed from the dragon's nostrils. "Little Shelly thinks she stands a chance against us. You picked the wrong fight, *girl*." Dark laughter punctuated the other dragons' agreement.

A frown appeared on her face. "Really?" she snapped "Of *all* the names you could have picked. Of *all* the witty comebacks you could've come up with you chose *Shelly?* Boys. You have offended me," the girl scoffed in the face of danger.

Ravin couldn't believe what he was hearing. It was perhaps the most intriguing and asinine thing he had ever witnessed. Was this puny mortal trying to pick a fight? Something inside him told him to go to her aid, not for the deal, but to see what she was thinking, and what she would say.

"You're going to shut your mouth, bitch," one of the underlings growled, "or figure out what happens when you tangle with fire. Do you have any idea who the hell you're talking to?"

The girl tapped her chin and studied the males around her. The thoughts in her head were so loud that they forced their way inside his mind. *'If I'm going to die young, I might as well go down swinging… she won't be completely alone without me…'* A mischievous smirk pulled across her face. "Let me guess," she said, turning to the other dragon who had spoken. "You're all assholes who think it's fun to gang up on cute girls, trying to push them around to make up for your tiny—"

"Enough!" the leader roared. He took in a deep breath; electricity crackled in the air.

Even from a few feet away, the hair on Ravin's arms stood on end.

This girl had pushed them too far and they weren't going to put up with it. Before the lightning dragon could get the shot out, a backpack flew into his face and he was knocked back a single step. Wrath flooded from the dragon like a venomous cloud.

"Good catch," chirped the girl. Her sarcastic taunt was unappreciated by her tormenters.

Sticks and Scales looked at his underlings and growled a command to attack. Ravin didn't have to read the dragon's mind to know what he was thinking. The bastard wanted her alive. He would show this insolent human to be afraid of his kind. Above all, he'd teach her to respect those more powerful. She would learn her place.

The girl got the hint. Her eyes darted around looking for an escape. However, they had created a wall around her.

It seemed as good a time as any for Ravin to step in. In a blink of an eye, he was between the girl and the vicious dragons.

"This is quite a pickle you have found yourself in," he quipped and offered her a wink. "How exactly did you get in a situation like this? Unless of course you're into the whole dragon orgy kind of thing. Personally, unless they're all pure fire I think it's a waste of time."

"It's Tuesday," was the girl's simple response.

"I see." The demon raised an eyebrow. "Now, if you know what's good for you, I would suggest that you accept my protection in exchange for somethi—"

He never got the chance to finish. A thick meaty fist connected with his jaw mid-sentence. Rage flashed through him as he glared over at his quarry. "Oh fuck that, it's on the house."

Without waiting for her response, he lunged at his new adversaries.

Nobody interrupted him, especially not when they hurt his beautiful face.

He fought viciously. Ravin used the dark powers of his species to cause damage that these punks would spend weeks recovering from. He barely caught himself in time to devote his wrath and pride to Sin. If he wasn't getting this girl's soul, he would at least use the emotions that this fight was causing to pay Sin.

Ravin's fists slammed into their brawny dragonic bodies. With each hit, he infused demonic energies that would sink inside of them to wreak havoc on their internal organs and muscles. He aimed for their sensitive spots with most of his power, and for more defended spots to cause distractions.

It didn't take long for the group of dragons to flee the fight. They were young and inexperienced, and had apparently decided that the girl wasn't worth this sort of abuse. Ravin had won the brawl and saved the girl.

Laughter erupted from the human; he suspected that she couldn't help it as they ran away with their tails between their legs. After all, it turned out much better than she could have ever hoped for. If not for him she would've been dragon chow.

The demon wiped some of the blood from his lips and spat on the ground. The stain on the porcelain tile vanished in seconds as the school's magic got to work.

"Good riddance." He snorted and crossed his arms. With a sigh he looked back at the human. "You alright?"

The girl brushed off her sleeves and gave the male a thumbs up. "Nothing broken, nothing bruised." She smiled. "Thanks for the backup."

With that she started to head off down the hallway. It would have been idiotic to stay around and wait for a round two. Ravin had a feeling that she often let her mouth get the best of her, but she clearly wasn't brain-dead. She was right to be a bit leery of a demon's help. Like the Fae, Demons would only help if there was something in it for them.

"Not a problem." He shrugged and started following her. Truth be told, he was a little bit disappointed. He had wanted to get payment from her, but his anger had gotten the better of him.

"Looks like you got off easy," the demon remarked. She could assume that he meant the dragons, but he expected that she would understand he had defended her free of charge.

"Just lucky I guess." The girl glanced up at Ravin, her expression unreadable.

"Lucky?" He arched a brow and decided to let it drop. "So tell me human, what the Hell were you thinking when you started taunting four massive dragons?"

"Michelle."

"Well then, *Michelle.*" The demon repeated her name exactly as she had said it. "What possessed you to sass talk dragons like that?" He was dying of curiosity. She was either very brave or very stupid.

"They started it." Her tone was bitter. "Okay, well sort of. They were picking on this girl and I figured, why not?"

The girl shrugged as she thought back to the event. "Class had ended and they had cornered a more timid flower. I made a split second decision to distract them." The only problem was her tongue had gotten her in over her head. Again. "Everything ended fine, so there was no real need to worry. I figured it was better me than her."

More than anything, this intrigued Ravin. Such a delicate mortal had raced to the aid of another being, knowing full well the consequences had someone not intervened. "You are either incredibly brave or have no sense of self preservation."

"Mostly lucky, I guess." Michelle nodded. Things had a way of working themselves out. If it wasn't a demon saving her life, it was something else. Maybe she relied a little too heavily on luck, but it had kept her alive so far. That was all that really mattered.

That made Ravin laugh. "Those dragons were going to take you alive, and precious little humans rarely last long in their dens. You are one of a kind, Michelle."

"And I am not falling for your sweet words, sir. Sorry, not interested in an easy monthly payment of my soul? Best you go find someone needier than I." Michelle didn't have time to sell her soul. She quite liked it where it was, actually. She didn't have a soft spot for demons, and didn't trust them either. Michelle had run ins with his kind before. It was always the same, and it was enough to be annoying. Yes, she was a human, and no, she didn't have an overwhelming need to buy anything that would cost her soul. Unless it was a fancy new holoscreen.

Wait, no, she already had one of those.

"Sorry for the punch in the face, but you sorta wasted your time." Michelle pointed out. "Unless you were doing it from the kindness of your heart, then you too can be one-of-a-kind. Good job."

A shrug was Ravin's initial response. He absently rubbed the stubble on his sore chin. "You didn't see me going in for the catch? Dick messed up my opportunity with that punch, so really I don't think you're too sorry about that particular hit." He crossed his arms.

A smile sparked onto Michelle's face. "No, not too sorry." She laughed. "You were all ready to throw in your tagline and everything. Maybe you should have cut to the chase." She let out a soft tsk and shook her head.

"Where's the fun in that?" Ravin offered her a crooked smile.

He quite liked the tag line: it let people know he was serious. "I don't really need your soul though." It was only half a lie. He didn't need it, per se. He'd paid Sin at least a little for her work, but more was always better.

"Good." She stretched. "'Cause you wouldn't be the first to try and get it anyway."

The girl glanced at a clock and cursed under her breath. She ran off without an explanation.

Ravin watched as she fled from him. His instincts told him to follow. The hunter inside of him wanted to track the prey that rounded the corner only a few feet ahead of him. Yet, he waited. The human deserved a nice head start.

Three

Cursing internally, Michelle trudged towards the exit. With her 'savior' left in the dust, she continued on, all but forgetting him. Before those rude dragons had interrupted her, she had been on a very important mission: picking her friend, Jo, up from work. It was unfortunate. Jo's transport had broken down, so Michelle was in charge of being taxi service.

As she patted her pocket, another swear left her lips. Her keys were missing. Had they fallen out in the fray? That was probable. Michelle had a knack for getting caught in the moment. Well, if they had been misplaced, the Lost and Found would have them by morning. There was no need to worry.

Lian would have the spare.

Michelle snaked through the many corridors. The convoluted

hallways were beautiful and decorated like a gothic palace. Her path was winding: one corner turned after the other. After a few semesters at Seneal Academy, she had learned the best routes. Getting lost was too easy. Michelle knew this from experience. With a well-tuned mental map, she found her way outside.

The moment she stepped out, Michelle was greeted by a fat raindrop to the nose. The magic firelight inside had been so bright, she hadn't even noticed that a storm had been gathering outside. Great. This was going to slow down her mission even more. On the positive side, the storm coming would make a great excuse. Jo might not question her lie. Michelle did have a tendency to have bad driving habits. So what if she liked to go fast? She had never caused an accident.

Yet.

By the time she had reached the human dorm, her clothes were soaked. The air conditioner tickled at her waterlogged skin and Michelle repressed a shiver. Okay, so there was going to be another delay. A change of clothes was going to be necessary. There was no way she was driving into town with her white shirt showing off the goods. She had not signed up for a wet t-shirt contest.

Pulling her arms across her chest, Michelle ascended the spiral staircase to the first floor. Despite the school's integration of all the species in the school, the Dorms were separated, with a few exceptions. Humans were the sole residents of the Light Dorms. This was more for safety concerns than anything. Putting the more fragile inhabitants with the carnivorous ones would have been a recipe for disaster. By the time she got to her room, Michelle was trembling from the cold.

When the door opened, warmth graced her. It felt amazing.

"Lian, I'm home!" Michelle entered and set her bag onto her bed.

"Aren't you supposed to be picking up Jo?" Michelle's little sister Lian called from the kitchen.

Michelle let out a groan. Like she needed a reminder. She went to her wardrobe and pulled off her shirt. The cold wet apparel had to go. Digging through her drawers, she found a graphic T, jeans, and a hoodie. Once they were on, she felt a lot better.

"Yeah I am, but I sort of lost my key, so I came to get the spare from you." Michelle sighed as she combed her fingers through her short dark hair. She meandered into the kitchen where her sister was standing, enjoying a steamy beverage. "I might or might not have gotten into a fight with dragons."

"Michelle!" Lian almost spit out her coffee in surprise. "You *have* to stop doing that."

"What?" Michelle shrugged and went to the holoscreen embedded in their kitchen wall, her fingers tapped on the buttons. "It's only happened twice—"

"Three times," Lian interjected

The wall chimed happily and a slat opened. A mug raised from a small platform and was filled with a decadent smelling drink. Michelle grabbed it and took a sip. "Okay, okay, three, but really, I'm fine. No need to worry. It won't happen again."

Lian let out a relieved breath.

"Today," Michelle added with a wink. Her sister let out a groan. Michelle put a heartfelt, soothing hand on Lian's shoulder.

With a sigh, Lian set down her mug. She turned and went into her bedside drawer and came back with the spare key. "I'm heading out to study. Promise me you won't do anything crazy."

Michelle gave her sister an earnest hug. In all honesty she replied, "I promise. I'm gonna go chat with Jo, and drop her off at her place. I won't pick any fights." She ran her finger in an X shape over her chest. Michelle took the key, and offered a smile, which Lian returned.

"See you tonight, Mischa?" Lian asked

"See you tonight Lia," Michelle affirmed.

With that, the younger girl grabbed her backpack and a jacket, then left to go study in her favorite spot.

When Lian had gone, Michelle heaved out a breath. Lian was a delicate flower. Since they had been little, Michelle had hated to make her baby sister upset. They had always been very close. Now that they were in college, sometimes it felt like Lian was the one taking care of her, in some aspects. Lian made sure their dorm room was clean, and on top of that, tried to help keep Michelle out of trouble. Tried was the key word.

Her eyes trailed out of the window. The rain was getting worse. Not wanting to be out in a torrential downpour, Michelle hurried out to her Holo brand transport. The Thing, as it was named, was an older machine. It ran great, despite its age. When she got into the seat, she placed her key in the ignition space, and her hand on the receptor. After the recognition scanner checked her identity, the Thing came to life. There was a slight jostling as the transport lifted from the ground. Newer models were a lot smoother. For now, Michelle would forgive the relic from her parent's past.

Once she gave the Thing time to warm up and get comfortable

in the air, Michelle took off towards Exskate, where her friend Jo worked. The solar powered roadways were lit due to the bad weather. The specialized roadway plates took in the sun's energy, and during the night or bad weather, they would light up making the road easy to see. Michelle was glad for that. The storm was raging. Her windshield wipers were working with furious speed. Was some weather spirit angry? Most of the time, it was hard to tell. Despite the peace Equilibrium had brought, there was always a touch of chaos. If it was a spirit, Michelle hoped they calmed their ass down. There was no reason for a storm this bad.

Luckily, Exskate wasn't far from campus. The outside of the rink was lit, so it was easy to see in the rain. Michelle parked as close as she could and pulled the key from its spot. Taking a deep breath, she readied herself for the mad dash to the door.

"One. Two." She let out her breath. "Three." With all her might, Michelle swung the door open and bolted. Droplets pelted at her like wet bullets. Dodging a large puddle, the girl battled through the storm. The moment she was under the overhang, Michelle was relieved. She didn't mind the rain when it was a light trickle, but the downpour was annoying. She found herself soaked through. Again.

Walking through the automatic door, Michelle felt instant respite. The entry space between outside and inside had a drying chamber. There was a burst of magically enhanced wind, and she was dry. The commodity was for safety reasons, but Michelle liked to think of it as a personal favor. With silent thanks, she continued on her path inside.

The doorman didn't stop her for payment. Student admission

was seven credits for entrance into the family fun center, but everyone there knew Michelle. She never skated anyway. When she was little, Michelle had owned roller skates, they were fun and she was decent at moving around in them. This rink was a Holoskating rink. It was all top-of-the-line Hover technology. Aside from her transport, Michelle was awful at anything Hover. Hoverboards, Hoverskates, HoverChairs, you name it, Michelle always found a way back to the ground. For the most part, she found it by the way of falling. There was a disconnect. Something about being suspended in the air didn't make sense to her body.

Michelle wandered to the manager's room and poked her head in. Jo was nowhere to be seen. With an impatient sigh, Michelle went down the line. First, the gift shop: standing there was a rather handsome lanky young man with messy blonde hair.

"Hey Beau, have you seen JoJo?" Michelle asked.

Beau looked around and squinted. He shook his head and replied with a thick overseas accent "We 'ave been short staved today. I zink she is making up for lost 'ands."

Of course. They were always missing someone. Michelle was not surprised. With thanks to Beau, she headed off. If she wasn't in the manager's den and Beau didn't know where she was, that meant one thing. Michelle trudged to the bathroom. Walking past the automatic door, she was greeted with the strangest of sounds.

"Did Cthulhu take a dump?" Michelle quipped. A sound of disdain reverberated from the middle stall. She had found her JoJo. The sound of the plunger continued with renewed vigor. There was the silence. A flush. Then, a sigh of relief. The door swung open. Michelle had to tilt her head back to look at her 6'1" friend in the eye.

"Score one for the Amazonians," Michelle winked, but Jo was not amused.

"Don't make me smack you with this thing, Mischa," Jo threatened, holding the plunger like a mace, "you know I will."

Michelle held up her hands in surrender. She had already dealt with the crappy weather. There was no way she was going to deal with a literally crappy plunger. Both of them started laughing, then together they walked out of the now clean bathroom.

"If I didn't know you, Jo," Michelle said, walking beside her best friend, "I would have actually thought you would have hit me with that." She looked over at Jo, who had a stupid grin on her face.

"I might have." Jo replied, "I mean, you are full of shit."

"Jo, I am offended right now." Michelle feigned a pout, "You are being so mean to me. I might complain to a higher authority."

"I'm the General Manager. I might charge you an entrance fee."

Michelle narrowed her eyes. Jo was one of the few people who could deflect her sass. It was one of the reasons they got along so well. Michelle needed someone to keep her in check. Jo was a kind soul, very caring: she gave to charities and often helped out in a local soup kitchen. The tall woman was one of the coolest people Michelle knew.

"So how long until your transport is fixed?" Michelle asked as they reached the concession stand. Part of their deal was that Michelle was allowed to get free food for her transportation duties.

"Probably tonight or tomorrow. They will be bringing it by

when it is." Jo put in Michelle's usual order. The cooks would have it done in no time. They were used to Michelle being there a good chunk of her day, hanging out or bothering Jo. Her friend had offered to hire her, but Michelle always declined. Even if she did help out from time to time when they were short staffed, Jo always got the same answer, "I don't have time, I have to look out for Lia."

"So, why were you late?" Jo grabbed Michelle's food from the window and handed it to her.

Michelle moved to a table, food in hand. With a proud sigh she admitted, "I might have picked a fight with some dragons."

"Again?" Jo's brow quirked.

"Why does everyone keep acting like it's a big deal?" Michelle huffed and stuffed a handful of fries into her mouth. "I mean, they started it. Sort of. I intervened so they didn't stick their dicks where they didn't belong."

"Michelle, you're one person. You don't have to save everyone," Jo pointed out. "You have enough on your plate with Lian."

"Well what about you?" The accusation came out harsher than Michelle had intended. "You insist on traveling in that old run-down thing. Your transport is older than we are and you *know* your dad would give you one if you asked."

"There is a difference between wanting to make it on my own and you putting your life in danger. You're right, I could have anything I could ever desire with a phone call, but that isn't what I *want*. I like being responsible and working hard for something." Jo crossed her arms defiantly.

"Maybe I like being the hero." Michelle dug into her burger. This wasn't the first time the two had this conversation. Michelle had a habit of trying to watch out for everyone, and in return, everyone did their best to watch over her. No one wanted to see her hurt. Michelle could be reckless, but it made her happy to stick up for those who didn't have a voice.

Jo leaned back in her chair and sighed. "Don't forget, you're only human."

"How could I forget?" Michelle smiled. "It makes the others drop their guard. No one would expect a simple human like me to take a stand. When I do, you should see the look in their eyes. For a moment, I'm not just *some girl* to them. "

Jo leaned over and messed with Michelle's hair, "Mischa."

"Yes?"

"You are absolutely and totally nuts." Jo returned her friend's smile. "And I love you for it."

Michelle couldn't help but laugh. Though she knew deep down everyone was right, she couldn't help herself. When she was younger, her sister had been in danger, and Michelle hadn't been able to do anything about it. Lian had once been a happy, optimistic sunflower. Michelle had watched as Lian wilted. With all her might, Mischa fought to keep her sister safe. She remembered the pain of seeing Lian injured and in a state of deep depression. Months had passed where Lian hadn't spoken. It had been the hardest time of their lives, and battling dragons felt like nothing in comparison.

If she could help it, no one else would ever have to suffer the way Lian had. Humans were the underdogs of Eartha. They didn't have extraordinary strength or speed. Magic was a rare gift, where in many other species, it was natural. Because of this, they were often looked down on as lesser and weaker. Michelle strived to break this notion. Even if her flesh was fragile, she would never let it show.

Thunder boomed directly overhead of the facility and Michelle suppressed a shiver. This storm felt off. A strange feeling of despair washed over her, but it was gone in a moment. She looked around but all she saw was patrons milling about.

"What's up Mischa?" Jo asked, noting a change in Michelle's expression.

"Huh? Oh nothing. The thunder spooked me, that's all." She grinned.

Jo nodded and laughed, though her expression was pensive. Something was worrying about her friend's reply. Something was wrong. As far as she knew, nothing scared Michelle.

Four

Ravin sauntered after the girl. His pace was leisurely enough to allow her to keep her head start. Of course, he did enjoy a good chase. Perhaps she would provide him with one.

By the time he reached the corner she had turned, there was no visible sign of Michelle. The demon let out a sigh, and sought out her energy. It wasn't hard to find. A thrill shot through his heart as he followed the trail of energetic mortal aura. It led to the double doors that revealed the courtyard. With a thought, he pushed them open, only to be greeted by the buffeting gale beyond.

He cursed. This wasn't a natural storm. There was a darkness to the tempest that could not have come from anything but another living creature. It all but obliterated Michelle's trail. It wasn't easy to find that dissipating energy, but he secured a loose grasp on it.

A quiet chime reached his ear. It only took that second and his focus was lost and the energy was gone. He extracted his holophone. A message flashed across the screen, 'Kaz Hockey Practice.' Tail twitching with annoyance, Ravin turned his attention to his dorm. There were many ways to find information about the girl, but he didn't have time right now.

Unwilling to get caught in the rain, he teleported outside his dorm room. The wards at the threshold prevented him from appearing directly inside. He unlocked the door with his key and strolled inside as if he owned the place. Well, he kind of did.

"Hey Kazun, miss me?" He winked at his roommate.

Kazun snorted and ignored the demon. He relaxed on their couch, guitar in hand. A melody filled the air, coaxed out by the human's skilled fingers. For a long moment he didn't respond. "Define miss."

Smoothly Ravin made a rude gesture at his roommate. "You so did." He walked into the kitchen and pulled out an old piece of pizza. "Anything fun happen while I was gone?"

A simple shake of his head was the only response that Kazun gave. Instead of giving an explanation of the great nothings that had happened, he finished the melody that he was strumming. The song was one of the ones that Kaz's father had written a few years ago. It was his father who had taught him how to play, and because of his teaching, Kazun was rather accomplished at the instrument.

Ravin examined his friend as he played. "So how's your dad

been?" He knew that the bond between father and son was a very powerful one!

The boy sighed, "Dunno, I haven't gotten to see him in a while." The fingers on his guitar strings stilled and the sound faded away into nothing. "I miss him." Kazun's tone was almost inaudible. There was melancholy sparkling in the boy's brown eyes.

"That's part of college." Ravin walked over and ruffled his hair. "With any luck you'll get to see your family again soon."

"Thanks, Rav." Kaz set his guitar in the stand and stood up with a stretch. "Hey, I have to go to practice soon." He absently ran a hand through his dark brown hair. "You gonna come with me, creeper?" One of his favorite things to do was tease his roommate and best friend. Kazun was well aware of the fact that Ravin could cause him great bodily harm if he wanted to. Happily, Ravin hadn't.

With a chuckle Ravin rolled his eyes. "I'd love to stalk you, though, you've got plenty of fan girls doing that already without my help."

A groan escaped his lips. "Don't remind me." If there was one thing Kaz couldn't stand, it was his rabid fans. He wasn't even sure how he had gotten them. He was a freshman! There were plenty of more interesting players on the hockey team. He was a defenseman, nothing special. Sure he had been one of the first picked for the season and had gotten a scholarship because of how well he had played in Focus School.

Ok, so maybe he could kind of see why he had attracted the fanatics, but that didn't mean he had to be fond of it. He was rather partial to not being stalked. He wouldn't have believed back in

Focus School that this would be one of the results of getting into his dream school. Most of the guys called them 'fan girls' behind their backs, but they'd overhead and taken it as a compliment.

It wasn't.

He grabbed his stinky gear bag and looked at his friend. "Shall we?" He gestured to the door.

Ravin pinched his nose. "You'd think after so many years they'd have a way to neutralize your man stank." The odor had permeated most of the ice rink. Their dorm was the only escape Ravin had from it.

"It's been years, Ravin, I thought you'd be used to it." Kazun retorted. "You could always be the one to try to find the solution."

The demon let out an offended sound. "I have a sensitive nose."

Kazun shook his head. "You're such a martyr."

"I'm going to pretend I didn't hear that, now get your ass out of here. You are not going to blame me for being late again." Ravin pushed Kaz out the door and pulled it shut behind them.

Kazun rolled his eyes and walked down the hall, away from their room. "You are a terrible friend."

"I'm the worst friend!" Ravin declared, probably more enthusiastically than he should have.

Kaz' laughter echoed. "I don't even know why I keep you."

"It's because I'm beautiful, isn't it?"

All Kazun could do was shake his head and push open the doors to the outside world. He braced himself for the storm that slammed into him like a truck. He pulled the collar of his jacket up to protect his neck. "I thought that's why you keep me," Kaz called above the hammering of the rain.

Ravin yawned lazily. "We have the perfect reason to keep each other. Nobody can beat our beautiful team." The demon cut himself off with a sudden gasp. "That's how you guys should win all your games this year."

"You are insane, Ravin." Kaz sighed, then again, what else did one expect from a demon?

"I'm going to go insane if the bounty keeps going up." Ravin kicked a puddle and grimaced at his soaked shoe.

Kaz paled and shrank into his jacket. "It went up again?"

The demon nodded. "It's been going up pretty regularly, Kaz." Ravin cast a wary glance around and fell in step with his friend. "We might need to skip town for a few weeks. A vacation would be nice, don't you think?"

"Didn't we come to Seneal because the conflicting energies would disguise me?" Kaz stuffed his hands in his pockets to protect them from the chill.

"They won't mean anything if there's more money on your head than most countries make in a year." Ravin's tail twitched. "We'll talk more about this later."

It took them a few minutes to reach the rink. They were greeted by a welcoming blast of cold air that embraced them like an icy hug. While the technology existed to make the building warm and the ice cold, old traditions prevented such modern interference. That was one of Kazun's favorite parts about this place. The scents of the rubber floor and old popcorn filled him with a sense of delight.

Even so far away from the locker room, they could hear the music blaring at full blast. The familiar tunes sent his heart racing and readied him for the practice to come. He supposed what he felt could be likened to nostalgia—hockey was one of his absolute favorite things to do in the entire world. Nothing would ever change that. He waved to Ravin as his roommate headed towards the bleachers.

Inside the locker room, he was greeted by the familiar sight of his teammates, some more dressed than others. He was used to being around half-naked men, so it no longer bothered him. He used to be so shy about changing in front of all the other people. Now it was a part of who he was.

His teammates came in all shapes and sizes. Their two star players were identical twin dragons who liked to switch identities and see who noticed. The 'enforcer' of the team, a massive werewolf, towered over all of them. Opposing players only messed with him once, and then they learned better. The team represented a fair cross section of the population of the town: vampires, fae, spirits, dryads. They even had a Foo Dog who served as a goalie. They weren't exclusively all male either, there was one female on the team, a Valkyrie who was their 'pest.'

Jaden—their goalie—stood in the corner with his arms crossed, shooting venomous glares at anyone who dared to glance his way.

Kaz raised a hand and offered a smile. "Hey Jaden, hey Hrist."

"It's about time you got here Kaz." Hrist poked her head out from behind her on-again, off-again boyfriend's back. She brushed some of her platinum blonde hair behind her ear and batted her wide blue eyes in an attempt to disarm him. "If you don't pick up your shit, you're going to get kicked off the team."

He flushed. "Sorry Hrist." He edged away from Jaden, who continued to glower at him. Kazun made his way to his locker and sat down in front of it.

There was a silvery chuckle from behind Kaz. The team's resident elf approached and placed a hand on his shoulder. Letvan was known for being graceful, powerful, and attractive as hell. With a pearly white smile, Letvan comforted Kaz, "Don't pay much mind to Hrist."

Letvan tossed his long braid over his shoulder and looked at the couple, emerald green eyes gleaming. "She likes to be the Alpha male, isn't that right, Jay?"

The bulky, dark-skinned goalie grunted, his jade eyes sharp. Uncomfortable shivers went down Kazun's spine.

"Such a sweetie," Letvan continued to tease. "Hrist, get your clothes on so I don't get turned into dog chow."

"Make me," the female challenged. Seconds later, she emerged from behind Jaden in full gear and made an uncouth motion. "Hurry up. You guys take forever to get dressed." With that, she exited through the door that lead to the rink proper.

Kaz shook his head and stripped off his shirt. "Thanks Letvan." He smiled at his friend as he started to pull on his gear.

The elf responded in his lyrical native language.

Even with only a limited knowledge of the Elvan language, Kazun knew that his friend had said 'You're welcome.' Kaz caught his reflection in the mirror and took stock of his damp self. Like the rest of the team, he had a bit of diversity in himself. Sure, he was a boring human and his mother's side had been in this country for generations, but his father had emigrated from Nippon.

Those features were prominent, to him at least. That could have been a reason that the 'fan girls' loved him so much. Not many people left their ancestral homelands anymore.

The loud pulsing beat of the bassline got his blood racing and his mind prepared for what was to come. It didn't matter to him that it was only a practice, he treated every moment he was on the ice with the same intensity. True, he kicked it up a notch or two for a game, but he always pushed himself so that his best increased. That is why he got his place on the team.

Once he had gotten changed into his hockey gear, he made his way out to the rink. His blades slid with flawless ease across the freshly resurfaced ice.

From up in the bleachers, Ravin had to admit his friend had quite the ability on his skates. It wasn't that the demon couldn't ice skate; he didn't have the grace that Kazun possessed. Most of the time he cheated, and used his mental abilities to hold himself upright.

He watched the multitude of pretty-boys (and girl) that made up the team proceed with various warm-up stretches and exercises. Soon they were skating and moving like a well-oiled machine.

It didn't take long for boredom to attack Ravin. He could hear Kazun's voice in his head, *'you have the attention span of a goldfish.'* He'd lost track of how many times his roommate had said those very words. Of course, his natural response was, *'Hey. I represent that statement.'* The demon rested his head in his hands. "Am I really having this conversation with myself?" he asked. When there was no response he added, "Yes. Yes, I am."

He glanced to make sure no one was listening to him. Much to his relief, the rink was pretty much empty. Very few people were permitted into the stands during practices.

That's when he spotted her.

Sitting across the way was the same dark haired beauty he had defended earlier. He couldn't believe his luck. What were the chances? He was quite the fan of this delightful fortune.

With smooth movements, Ravin padded along the bleachers towards her. "Hey." He waved a hand as he approached the girl. "What are you doing here?"

A deer-in-the-headlights look appeared on her face. She brushed the hair from her eye and behind her ear. Without reason, she began to tremble like a leaf. She looked up at the demon. It didn't take a rocket surgeon to tell that she wasn't Michelle, but the resemblance was uncanny.

"I-I'm s-s-sorry," she whispered almost inaudably. "I-I will leave... I-I d-didn't mean to be i-i-intruding." The girl stood and began to gather her things, packing them delicately into a pristine white messenger bag. Her eyes stayed locked onto the bag and dared not look up at the male who had horns atop his head.

If Ravin could smell fear, it would be more overpowering than the stink from the locker rooms. He was taken aback by the female's reaction. "Whoa. Hey. It's okay. You're not intruding. I thought you were somebody else." He reached out a comforting hand.

The girl glanced up at him and began to shrink even smaller as her sight lingered for more than a second on his face. Tears of pure fear bubbled in her eyes. An involuntary whimper escaped her mouth and she tried to back away, as if Ravin was some sort of rabid dog. Her bright blue terror-filled eyes locked onto the small dark horns he possessed.

He cringed a bit as the girl's emotion of terror washed around him like an acrid wave. The energy almost suffocated him. It was far too much to handle. Ravin could feel her staring up at his horns, he absently rubbed them. "Hey, it's ok... uh... female person." Oh lord, he hoped that she would calm the hell down. "Do you know a girl named Michelle? You guys look a lot alike."

"M-my sister?" The girl asked in a quiet whisper. Her anxiety only seemed to grow at the mention of the other girl.

Sister? Well that explained the resemblance.

"Yes, do you know where she is?" He tried to make his voice as nice as he could before he scared her even further. He hadn't even done anything to her, "I have something to discuss with her."

Silenced surrounded them as she stared the demon with eyes full of mistrust. She didn't know what on Eartha a demon would want with Michelle. Was her sister in trouble? This wasn't good, or at least, that was what she thought. As far as she knew, anything that had to do with the dark race was not good. She shook her head.

Ravin knelt down next to the frightened female. "Pretty please?" he soothed. "I would very much like to talk to her. She's not in any trouble of anything, I promise." Not that his promises meant much to anyone.

When she didn't respond, the demon poked her in the side. "I don't have malevolent intent, I'm trying to figure some stuff out and she can help me out," he whined, hoping that groveling would help his cause. He didn't like his progress with her, and by progress he meant several giant leaps backwards. If they hadn't looked so similar, he would have bet money that they weren't related at all. This girl and Michelle were light-years apart in terms of temperament. In addition, Michelle had a far more delightful curvaceous figure.

"C'mon," He struggled to keep his voice light as he poked her more.

Without warning he felt a hand grip his horn then yank down. His neck was jerked at a painful angle.

"Leave her alone, Ravin!" an angry voice grated.

Five

The demon tried to pull his horn away, but it was impossible. The intense, irate Kazun was gripping him with all his strength. If this hadn't been a clear display of aggression, Ravin may have been a little bit turned on. It wasn't his fault that his horns were sensitive.

"You wanna let go pal?" he asked in a low tone. His neck was crooked at an awkward angle and it hurt. If there was one thing he hated more than anything, it was pain. This was all his stupid roomie's fault. Who ran off the ice and up the stands in hockey skates during practice and grabbed people's horns? Kazun, apparently. How rude. Ravin thought he had trained his human better than that.

Kazun ignored the demand and gave him a sharp glare. "You

need to get out of this habit of messing with girls, Ravin." He growled and jerked on the demon's horn again.

"I wasn't messing with her." Ravin was unable to lift his head to look his friend in the eye. "I was asking her if she knew where her sister was."

Another wrench on the horn silenced Ravin. "Why does it matter where her sister is?" Kazun huffed. "You'd better not be making deals on school grounds. You know how absolutely stupid that is. The headmasters will kick your ass to Hell in an instant."

"Ow!" Ravin whipped his tail back and forth like an agitated cat. He whimpered, "I swear I only wanted to talk to her sister." The demon writhed and tried to escape from his friend. "Scout's honor."

A scowl crossed Kazun's face. "You were never a scout, and we both know it. Why do you want to talk to her sister?"

"Let me go and I'll explain," Ravin half-begged, wanting more than anything to be able to stand up straight. He knew he looked like a moron being bent in two at the whim of this human. No respectable demon would allow such behavior. He didn't want rumors flying around that he was some human's pet.

The hockey player released him.

"Go on." Kaz crossed his arms and kept a close eye on Ravin.

Relief spread through Ravin as he rubbed his sore neck. "I was on my way back from a little meeting with a friend." He cast a glance at the shy girl. "Purely platonic of course, and when I went through the school and found Michelle—her sister—staring down four big ol' burly dragons. I saved her, no strings attached, but then she ran off."

"And you lost her?" Kaz was far from convinced.

Ravin simply shrugged. "It wasn't on purpose. I got cocky." He took a step back as the hockey player moved towards the girl.

Kazun sighed. "Fine, I believe you, but that doesn't mean you had to take it out on her sister." He turned to the girl. "Hey, I'm sorry about him, are you alright?" His cheeks reddened.

His voice was calm and his face gentle. Of course, once he remembered that he had a pungent powerful man-stank, his cheeks' color grew deeper. It would be his luck to scare off the girl he had saved with his terrible smell.

The girl had watched the entire conversation. She was more than relieved that the boy had saved her from the demon. Her cheeks were stained with tears. She quickly rubbed her eyes and in a near-silent voice replied, "It's okay." Even if she was scared to death.

Though, the boy, unlike many others, made her feel a bit safe. Not that she felt comfortable with him, no far from that. It was more like she trusted him not to come after her violently. Probably because he had tamed the demon and made him stop poking at her. Now that she knew the boy had a bit of control over the scary creature, she felt herself breathe regularly and her heartbeat slowed.

A smile came to Kazun's face when she spoke. "That's good to hear. Don't worry about him, he's more bark than bite." The boy knew he only had so much longer before he was needed on the ice. "My name is Kazun, what's yours?" He had seen her around the rink before, she was up in the stands a lot. But, she wasn't one of his dreaded fan girls. That was a very strong plus, even if she did still look wary of him.

"Lian," the girl murmured in a near noiseless breath as she peered down at her toes. Lian rubbed her arm for a bit of comfort. Her timid face warmed with a fine painting of pink. As she fidgeted, she dared not look at either of them, though she was somewhat grateful. That didn't ease the tension growing and the tempest of anxiety that welled within. Lian's fingers dug into her sweater. There were two of them. They could overpower her. They could hurt her. With a shaky step back, the she attempted to widen the distance. Lian quivered on the wind of fear.

"It's very nice to meet you Lian," Kaz replied as sweet a tone as he could muster. But before he could, continue he was cut off by a shove from his roommate.

Ravin scowled down at his friend. "That is so bogue." One hand ghosted along the smooth of the horn that Kazun had jerked. "What, do you carry a torch for this dame even though you didn't even know her name? Are you doing the bear? What is this, a batty-fang? You said yolo then grabbed my horn bro? GG, broseph, way to 360 noscope me. Can you dig it?!"

Both humans fell silent. Most of the tirade had gone in one of Kazun's ears and out the other. He cast a glance at Lian. The girl had fallen another pace away and looked as confused as he felt.

"What century are you in?" It felt as though Kazun's mind was melting as he tried to process Ravin's babble. Instead of trying, he shook his head. "Doing the bear?"

"It's courtship with hugging." Ravin stuck his nose in the air and crossed his arms.

"Ravin you're not helping," Kazun snapped as his cheeks

burned. "You need cut it out," he ordered. "I don't have time for your nonsense right now, my break is about to end. So sit down and shut up."

Ravin's eyes narrowed. For a moment he mulled the human's words over in his head. Then, at length, he plopped down onto the steel bleacher bench.

The boy turned his attention to Lian. "See? All he needs is a good smack across the nose and he stops his barking. He's not too scary. He'll stay like that until I get back."

Before he could say anything else, the grating voice of his coach reached his ears. His break was done. "I'm so sorry, I've got to go. Could you stay here and keep an eye on him? Practice won't last too much longer and I'll beat him if he does anything bad, but I can't keep an eye on him and skate at the same time."

Lian blinked and shuffled her foot. There was a long awkward pause, but eventually she nodded. Not like she could get far. The demon terrified her, but her decision was a tactical one. As scared as she was, at least if she stayed here there would be witnesses. If the demon or the boy tried to harm her *someone* would notice. If she ran away and they chased her to a dark hallway— there was no guarantee. With a careful step, Lian moved to the other side of the aisle away from the demon and sat. There was no point in continuing her work. So, she sat and kept her careful gaze on the ice and watching the monster who sat a yard away out of the corner of her eye.

"Thank you," Kaz called as he worked his way out of the stands. He did his best to avoid his teammates' gaze.

The Valkyrie's eyes flickered with a mischievous glint. "It's so cute. You finally worked up the courage to go talk to her, Kaz." Her lips quirked into a smirk, "So, when can I expect the wedding invitations?"

He shot her a glare as he felt his cheeks turn cherry red. "Bag your face." The burning on his face only increased. "Damn it Ravin," he murmured to himself. The slang hadn't been used in how long and yet Ravin still remembered it? "Shut up, Hrist."

"You're adorable." She stepped out onto the ice and slid effortlessly to her position.

Coach picked up their drills to a fever pitch so none of the other guys could taunt him further. It also meant that he had little time to think of the ever so wary Lian. He would feel better about talking to her once he didn't smell like a heaping pile of hockey stank.

She'd shown up sometime during the previous semester. Like clockwork she appeared and did her homework without any interruption. At first everyone had assumed she was another one of the 'fan girls' and had done what none other could. The fan girls were banned from practices ever since the notorious octopus incident two years ago. He hadn't been there for it, and he was grateful beyond measure.

Yet, never once had she displayed the characteristics of a typical fan. He'd spent more time than he would admit watching her and as time went on, he'd developed a petite crush on her. Kaz knew that with his track record, talking to her would be bad.

He supposed he had to thank Ravin for picking on her. Yet, he couldn't condone bullying. Especially against cute… adorable… defenseless girls. Or, he assumed that she was defenseless. Few creatures at this school were truly and honestly without a means to protect themselves. Everyone had secrets here, even him.

A quick glance confirmed that Ravin was, in fact, behaving. He couldn't wait to talk to her again. Well, have her whisper in his general direction. Or in the general direction of her feet. Really, anything worked. He wouldn't complain.

Practice went by at a fast pace, much to the human's relief. So, once he was done he raced off the ice, stripped, then jumped into the shower.

"Hey Kaz did you get the shot?" Axel, one of their two dragons asked. Before the human could respond his identical twin Ace added, "cuz you've got the luuuurve fever." Both twins burst into booming laughter that drew in several others.

Kaz shoved his head under a showerhead and did his best to tune them out. After a few minutes they quieted so he dared to emerge.

The second his head popped out, Mark the werewolf shot him a grin. "So did you finally find a bun for your hotdog?"

Embarrassment bubbled inside him. His skin burned with the fire of his flush. Black spots swum in front of his eyes as his teammate laughed at him. For a moment everything swayed around as unconsciousness nipped at him. He had to squeeze his eyes shut to keep from getting sick.

Then one by one they fell silent. Kaz dared to peek open his eyes and found himself face to face with their team captain.

"Is everything ok, Kazun?" Letvan asked in a soothing voice.

Kaz nodded, "Y-yea." He rubbed his face and felt his tears melt into the shower water cascading over his head. "Thanks." The boy turned his gaze to the wall and focused hard on not existing.

"So did you have a nice time talking to Lian?" Letvan shocked Kaz out of his funk. Unlike the others, he was sincere and made no attempt to mock the youngest member of the team.

Kaz's brown eyes widened in shock. "You knew her name this whole time?"

"Of course, she's in my Natural Remedies 104 class," the elf shrugged.

Kazun's jaw dropped. "Why didn't you tell me?"

"You didn't ask."

Frustration replaced all lingering embarrassment. "You know I've got a crush on her, how would I even know to ask?"

"You needed to have faith in yourself." Letvan brought back his shoulders and gained an aura of unshakable confidence. "Not everyone is born with bravery. For some, it is forged by their actions. This small act will only help you later in life. It's a lesson that had to be learned."

The human thought about his friend's words. "Thanks then… I guess."

"You're welcome."

Kazun grabbed his towel and left the showers. He changed into the clothing hanging in his locker, then shoved his gear into his huge bag and raced back rinkside. It was only a matter of time before he returned to the two who waited for him.

The boy waved. "I'm back," he said with a grin.

"About time." Ravin leaned onto the row of seats beside him as he stretched out his body.

Lian, who had actually remained, lifted her hand in silent

greeting. She cast a wary glance to the two males.

"So now that he's here, could you pleaaase tell me where your sister is?" the demon begged theatrically. He wasn't used to not getting what he wanted, when he wanted it. He was able to get things with ease, and Lian holding out was most definitely not cool in Ravin's opinion. Kazun had been on the receiving end of such acts in the past.

Kazun knelt down in front of Lian. "He's not going to stop asking unless you tell him, which can get pretty annoying. I know, I have to live with him." He chuckled and shook his head in a 'can you see what I have to put up with?' manner. "I promise that I'll go with him to beat him up in case he causes any trouble. See, I know all his weak points."

"Kazuuuun!" Ravin whined and wiggled in his seat. "You're so mean to me."

"Well…" Lian paused and gave the demon an unsure look. A moment passed and she spoke under her breath to Kazun, "she went to the roller rink to pick up our friend Jo and give her a ride home… also to get free cheese fries..." Her voice trailed off and she looked at her shoes. It had taken a lot to tell Kazun that. The thought of a demon trailing her until she told him was more terrifying than placing a single shred of faith in this human. Plus, he could be dropped by the hockey team if he dared to do anything to her.

Kazun smiled, "Thank you very much." He almost laughed at the happy coincidence. He loved rollerblading as much as he loved ice skating.

Ravin jumped to his feet and put his hands on his hips.

"Onward to the Exskate!"

Kaz sighed and shook his head. What was he getting himself into? He couldn't believe how bold he was being in this situation. He didn't have the most ease when it came to talking to women. Or at least he hadn't before he started college.

In school, he had fainted more than once when he had tried talking to pretty girls, which had come with being a hockey player. He blushed so hard that his vision grew spotty and if he didn't calm down enough in time, he passed out. So he avoided the opposite sex. As a result, his schoolmates had started the rumor that he was gay. It hadn't bothered him. It was only gossip.

While the roommates were distracted with their excitement, Lian quietly slid away. They had gotten what they had wanted from her and now she would be left alone. Michelle would be able to handle both of the scary men. Michelle probably wouldn't have any fear—she never did. Michelle was brave. This was a simple fact of life. It was something that Lian had always been grateful for.

Dark memories tugged at the recesses of her mind. Pain bit into her arms, and it took Lian a moment to figure out it was her own fingernails gripping into her skin. A storm raged outside and it only reminded her of a time she wished would wash away forever.

How old had she been? Five. How could she ever forget that night? Though long worn from the years that had passed, the scar she had been left with had never faded completely. Despite wanting to push it into the corners of her mind forever—the memory was too strong to be contained. It haunted her still.

Lian stood at the threshold of the rink and stared out into the torrent. Her thoughts forced her to a different time and place.

It had started out such a beautiful day despite the rain. Of course, it could have been a tornado and the young girl would have been excited all the same. After all, it was her fifth birthday. There was no party planned because Lian had begged to go to the Summer Botanical gardens. The trip had been planned. Even the storm wouldn't stop them. The gardens had an indoor exhibit. Lian still got to see pretty flowers—and that was all that had mattered to her.

On the way, Lian had fallen asleep. It was the last time she ever slept in peace again. It was a memory she cherished. The innocent dream had been lost with age, but Lian could still remember that it had been a happy one filled with sunlight.

When they reached the Gardens, her Mom and Dad let her pick wherever she wanted to go. First they went to see the flowers of the palace exhibit. One of the lovely elves who worked there had given her a beautiful flower crown for her birthday, woven from the royal species of flowers. The floral smell still lingered in her mind and her heart clenched.

It had been the highest point of happiness. How could five-year-old Lian know that it would be the last moment of peace in her life?

Lightning flashed through the dark sky and the outside world tinted purple before the gloom overtook the air. Lian hated lightning. She began to tremble. She knew there was no escaping it. Reminding herself that the sooner she got it over with, the sooner she would get it done, Lian pushed herself out into the rain.

A cold spray pelted her skin. It could not compare to the ice she felt in her veins. The lightning had made all the lights go away all those years ago. The lightning had made the power go out, and because of the confusion, little Lian had gotten separated from her parents. She was so lost and so afraid.

The torrent of water masked her tears. If she could have a single wish, it would be to make it go away. If she could make the visions stop....

Looking at the tall man, she had thought nothing of him. His face was beautiful, and his dark horns were new and interesting. They were so well kept and polished. He held out a flower to her, the petals white as snow. His words were gentle and his hooded cloudy eyes spoke nothing of the storm that lay behind them.

She shouldn't have gone with him, but he had said he knew where her parents were. Why shouldn't she have trusted him? She was only five. The others had given her flowers and the soft petals made her so happy.

Thunder boomed and the girl's nails dug further into her arms. Surely they would leave marks by the time she made it home. Her lip trembled as the storm reached its climax. Air twisted around her delicate frame.

He had led her off the path and made her touch his horns. How was the five-year-old supposed to know the implications of such an act? She didn't understand when he told her to take off her jacket. It was chilly, but he said he could make her warm. Lian had trusted him. He was an adult, and she had never known an adult to be bad.

When he was done with her that day, the demon had taken

her flower, her trust, and her innocence. Lian didn't remember what happened past then, but Michelle had been the one who found her… everything else was a painful blur.

Lian bumped into a dark figure, stopping her in her tracks. In a slow motion she looked up and into storm colored eyes. The air went quiet and cold. She couldn't even let out a scream as a smile came to the man's face. His smooth, petal soft hand touched her face. His honey sweet voice tickled her ears. "My, my have you blossomed."

Six

It took some time for the two to realize that the girl had run off. Kazun couldn't help but feel his spirit sink in disappointment. He couldn't blame her for fleeing. However, if he had a choice, he wouldn't spend so much time with Ravin either.

"Can we drop my gear off before we go on your adventure?" Kaz shifted the massive bag that was almost as tall as he was. "I really don't want to lug this thing around."

Ravin arched a brow. "Afraid the odor will scare everyone off?"

Kaz rolled his eyes. "Can you stop? I almost fainted in the shower and I really don't want to deal with this right now." His shoulders sagged. For a moment his umber gaze dimmed with exhaustion.

"Sure, come on." Ravin grabbed his roommate's arm, then teleported them inside the dorm building, outside their threshold. He unlocked the door with a flick of his key. With one hand he held the door open so Kaz and his bulky burden's progress were unimpeded.

Kaz reeled on his feet until his vision focused again. "Thanks." Even after eleven years, teleportation was more than his brain could comprehend. He pushed through the doorway. The sports bag fell to the floor with a careless thud. He proceeded to raid the fridge. In his search he recovered a half-eaten sandwich and an energy drink.

"So what happened in the shower?" Ravin leaned against the wall while he waited. The human heaved a sigh, seeming to ponder the question.

The loud sigh was his only response for a while. At length, Kazun explained, "They were teasing me about Lian." He stuffed the last corner of the sandwich into his mouth to deter Ravin from inquiring further.

For the briefest of moments Ravin's eyes widened. "Wait, was that her?" he asked in hushed awe.

Kazun rolled his eyes and popped open the drink. He took a quick swig. The drink came in too quickly and he found himself sputtering and choking. Kaz coughed a bit of the sickly sweet liquid onto the counter. His foot connected with the cabinets in frustration. He mopped his mess, then ran a hand through his hair.

"Of course it was, you complete and utter idiot!" The edge to his voice was sharp as a blade.

Ravin cringed. "I'm sorry Kaz, I didn't know."

The human held up a hand. "Don't." He shook his head. "It's probably for the best anyway." Kazun stared down into his drink. "With the crap with the bounty it's not safe to have anyone close… let alone let a crush be anything more than a crush." His voice was somber. After a few more sips, he placed the empty container on the counter.

Ravin looked Kazun over; quite a bit of the demon's previous excitement had diminished. Taking souls had put them both in this position. Sometimes he forgot that. No matter what he said, Kaz probably believed this was in pursuit to a soul. He fingered the key in his pocket. It was an excuse to see Michelle. Yes, he could have given it to Lian, but he didn't need the backlash that could cause. There was no doubt in his mind that she would think he'd stolen it. There was no guarantee Michelle wouldn't think that either. Yet, out of the two sisters, Michelle would smart-mouth him instead of cry. He could deal with sass. In fact, he quite liked it. Tears were messy and could get him in massive trouble with the higher-ups at the school.

"Are you still going?" Kazun's energy seemed to have returned, thanks to the drink and snack.

A cocky grin worked its way onto Ravin's lips to hide the tumultuous feelings inside of him. "Of course, let's go."

Kazun shook his head, then reached for his friend's arm. Before he grabbed it, Kaz pointed at Ravin's face. "You have to buy me nachos for dragging me along," he ordered with a stern look.

The demon rolled his eyes. "Yea, yea." Ravin snatched Kaz's hand. In his mind he pictured Exskate. The mental image was fuzzy. He could remember the solid overhang with the flashy logo plastered on the front and automatic doors. Yet, it was all he needed. With a pop of energy, the two boys appeared outside, safe from the downpour. He repressed a laugh as Kazun stumbled against the building.

"Next time give me a bit of a heads-up." Kazun looked a bit green as he attempted to center himself.

"There's no fun in that." Ravin sauntered inside and enjoyed the warming sensation that surrounded him. The spade on his tail fluttered in the slight breeze. Cold braced his back as Kazun joined him.

They stepped past the second set of doors and Ravin fished out his wallet, paying the fourteen credits to grant them access to the building.

The demon glanced around. "Do you see her?" he asked Kazun. Though their vantage point wasn't the most advantageous, most of the rink was a sea of swirling faces, most of which were going too fast to recognize.

"No," Kaz replied. "Lian said she'd be getting cheese fries, so let's go get me some nachos and she could be there."

Ravin gave Kaz an odd look. "She said that?"

The human nodded. "Yeah, you didn't hear her?" He arched an eyebrow.

Ravin scoffed. "She barely even squeaked at you, I almost didn't even catch 'roller rink.'" He threw his hands into the air.

"Someone needs to listen better," the human teased. He fished the wallet out of Ravin's pocket, then made his way to the concession stand. He leaned over the vaguely sticky counter and looked at the various options they had to offer. "I'll have nachos please."

He gave a smile to the man working there, eyeing the nametag the boy wore, he added, "Beau."

Beau gave him a smile. "One order of nachos coming right up." His voice was painted with the tones of an overseas accent. "Zat'll be three credits."

"Thanks," Kaz replied.

Within a matter of moments, they had exchanged the money for the cheese smothered chips. "Enjoy," Beau beamed.

"You rock," Kaz replied as he lifted the tray. He slipped a couple of credits into the tip jar before he turned to face Ravin, who had followed him. "She's right there." He pointed over to the chair Michelle was sitting in.

Ravin glanced over and arched a brow. "How did you know it was her?"

"Well, if you confusing Lian for her was any indication, then they look a lot alike. It's not hard to put two and two together," Kaz explained in a bored voice.

Well damn, he hadn't expected the kid to be useful. "Thanks. I might have to keep you." He strolled over and slid into an empty chair at the table. "Found you," he chimed.

A pair of bright blues accented by neon lights looked at the demon. Michelle twisted her gaze down at her wrist and nodded once. "Wow that took a lot longer than I expected." Her gaze turned back to the tall girl sitting beside her "Some demon he is, right, Jojo?"

The manager let out a laugh. "Plus he brought reinforcements," Jo nodded towards the nacho-eating boy. "But that's understandable when dealing with you, Michelle." She winked a forest green eye.

"That's not fair. You had magic rain that hid your energy." Ravin countered. "As for the sidekick, the kid is semi-permanently attached to my hip, so he's almost always with me. That's what I get for getting a human instead of a puppy."

Michelle looked between the males. The not-puppy seemed content with his food. He either didn't notice being likened to a dog or didn't care. Then again, he was probably used to the demon being disrespectful. Many races treated humans as the underclass. Many learned to put up with it. Michelle wasn't one of those people.

"That's great." Her eyes narrowed into sharp points, "But at least you can bring this pet into establishments, right?"

"We do have a 'no animal' rule." Jo placed her lips on a straw and blew air into the cup, causing the liquid to bubble, "Well, really, a 'no anything that will poop on the floor' rule. Babies are excused because you can throw a diaper on them."

Michelle turned to Kaz. "I think he looks potty-trained. Do you think the demon potty trained his pet? It is swell that you would take him out for a walk, anyhow. Very sweet. I hear we humans need daily exercise." Her fingers tapped agitatedly on the table top. Michelle felt like a stick of dynamite, and there was no telling what would light her fuse.

Ravin chuckled and ran a hand through his blonde hair. "Found a sensitive spot did I?" He leaned forward and rested his arm on the table. "Well sweetness, he's actually my roommate. Sorry to get you worked up over nothing."

Kazun shrugged. "Feel free to smack him if he pisses you off.

He's trying to get a rise out of you. I've learned to ignore it." He munched on another chip as he turned his attention back to the people skating. His head bobbed to the catchy tune that played over the sound system.

"We could always kick him out for disturbing the peace," Jo offered.

Michelle nibbled on her thumbnail for a moment, "Well, my peace is pretty disturbed."

Jo let out a laugh and leaned onto the table with her elbows. With a playful smirk she continued, "then again, it isn't like you are a paying customer." There was no fun if she couldn't pick on her best friend every once in a while. Michelle should have known by now that Jo would take every opportunity she could get to enact payback for the amazon jokes.

"I pay!" Michelle crossed her arms over her chest. "Sometimes."

Ravin watched them with amused eyes. "Well aren't you two a pair?" He leaned back in his seat once again. "So as it turns out, cupcake, I do actually have something that you want." The demon flashed a grin. "And this time it isn't a 'get out of dragon torture free' card. It's something you probably don't want me to have."

"Really? Nicknames?" Michelle rolled her eyes. If there was anything she couldn't stand it was nicknames. Well, nicknames she didn't approve of. Like Shelly. The gods help anyone who dared call her Shelly. Her parents had put a lot of time and effort into looking through a baby name book. Of course when they saw "Who is like God," they knew they had found the best option for their girl.

It wasn't like they had been expecting to have a son and a little girl popped out instead. It wasn't like she was supposed to be named after her grandfather. It wasn't like they had made a little sign that said: "Welcome Mischael" for the hospital door and had to change it. No, it wasn't like that at all. She had been named because her parents knew from the moment of conception that their baby was going to be something special. Nothing like the other stuff.

"And I doubt whatever you have in your pocket is worth my soul or my time." She stood.

Jo blinked, then offered a complimentary backup 'Z-snap.'

Ravin gave a lazy grin. "That's alright then, I'll come visit whenever I feel like it." He reached into his pocket and held the key. "You know, I actually considered giving it back, but then you went on your little sass spree, and what can I say? I'm 'trying to get a rise out of you.'" The demon winked at her as his tail twitched behind him, reminding her of a cat who had cornered its prey.

For a moment her eyes went blank. Her key? He had her key? Immediately her fingers balled into fists. She felt the playful energy that had bubbled around her pop and transition into something much more serious, "You stole my key?" she accused.

Jo put her hand on Michelle's shoulder. "I'm sure he found it and is going to give it back." The tall girl's voice had changed too. It was soothing. "Because if he doesn't, you can go to the headmasters because that can be very dangerous and you can report it."

Michelle, who liked this little bit of information held out her hand. "Give it back and or I swear you'll regret it." Humans of all the species had to be careful with their safety. One wrong move and a demon could come bouncing into their safe area with ill intentions. Michelle wouldn't have minded the joke so much if it had only been her it was directed at. Her hand clenched so tight, so her knuckles went white. But if demon boy thought he could even joke about making his way into her sister's safe area, he had another thing coming. This demon had a key to her room. Gods above, she could only imagine if Lian knew. The girl wouldn't feel safe in her warm haven.

It had taken Michelle months to prep Lian for coming to college. A college that allowed demons. Hour after hour, Michelle had worked her ass off to make her room a safe, comfortable place for her sister. This demon wasn't going to ruin all that.

If he wouldn't give the key back, she would not hesitate to get the headmasters involved. It wasn't that she couldn't take a joke. Hell, Michelle loved jokes. No. This wasn't funny, because at the end of it, all Michelle could think about was the fear in Lian's eyes.

"You have three seconds before I make a very, very serious phone call, cupcake." Michelle's outstretched fingers made a 'give it here' motion.

For a moment Ravin hesitated, and that moment was all Kazun allowed. He grabbed Ravin's horn and jerked his head down. "Do what the lady says, now. She's not messing around and you know I'll keep my promise to Lian and kick your ass if you don't." His brown eyes shone with a seriousness that showed he meant every last word.

Ravin managed to free himself from Kazun and ran a hand over his horn. "For fuck's sake will you people let me get a word in edgewise?" He gave them offended looks. "You both monologue more than super villains." The demon tossed the key into Michelle's outstretched hand. He shook his head. "Seriously though, don't grab my horn," he scolded Kazun. "I don't like you that way."

He fixed the girl with a serious look. "I took it too far," he admitted. "But I wasn't actually going to show up one day and rifle through your fridge. I've got my own perfectly good fridge back in my dorm and it's stocked with all the niceties. There's even chocolate milk. You dropped the key when you went skipping off into the storm. There's a reason I talked to Lian. I thought she was you—it's an easy mistake to make. Yes, I played relatively nice. As nice as I get."

Kaz rolled his eyes. "You've said more now than the three of us put together, who's the one monologuing?" He turned his attention to Michelle. "I can at least back him up on the being nice to Lian front... kind of."

"No." Michelle breathed, "You did not go and talk to Lian." Stuffing the key into her jeans pocket, she patted her sweatshirt, trying to find her holophone. There was no telling the kind of damage that such a conversation could cause to her delicate sister. Once she found her mobile, she looked at it. There wasn't a missed call or messages. For a moment, Michelle's heart settled. Generally, when there was a problem or Lian had an anxiety attack, she would call Michelle immediately. There was a possibility that she had gone back to the room to hide. If that was the case, Michelle would be lucky if she could wrench Lian out from under the bed.

This demon was a lot more trouble than he was worth.

"If you ruined months of work, I am going to be so pissed." Michelle seethed. Every day was a challenge. Michelle loved her sister to no end, and slowly the girl had found herself able to go out by herself. If they went back five steps because of this guy…

"She has come quite a way since she got here," Jo reminded her, "and they didn't know about her demonophobia. Deep breaths Mischa. Deep Breaths."

"I don't know if this helps at all," Kaz chimed in. "But I showed her how much of a pushover he can be, and told her I'd kick his ass if he did anything. She's been sitting in on hockey practice, so she knows that I potentially could. She actually spoke to me, so that's got to count for something too." He offered a nacho to the protective older sister in attempt to maybe make her feel a bit better.

Ravin ran a hand through his hair. "I didn't know. Some things now make a lot more sense. I'm the polite sort of demon who doesn't intrude in thoughts, though I probably should have in this case. For what it's worth, I do feel bad." He did look distinctly guilty.

Michelle sighed and turned around away from them. She didn't fully accept the apology, but she didn't decline it either. Then again, she didn't take the world peace nacho. Her worries were escalating. Lian hadn't called after meeting face to face with a demon. This was the tamest demon Michelle had ever met, but that didn't matter. One time when they went out shopping, Lian had gone into a panic after seeing a ram spirit with exposed horns.

Not able to stand the radio silence, Michelle dialed her sister and waited for an answer. The holodevice let out a happy chime into her ear. Why wasn't Lian answering? After the fifth round of the tone, Michelle bit her lip. Something was wrong.

There was a click. Michelle let out a breath she hadn't realized she was holding.

Her relief didn't last long as she heard her sister crying on the other end of the line and the static sound of rain.

"Lian? Are you okay? Do you need me to come get you?" Michelle turned and cast a glance at Jo. The crying got harder, and Lian's response was nearly unintelligible. Michelle bit her lip and continued in a very gentle motherly voice, "Lia baby, it's okay. Take a deep breath. I'm going to come find you."

The younger sister was still crying, and Michelle knew her words would do little to quell the fear.

"Do you think you can make it back to our room so you are out of the rain?" Michelle soothed, but Lian's response didn't offer any clue that she would or wouldn't. "Want me to stay on the line with you until I get there?" The static got worse and worse, and Michelle wasn't entirely sure that it was rain she was hearing. There might have been some magic interference.

"I will be there as fast as I can." Michelle grabbed her key out of her jeans pocket and stormed off towards her transport, not even saying goodbye to her friend or new acquaintances. She didn't have time. Michelle knew Jo would understand and find a different way home. Right now, she had to get to her sister as fast as she possibly could.

"Something is wrong," Jo whispered to the males. "Something is very, very wrong."

 Seven

Kazun's fingers felt numb. His mind raced as he tried to process both girls' words. His heart hurt with the idea that something he had done had caused Lian some kind of harm.

"Did you know?" he asked his demonic friend.

Ravin raised his hands in surrender. "I swear I had no idea. I wasn't trying to cause any problems." He at least had the decency to stay out of other's minds. It was a courtesy thing for himself, too many voices in the brain made one start to lose it. "You know I'm not trying to draw attention."

Kaz's fingers curled tight around the container. "Michelle will help her, right?"

Jo regarded the boys and she sighed, "Lian has a lot of anxiety issues. It may be another episode. If anyone can calm her down, it's Michelle." She shrugged and looked around. "Now I have to find a ride home. If there is anything else I can help you with, let me know."

Ravin stood. "I'd offer, but I doubt you'd want demonic help." He stretched his arms. "The public transportation system here is pretty reliable, so I could toss a few credits your way because I seem to have cost you your ride."

"It's alright, I have credits," Jo responded. "Thanks for the offer though."

The demon was about to respond when an unfamiliar shadowy energy slithered up his spine. He turned and scanned every inch of the building with his mind. Auras from elves, vampires, werewolves, a handful of mages, nymphs, a few fae, a dragon or two, and a smattering of other miscellaneous creatures assailed him. None of them had caused this strange obscure sliver of power.

It was dark, something more powerful than the others. Something that made his heart freeze. The sensation was as though a slug were making its way down the center of his back and leaving a trail of evil behind. Yet, he couldn't find the source. It was as if they had erased their very presence, just to mess with him.

The feeling struck him as familiar, yet he couldn't place it. While the owner was unknown, the kind of energy was not. It was one he knew all too well.

Ravin turned to Kazun. "We need to go," he snapped. "Now." The demon grabbed the boy's arm. "Bye," he said to Jo before he teleported them both from the rink. When they appeared outside their dorm, he threw open the door. He shoved Kazun inside, then locked the bolt behind them. With a flick he turned on the extra protection wards that would prevent those with malicious intent from entering.

"What is going on Ravin?" Kazun demanded as he struggled to keep his balance.

The demon double checked the wards, then all the windows. "The bounty gets doubled and there just so happened to be a demonic presence in Exskate."

Kazun shook his head. "It could have been a student," the human dismissed. "You've jumped at them before. This could be another misunderstanding." He wanted to hope that whatever Ravin was doing wouldn't have failed already. The guilt was more than he could bear. His life wasn't worth more than anyone else's, yet he didn't want to face the day that he knew would come in time.

"No, I didn't recognize it." Ravin paced towards his room, then stopped half way. "It's too much to be a coincidence."

The human closed his eyes and let out a long breath. "Fine." The paranoia might pass in a day or two. Maybe things would go back to normal. Or so he hoped. "I've got my normal schedule tomorrow, plus study group. We were planning on getting some—"

"You're not going anywhere without me until I know it's safe." Ravin interjected. His stern gaze held the human in place.

"I know it's bad, but I want to get lunch with friends." Kazun lifted his bag from the middle of the floor. "You can come too, I won't say no." He shrugged then shoved the large bag into the hall closet.

Ravin watched his friend with a wary glance. "No. You can go to class and practice and that's it."

Frustration got the best of him. "Really? This again?" Kaz shoved his hands in his pockets to keep from doing something he would regret. "Ravin, let me go get food and enjoy myself."

"I told you less than two minutes ago that the bounty on your head skyrocketed and you want to go gallivant about with a giant target on your back?" the demon retorted. "If we had gotten to Exskate any sooner, we would have been caught. What would you have done then?" he demanded and threw out a hand toward their front door. "There were no wards to protect you there. Whoever it was just so happened to be a league above me."

Dark brown eyebrows furrowed. "I would have met it head on instead of hiding." He took a step towards his friend. "I thought you were paying to have my energy masked. Doesn't that count for anything?"

"I can't afford the most expensive protection that Sin has to offer," Ravin admitted, though Kaz knew it pained his pride to do so, "or do you want me to get her more souls so that I can buy you a few more weeks?"

Kazun didn't flinch, though the façade cracked. "Don't throw that at me," he growled. "I don't want you to steal souls to hold off some looming deadline. It's only been a year and you can barely keep from drowning. Yet I get to live with the knowledge that people are dying because of me."

"If I didn't get to half of those people, someone else would," Ravin countered. "I give them more than they would get from anyone else."

Kazun threw up his hands. "Stop, don't act like you don't enjoy it. Oh, poor Ravin has to do exactly what he was doing for his whole life before he met me." He firmed his stance and gave his friend a challenging look.

The demon's expression darkened. "My nature compels me to gather souls to further myself, and the rest of my kind, yes. It's something that I can't help. You don't know how long I fought it."

"Stop making this about you Ravin," Kazun snapped. "And don't pretend you're doing this for anyone but yourself. I'm just an excuse." He had to hold onto the counter with his hands to prevent himself from throwing a punch straight into Ravin's stupid mug. He wanted to see the demon suffer for once.

Instead of trying to make things better, the demon growled, "Keep that crap up and you'll lose more privileges."

"What, you'll ground me?" Kazun sneered. "I already can't go to the bathroom without you checking in on me twice. What else could you possibly get rid of?"

Ravin lifted a lip into a smirk. "I could toss you in a bunker and not worry about letting you have social interactions."

"Don't act like not imprisoning me earns you a medal," Kazun barked as he tightened his grip on their countertop. He couldn't remember a time that they'd fought like this before. It had been building, though, and the kettle was screaming, ready to burst with steam.

"Would you rather only get to see the light of the sun once a week?"

The final push made Kazun snort indignantly. He stormed over to the couch. He snatched his game controller and flipped on their holoscreen. He wanted to engage further. Yet, a quiet, rational part of his brain knew that the only possible outcome of the fight wouldn't be worth it. So instead he allowed himself to sink into the arms of his familiar mistress, video games.

Ravin growled under his breath. With his mind, he made a beer fly out of the fridge and into his outstretched hand.

"I want to meet Sin," Kazun half-yelled over his shoulder.

"No," Ravin snapped.

It took a lot of energy to keep the controller firmly gripped in his hands, instead of lodged in any of a number of things, including, but not limited to the holoscreen, the wall, and Ravin's face. "It's my ass she's protecting, I should be allowed to talk to her."

"You're not going to that place." Ravin put his foot down, and his tone let Kazun know that there would be no more of that.

"Well gee thanks, *Dad.*" Kaz forced his voice to be both mocking and pleasant.

"Shut the hell up, Kazun." Ravin stalked into his room and slammed the door shut.

The two males allowed time to pass in silence. Kazun beat up imaginary enemies in his game. Each strike let out a bit of frustration that otherwise would have remained bottled inside until he exploded. More than anything, he ached to call his dad. Yet, he knew that this radio silence was for the best. The less his dad knew about the situation the better.

In his room, Ravin held his head. His fingers raked through the shaggy blonde locks and slid over the rugged stubble he hadn't bothered to trim. This was going to be the end of him one day, he could feel it. The train was at the other end of the tunnel, and he was the damsel strapped to the tracks. Yet it hadn't been some dastardly villain who had tied him down, it had been himself while he tried to rescue Kazun, the other damsel who had resigned himself to his train bound death some time ago.

He could feel Kazun's anger diminishing, even as his own had wiped him out. He hadn't known that this would come. Kazun didn't know the pressures on Ravin's shoulders. It was offensive to insinuate they didn't exist.

Yet, he knew that it had been a mistake mentioning all the souls that had been lost in the name of protecting Kazun. The guilt sometimes poured off of the boy thick enough to bog down Ravin for days. When that happened Ravin did what he could to offer the intense emotion to Sin, but guilt always struck him as a Heaven thing.

The demon stripped off his shirt and paced a bit.

When he knew that his temper had cooled off enough to return to the living room, Ravin eased open the door, and watched Kazun for a little bit.

Kaz had calmed enough to have sprawled out across the couch. His face was drawn with the focus of a hardened gamer. He even leaned forward a bit, which meant something intense was happening.

While Kazun was diverted by the fascinating fight before him, Ravin strode in the living room, then flopped into the recliner. He watched his roommate defeat the enemy he was fighting with expert precision. By the time the computer was defeated, Kazun hadn't taken a speck of damage.

"You should go easy on the poor computer, it doesn't know any better," Ravin chided.

Kazun shrugged. The tension was gone from his shoulders.

"It's the hardest they have programmed, it's not my fault that they're not ready for me."

The demon hazarded a chuckle, and felt himself at ease when Kazun joined in. All he did was watch as the boy mercilessly beat other competitors with the same ruthless precision.

After a while Ravin asked, "Do you remember how we met?"

Kazun rolled his eyes, then focused harder on his game. "Of course I do. It's impossible to forget." That moment had changed his life forever, even if he didn't know it at the time. How could a seven-year-old comprehend life-altering decisions? It was an unreasonable burden to put on such a child, especially one who had experienced the loss Kazun had by that age.

"For what it's worth, I'm sorry." Ravin took a long swig of his drink.

"You're just sorry it turned out this way." Kazun couldn't hold back the snide remark, or the subsequent grunt that followed it.

The demon shook his head. "No, I'm actually sorry about this whole thing."

Silence passed between them again. Neither were too eager to break their little truce and take the chance of saying something that made them cross the line back into anger. When Kazun beat the next foe on the list, he placed his controller down and looked over at his closest friend.

"Why did you stay?" he asked.

Ravin stared down at his bottle. He couldn't tear his gaze away from the bubbling liquid inside. "You know why," the mumble ground out.

Kazun sat up a bit. "No I don't. That's the one thing I never quite understood."

Hurt crossed Ravin's features. The bottle cracked beneath the pressure of his fingers. Again, he didn't say anything for a while. A wide range of emotions passed behind the quiet outer visage. His bangs fell before his dark eyes, obscuring part of his face from Kazun's gaze. After a lifetime of silence, Ravin responded, "Because you're my friend."

The human got to his feet and padded over to his roommate. He squatted down next to the demon and looked into the familiar face. "You're my best friend." Kazun offered a consoling look and half smile.

"Don't give me that cute guise." Ravin pushed at Kazun's head without malice. "You know I can't handle those puppy dog eyes." He did his best to block out the wide brown chocolate stare, begging for attention.

A bigger smile worked its way onto Kaz's lips. "Is that why you went with a human instead of a puppy?" he teased.

"Should have gotten the damn puppy," Ravin murmured as he took another draft from his beverage. "They give those, 'I'm cuter than anything you've ever seen and can manipulate you into anything' looks less often than you do. Yet you still wonder how you have a drove of girls tailing you. The puppy at least appreciates the attention."

Kazun opened his mouth to retort, but closed it again. "Yea, but those people tailing the puppy aren't likely to try and molest it."

"That's true." Ravin finished his drink. "And someone might make me share a puppy if I had one. I don't have to share a best friend."

"I think best friend is a bit presumptuous Ravin."

"On please, you softie. You're the one who said it first," Ravin complained.

Kazun leaned on the armrest of Ravin's chair. He crossed his arms on the supple leather, then rested his chin atop them. "True, so I guess it has to be so."

"I know I seem unreasonable, but I'm trying to be cautious." Ravin shrugged, though he had a feeling that his friend was already long past the initial anger. "I don't want to get you caught over something stupid."

Kazun heaved a sigh and rolled back onto his haunches. "Fine, I'll be low key for a few days until it all boils over."

"There's a good sport." Ravin fished a ring out of his pocket. "Put this on." He passed a simple silver band over to his friend. It glittered many colors in the light coming from the holoscreen.

With a quick motion, Kazun scooped the ring and slipped it on his right index finger. "What is it?" He asked.

The demon gave a mischievous grin. "Pretty, that's what."

"Yea, because I need something pretty," Kazun sneered, but did not press the issue. "What's the occasion?"

"Best friendship?" Ravin shrugged.

One dark brow shot up. "So you're claiming me?" The human teased as he examined the bit of jewelry.

"Are you trying to imply that I hadn't already?"

While the human laughed, Ravin gave a halfhearted chuckle. In his mind, he ticked another one of the magical objects he could use to protect his friend off the list. There were still a few more left, but they wouldn't last long. After that, he didn't know what he would do to make sure he didn't lose the one person in the world that mattered to him to a fate that Ravin himself had condemned the boy to.

He was thrown from his depressing thoughts when he felt a vaguely familiar energy approaching. He arched a brow and rose to his feet. His mind only dwelled for a moment on the fact that he hadn't pulled his shirt back on.

Regardless, he waited, and suppressed a laugh. With his mind he pulled the door open. His lips curled into a smirk. Well wasn't this a treat?

Eight

Michelle locked all the doors and made sure the curtains were closed. This was bad. With a gentle touch, Michelle ushered a semi-catatonic Lian to her bed. Panic rested in the older girl's stomach as she made a show of ensuring the perimeter was safe. Even if it was mostly for show, Michelle wanted her little sister to feel safe. She went to the wall and flipped on what looked like a light switch.

As if a spark was ignited, etched markings in the floor began to glow. Precise geometric patterns lit the surfaces like stars. Every human dorm had its own small defense system. The wards that littered their room would keep those with impure intentions out. It even worked against petty thieves. The downside was they wouldn't keep out the worst of the worst. Michelle didn't know what she was dealing with, but the wards were the best protective measures she had.

Lian had been dead silent since Michelle had found her out in the courtyard. The girl had been curled in the mud, sobbing. A few people had gathered around her to try and help, but Lian had started screaming hysterically at their sympathetic touches. Luckily, Michelle had gotten to her quickly and calmed Lian down enough to move her back to their room.

"Lian, we are safe." Michelle kneeled next to her sister. "Let's get you cleaned up and we'll talk about this okay? Was it the demon?"

The instant Michelle said the word, she regretted it. Loud terrified screams escaped Lian's mouth. In a frenzied motion, Lian flailed, trying to strike an unseen assailant she crawled to the other side of the bed and hid against the wall, cowering.

Michelle rubbed her now reddened cheek. Gods, Lian was sweet as honey in nature, but she could sting. This wasn't typical Lian behavior. With a slow controlled movement, Michelle got up and sat on her sister's bed. She put her hand on Lian's back. The wet fabric of her shirt was frigid.

"Shhhh it's okay. Let's get these wet clothes off and get you into something comfortable." Michelle's voice was as soothing as she could manage. Her general disposition was abrasive and sassy. It took everything she had to be soft and caring. For her sister though, she would do anything. Lian didn't move, she laid there, eyes distant.

The two sat for a long time. Michelle rubbed Lian's back and tried to be of some comfort. Something then caught Michelle's eye. The wet clothes that clung to Lian's skin were riding up, revealing her lower back. Red welts lined the younger girl's skin and the area looked irritated.

Michelle had to resist exclaiming in surprise. Drawing attention to anything wrong might set Lian off further. The current objective was to get Lian calm enough to speak actual words. In the common language. Michelle had to understand what was going on.

When she was sure Lian wouldn't strike out again, Michelle sat her sister up. With every ounce of tender care that she possessed, Michelle undressed Lian and got her into a warm night gown. Then, she wrapped a warm blanket around her sister's shoulders.

"It was him," Lian whispered, as she pulled the blanket tighter around her shoulder. "It… it was *him*."

"What?" Michelle's body tensed and immediately became alert, *"Him?"*

Lian nodded and averted her eyes.

Michelle's mind was racing. How could that be? How was he here? Michelle wondered if she could put the wards up any higher—or if she should tell the headmasters. Assuming, of course, if he was even following them. Had it been a coincidence? If that man was a demon, it was more than possible he was here because, this place was saturated in anything supernatural. The likelihood of a demon prancing around was very high. Sure, it did seem strange that Lian would see the man who had destroyed her… but Michelle wouldn't question it. She had seen much stranger things.

"What happened? What did he do?" Michelle tried to keep her voice as calm as possible. She was feigning a brave front, but hell, that wasn't how she felt at all.

"He talked to me…" Lian murmured into the blanket. "Then…" Her voice tightened, "Then… he kissed me and he left." The fragile girl's eyes went distant and her body sagged against Michelle's. She was trying to push away every thought of the dark haired demon. His face kept coming back and haunting her. His smile was seared into her mind.

"It's going to be okay, Lian," Michelle soothed. "I'm going to call the headmasters and they will send a mage to strengthen our wards. I will keep guard all night and day if I have to." The older sister wrapped an arm around Lian comfortingly. This was turning out to be a pretty sucky day.

"Thanks Michelle," Lian whispered and hid her face.

Michelle knew it wouldn't be easy for her sister to calm completely, but it was a step in the right direction. At least she wasn't screaming or flailing anymore. Stillness was A-Okay in Mischa's book.

"Hey, no worries, 'kay?" Michelle said with a smile. "Why don't you get some rest?" A few moments passed before Lian nodded.

Michelle thought about making some nice hot cocoa. Warm beverages were soothing, someone had told her once. With a smile, Michelle decided on her course of action. She stood and went into the kitchen. With a few button pushes, the drink dispenser opened and began to make hot cocoa. The drink steamed. Michelle grabbed some whipped cream and a bottle of chocolate sauce from the fridge. With the best of her artistic ability, she made a sloppy whipped cream flower and drizzled the chocolate in a sketchy spiral.

Proud of her work, Michelle brought the drink back to her sister. She would worry about the clean up later.

Lian took the mug and sipped the rich contents. It didn't take long for the pacifying cocoa to do its job. Lian was composed, if exhausted looking. The day had been long. Once she was done, Lian handed Michelle back the mug. With slow movements, her head found the pillow, and she rolled onto her side so her back was facing Michelle.

"Sleep well Lia." Michelle let out a breath. As she was about to cover Lian with her feather comforter, she stopped in shock. The welts were gone. Instead, printed on her sister's mid-back were words. Or at least, Michelle assumed they were words. Thick dark ink scrawled a tattoo across her flesh. Now, Michelle was used to crazy. A bit more so than any person should have been, but this… this was on a whole new level.

This wasn't a tattoo. Michelle knew for a fact that it couldn't be. It hadn't been there moments ago. As much as she didn't want to admit it, the only course of action she could think of was going to talk to that demon from Exskate. The dark words embedded into Lian's skin looked evil. Ravin had claimed to be "polite", so perhaps he could tell her at least something about it. Luckily she remembered the demon's name. Ravin, it was close to Raven, so it wasn't hard to remember. If she went to the school directory in the library and typed his name in, chances were he would pop up. Unless that was a nickname…. Then she would have to brave sticking her neck out and ask around.

Hopefully that didn't mean vampires.

Michelle was trying not to freak out. First, *He* returned and then this demonic tattoo appeared. What was next? Honestly, Michelle didn't want to know. Seeing the long absent demon today wasn't a coincidence. Michelle was sure of that now more than ever. Could he be the source of the 'tattoo'? Ravin might know. She tried to bring up a mental image of the dark words, maybe he would know what they meant. Michelle wasn't really an art student, but she hoped she could recreate it.

Michelle went to her side of the room and pulled out an unused notebook. It was supposed to be for her humanities class, but it was rare that she ever actually did school work, let alone taking notes. After finding a marker she got to work. Could she get it right on paper? Hopefully, with enough effort, she would.

Long moments passed in silence as Michelle worked on drawing out what she could remember of the tattoo. Three drafts later and it looked decent enough to get the message across. Once she was done, Michelle threw away the crumpled mistakes and put the remaining one in her pocket. She grabbed the notebook again and wrote down a quick scrawl of words.

Hey Lia.

If you wake up, I went to do stuff and talk to the Headmasters and things. No worries.

Mischa.

It was a vague note, but Michelle was proud of it. Lian wouldn't expect there was anything else wrong because, well, that was the type of note the older sister always left. Sometimes on the rare occasion, she'd leave a pastel sticky where Lia could find it saying, *'Gotta do things'* and it was never questioned.

Once Michelle was sure that Lian was deeply asleep, she headed out. Her first stop was to find the school directory. Once down in the main lobby of the human dorm, Michelle held a large tome. It was at least fifteen pounds and the book was filled with names of the students. Michelle had forgotten how big the school was.

"Better get started." She flipped through the book. Her first course of action would be to look through the Dark Dorm list. Seneal had six different on-campus dorm sites. Each held a specific type of student. It made things easier when certain types of creatures had certain needs. It wouldn't be wise to house the vampires and werewolves together. For one, vampires had good senses of smell, and werewolves were known to leave a pungent dog odor. Same was true about putting humans and demons together. The separation of the species was not only for comfort, but for safety.

All of the dorms held a variety of students, even the Light dorm where the humans lived. It was rare, but other creatures managed to get spots here and there. However, when that happened, waivers had to be signed and it was a daunting bureaucratic process. Similar creatures were supposed to stay together. That was how it worked.

Michelle was grateful for it too, at the moment. That meant that somewhere in the Dark Dorm pages, there would be the name Ravin. She flipped through the pages, scrolling through each name. She found a Ryan, a Raj, a Ravier, a Ralven, and even a Raven, but after almost a half an hour of looking through the directory, not a Ravin could be found.

A loud curse escaped Michelle's mouth. Okay, new plan. The holonet was sounding like a much better idea. Who needed old fashioned paper-based books anyway? With a change in direction, the girl hightailed it outside and to the main school building. It wasn't far away, but Michelle was careful not to let her guard down. Night owls were stalking around and she wouldn't want to get caught between a rock and a vampire.

Once she was in the main halls of the school, the girl felt a little more at ease. If something decided to attack her, she had the hopes of being heard by a teacher, or a headmaster.

Luckily the library wasn't too far away. Normally Michelle wouldn't go to this length to get on a computer. Hell, she owned a laptop, but she didn't want Lian to find out anything. She knew if her sister caught wind of the fact she had a demonic tattoo on her back, Lian would flip out. The poor girl already had enough stress in her life.

The longer Michelle could put off Lian knowing about the tattoo, the better it was for her.

The library was certainly a beautiful place. Michelle allowed herself to breathe easy again once she entered. The walls were filled with ancient tomes of their time and preequilibrium. Old texts filled the room with a pleasurable dusty aroma that sung with inspiration and pure history. Even to someone who wasn't a book worm, the library was a pretty cool place.

Michelle hopped onto one of the many computers that were tucked around the library. Despite the old timey feel of the place, the academy tried to keep things pretty top of the line and up to date. The girl opened a web browser and stared at the blank search line. Okay, how to find a demon on campus.

Might as well try the obvious first. She typed in his name,

"Ravin". The first thing that appeared was a large box that had a definition of the word Ravin.

rav·in

noun

archaic literary

1.violent seizure of prey or property; plunder.

Michelle almost found herself laughing. Great name for a demon. Did he pick that out himself, or did his mother have plans for him growing up? Well, that certainly wasn't going to work. So, she then altered her search. She typed in "Ravin Demon" hit enter and waited for the screen to load.

"Did you mean 'Raven Demon'?" The machine asked her.

"No, I meant *RAVIN* you stupid piece of—," Michelle started to curse out the holocomp. She was getting frustrated. Right now wasn't a good time to hit a dead end. So, she had to think about a different way to approach her problem. Thinking outside the box wasn't easy, especially with the amount of stress she was under. The unknown demon who had hurt Lian had returned and now Michelle was being forced to gallivant all over campus to find information about this dark tattoo. Sure, she could have stayed at home and watched over Lian, but Michelle figured that would be a useless endeavor.

If the demon did show his face at their place, there was nothing that Michelle could do to protect Lian. Being a human meant Michelle was fragile. Mortally so. She rolled her wrist. The aggressive key strokes were causing tension on her bones.

Michelle leaned back in her chair and closed her eyes. The demon Ravin was giving her nothing. There was a possibility she could go asking around, but at what cost? Most people didn't like to waste their energy without getting something in return. Most favors could end up costing an arm and a leg. Literally.

No, Ravin wasn't the path to follow. Then it struck her. The puppy-boy. He had been following Ravin around. Michelle's brows furrowed as she struggled to remember the face. It had been so familiar, why couldn't she place it. Then it struck her.

"Hockey Hallelujah!" Michelle's finger's flared on the keyboard with excitement. She immediately went to the school's holosite. It didn't take her long to find what she was looking for. On the front page there was an advertisement for a hockey game coming up, and the almond eyed boy was standing front and center. The posters for the game were plastered all over the school bulletins. How could she have forgotten.

Clicking on a link, Michelle was brought to a roster of players and there he was, "Kazun, huh? Well, look out buddy cause here I come." This kid would help her find Ravin. Most humans were pretty good when it came to asking for help. So even if he didn't know where Ravin was, he would be able to give her some idea of where to look.

Michelle took a pen from her pocket and wrote the dorm name and room number down.

Light Dorm 476.

The girl got up and looked around. The library was quiet, and there were only a few students around. They stirred as she moved, but their attention was drawn back to their work. Michelle was weary, but decided none of them would follow her. They all seemed too enthralled with their screens. She was on a mission that was taking too long.

Not wanting to waste any time, Michelle began the dangerous journey back to her dorm. The night air was cold, the rain had left it chilly. The girl rubbed her arms as she tramped through the grass instead of taking the pathways. It was faster that way.

Moments passed and she was entering the lobby of the human dorm. A few people were up and about, talking to one another. A few were obviously mages. They looked too old to be students. Michelle's best guess was that they were sent because of the lovely storm that had subsided. Many people were on edge—including Michelle. The girl offered small smiles to the others, but kept on her path. She entered the boy's stairwell, and she was sure to have gotten some looks.

How indecent of her.

Not that she cared what other people thought, she was working her ass off trying to keep her sister safe. Perverts. There were bigger things out there than trying to get with *some guy*. Sure, Michelle had had a boyfriend or two in the past, but they had turned out to be duds. Right now, the only thing she was thinking about was surviving college. Literally. If she could get herself a degree in one piece, then that was all she cared about. Sure, she had her moments of skipping classes, but she hadn't really failed a class yet. She had come close, but no cigar.

More than graduating, Michelle wanted Lian to be safe. Since Lian was little, Michelle had fought tooth and nail to make her happy, to see her smile again. Every time the young girl had gotten close to being normal, something came and stole it away. Not this time. Michelle would make sure of it. She would put everything right. There was no other option.

After climbing the stairway, Michelle trudged her way down the hallway. She counted the doors; they were all even numbers. Boys even, girls odd. That made it easy to remember. After a nice long walk to the far corner of the building, she finally found room 476. She let out a sigh of relief. Here, at last.

So this was where hockey star lived? It seemed so modest for one of the most popular faces in school. Michelle lifted her hand and went to knock, but before her hand could touch the door it swung open and she was graced with a half-clothed body.

"Well, well, well Princess, now it seems like it's you looking for me," purred an oh-so familiar and oh-so confident voice. Yup, she had found it all right.

Nine

The door had swung open all by itself, and Michelle was granted quite a sight. The doorway was a perfect window into the demon's home. And she had not been expecting it at all. She had forgotten that demons had mental abilities, such as telekinesis and mind reading. Well that wasn't fair.

Luckily for her, he was quite the sight to see. A roguish grin painted his handsome face. "So to what do I owe this pleasure?" His sculpted chest was bare and his pants slung low on his hips.

Of course, he didn't care. Modesty wasn't one of his strong suits. Ravin had taken good care of his body, and he liked to show it off. Some demons weren't as blessed as he had been. As a deal maker, he had to be pretty. People were more likely to trust someone who was attractive. That was how the human mind worked.

It amused him that she had come to his humble abode. It would only take a few moments to discover what the strange human was after, but he wanted hear it from her. He always got a kick out of non-mind readers trying to explain themselves. This was a treat, and he would enjoy it as such. He leaned against the door frame as his tail flicked like the cat-who-caught-the-mouse.

"I need you to look at something," she stated, holding the small slip of paper tight. "And it's important."

"Alright, go ahead." His dark eyes flicked over her face. Something had spooked her. Was this somehow connected to the phone call she had received at the rink? This was an interesting development.

Michelle all but shoved the paper into Ravin's grasp. Her movements were as short as her temper. She crossed her arms. Her stance demanded answers. After all of this work of finding him, it was about time she got them.

He eyed the drawing. It was familiar, but not in a good way. Discontent swirled in his stomach. His sable eyes moved from the symbol to the girl again. "So what's this information worth to you?" He expertly hid his churning emotions. "Other than your soul of course."

There was a price for everything, and she was going to have to pay.

She knew the agitation was plain to see on her face. Always a damn price. Her fists clenched, but she refrained from acting brash. If she, for some reason, ticked him off, she wouldn't get her information. That wouldn't be good.

Under her breath she commented, "stupid monsters and your

stupid prices…" Her eyes closed. "I'll do anything."

Ravin leaned back and folded the paper. "Well I'm always in need of rare, expensive, and pretty things." Mostly expensive. Anything to pay Sin to keep his end of their deal. "Oh, and a French Silk pie."

"A pie?" Her brow quirked. "Do you want fries with that?"

This only spurred the demon on. "Why yes, I do." He winked.

Michelle wanted to scream, but instead she bit her tongue. If she continued on with her sass, before she knew it, she would have had to get a gallon of juice, three bouncy balls, and a paperclip. Begrudgingly, she muttered a simple and bitter, "Whatever, I'll get it."

She turned around and headed towards the exit. Her mission now was to go find him what he wanted. She would figure something out. She *had* to. For Lian… for her sister's safety. A dark moody cloud hovered over her head.

Ravin lazily thumbed the edge of the paper. "Oh, you know what? Kazun might get bored, so, go ahead and get those bouncy balls while you are at it."

Resisting the urge to flip him off, Michelle continued on. Stupid mind readers. Fuck him and the bouncy balls. As if she was *actually* going to get those for him. Okay, so, finding some rare pretty whatever, and a pie. Where on Eartha was she going to get a rare pretty something? Of course, she could ask someone, then she'd have to go on another wild goose chase into infinity. Great. This was turning out to be peachy. Desperately, she tried to think of something, but what was there to find? She had a few pieces of jewelry lying around in her dorm, but she figured a Focus school class ring and a birthstone necklace wouldn't be worth much to anyone but her.

The holonet was always an option, but she would have a hard time explaining why she spent a shit ton of money to her parents. She didn't think telling them, "Oh, Lian got a magical tattoo and I had to pay a demon to tell me what the fuck it meant," would work anyway. The only other option she could even begin to think of was asking Jo.

Her best friend was one of the richest people she knew, second only to the royalty that came to the Academy. Jo's mother was a famous fashion designer and her father ran one of the largest corporations in all of Eartha. Both dragged in ridiculous amounts of money through their businesses. Enough so that Jo and her brother Clarence were set for life.

Michelle dug her phone from her pocket and speed dialed Jo. The other girl was off work and probably relaxing. Since Jo was the day manager of the roller rink, she didn't often stay awake too late. For a brief moment, Michelle felt a pang of guilt. She didn't like asking Jo for favors, but on top of it, Michelle had totally abandoned her earlier. The phone rang once… twice… Michelle was about to kick the wall.

Then her friend's voice sounded on the other line.

"Hello?" Jo yawned. It sounded as if she had nodded off while watching a movie. Michelle could hear explosions and one-liners in the background.

"I need your help, Jo," Michelle stated bluntly. There was no time for beating around the bush. The quicker she could know what was on Lian's back, the quicker she would know if the girl was safe or not. Though she had a terrible suspicion that her little sister was in harm's way.

Jo's voice abruptly sounded more awake. The sleep had been shaken off by urgency. "What's wrong, Mischa?"

Not many people called her by that nickname, but hearing it made Michelle calm a bit. She hated being called Shelly, but Mischa had a nice ring. Plus, her little sister had made it up when she was learning to talk. Michelle was a hard name to pronounce for a two-year-old. "Lian might be in trouble, and the only way I can know for certain is by giving a demon 'a shiny.'" It was hard to ask for her friend for this sort of a favor. Jo didn't like people mooching off her cash; hence, not a lot of people knew she had it.

Michelle continued, "You have to know I wouldn't ask unless I literally had no other way and I can't let Lian be in danger, I can't." A single tear threatened to leak out at the corner of her eye. She wasn't a crier. Michelle *hated* feeling weak. A ragged breath escaped her lips, and she knew she had to calm herself down.

"I know. I will do what I can. What sort of shiny?" Jo asked. On the other side of the line, Michelle could hear her friend shuffling through drawers.

Michelle shut her eyes and shook her head. All she knew was it had to be something valuable.

"Something a demon would want," was the only answer she could give. It was hard to tell what could be valuable to another person. Did he mean with a bigger price tag? With more use? What? It was a bit annoying, and she hadn't thought to ask. She was pissed off, and that didn't lend well to her plight. Michelle was known for acting before thinking. In this case it was doing her a disservice.

"I think I have the thing," Jo gasped. "You owe me for this."

A slight smile appeared on Michelle's face. "I will add you to the list, then."

Jo told Michelle she would meet her in the parking lot and hung up. Michelle always knew how good a friend Jo could be. Literally, she was the best.

Michelle headed down the stairs and to the doors that lead to the parking lot. It would be a few minutes at least for Jo to get there since she lived in an apartment not too far away. As she waited, Michelle tried to calm herself a bit. It had been a long time since she had gotten angry like that, and the tornado of emotion surprised her. After everything demons had done to ruin her life, it was too easy to be mad at them.

Maybe somewhere, deep down, Ravin was a decent guy.

Of course he wasn't, Michelle decided. There was a reason he was a demon after all. They were all the same. Sure, he had massive sex appeal. Good for him. So did most of the guys who went to Seneal Academy. Not like it mattered. After she got what she needed to know, she would never have to see him again.

Her toe tapped on the ground as she waited. Where would she get a French Silk pie at this time of night? She didn't want to ask Jo for the pie, since her friend was already doing too much. Maybe there was a bakery close by that would deliver. Then again, it was pretty late, especially for bakeries. It was possible the school's cafeteria might have had some sort of pie, but there was no guarantee that it would be French Silk.

Michelle pulled out her wallet and inspected its contents. A happy ten credit bill sat inside. Slowly, a devilish smirk popped on her face. Maybe she could fold it into a paper airplane and throw it at his overly smug face and tell him to go buy it himself. She didn't have time to go run around town to buy pie. Amusement rolled through her mind, keeping the girl preoccupied as she waited.

The more she thought about it, the delight faded. Each student had a food fabricator hooked up to their counter unit. With a code, Ravin could have gotten his pie instantly. It was a wonderfully complex machine that was so easy to use. Modern technology was the best. Not that Michelle had any idea how it worked. She just knew what buttons to press.

Lucky for her, the wait was short. It wasn't more than fifteen minutes before a pair of familiar headlights could be seen in the parking lot. Beau. Oh, that boy was a life-saver for driving Jo over. Michelle was glad that he and Jo were friends. The tall girl climbed out of the vehicle and loped off towards the dorm building. Michelle met her outside on the sidewalk. The air was cool with night. It felt good.

"Delivery for one 'Mischa,'" Jo smiled, and held out a pendant on a leather chain. Michelle blinked, and Jo took her opportunity to explain. "This is an artifact found in ruins of Old South America, now the Summer Kingdom. My parents got it at an auction and I've been using it as a decoration, so, I guess you need it more than I do."

Michelle embraced Jo. She couldn't express how much this meant to her. The glittering pendant was perfect. She didn't figure demons would be too interested in common gold, but a pendant from *Aztlan* was a different story. Earth's Old South America was long gone, now the region had shifted into the Elvan lands. The fact this piece of treasure had come from the long lost continent was remarkable. Michelle held it gently. Her eyes traced the complex lines. If nothing else, it was beautiful.

"Now, it's time for you to repay me," Jo huffed. "You have to tell me what in God's good name is going on."

"I don't think God's name has anything to do with this," Michelle quipped. "There is a demon who wants something with my sister. The one who…" She trailed off.

Some things were too hard to say, and she knew Jo understood. Her friend comforted her with a hand on the shoulder. Michelle looked into reassuring eyes.

"Tonight, I saw this weird tattoo on Lian's back. It was in demonic, I'm positive. It appeared after she swore she saw the demon… It's too much to be coincidence." Michelle's voice was strong and sure. As much as she didn't want there to be anything wrong, she knew she had to be prepared for the worst. She had to do whatever it took.

"Keep me updated," Jo ordered. "And if you need *anything*, I am here for you two." She wanted to help. Jo would do anything in her power, and she knew Michelle would too. The sisters were her best friends in the world. Both of them had a certain charm that kept them close in Jo's heart. Mischa was delightfully sassy, and Lian was so dainty and kind. Jo didn't care about money; it had no value to her. Friendship on the other hand, was the greatest gift of all.

"I will," Michelle swore. "Thanks Jo. For everything." After a quick hug, the girls parted ways and Michelle walked with haste back up the stairs to get to the fourth floor. Clutching the pendant, she was ready for answers. She deserved them. At least to know what she was dealing with.

On swift feet, she walked down the hall and towards the light at the end of the tunnel.

Michelle stood in front of the door, but didn't bother knocking. Nope, she thought really mean things, really, really loudly. If this guy wanted to play mind reader, sure, she'd play. At the full power of her thoughts, she roared into the chorus of a really bad song she had heard on the radio.

"Ding dong," she muttered, waiting for the door to grant her entrance. Answers awaited, and as scared as Michelle was to know the truth, she knew she could have no less. Lian had already been through so much, and if the man had returned and done something to her. The girl didn't even want to think about it. As messed up as Lian was, Michelle had seen her at much worse. Lia was a sweet, carefree girl who had been forced into fearing her own shadow. Happiness was always a step away.

It wasn't fair. Life wasn't fair, and Michelle knew that as well as anyone. As soon as they took a step forward, they were thrown fifteen back.

Silence surrounded Michelle. The demon didn't answer. Maybe he had fallen asleep? Tapping her toe, the girl waited longer and longer. Minutes passed with nothing. Okay, well this was strange. She figured the Ravin would be at the top of his game. He wasn't answering. Had something happened to him?

With a soft rap on the door, Michelle knocked. Silence. She waited a few seconds before knocking again. No answer. What was going on? Was he messing with her? If he was, he was so going to get it. Feeling impatient, Michelle knocked again, harder.

"Open up, you prick," she growled.

Then suddenly the door opened. Standing there was a sleepy boy with shaggy hair. He rubbed his tired eyes, and he yawned. It was the hockey player.

"Where is Ravin?" Michelle demanded.

The boy stood there for a while. He looked back inside then to the girl. It was obvious he had just woken up and he was groggy. He tilted his head questioning what was happening.

"Ravin. Where. Is. He?" She pressed.

"He's not here?" Kazun questioned, confused.

Ten

Ravin dropped his facade the minute Michelle departed. He understood her discontent. He'd be angry, too, if his sister acquired an unholy tattoo out of the blue. Of course, he didn't have a sister—that he knew of—so this was not his concern. He had to figure out if this mark meant what he thought it did. Danger. They were evil, even in the poorly rendered drawing. Ravin felt the energy welling from the symbol. Cool clammy tickles crawled up the skin of his hand. He repressed a shudder.

There was only a slight chance that he was wrong. Never before had he ever wanted that so much. He resisted the urge to crush the paper. Despite that initial reaction, he still needed the image to get some information.

At length, he returned to his room and closed the door. He

grabbed a shirt off the floor, and pulled it on. There was business to be done. The demon headed out to Sinsation. It was the only place he could get consistent information that wouldn't cost him an arm and a leg.

It wasn't as if he needed this cluster fuck right now. However, he was glad to be able to use Michelle for payment. Every part of what he asked for was going straight to Sin. Hopefully, Sin appreciated the payment that Michelle was bringing. Life was becoming this vicious cycle for him. It was all because of that damned bounty. If he hadn't been trying to find souls, he wouldn't have run into Michelle. If he hadn't run into Michelle, then he wouldn't have to deal with this damn tattoo thing. If his instincts were right, all of it was above his pay grade.

A simple thought put him outside the bar. Absently, he clenched his free hand into a fist. Somebody inside was going to get him what he needed. He hoped the price wasn't too steep.

He shook his head as he was granted access to the bar, the familiar aromas of drink and fried food assailed him, intermixed with the scent of wood varnish. With a quick scan he saw a few familiar faces. Each one that he knew was associated with an amount of money or a specific task that they required. Some of these beings were so predictable. They were frustrating, and not worth it. Plus, they weren't skilled enough to confirm or deny what he already knew.

There was one unfamiliar face that stood out. Oddly, he felt a connection, like he knew this person. It wasn't the similarities that some said all demons possessed. No, he'd seen this demon before, but he couldn't place when or where. His energy stunk of the rain that had poured down all night, though Ravin was certain that if this new demon had been causing it then there'd still be a downpour. The tall horns on his head warned Ravin that this wasn't someone to tango with. Yet, he surmised, if this stranger was a bounty hunter then he wouldn't be at the headquarters of the very person who was trying to foil all other hunters. It couldn't hurt much to test this newcomer. Plus, he had good reason to want to procrastinate.

Ravin grabbed a drink and walked over to the demon. "You're new around here, aren't you?" Casting a roguish grin, he slid into the chair across from his kin. The hardwood was cool so he knew that the other hadn't recently had company. All the same, he took in every detail of the other demon that he could.

This man had horns far larger than Ravin, though they weren't nearly as large as Sin's. The sable projections protruded from his jet black hair, and grew straight back over his head, curving back into sharp dangerous points.

"I am." The man's piercing pale grey eyes glittered as his lips curled into a slight smile. "It's always nice to see a friendly face."

There was a dark edge to his tone that most people wouldn't have noticed, but it was quite apparent to Ravin. The man rubbed the stubble that marked his strong chin.

"Isn't it?" Ravin took a swig of his drink. There was always something with his species; this guy was here for a reason. "The name's Raven," he offered, purposely giving the wrong name. Names held power in the supernatural world. To give out a true name was asking for trouble.

"You can call me Ira," the demon across from him said, running a hand through his dark hair. Ira was silent for a long few moments as he downed some of his own amber ale. Those light grey eyes scrutinized Ravin, then in a concerned voice that came off as condescending—he sighed. "You must have it so hard with that warrant hanging over you." His grey eyes pierced into Ravin, reading him like a book.

Tension shot through Ravin's body, like lightning. Ira knew. Of course he knew. There wasn't a soul in Hell who didn't know about his predicament. Instead of being intimidated like this being wanted, Ravin used it as an affirmation to remind him why he was working for Sin.

"Well I suppose after this long, I'm used to it." Ravin brushed off the other demon's fake concern with little more than a shrug.

"I might be able to help you," Ira said in a honey smooth tone. "It wouldn't cost you very much."

Ravin suspected that Ira was lying. Nothing was cheap anymore. Everyone had their price, and even Sin hadn't helped get rid of the bounty. She just kept doubling the price for protection. "Oh I bet." He suppressed a snort of derision. "Do go on, don't leave me hanging."

"You really want me to tell you?" Ira's brow quirked as he asked in a calm tone. There was a strange edge to his voice that Ravin couldn't quite identify.

After a few moments of consideration, Ravin nodded. "Sure, why not?"

Ravin decided there wasn't actually a snowball's chance in Hell that this Ira could, in fact, help him. It was more likely he wanted to deceive Ravin and claim Kazun's head in one fell swoop. The compensation was more than money; the higher-ups offered power. To an average demon like Ravin, it was so deliciously tempting. More than once he'd considered turning himself in, but even he had standards.

The dark haired demon leaned back in his seat. "Why should I?" he yawned lazily. "You don't honestly believe I can, so why waste my time explaining?"

"Because perhaps you can convince me otherwise." Every molecule of Ravin's body screamed at him to get up and leave. Only terrible things could come of this demon's company. Yet, he couldn't shake the feeling that Ira held some kind of secret that could ultimately aid him. After all, in no time flat, the reward would be so high that even Sin couldn't throw people off his trail. At least, that's what she claimed.

Ira shook his head. "I don't think you're ready to take it seriously."

The words sent a flare of anger through Ravin.

Ira reached into his fine jacket and slid a business card across the table. "When you're ready to hear what I have to say, why don't you give me a call, and we can discuss things further. After all, you already have the answer, right there, in your pocket."

Ravin's fingers brushed the outside of his pants. He felt the folded rectangle Michelle had given him. The symbol could fix it all? He knew the mark was dark in nature and dangerous, but in truth, he didn't know the exact words depicted. That's what Sin was for.

Before he had the chance to ask any further questions the oh-so familiar feel of Sin's energy struck him like a bolt of lightning.

He turned to her and half stood. When he looked back at where Ira sat, he was gone. Of course, the other had been flighty. Most of his race were when they knew they couldn't achieve what they set out to do.

"Twice in one day, Ravin? Oh you spoil me." Sin had a wicked smile on her beautiful face. Her long tail swayed lazily as she approached. Each step was silken grace.

"Now to what do I owe this visit, my dear?" Her voice was as delicious as a decadent dessert. Every rich word she spoke was like warm molten chocolate to the ear. She leaned tantalizingly close to him. Of course she could easily read the other's mind to figure out what he wanted, but she preferred talking. There was a reason she owned a bar. Socializing was her specialty.

His eyes drifted over her perfect caramel skin and her thick black hair. "You know I love to spoil you, my dear." He enjoyed her closeness. Sin was one of the most gorgeous women he knew and it would be a crime not to appreciate her. "I need to ask you to help me with a translation."

"Oh sure." Always work and no play. "Let me see what you've got." She held out a flawless hand. Sin was being more than nice and not even asking for something in return. Ravin did a lot for her, so it was the least she could do.

Ravin pulled out the picture Michelle had drawn. "So, I'm not going to lie, I don't have any idea what it means. It's dark in nature that's about all I can figure out."

Sin's fingers were precise as they retrieved the paper. The smile on her face faded the moment she read the words. Her eyes traced the marking. There was a mixed emotion floating around in her dark expression.

"Where in Hell's name did you find this?" she hissed. Before she realized what she had done her hands clenched around the delicate drawing, crushing it with wrath. It was imperfect, but it was clear to her what it was supposed to mean. The marking was one of a kind.

"A *human* asked me to translate it for her," Ravin growled in a low tone. He didn't want to get the attention of other patrons. The demon already had one of his fellows trying to get in on this worrisome piece of paper. Like he really needed more of them on his back. No, this was only for Sin's eyes and ears. Luckily, when she crushed it, the quiet cold energy it exuded ceased.

Sin rubbed her temple as she grabbed Ravin's hand and pulled him into the back room where she took care of the business aspects of her bar. Files lined the shelves along the walls and simple books were filled with numbers and payments. She figured this was a conversation better not overheard by others. Once they were both inside, she shut the door and locked it. Her eyes fixed straight onto Ravin.

"This is the Word of the Marked," Sin whispered, tail twisting, "Ravin, you do know what that is, correct?" It was old, old lore. The Word of the Marked was a story about the rise of Darkness. It was a bedtime story for baby demons. Though, she had never seen any true evidence of it crawling around the Eartha.

Ravin shook his head. "I don't, actually." Many things had been lost from his mind over the years. There was a point where all memories had disappeared everything from before Sin finding him in a field was long gone. If he had heard the stories at one point, it had been a time long lost to him.

"The Word of the Marked means great and terrible things. Tell me your familiarity with angels?" Sin sat on the edge of her sturdy mahogany desk. Her gaze seemed to get distant as she tried to recall whatever information she could.

Ravin cringed internally. "I know that they are our mortal enemies and our opposites in every way. They reside in *Heaven* and serve their Father." He shuddered and scrunched his nose. The thought of angels left a bad taste in his mouth. "They tend to terminate us on sight."

"Have you heard of the Dark Angel?" Sin continued, her tone light, but her eyes were grave.

"No." Ravin leaned against the wall and crossed his arms.

Sin leaned back in her chair. After a long sigh, she opened her hand and let the crumbled scrap fall to the desk. With lazy strokes, her fingers traced the lines and smoothed it out again. "A long time ago, there was an angel race born of darkness. The light bearers feared them and a great war erupted."

"A war of angels?" Ravin's brow quirked.

"One like you'd never imagine. There was blood that rained from the heavens. And after it all, one dark angel was left. With a scythe made of moonlight, she single-handedly destroyed platoons of angels." Sin sat up straight, her eyes wild as she recounted the story. "She cracked the Earth and sent torrents of death among the human race. She killed and slaughtered and swore to kill all that the beings of light had created." Her voice tapered off. "The world had never seen such dark days since..."

"By the grace of their Father, she was locked away, but she

swore she'd return. This, The Word of the Marked, is her emblem. This symbol is said to be one of the only things that can free her from her prison."

Ravin was slowly beginning to comprehend how much worse the situation was than he had first thought. Michelle was not going to like this news. Could she handle it? Did she even know that angels existed? The lofty beings from heaven didn't often find their way down to Eartha. They much preferred their residence in the cloud temples above.

"How can a mark like that free her from an angel cage?" It all seemed too farfetched for Ravin.

"Like any other angel, she can link herself to a human. This mark gives her a human to link to." She watched him with careful cat eyes.

His blonde brows furrowed. "But since there's only one dark angel left, there's a chance that they'd never even see the angel in their lifetime, right?"

"The fact that this mark has appeared on someone isn't an accident. There is a very, very specific ritual. It takes time and planning. Ravin, someone wants the dark angel to be released, and unless you can find out how to stop them..." she trailed off. She didn't have to spell out where this was going. It wasn't good for the poor little mortal. She stretched a little. "I understand you care about your little humans Rav, but you have that outstanding bounty hanging over Kazun's head. Do you really need something else to worry about? In my expert opinion, you need to walk away from this." She held out a caramel colored hand, offering the drawing back.

"Where's the fun in that?" Ravin teased as he took the paper. Internally he was a wreck. Life was dealing him the worst possible hand. He always tried to keep the calmest demeanor, even in situations like this.

Now he had to figure out what to tell Michelle.

"I guess that's why I do business with you Rav," Sin said with a whimsical smirk. "Always willing to go above and beyond." The woman hopped off of the desk and ran her hand across Ravin's cheek. "I guess it wouldn't hurt to check out the situation. If you don't mind me tagging along. A dark angel may be bad for business, so it is really for the best." She winked.

Part of her decided to help the other because it was true. A dark angel had the potential to make her near obsolete, and on the other hand, she was curious. Plus, it was considered polite to offer her assistance to someone so loyal.

Ravin nodded. "Sounds excellent. Let's go back to my dorm, Michelle might be back soon." He ran a hand through his shaggy blonde hair.

Sin gave him a smile and a nod before disappearing into a puff of smoke and energy.

The demons appeared outside Ravin's apartment and quickly entered. A few moments later a sleepy, and slightly irate voice chimed. "You want to explain what the hell is going on here?" Kazun rubbed his eyes tiredly and glared at them.

Eleven

Michelle's brows furrowed. He was with a female demon. This was frustrating. Her sister's life could have been on the line and what was he doing? She frowned and crossed her arms. With an aggravated toss, she threw the pendant that she had retrieved for him at Ravin's face. To her dismay, he caught it.

"There. Take it you arrogant fuck-boy." Her eyes pulled into a dangerous glare.

"She's quite the cute one, Rav," Sin purred with a smirk. "I can see why you're helping her out." Sin's long tail swayed back and forth with interest. This human had a bit of zing to her, which was delicious. She approved.

Ravin grinned and turned to Sin, ignoring Michelle all together. "Why thank you." He offered the amulet over to Sin. "Does this work as adequate payment?"

Sin took the beautiful shining pendant in her hands. It was quite the delightful treat. Sweet magical properties oozed off of it like molten chocolate. It was from pre-equilibrium. Sin brought the amulet to her face and dragged her forked, pierced tongue across its grooved surface. The magic sizzled and popped like fizzed candy against her sensitive flesh. "Oh yes, Rav, this is quite nice."

Michelle blinked as she watched the two. Her cheeks were a little red from the she-demon's comment. Not from embarrassment, but from anger. Her blue eyes flared with aggravation. "Will someone tell me what is happening?" Her hands clenched.

With a swish of his tail, Ravin held out the drawing and looked at Michelle. "Lian has this tattoo, doesn't she?"

"Wait, what?" Kazun asked in a more alert tone.

Michelle looked at her feet, sighed and nodded. There was no use hiding it. The mind readers in the room knew it anyway. How could they not? It was blaring in her thoughts louder than a foghorn. "Yes," she reiterated. "Yes, she does."

Ravin nodded. "It is the Word of the Marked." Michelle's glare made it clear she had no idea what he meant. "Typically the Word of the Marked indicates that one is targeted to be tied to an angel. In fact, at some point you could get one, too."

"Angels?" Michelle questioned, "That marking didn't look very holy."

"Well, if you're an angel expert now, then you didn't need to waste your time getting me that amulet. I can see you don't really need my help." Ravin flopped back onto his couch and reclined.

"Now, now Ravin, So rude." Sin stretched, her body lithe like a panther. Her exotic eyes smoldered. "I remember when you came to me looking for help like a lost kitten. Perhaps you should show the woman the same courtesy and kindness." The female demon stepped over to Michelle and sighed. Her hand trailed against Michelle's short dark hair. With a gentle tone, Sin addressed Michelle. "Because it isn't Haelic, the angel language. These words are dark in nature." With the grace of a butterfly, the demon slid her hand down to Michelle's shoulder. Then Sin turned to Ravin.

"Now help this young lady," she commanded him.

Ravin sighed and leaned back. "She should be alright, Lian that is." Yes, whatever ritual it was had been performed, but the only dark angel left was bound… somewhere. "I'd keep an eye on her."

"That's it?" Michelle questioned, "Seriously?" A part of her was really relieved, but another told her that it was complete and utter bullshit. Then again, if the demon had decided that was what he was going to inform her of anything more, then there was no way for her to change his mind. She'd accept it grudgingly, but she still had a bad feeling in her gut. A really bad feeling.

"Seriously." He kept his demeanor as calm as possible. "Watch her."

Michelle shrugged her shoulders and looked over at Kazun. This didn't feel right. Something seemed off. Like…she wasn't getting the whole picture. They were keeping something from her. Sin seemed likely to tell her, but Ravin's information wouldn't help a five-year-old. Then again, maybe she didn't want to know. It was frustrating, but there was nothing to be done about it. Here anyway. She would do research of her own. "Thanks… I guess."

Kaz looked between everyone in the room. Everything was weird. He knew Ravin was hiding something, but he didn't know exactly what.

"Thanks Sin." Ravin nodded, she had assisted him and he was grateful.

"I guess that's my cue," Sin purred. "It was my pleasure." She took one last long look at Michelle before disappearing into nothing.

The human watched as she left, then glanced back to Ravin.

Ravin peered at Michelle. "Thank you for the amulet," he said in a calm tone. She wouldn't understand what he had done or why for that matter. Not that he really cared at all, as long as the other demons stayed away from Kazun. Nobody was claiming the bounty while he still drew breath.

"Yeah, thanks for nothing." Michelle turned and stormed out of the room. It was obvious that something else was happening… something wasn't right. She could feel it. Her sister was in some sort of danger and the only answer she had gotten was that it was a dark angel… whatever that was. She'd find her own way to keep Lian safe. However, it had put this "mark" on her sister, it wasn't going to get her.

Michelle had failed to save Lian once. She couldn't stop the bad things from before, but now she had a warning and a name for the tattoo. Plus, she was stubborn as hell. It wasn't a safe combo, but it was all she had. If Lian was hurt again, Michelle didn't know what she would do. Hopefully, it wouldn't come to that.

"I could help you know." Ravin called after Michelle. Hell, he might even give her a discount. Ira's offer was still fresh in his mind... and he knew it had something to do with Lian now... it would be smart to keep the two girls close.

"Help?" Michelle questioned. *"Help?!"* Her frustration had hit its climax. If she was a kettle, steam would have poured from her ears. "If your version of help is 'find me something expensive, then I will tell you to babysit your own sister' then your help is *useless* and I don't want it." She was fuming. Desperation and worry fueled a dangerous fire. "Let me guess, for nine-ninety-five I can get a 'make good choices, don't do drugs'."

A muscle ticked in Ravin's jaw. "We all have something we need to protect." He stood and took inhumanly smooth steps towards her. "I took *payment* so I didn't lose what was important to me." There was a dark edge to his voice. "In my situation, you would do the same." He used his height to loom over her. "Now do you want your sister kept safe or not? Because I don't have to offer. There are other places I could offer my talents, but there aren't many as nice as I am to do it with *limited* payment."

The human girl looked at him, and her piercing blue eyes did not waver with fear. "If you are protecting someone, wouldn't you want to know all you could to keep them safe? Wouldn't you want to know if there was anything you could do? I know you aren't telling me the full truth. I'm not an idiot. In a few hours, Lian is going to wake up..." Tears bubbled in her eyes and her fists clenched, nails biting into her palm. "And she is going to go take a shower, like she always does, and she is going to see that *thing* on her back." The tear escaped and rolled down her cheek.

"She will freak out, and come looking to me for answers that

I don't have. Because I am one of the few people who believed her when she told me one of *your* kind hurt her." Michelle reached up and rubbed her eyes. "And I get to look her in the eye and say 'Guess we'll have to wait and see what happens.'"

Michelle's single tear hit Ravin harder than he had expected. He hated tears, but not in a violent way; they were one of his weaknesses. The demon ran a hand through his hair. "When she starts freaking out, demons are going to come looking for her, Michelle," he told her in complete honesty. Of course, he left out the detail that there was at least one demon searching for her already.

"Then tell me what to do," she begged, voice wavering. "Please."

Ravin reached out and put a hand on Michelle's shoulder. "You need to trust me." He cast a quick glance at Kazun, his eyes soft in a moment of weakness. "I know it's hard, but you have to."

"I don't know if I can," Michelle sighed softly. "Trust doesn't come cheap." As scared as she was at the prospect of demons looking for Lian, at least she could fight to have the upper hand.

A snort escaped Ravin, "I'll get right on that then." He winked at the human. "In the meantime, go get some rest. I'll get her a necklace that'll disguise her energy." That wouldn't be too hard to find. He had several different items that served the purpose of hiding beings. They were all different pieces of jewelry that he'd collected over the years from unsuspecting or complacent victims.

"Thank you," the girl said, her voice sincere. "See you tomorrow then?"

He nodded. "Of course," He put a hand on her head. "Sweet dreams." It felt as though a weight had been lifted from his chest, even though he knew that his burden had increased exponentially.

She nodded and replied, "You too, Ravin... and," she looked over at Kazun. "Sorry for waking you." She brushed Ravin's hand off her head and she smoothed her hair a bit.

"S'ok," Kazun said with a sleepy yawn, "Night." Yes, he was disturbed by what was happening with Lian, but he was too exhausted from his day for it to sink into his mind.

With a wave, Michelle started her way back down to her own dorm. It had been an overly exciting night, and she was ready to get some rest. Her bed called to her every step of the way. How nice it would be to get all cuddled under her blanket. She knew that it would be impossible to actually sleep. In the morning, she would have some questions to answer.

At least at this point, she had some vague idea of what was happening. The Word of the Marked, eh? Well, at least it had a cool name. If it had been something like the Bunny Paw Print of Death, well, that would have almost been insulting. Her thoughts made a frown appear on her face. Frustration returned. What was she going to say if Lian found out?

Ravin was trying as hard as she was to keep someone safe. Though she could respect the action, she found herself angry at him once again. He could have least offered her something to go on.

A bit of fear splintered through her thoughts. If demons wanted Lian, what was stopping Ravin from turning the tables on her? What if he was after her too… or if Sin was? A shiver rolled up her spine. Okay, no more bad thoughts.

For now, she would keep it in the back of her mind. If Ravin made any moves against his sister, Michelle would be ready. For a while, she would humor him and keep tabs on him. He was the only lead she had. Betrayal was the only thing that could make this situation worse. No. It wouldn't be betrayal. She would have to have given him an ounce of trust for that. He hadn't earned it yet. No, Ravin was first on her radar, and after him was that Sin woman. Michelle would keep her guard up. She would allow Ravin's help for now. Not because she thought he was a decent being. Because he was the only shot she had at keeping Lian safe.

As she approached the door, the sound of coughing hit her ears. It wasn't until she got it open that she realized the sound she was hearing was her sister. Michelle rushed into the room and found Lian laying in the middle of the floor, coughing and hacking.

"Lian!" Michelle cried out and kneeled by her sister. Carefully she placed her hand on Lian's forehead. Pure heat radiated off of the girl's skin. With a quick step, Michelle ran to get a damp cloth to try and cool her off, if only slightly.

"Michelle..." Lian whimpered. "I don't feel good..." Another round of coughing struck her hard and she curled tightly into a ball. After a few moments, her sister returned and she was helped back into her bed. Michelle placed the cool cloth on her head.

"It's okay," Michelle whispered. "I'm here. You're safe now."

Twelve

The morning came far too soon. It appeared Kazun got plenty of rest, while Ravin got very little. His knowledge of what was happening kept his eyes open throughout most of the night. There was a chance that Lian could be the key to getting rid of the bounty. That same bounty that had been the bane of his existence for the past few months. It would be nice to wake up one day and not have to think about Kazun's safety.

Now that would be swell.

He slid out of bed with a groan and pulled on a fresh shirt, being careful to avoid catching the cloth on his horns. For a few moments, he studied his reflection in the mirror that hung above his dresser. He could see the bags under his eyes from lack of sleep.

With a heavy sigh, he crossed over the plush dark carpet that covered their floor, and strode easily into the living room. His roomie was eating a bowl of cereal without a care in the world.

"Morning," Ravin grunted.

"Morning," the human yawned in reply.

Ravin slid into one of the chairs that surrounded the table and shook his head. "You've got no excuse to be tired, you wimp. You actually got some sleep." He brought the cereal box over with his mind and grabbed a handful of O's, and popped them into his mouth.

"I guess that's true," Kazun shrugged. "So what was with last night anyway?"

The demon sighed again. "Well, apparently your little girlfriend has got a target on her back. I agreed to help her and her sister out."

A flush covered Kaz's face. "She's not my girlfriend." Of course she wasn't, he'd barely known her for a day. She hadn't even been able to talk to him. Dating would be impractical… and awkward. "I'll go check on them after practice, it can't be easy to cope with something like that." He of all people knew what that was like to be under constant scrutiny.

"That sounds like a good plan." Ravin rubbed his tired eyes, then stretched. "You and your girlfriend are perfect. It's so sweet I think I'm going to get super diabetes!" he jibed and popped a few more rings of cereal into his mouth.

"I swear to everything that is holy and unholy if you call her that again I will punch you out Ravin," Kazun growled and flushed deeply. "And what in the star's name is diabetes?" He hated being teased, by Ravin more than anyone. The demon knew all of his weak points.

Ravin laughed and leaned back. Of course Kazun didn't know what the old world disease was. How precious. "You're so sweet to me, Kazun." The demon made wheat rings float around him like an asteroid belt of nutrition. "It's a matter of time, cutie pie." He flicked his tail in delight.

Kaz finished the milk in his bowl and went to rinse it out.

"Don't be such an ass," he called over his shoulder and put his dish in the sink. "I've never dated anyone. I highly doubt that will change." The human walked into his room and grabbed his workout gear.

"You never know!" Ravin shouted after him.

"Drop it." Kazun pulled his bedroom door closed. "I'll be back in a few hours, please don't cause too much trouble." He walked over to the table again. "While you're at it, give me their room number."

The demon shook his head. "Do you honestly think that I have it? That would be invading their privacy and ever so rude. Plus, when would I even have the time to figure that out?" Ravin put the back of his hand against his forehead.

Kazun rolled his eyes. "I know they're in this building, just not where."

The demon tapped his chin, then shrugged. It had been stamped on her key, "it's room 143." Ravin narrowed his dark eyes. "You owe me." Had Kazun not known his friend so well, he would be sure that Ravin meant it.

"Yeah, yeah," the human brushed the threat off. "But seriously, stay out of trouble."

"Oh Kaz, you know me so well." The demon tossed his blonde hair, but didn't disturb the ring orbiting him.

"I know, that's what I'm afraid of." With that, he left their room.

Kazun headed down the stairs and to the gym on campus. Today's agenda was lifting weights to build their muscle mass. Not that half the team needed to. Both of the fire dragons could lift the whole team without even trying. Single-handedly.

Once again, his teammates blasted loud music with a pulsing beat that matched the rhythm of the reps. After two hours of pumping iron, Kazun felt both energized and drained. His skin was slick from sweat and he could swear that he smelled like Hell, but he loved it.

"Good form Kazun." Letvan rubbed the top of his head with a towel, his voice was tinted with the ever so sweet accent of his people, "Your vigor never seems to diminish." With careful fingers the elf traced the lines of a small braid he wore on the side of his head.

Kazun beamed at his team captain, "Thanks Letvan, I try!"

"Got any plans today?" Letvan asked with a pleasant smile as he used the towel to wipe away some sweat from his face.

The human nodded. "I'm going to check on... a friend to see if they're okay. Apparently something is going on in their life and they need support."

He was intentionally as vague as possible for a few reasons. One, he didn't need his other teammates hounding him for checking on the *girl*, especially after the flak they gave him for talking to her yesterday. Two, if they found out *why*, then it could jeopardize poor Lian's safety. And three... Well, some of them wouldn't leave her alone if they found out who she was she was and the poor girl was so very shy that it could destroy any chance he had at becoming friends with her.

"Aww, well wish them well for me," Letvan replied. "I have to go train my young pupil. So that should be fun."

Kaz blinked, confused for a moment about who Letvan would be training. He vaguely remembered Letvan saying something about this before... "Isn't that the kid you're teaching how to be an Elf?"

"Ah yes," Letvan lilted whimsically, "Marius. He's my little pet project."

"He was raised by humans even though he's from your Court, right?"

At Kazun's response, the elf nodded as he moved over to his water bottle. Letvan poured a small amount on his head to cool off. "Real tragic case," the elf continued. "But he is eager to learn, and hopes to join the Summer Court after I get him prepared."

Letvan's story warmed Kazun; it was uplifting. He was glad that his teammate would be so kind to someone he barely knew, even if they were the same species. "I wish you both the best of luck." He grinned at the elf.

"You too, Kazun," the other said with a thumbs up, then he left to go change.

When he was done changing into fresh clothes, Kazun left the gym, using the side exit to avoid the fan girls that he was sure would be waiting for him. He headed to the cafeteria to pick up something quick to eat. His stomach grumbled, reminding him that he hadn't eaten very much that morning.

Sitting on the far edge of the lunchroom was a girl wrapped in an overly large soft pink sweater. She wore a pastel knit hat, and a matching scarf. Looking around, the girl appeared very nervous. A sneeze escaped her nose and she rubbed her face with her long sleeve. As Kazun passed, their eyes locked. There was a question in his gaze, as a response the pair of shy, blue eyes looked down.

Kazun raised a brow, then went into the lunch line to get some food. As always, the cafeteria was filled with a plethora of choices. On one side they had classic pre-equilibrium 'American' food, burgers, chicken strips, and the works. Down another line was sushi, pasta, and Elvan delicacies. In the far corner was a cooler where vampires could find a meal. The academy had anything that anyone could want to eat, within reason. The large amount of choices was nice, but sometimes made it hard to pick a favorite.

Kaz grabbed some pasta. He needed the carbs that he had burned while working out. He put the plate on his tray then added garlic bread, and went to the cashier. All he had to do was swipe his student ID card and it was paid for. Food in hand, he started back for Lian's table. As he approached, the girl lifted her hand in silent greeting before sneezing again.

"Everything ok?" he asked as he pulled out one of the chairs to sit. Kazun lowered his voice even further, "I wanted to apologize again, for Ravin yesterday. He's sort of an idiot. Probably the *biggest* idiot, with filter issues." He did his best to keep his tone even and his expression calm.

"I… I'm sick," Lian responded in a muffled voice. She rubbed her nose with a tissue before sniffing, "it could be… um… worse." Her face was flushed, it was hard to tell if it was from her illness, or if it was from a blush.

"I'm so sorry." He stabbed his fork into his pasta and gave her a sympathetic look. "I hate being sick."

Lian didn't respond. Instead those wide blue eyes were centered on him, examining him.

Kazun felt awkward, like he was on display. He cleared his throat, and swallowed another bite of food. "So, what are you doing out here?"

"Michelle is getting me something to eat… she hopes it will make me feel better," she informed him in a whisper. She gave a quiet sniff, silently wishing she could smell his pasta, and watched him for a moment.

He nodded. "That's really sweet of her." The boy really did hate being sick, but his father would always make him soup when he had been home. Kaz let out a laugh. "Sorry about my stink. I had a work out a bit ago, so I'm probably pretty rank."

Lian rubbed at her nose a little and shook her head

"I can't smell anything, and sweat smell isn't so bad. It makes me feel better after I work out." Timidly she rubbed her arm. Was that weird? What if it was, oh she was not good at talking to people. Wiping her face, the girl took a deep breath and started coughing.

A smile crossed the boy's lips. "I don't think it smells that much. Ravin always teases me though, so I guess I'm a bit self-conscious." His cheeks flushed as he took a bite of his pasta.

"It's…okay," the girl's tiny voice replied after a few seconds. "Don't worry—" her sentence was stopped by a second stream of coughs. After regaining her air, she touched her sore throat and let out an involuntary whimper.

Kazun frowned. "Shouldn't you be in bed?" he asked in a gentle voice. She appeared so tired, she looked like she was ready to keel over.

"I was hungry…" Lian explained, "and Michelle can't cook…" So, Michelle had piled a ton of warm clothes on her and had placed her there while she looked around the cafeteria for decent sustenance. Most likely her big sister was still in the line being indecisive trying find the correct this or that. There were always so many choices…

Kazun gave her a strange look, "Why not use the holopad in your room?"

"You don't know my sister, do you?" Michelle had tried earlier, but had somehow managed to jam the equipment. So here they were.

He nodded knowingly. "I'm sorry about that…" His cheeks tinted darker. "I seriously hope you feel better…"

"Alright! We have chicken noodle, tomato basil, creamy cheese broccoli, two different kinds of juices, a grilled cheese, some water, and whatever this weird looking vegetable is… I think it's an albino broccoli." Michelle chimed in a peppy tone as she approached the table.

"Michelle…. that is a cauliflower…" Lian stared at the large tray of food. How on Eartha was she going to eat all of that? Sure she was hungry… but that was so much. She gave Kazun a 'there is no way I'm eating all this look', then she turned her attention back to her sister. "So much…"

"Eat what you want, Lia," Michelle said. "We gotta get your

energy up so you can fight your cold. Oh, hey, Kaz." She plopped down in an empty chair and grinned. She was being such a good big sister, taking care of Lia and everything.

"O-okay..." Lian began to pick quietly at the food. She could feel her face was even more flushed with embarrassment. People were staring now, weren't they?

Kazun nodded in acknowledgement of the older sibling. "Hey, Michelle," he waved his fork and spun some more noodles onto the utensil. They were quickly devoured, and followed by large bites of garlic bread.

"Didn't expect to see you," Michelle commented. "Is your roomie bumming around somewhere or is it only you?" She picked off a bit of food from the large amount on the tray.

"I got done with weight lifting," he explained between bites. "Ravin was still at home last I checked, but I was out for an hour or two since then, so he's probably found some trouble." The boy laughed as if sharing a private joke. Of course Ravin would find trouble. He always did.

"Ravin getting into trouble?" Michelle taunted. "I could *never* imagine that." She let out a chuckle, and even Lian gave a weak smile. It was nice to see that, despite how sick she had gotten. Even if Michelle didn't look it, she was really worried. Lian rarely got sick. When she did, it was like a cough, not some sudden fever… It was more than a little perturbing.

With a chuckle, Kazun finished his large plate of food. His belly felt warm and full, which made him content. "He'll probably show up before too long."

Truth be told, Ravin had a way of appearing when he was

mentioned.

Lian blinked as she took in a spoon full of the broccoli and cheese. She stared past Kazun's shoulder and tilted her head. She seemed to be watching something. Quickly, she looked back down and ate faster as if she had seen something she shouldn't have.

Kazun tilted his head and looked over at the shy girl. "Everything ok Lia—"

His words were cut off as a pair of hands jabbed into his sides and a voice made a loud sound in his ear. He half-screamed, half-yelled and thrust his elbow into the stomach of his 'attacker.'

"I deserved that," Ravin choked out and held his gut. He slid into the seat next to Kazun and pouted at his friend. "You're so cruel to me Kazun!"

The human knew he was red with embarrassment. How many times was Ravin going to do this? It was always the same result when Ravin tried to scare Kazun, and the demon always complained when he came out injured. "Stop doing that Ravin," Kaz ordered in a stern tone as he tried to calm down.

"I guess it's appropriate to say 'speak of the devil'," Michelle commented dully, but she held an amused smile. It was fun watching Ravin get hurt.

Lian on the other hand looked very, very concerned. So concerned, that she let out a few coughs.

The demon let out a strained chuckle. "Well, it is appropriate, I am a handsome devil."

He glanced over at the small sick sounding girl. He frowned. She was sick. So soon? This wasn't good, not good in the slightest. He didn't have to be a doctor to know that this wasn't a natural illness. With a glance, he could tell. The Angel Syndrome had already begun.

Thirteen

He did his best to hide the tension that this new knowledge caused. "You know, it might be best to get Lian back to bed soon." Ravin tried to appear as if he was concerned about the girl's health. Of course, he was worried about the sickness, but not for the same reasons that Michelle and Kazun would be.

The girl was tied to a dark angel, but her fragile mortal body was rejecting the new energy. It wasn't uncommon for someone tied to an angel to experience some side effects. Most people called it "Angel Syndrome." Most showed the outward symptoms of slight fever, a cough, sniffling, and in extreme cases, nausea. He had a feeling that this was only the start of her symptoms. This dark angel was a powerful, ancient being, feared by all. Even a sliver of that potential could ruin a human.

From across the table, he could feel the dark energy emanating from Lian's body. He knew what to look for, and perhaps if one didn't know the energy, they would ignore it. But soon, that energy would be more potent and demons would flock to it.

Lian was scared of demons as it was. It would only get worse as the energy grew stronger because those demons would be drawn like moths to a flame.

Michelle looked over at her sister. Lian was looking pathetic. Maybe the demon was right. "You finished with your grub, Sissykins?"

Lian looked down at her half eaten bowl of soup, then at the grilled cheese with a single bite from the center. After taking a last bite from the sandwich, she gave a sheepish nod.

"Let's all go together," Kazun offered in a light tone. He didn't want these two walking around on their own, in case Lian suddenly passed out. It was an excuse to keep them safe, if anything happened.

"Perfect idea," Ravin praised his friend.

"Lian, would you mind a couple of house guests?" Michelle asked. She wanted to talk to Ravin anyway. She had a suspicion that this sickness was due to the dark tattoo on Lian's back. She was certain the demon would know.

Lian looked around for a few moments before finally whispering, "But our room is dirty."

"They don't care, and when you say the room is dirty, that means you've been sick and can't be anal about everything. Trust me, sis."

The older sister messed with Lian's hair. Her response was a single squeak of protest. So what if she liked things really clean? When things were out of place it made her anxious. Then again, most things did.

Kazun offered a friendly smile. "It can't be worse than how Ravin leaves our place. I feel like a maid sometimes."

"It's not my fault that you don't understand my genius organizing style." Ravin put an offended hand to his chest.

"If by 'organize' you mean throw everything on the ground until I pick it up for you, then yes, you're a genius." If there was one thing he could do without, it was Ravin's 'cleaning style.'

"That sounds familiar, doesn't it Lian?" Michelle laughed with a wink. Her little sister was always cleaning Michelle's messes. Not that Michelle was overly unorganized, but Lian could be a bit over attentive to details. She liked things how she liked things. If one thing was out of place, Lian would notice and fix it.

Lian gave Michelle a warm smile. She yawned and hid her face with her fluffy sleeves. She looked ready for bed. Her blue eyes were dull with exhaustion, and dark rings bloomed below them. The tip of her nose was red from using too many tissues. The poor thing looked ready to fall asleep in her bowl.

Kazun stood and offered Lian his hand, "C'mon." He spoke carefully to avoid alarming her. "Let's head back to your place." In a situation like this, he would like to have a friendly face and a helping hand to get right back into bed to sleep off the sickness.

Ravin regretted the new time crunch he was under. This was yet another countdown he had to deal with. He hated his kind so much sometimes. They could be greedy, selfish bastards. If there was a chance for power, they would make a grab for it. If there was even the narrowest chance of increasing their standing in the demon hierarchy, then it was the most important thing in the Under. Maybe if they stopped being so greedy, and had the ability to understand what it was like to have someone trying to take something—other than power—from them, then maybe they would lay off for once. Maybe then he could get a good night's sleep.

Before he had Kazun in his life, he had been completely carefree. There had been no limits, other than the ones Sin put on him. He could do whatever he wanted, whenever he wanted. Stealing souls had been a breeze, and had required no thought whatsoever. Nobody put looming deadlines over him or wanted his head on a platter. This weakness that had resulted in the bounty on his head, the weakness that made him promise to protect this human… if he had known back then, maybe he would have turned his back on Kazun.

More so now, than in the past ten years, he was beginning to doubt himself. Demons were typically harbingers of chaos. It was in their nature, but Ravin wasn't compelled to cause trouble. He had to protect these pathetic humans whose lives were little more than a blink in his thousands of years of life.

Something inside of the demon had always pushed him towards defending humans. It used to be weaker than his desire to steal souls. Over a thousand years ago, he wouldn't have given humanity a second thought. Now, the situation was different.

He couldn't fight that humane part of him, and he didn't know why. Most of the time, he was left wondering, "what in the name of the Under am I thinking?" That thought came daily now.

"Ravin?" Kazun spoke in a concerned tone.

"Hm?" The demon looked at his friend with what he hoped was a bland expression. His thoughts did not need to cause the others worry. He needed to keep calm for their sake. They didn't need to know that in the back of his mind that he was considering the strange "Ira's" offer.

"We're about to head out," the human continued and raised an eyebrow. Standing beside him was the cute girl, holding his hand for stability. "You coming or not?"

Ravin nodded. "Of course, you'd get lost without me." He masked his unease. It was one of the skills he considered required for his job. To reveal his true feelings would cause panic. The demon stood and glanced over at Michelle. Should he tell her about the sickness? Yes, it would be good to do so.

"Because we don't know the way to our own room," Michelle retorted and gestured for them to follow her. Her stomach filled with the wings of thousands of butterflies. Lian was accepting help—from a boy nonetheless. She cast a glance over at Ravin and thought to him, *'Your pretty boy better play nice.'* Her eyes narrowed.

He acknowledged her directed thought with a subtle nod.

The others followed Michelle at a snail's pace, ensuring that Lian didn't exert herself too much. Ravin fell in step with the parade leader.

"Oh, he will," Ravin muttered to Michelle. "He's a huge puppy dog."

Michelle glanced back at the two. Lian looked really tired, and she was using the boy as a crutch. Lian was sick enough to not care that she was leaning on a stranger. *'Good,'* Michelle replied mentally.

It wasn't a long walk outside to the gardens. From there, it was a short hop, skip, and a jump over to the human dorms. Lian would be in bed before she knew it.

Lian sneezed and shivered. Despite all the layers of clothing she was wearing, she couldn't get warm. Huddling into her sweater, she tried to get comfortable.

Despite everything that was going wrong, the entire campus seemed even more beautiful than it ever had. The trees that lined the pathway were tinting orange and red, full of fiery life. Chirping birds sounded like the songs of angels. The calm, cool breeze embraced and whisked away the lingering worry.

That wasn't to say that the school grounds weren't beautiful on a normal day. Some said that the gardens were designed so magnificently that even the Elvan kingdoms harbored jealousy for Seneal.

"It's such a nice day," Kazun muttered to Lian to make sure she was still conscious beside him.

A dark energy filled the air, one that did not originate from the small human girl the three were guarding.

Ravin tensed. He held out his hand to stop the others.

"Something's coming." Shivers ran up his spine.

This malicious energy was sharp and dangerous. It wasn't quite to his level. However, he had to protect more than one human, and that was never easy with their lack of defense.

"Well isn't this adorable?" a silky smooth voice called from behind them. They turned to face a lithe looking demon who stood with confidence. She wore barely anything. Ravin couldn't help but think she looked like a videogame character from before equilibrium. "Corralling humans now Raven?" she purred and swept her eyes over them. "Which one of your sheep has the delicious energy? I want it."

"You had best be leaving," Ravin ordered in an even voice. "You won't like what happens if you don't. I don't have time to deal with you right now."

The new demon laughed. "You college children are so adorable, just because you're learning, doesn't mean you are better than everyone else in the world." She strode towards them, hips swaying. "Now how about you hand it over."

Kazun shifted Lian closer and wrapped a protective arm around her. The girl was trembling in his arms. She stopped moving on her own. Ravin could kick the woman's ass, Kazun was sure of it. Right now, he knew he needed to keep Lian safe and to get them back to the dorms where there were wards.

"Get out of here." Ravin took in a deep breath to focus his energy. "Or you won't live to regret it."

Instead of offering an answer the demoness lunged at Ravin, her fingers outstretched. In a flash, pain seared Ravin's forehead. Hissing, she came at him in a flurry of movement. She reached for anything she could grab. Her eyes were wild.

With a thought, the Ravin threw her away from them. He panted and touched a bloody scratch on his face. Darkness filled his eyes as he spied the crimson on his fingertips. "Oh, I'm going to make you regret this."

In the blink of an eye, he was in front of the recovering demoness.

She blocked his attack with her arm, but barely. Even from a distance, the humans could hear her bone snap. An inhuman howl escaped her lips as she swiped her leg to throw Ravin off his feet.

He easily jumped over the outstretched limb and aimed a kick at her.

The girl rolled to the side and scrambled away. In a pop of energy, she appeared in front of the humans.

"Which one of you is it?!" she demanded and lashed out with her nails, fangs bared.

Kazun shoved Lian out of the path of danger and felt a sharp pain as the skin on his arm was torn. He launched a fist at her face and felt satisfaction at the crack of her nose as it shattered under his assault.

"Back off," the human growled, his eyes dark. He wouldn't let her touch either of the girls.

The demoness' gaze darted between her two attackers and she let out a low yowl. She dove at Kazun; she could feel the humanity wafting off of him. The woman dug her nails into his shoulders. "Tell me," she shrieked.

Ravin grabbed her by her long locks and threw her into the nearest tree. "I don't like people touching my things," he snarled.

The mighty tree cracked, but held true as she slammed back first into the trunk. The demoness tucked her feet under her and launched off the torn wood. Her body hurtled through the air, straight for Ravin.

With a simple sidestep, he dodged her attack, and grabbed her around the waist. It was all too easy to slam her down into the ground and grind her face in the dirt. He sank his heel into her spine and held her down with his foot.

"You tell the others to stay the hell away from us." Ravin's voice was low and dangerous. "Trust me, you are getting off easy. Show your face to me again and I'll be the last one to ever see it."

She nodded quickly and squirmed.

"Do you understand?" Ravin demanded and shoved his heel deeper into her spine.

"I understand," the demoness screamed.

"Good. Now get out of my sight before I change my mind." His voice was venomous as he released her.

She disappeared without another word, or even a second glance.

"Now, let's go to your dorm." Ravin spoke in an angrier tone than he intended. He turned his dark gaze to the humans. "Post haste," he added. The urge to laugh rose in his throat.

Michelle was bent over, doing her best to assist Lian up from the ground. The younger sister looked like a turtle, tipped over on her back. No matter how hard she tried, Lian couldn't get up. She was in a panic. A demon had appeared from nowhere and attacked. That was one of her worst nightmares. She cried and huddled deep within her plush shell.

Michelle tried to coax her up to her feet, but Lian had shut down entirely. So, Michelle did the only thing she could do. She picked her sister up. Lian wasn't all that heavy, but that didn't make it an easy task. Michelle didn't have the greatest upper body strength. Despite that, she was the only one who could have done it. If either of the males had tried to touch her, Lian might have gone ballistic.

Ravin gave Kazun a hand, and yanked him to his feet.

They walked back to the dorm with Ravin at point. He was on edge.

He ensured they reached it safely and locked the door behind them. This was the last thing he wanted to have happen. Getting messed up in this crap was going to jeopardize everything he had done to make sure Kazun got to live.

Michelle wasted no time and flipped the ward switch on as soon as she set Lian down. Faint lights shined as their protection was activated. The girl looked over at her sister who was on her bed, trembling with fear and exhaustion. This had been a long, hard day.

"Thank you, Ravin," Michelle said under her breath, rubbing her arm, "for keeping us safe, but you can't stay." She nodded over to her sister. If Michelle was ever going to get Lian to calm down enough to rest, a demon couldn't be there.

The demon nodded and reached into his pocket. He removed the necklace and held it out to Michelle with a calm expression. "Have Lian wear this. It should work until I can find something stronger." He looked over at the pitiful lump of curled up human on her bed. It would have been so easy to take her out from under her sister's nose if he tried. It could fix everything. It would mean he could save Kazun with only one more soul.

"You should have somebody over to help you watch her; anyone really. This is getting more and more serious," Ravin explained and cast a cautious glance at Michelle. "I didn't expect it to progress this fast. She's experiencing Angel Syndrome. Her body

141

is rejecting the angelic energy that's assaulting it. She's only going to get worse from here on out."

Michelle nodded and dug out her phone. For a few moments, she stared at it before looking over at the demon. There was one person who she trusted with her and her sister's life. The choice was obvious. "I'll call Jo."

Fourteen

Jo woke with a start. Her alarm blared its good morning siren. She let out a groan. It was time to get up and get ready for work. Rolling over in a heap, Jo smashed her hand on to her clock, and the dreadful sound ceased. With her face in the pillow, she fought to stay awake. It was so nice and warm in her personal blanket cocoon. She didn't want to break out of it.

Of course, she knew she couldn't lay in bed forever. She had work to do. Important work at the skating rink. Being a manager was fun, if you didn't want a life. She had stayed awake too late getting Michelle that amulet, and now she was bone tired. More than anything, she wanted to lay in bed and fall back asleep and bring back the dream of the muscular man and his speedo. It was bright pink and she approved.

Her phone began to ring. Its loud, overly cheerful tone begged to be answered. She groaned, being dramatic, knowing that no one was there to hear her complain.

"Hello?" Jo yawned, sitting up and rubbing her crusty eyes.

"Hello!" An exuberant voice chimed on the other line.

Jo flopped back onto her pillow. Holomarketers. Somehow through the thousands and thousands of years of telecommunications, they never went out of style. The only difference was that, instead of outsourcing to another country, they now outsourced to another plane of existence. The Under, or Hell as most knew it, had *the* largest holocom telemarketing industry in existence. Jo liked to imagine that there was an infinite building filled wall to wall with cubicles and pencil pushing demons. They would all gather around the watercooler and talk about what kinky sex dungeon they had visited the night before, how many things they had killed, or brag about how they had kicked a cute puppy.

It was a rude stereotype, and she knew it. At the moment, she was allowed to think such things. It was their fault for calling when she was groggy.

"What do you want, Hell-a-marketer?" Jo sighed and forced herself to her feet.

"Well, would you be interested in a very special offer?" The demon was very peppy as he ignored her sass. Jo could imagine him lying on a pink plush bed, twirling his tail in his finger. The thought brought a smile to her face. She would entertain him.

"Oh yeah? What kind of offer?" Jo went into her bathroom and sat on the counter. Her long fingers pulled through her matted hair. It was a bit greasy. Definitely a shower day.

Her friend on the other line wasted no time in his sprightly response, "Are you sitting down?"

"It's like you can read my mind." She smiled.

"Bouncy castles. I know someone's birthday is almost here."

"Mine? Is it my birthday?" Jo gasped and put a hand to her mouth. "You know what. I think that this is a *wonderful* offer. I have a few questions."

"Oh of course! I am more than happy to answer any questions," The demon sounded like a cat who had caught his first mouse in months.

"How did you get my number and my information?" she demanded. "I am supposed to be invisible to all Holomarket listings."

The line went quiet, then there was a click.

Jo sighed, shaking her head. She put her phone in her sweatpants pocket and hopped down from the counter to the shower. Once finished, she shuffled to the kitchen. While looking through her pantry, she decided today was a cereal day. Nothing beat breakfast, or really, any other meal of the day. Eating was one of her favorite pastimes. Not only was food delicious, it gave her energy.

Being a manager at a skating rink required quite a bit of physical activity. She was on her feet most of the day making sure everything went smoothly. When she wasn't at work, she was off cavorting with Michelle and Lian. If she didn't have the fuel, she couldn't maintain her franetic lifestyle.

Jo sat down and enjoyed her breakfast. She even treated herself to a slice of toast with jam on it. Since she had given Michelle that amulet, she felt like a good citizen. Helping those in need, what an achievement. People who did good things deserved good things. She crunched the flakey crust of the toast. Sticky sweet strawberry clung to the corners of her lips. The butter and fruit flavors danced in her mouth. It was amazing.

After breakfast was devoured, she left for work. It promised to be an uneventful day for the most part. She kept her phone close, waiting for Michelle to contact her. After what had happened last night, she was ready for anything. Michelle had promised to keep her updated. Her best friend might be quirky, sassy, and a bit on the irrational side, but Mischa was good about keeping her word.

At the rink, Jo whizzed around on a pair of skates doing her managerial duties. There were quite a few tasks she had to complete. First she had to check stock, and make sure everyone was on task. For the most part, they were.

Of course, they were missing one member of their team *again*. Jo would have fired him if they weren't understaffed. In the next few, days she would get around to making a 'Now Hiring' sign for the front door. A lot of students in the town were looking for a job that paid better than minimum wage. Since a great number were supernatural they got supernatural jobs, which made sense. A vampire working at a fast food joint didn't seem right. Of course, there were humans available, but most of them were magical too. There were only a select number of people willing to do a service job. Too many slots to fill and not enough mundane people.

A lot of folks had more than one job, trying to supplement their ever diminishing wallets. Jo was thankful every day that she never had to worry about money. It was nice. She worked hard and did her best to give back to the community. No, she wasn't perfect. Hell, she had flunked out of college and she was working full time at a skating rink. Her mom wanted her to be apprenticed under her, but Jo wasn't into fashion. Even worse than that was the thought that she would have had to work at her dad's company. Luckily, her brother had that covered.

Work would pass without much excitement as it always did, then she would go home. Fortunately, her weekend was only a few hours away. She would only need to come in for the interview she had with a potential applicant, but even that was easy. That meant she could hang out with her friends or catch a movie. There were a few good ones being played at the full sensory theater. Those were always fun and immersive. It beat doing nothing or the alternative, doing too much.

The day was slow, for a weekday. Most people were at work or school but there were always people who loved to play hooky. The rink was a quiet place during 'office hours'. Later, though, it got active. The college kids liked to hang out, have fun, and listen to the music that played.

For now, the most exciting thing happening was an elderly couple jam skating. They were regulars. Jo sighed and looked at her phone. Maybe it was a good thing that Michelle hadn't contacted her. That meant all was good. Right?

Suddenly, it started to ring. It took less than a second for her to answer, "Hello?"

"Hey Jo!" It was Michelle. "Want to have a sleep over?" The girl sounded concerned. Something must have happened, but she didn't want to say what. Jo nodded despite the fact the other couldn't see it. Her finger twirled a long ringlet of her dark hair.

"Sounds like fun," Jo chirped. "Do I need to hurry over?"

"The sooner the better. Lian isn't feeling well. She needs some cheering up," Michelle replied.

Jo felt a pang of worry. Lian was sick? That was something new. She had never seen the delicate girl ill. At least in body. Lian had plenty of psychological problems, but never physical ones. Lian was the type who never forgot to take her vitamins. She worked out daily and ate her greens.

"Be there as soon as possible," Jo said, and hung up. Now things were getting interesting. No more of this sitting around and waiting. She couldn't stand it. Action called, and she was more than ready for it.

After finding a replacement, Jo went out to her freshly fixed transport and drove towards the school. It was a reminder of her failure every time she went there, but she tried to not let it get the best of her. She had wasted a lot of time and money, and she still had no idea what she wanted to do with her life.

Okay, maybe she did know. Above all, she liked helping people. But how could she really help people other than volunteering or giving away money that wasn't even hers? There were a plethora of jobs out there that required a college degree, but she wasn't cut out for difficult classes.

As she parked, Jo looked at the building. Her determination spiked. No time to worry about the future; she had the present to deal with. She walked down the familiar hall until she arrived at Michelle and Lian's room. From the inside, she could hear coughing.

It didn't sound good.

Jo knocked a few times before Michelle answered.

"Hey Jo," Lian called. She waddled to her sister and looked up with sleepy blue eyes. "I'm sick, but Michelle says having you over might make me feel better." She rubbed her eyes, then turned and walked away. Once again, she flopped into her bed and snuggled under a pile of blankets. Once in her cocoon, she was content.

"What's with that silly grin?" Jo asked Lian, sitting on the edge of the bed next to her. "You look too happy to be sick."

Little Lian sat and gave Jo a big hug, but she shook her head, not willing to answer.

Jo couldn't help but laugh, "What's his name?"

Immediately, Lian looked horrified. She shook her head quickly and pulled the blanket over her face to hide.

Well that wasn't hard to figure out. Lian had a little crush on someone? So cute. Jo couldn't really imagine Lian with anyone, or crushing on any boy, but it was nice that it was happening. After all the things that had happened to the poor girl, she deserved to have a relationship.

"His name is Kazun," Michelle sighed melodramatically. "The hockey star extraordinaire." Michelle watched with great care. It had taken all of her energy to calm Lian down after the afternoon's trauma. For once, luck was on her side. The cough medicine Lian had taken was making most of the day fuzzy for her. The Angel Syndrome was still taking its toll.

"No!!" Lian whined back and buried her warm face into Jo's arm. "Shush."

The name was familiar to Jo. Where had she heard of a Kazun

before? At the skating rink! She had seen him there many times with the other hockey players. He was rather popular with the crowds, human and inhuman alike. It wasn't often someone like him found a place on any sports team. Humans rarely made the cut. That made him somewhat special.

Jo wrapped her arm around Lian's shoulder. Lian had a way of endearing herself to people. It was an honor once she started talking to someone. When Lian had said her first quiet sentence to Jo, she had felt so special.

"You shouldn't be ashamed by it," Jo said in a matter-of-fact voice. "He's a nice lookin' guy. And I mean from what I can tell he's genuine. He's always really polite when he orders his snacks and tickets."

In response, Lian let out another embarrassed whimper. She didn't like being the center of attention. "Well, Michelle likes Ravin," she threw the game her sister's way. Michelle was not prepared for this.

"I do not," Michelle snapped. "He might be Mr. Hotshot, but no. Just. No. Ew."

"Aww," Jo sighed. "My little girls are growing up." She faked a sniff and rubbed her eye as if removing a tear. "Next thing you know, they will be kissing boys and…"

"JO!" the sisters yelled in unison. Jo could only laugh. Once you got to know them, Michelle and Lian were so similar. She knew how to mess with both of them at the same time. It wasn't difficult, but it was fun nonetheless.

From her bed, Michelle crossed her arms and pouted. Jo was being mean. She didn't like Ravin. Even if he thought he was good looking. Sure, it was great that he was helping her out, but he was a *demon*. First of all, their ages were probably so far apart, the Grand Canyon looked like a kitten. Secondly, even if she *did* like him for some reason, it wouldn't matter. She didn't have time for men, nor did she have the energy.

Lian had a shot with Kazun since they were both human.

"Don't think about it too hard," Jo was rubbing Lian's back. "We're messing with you."

"Yeah, yeah," Michelle sighed, resting her head on her knees. She looked over as Lian let out a little sneeze. Her main focus right now was to keep Lian safe and happy. She didn't have time to worry about the other things in her life.

Lian shifted from beside Jo. A petite smile appeared on her face and she whispered, "He isn't so scary. Even for a…." Her words drifted off and her eyes looked down. She couldn't say the word. There was such fear attached to it. From what she had seen, Ravin was okay. No, she didn't trust him, she couldn't, but he didn't make her want to hide in a ten-foot hole. Only a five foot one.

Jo got up and let Lian lay down.

"How about I call us in some pizzas?" she offered with a smile. "You can each get whatever you want. Does that sound good?"

"I want pineapple pizza," Lian said quietly, smiling at the thought. She loved how sweet the pineapple was in contrast to the tangy tomato. Michelle, on the other hand, demanded a meat lover's pizza.

Jo giggled. These two were her precious sweet cinnamon rolls. It was no wonder why she kept them around. She loved being able to spoil them. That was a fun part about having money. The best part of it all was, she knew that the two girls didn't want to be around her for the number in her parent's bank account.

She never felt like she was being used.

Most relationships Jo had been in, friend or otherwise, had gone terribly wrong when they found out how much money she had. They wanted expensive things, and extravagant dates. Jo ended up paying for everything. It happened more times than she dared count. These friends were the best. If anything ever happened to either of them, Jo would never forgive herself. They were good people and deserved the best things in life.

"Sounds delicious," Jo chimed and pulled out her phone, "I think I want..." She tapped her chin as she thought. Jo loved variety. What sort of pie was she in the mood for? Not meat lovers, too much... well... meat. Not veggie only for the same reason. "Supreme." That would give her a nice mix of everything.

"Michelle was right," Lian spoke. "Having you here is making me feel a lot better." Her eyes sparkled with happiness. After another cough, the girl settled back into her blankets.

"That's 'cause I'm *always* right." Michelle stated.

Jo couldn't help but chuckle.

"Always?" She questioned. Her green eyes gazed at her holophone as she searched for the number for the pizza place. It was then she noticed something out of the corner of her eye. A shadow appeared on the blinds. There was someone crouching outside their window.

The girl tilted her head, and watched as the shadow moved, as if standing. Who could it be? How strange. There was a yelling, then silence. Moments later, the glass on the window shattered. Jo simply blinked, and when she opened her eyes, there was a sword stuck into the wall.

It was less than three inches away from her face.

Fifteen

His day began as it always did, at 5am sharp. He woke up, changed into something suitable, and lifted his light-as-air holopad. With a push of a button, he connected to a video chat. Only a few moments later, his parents joined from the neighboring country of Denvar. "Good morning, Mom and Dad," he sang with a smile and waved.

"Good morning Marius!" they chimed back and beamed.

"How has school been?" his mother asked, her sea blue eyes glittering. She looked as he remembered her: brown hair, graying slightly at the roots, soft wrinkles gracing the sides of her eyes. Her round face was like the sun on a cold day.

"It's been fun," Marius replied in a light tone. "I really enjoy all of my classes, though I can hardly find the time to breathe."

"It's important to take a break every now and then," his father reminded him. "Work too hard and it's not fun anymore." He, too, was as Marius recalled: his soft dark hair was rapidly gaining the salt and pepper look, and his wrinkles were more pronounced. But his eyes were full of jovial energy that years couldn't leach from him.

Of course, he had no reason not to remember. He talked to them almost every morning.

"I know, I know," the boy brushed some hair behind his ear, and hesitated as he glanced at their round ears. A cold sadness settled in his stomach as he got lost in a train of thought that never went anywhere good...

"Is something wrong?" his mother noticed even the slightest change in him.

Marius shook his head. "Of course not, but hey! I've got to go get ready for my practices!" He glanced at the clock. Even though he hadn't been talking them for as long as usual he was already behind on his morning routine.

"Alright, baby boy, have a good day!" His mother's smile warmed him.

"Make sure you get your homework done!" his father added.

"Will do!" Marius laughed softly. "I love you."

"Love you too!" The screen went dark.

Marius flicked off the holopad and stood. His muscles protested just the slightest, but he chose to ignore them. He sighed and ran a hand through his shoulder length blonde hair. He caught his reflection out of the corner of his eye and turned to stare. Ever so gently he tapped the tips of his pointed ears.

He still didn't know how to tell them that he was learning about his Elvan culture, the same one they had never so much as introduced him to.

Shaking the confusing thought from his head, he grabbed his gear. He had two hours to practice with the soccer team, and then he had to run to the gym and do some gymnastics—a sport he'd been participating in since he was four. Once he finished, he had a three-hour cooking class, then pastry class, and an Elven language class. Then he was going to meet his teacher for meditation followed by swordplay and hand to hand combat. After he got his homework done, he hoped there would be time to squeeze in fencing.

Sometimes, he felt like he was doing too much. He probably was, but he could handle it. His parents had been signing him up for all sorts of sports and activities since he was little. In hindsight, he knew now that it was because he always had more energy than the average human child. Because he wasn't human.

He jogged to the cafeteria for breakfast. He couldn't very well practice on an empty stomach. Most days he used more calories than he took in, and he was shoving food into his mouth at every opportunity.

No matter how hard he tried, he never grew outwards. His body was lithe and willowy, even if he ate nothing but junk food and dessert all day. That too, he attributed to his Elven heritage.

Inside the cafeteria, his gaze glossed over his oh-so-many options. There was the food he wanted, and the food he should pick. He was an Elf of Summer, and in Summer they were vegan. There was even a special area that the food that Summer elves would pick, away from the meat and dairy filled products. Away from the food Marius wanted to eat. He'd been raised by humans, so he quite liked meat, dairy, and all the delicious variants that came from those categories.

Bacon beckoned to him with its delectable smoky aroma. Never had he smelled anything so heavenly. The scents of ham steak and sausages tickled his nose. There was absolutely no way he was going to be able to resist today. He had to have it. He was already salivating.

With a suppressed sigh, he grabbed a meat lover's plate piled high with the delightful forbidden fruit and lightly fried eggs, along with toast points ready to be smothered with real butter.

'As long as Letvan doesn't find out I should be fine,' Marius reasoned to himself.

He always made an effort to be vegan when his teacher was around. But, what his teacher didn't know wouldn't hurt him. It wasn't as if he went out to kill innocent animals for fun. He treasured the gifts they gave with the loss of life. After all, the animals had happy lives before they passed.

The elf plopped down and devoured his meal, along with a cup of mocha coffee with a generous dollop of milk.

He ate as quickly to avoid getting caught with meat. The Queen certainly wouldn't allow him into the court if he continued his carnivorous ways. It was so hard to stop. Twenty-six years of eating meat made it insanely difficult to abandon the practice.

His parents had raised him to be a carnivore, which was shameful now.

Marius sprinted out to the soccer field. He only had a short amount of time before he had to get there.

It felt as if the rest of his day went past in the blink of an eye. He showered after soccer and again after gymnastics. He was almost late to his cooking class, which went by without much concern. His mother had done well to teach him in the ways of the chef.

Then he had to run to pastry class. Oddly, baking was hard for him. There was so much stuff going on, but it didn't feel much like work. The fun made his day go by so much faster. That is, of course, until he reached the point in his busy schedule when he met up with his teacher.

They would meditate and that would help center him after all of the running around. The opportunity to sit down and clear his thoughts was his favorite part of the day.

Marius walked into the peaceful, perfect gardens. It was the most majestic place he'd ever seen. He waited amongst the trees until his teacher arrived. It was times like this that he really wished he could go visit Summer. It was a truly amazing place. At least that's what he'd heard.

There was plenty he had learned about Summer, but he had never been able to visit it. As far as they were concerned, he wasn't even an elf. Not yet at least. He was raised by humans in the human capital of Eartha, so what value did he have in Elvan society?

When his teacher did not show up, Marius took it upon himself to start alone. It would not be the first time he meditated on his own. However, he preferred having his teacher there. He was less likely to fall asleep with the intimidating presence of a mentor to ensure he stayed awake. It wasn't that he was scared of Letvan, it was that his teacher had a way of motivating him.

The elf took a deep breath and sat down with his legs crossed. He closed his eyes and tried to clear his mind. As always, it was difficult for him. The need to sleep was right behind his eyes, threatening to take him at any moment.

Despite that, he fought to stay awake. It was nearly impossible with an empty mind.

He felt himself slipping into an extremely relaxed state. His energy felt centered and his mind clear. There was nothing like it in the world. Everything in the universe was at peace. So peaceful that everything disappeared.

Marius was brought back to reality as a hand struck him.

Letvan stood before his pupil, in silken Elvan training garbs. He cocked his hip to the side and sighed, "Sleeping? I thought I trained you better." He kneeled down and messed with his student's hair. A smile appeared on his face.

Marius's cheeks burned in shame. "Sorry teacher." He rubbed one eye. "I didn't mean to."

The last thing he wanted to do was to disappoint Letvan.

"It's alright. Come on, We're going to do some sword training." Letvan offered Marius a hand that was surprisingly smooth, for a warrior. They both stood and the mentor began to stretch. On his belt were two beautiful Summer-crafted swords. A sly grin appeared on his face.

"Left or right, Mari?" Letvan placed his hands on each sword, feeling their grips beneath his touch.

They were Letvan's swords, ones he had made himself. Once Marius was accepted into Summer, he too would make his own weapon. When that day came, the young knight, Letvan, would be so proud of him.

Marius watched his mentor and stretched a bit. After a few moments of consideration, he spoke. "Right."

"Good choice!" Letvan took the sword from his belt, and handed it over to Marius. It was honestly the better sword, and he was proud of his student for making the best selection.

The student beamed and took the weapon. "Thank you."

Every time Letvan praised him, Marius felt so proud. It was clear in those moments that Marius was making progress.

Once he had grown accustomed to the weapon, his teacher started to swing at him. It hadn't been long enough that Marius hadn't been caught off guard by the sudden attack. With a quick movement he dodged the strike, rather than blocking. He knew his teacher was far stronger and would be able to overpower him.

When another attack came, it wasn't nearly as strong as he feared it would be. His teacher was going easy on him, at least for now. That could change in a split second.

They clashed on and on. Marius could tell his teacher was dumbing down his skill. In a real fight, Letvan could have gutted him with little effort. Still, Marius liked to think that he was making vast improvements. The Elvan style was different than fencing, but at least his experience had helped him learn his heritage.

Then again, he supposed he shouldn't compare himself to Letvan. Even though he was young for an elf, Letvan was already top of his field. Marius would be hard pressed to surpass Letvan in his lifetime. Still, the boy would try to make him proud.

"Nice block," Letvan praised as their swords clashed with a

satisfying chime of silver. "You're being quite fluid today. Very good job."

Without wasting any more air on compliments, Letvan twisted gracefully and tried to get the upper hand on Marius.

Marius grinned as his teacher boosted his confidence. He didn't waste his words with thanks. That could cause him to lose focus, and make him lose. He struggled to keep in the lead, but already he could feel his long day wearing down on him. The entire morning had been spent on his feet, working hard, and he was beginning to feel it.

He blocked a punishing blow delivered by his teacher; his face twisted with pain as his wrist took the brunt of the force.

The boy didn't have time to react as Letvan bent down and swept out with his legs. His feet went tumbling out from under him, and his back met the hard, unforgiving ground. All his breath rushed from his lungs, and his skull cracked against the earth. He sagged and let the weapon fall from his hand.

"Y-You win again," Marius panted as sweat trickled down his face.

"Damn right I do," Letvan laughed, "I'm impressed though. You're really coming along."

"Thank you, teacher." He let out a breath and sat up. "Couldn't you have been a bit gentler though?" Marius rubbed the tender part of his head. It wasn't the worst defeat he'd ever suffered. Letvan helped Marius up.

The proud knight commented, "If I could have, I would have."

Marius sighed, "At least you're honest." He rubbed his arm. "Did I do better than last time?"

"You did," Letvan assured his student. He smiled and stretched a bit, making one of his bones pop. Sparring was always such fun and was quite the workout. It always hurt so good. Then again, he was never on the losing side of it. "I'm sure you'll be getting your letter any day now."

Marius's eyes widened. "Are you serious?"

To get a letter meant that he could start the basic training in Summer for becoming a knight. It was the highest honor someone like him could ever get. It was the highest honor any Summer elf could get! To be accepted into the court would have blown him away, but to be told by one as amazing as Letvan that he might get that letter made him lightheaded.

Letvan's eyes drifted past Marius's shoulder. There was a young man looking into a window on the ground floor of the human dorm. The mentor got his student's attention. "What do you make of that? Isn't that the girl's side?"

Marius looked where his teacher directed. "That's a pervert staring in a girl's window." He was appalled. That was wrong. The humans had no natural defenses to alert themselves to the peeping Tom. "We have to do something."

"Why don't you just go throw your sword at him." Letvan commented dryly.

The pervert stood, and glanced over at the two elves, as if he'd heard them. Without really thinking, Marius did as his master said and threw the sword at the disgusting man.

"Is that a sword?" The man shouted moments before he disappeared. Time slowed for Marius; the weapon broke through the window, sending glass flying. His heart stopped as it disappeared into the room.

Oh Summer, what if he'd hurt someone?

"Marius! Why the Hell would you actually throw your sword?" The mentor cursed and took off to go make sure whoever might have been inside was okay. He gave his student a 'you're following me' look.

Marius squeaked as his teacher yelled at him. "I thought you were serious!"

So, his ability to understand sarcasm wasn't the best. He took off after Letvan and up to the window. The elf avoided putting his hands on any glass as he leaned in, wide eyed.

"Oh my Summer, is everyone okay?" Cold fear filled his heart. What if one of them had gotten hurt because of him?

"Everyone's okay, no thanks to you, you crazy damn elf," the peeper shot at him.

The elf's eyes narrowed. "You were spying on them."

"Ravin. What the hell is going on?" One of girls inside snapped, she pointed over to a girl who was inches away from having a sword impaled on her, "And why the hell was Jo almost shish-ka-bobed to death?"

Ravin looked at the people in the room. "I was keeping an eye on you guys. I thought it would be a good idea but, obviously it backfired. That's not the point." The demon cast a venomous glance at Marius. "That crazy ass elf threw a damn sword at me!"

Marius didn't hear what the demon was saying, all he could see was the human he had almost skewered. She was stunning, despite the fear. He swung into the room avoiding the broken glass and walked over to her, and then knelt down in front of her. "Are you okay?" the elf asked in a quiet voice.

"C-Could be worse," Jo chuckled nervously, "About three inches worse to be exact."

"I am so sorry," the elf's voice broke. He couldn't believe that he'd almost taken a life.

"It's okay," Jo accepted his apology, and it was then she noticed something strange. She wasn't the only one. A silence fell upon the room. It was unsettling. There was no sniffling or coughing. Jo and Michelle glanced around, and it was then they noticed that Lian wasn't in sight.

Michelle got up and searched. Maybe she had gotten scared from all of the commotion and went to hide. That was a very Lian thing to do. Though, as she looked under the beds, in the closet, the bathroom, and other various places, she noticed a recurring theme.

"Lian?" Michelle called out, "Lian! Where are you? Come out this isn't funny."

Marius looked over at the others. "What is going on?"

A dark look covered Ravin's face. He'd just realized girl's presence was gone from the room. The darkness was nothing but a lingering whisper. "She's been taken."

Sixteen

Anger unlike any she had ever felt before flashed through Michelle's veins. Her eyes locked onto Ravin, "What the hell do you mean by that?" she snapped and continued to look for her sister. Pillows flew across the room. Lian couldn't be gone. How could she have been taken? They had wards.

Tears threatened to flow as she threw all the blankets and pillows off Lian's bed. Lian had *just* been there a second ago. It wasn't possible for her to be gone. How could she have not kept Lian safe? How could she have failed?

"Keep looking," the girl demanded, "She can't be gone!"

Ravin let out a breath and peered into Michelle's eyes. "Her energy is no longer here. Someone took her, it won't do any good to keep wasting time." As much as it would hurt the human, she had to accept the truth or else she would get stuck in a never ending loop. They didn't have time for that.

He turned his attention away from the humans for a moment and looked at the elf outside the window. "Was your sword enchanted, Letvan?" Ravin asked in an even voice.

Letvan nodded a little, "Nothing that powerful though. Shame to say my magic isn't the best." He shrugged. Well this was strange. Positively puzzling, to say the least. He was used to a lot of things magical. Spells were as common as ants in an ant hill here at the school. What he found to be inexplicable was the fact that this missing person was gone without a trace. All magic that he knew left a distinguishable signature. Was there one that the demon wasn't picking up? He looked over at his pupil, then back at Ravin, "Why?"

"Because I think your magic was powerful enough to break their wards." Ravin could feel the protective circle had weakened exponentially. "Someone is going to have to speak with the school magister about these lackluster seals."

It was borderline shameful that the shielding markings had been crippled by a sword. The magister needed a stern talking to. The wards were the only things that kept the squishier species safe. If anyone found out that they had been neutralized so easily, then there could be extreme danger for everyone.

Marius' face fell. Someone had gotten kidnapped because of him? This was not good. Not good at all.

"I will," Letvan said. "If it was my sword that broke it, then I shall fix what I can." He bowed his head. "If nothing else is needed of me, I will go speak with them. Immediately." The elf's gaze landed on his sword. "Marius. Return to me my blade."

Marius gripped the sword hilt before going over to his teacher. "Here." He tried not to think about the trouble he caused. Before he returned the sword to Letvan, he grabbed a piece of blank paper from a desk and wrote down his phone number. He offered it to Jo. "Call me and I can try to make up for almost taking your life." With that, Marius handed over the blade, then vaulted out of the broken window, his face redder than a cooked lobster.

Jo glanced at the paper as Letvan followed his student. Most guys would stop at 'here's my number, so call me, maybe?' She rubbed her neck, then looked over at Michelle. Her eyes softened. Michelle's eyes were glistening. Jo felt her heart drop. She could feel the panic in the other's stare.

"I failed," was all Michelle said, staring at the floor, lost in a pain that ran deep. Lian had been taken and there was *nothing* she could do. Her sister was lost, afraid, and alone in a den of lions. More than anything, she wished it was her who had been taken. Lian didn't deserve this. Rage exploded and Michelle punched her pillow with everything she had. She wanted to kick and scream. She wanted her sister to be safe.

"She's gone. And I failed." Michelle's voice echoed in the small room. Her broken blue eyes landed on the demon. A single tear escaped. Her voice was quiet as the calm before the storm, she repeated, "She's gone."

Ravin watched Michelle. "She is, but you can still get her back," he said in a determined voice.

Lian posed a threat if she wasn't close to her sister. Someone could use her to her full potential if she wasn't safe and sound.

Having a dark angel on the loose could cause major havoc.

Michelle clenched her teeth. Her fingernails bit into the soft flesh of her palm. "How?" she grated.

She stormed to Ravin and gripped the front of his shirt. It was the only way to avoid punching him. Sure, this wasn't his fault—as far as she knew. She wouldn't take him out of the equation. He was a demon. His kind ruined everything. "I will do anything."

"I will do whatever I can to help, too," Jo announced. A sword had almost killed her, sparking a 'you only live once' mentality in the young woman. Having bottomless pockets would surely help their cause, she reasoned. If she was going to die, this was as good a reason as any.

The demon tilted his head down to stare at Michelle. He patted the fist that was trying to ruin his favorite shirt. "Good, because I can't do this alone." Ravin used his mental abilities to uncurl Michelle's fingers and free himself. "First things first." He crossed his arms. "We need to figure out who took her."

He was sure it was going to be more difficult than he made it sound.

He couldn't sense anything about the kidnapper. Whoever it was had far more power than Ravin. It was someone that he would not want to clash with on any day. However, these were special circumstances and that would negate his base instinct to avoid such a dangerous foe.

"How do we do that?" Michelle questioned. There was no doubt that whoever took Lian was a supernatural being. Michelle wasn't that search savvy when it came to those. Finding humans was easy. You called up the police, the police worked their magic, and sooner rather than later, your missing person showed up.

A demon on the other hand, that was different. Playing by their own rules was in their nature. Even Ravin did his own thing. She eyed him, mistrusting his motives. Why was he helping? What was he getting out of it? She wouldn't, no, she *couldn't* believe he was doing this out of the goodness of his heart. Not that he even had one.

The room was still. A strange silence hung like a stifling cloud heavy in the air. Pressure weighed down on Michelle's shoulders. She was ready to go into Oblivion if she had to.

As much as he hated to admit it, Ravin knew he couldn't do this on his own. He needed to get help. "We need to go talk to Sin," the demon said through gritted teeth. Like he needed to owe Sin more. At this rate she was going to own him. Completely. Never-ending servitude didn't suit him well.

With a backwards glance at his companions, Ravin took off. If they knew what was good for them, they would follow him. More than little Lian's life was at stake here. The fate of countless beings hung in the balance if the dark angel got free, which would happen if Lian was in the wrong hands. It remained to be seen if that was the current case.

The walk made Ravin feel uneasy, as if there were dozens of eyes watching him. He knew at least two pairs of eyes were on him, but any more than that was speculation. His body was tense, yet he tried to put on an air of ease for the girls. Perhaps they might be able to fathom the significance of their predicament, but probability stated otherwise. Neither of them had heard of dark angels, so they couldn't even begin to comprehend the severity of the situation.

There was a reason that there was only one dark angel left in the world.

At one point, there had been many. In the Beyond, or Heaven as it was often called, they had lived side by side with the Angels of Light. There wasn't much known about them, except for the tales of the Great War. The three sects of Light angels banded together to exterminate the dark ones. Much destruction befell the Beyond and it trickled over to Earth.

One by one, the dark angel tribe had been slaughtered. Except for one. The legend told of the Mother. She was a fierce warrior who destroyed any and all who faced her. She threatened to block out the sun and cause the apocalypse. Her ultimate goal was to eradicate all life.

The dark angel was so great that all the powers in Heaven could not kill her. So, they shackled her in the core of Earth. To this very day she was still there. If she were to get free... Ravin shuddered at the thought.

He glanced around as they walked the familiar streets to Sin's bar. Nothing was out of the ordinary. In fact, everything was almost far too normal for the heavy burden that weighed on his mind.

'Way to get yourself in way too deep again, Ravin,' he mentally scolded himself.

Maybe this time, things would go well. After all, if he gave up hope then he would have nothing left.

When they arrived at the bar, the heavy metal door loomed over them. The cold steel shimmered in the overcast light. The building stood proudly, and even from the outside, the faint sound of music could be heard. The metal slat opened up and a pair of cold eyes glanced over the crew.

"Denied," a bass voice rumbled like muted thunder.

The girls looked to one another questioningly, then at Ravin. What did the voice mean by that? Both of them were old enough to have liquor. What was going on?

"What do you mean, 'denied'?" Michelle shot. "A girl can't grab a drink?"

"A *human* can't go in to drink," the thunder spoke, the dark eyes behind the slat squinted.

"Scared that us little human girls are gonna hurt you? Us little fragile creatures? Huh, maybe you monsters aren't what you're cracked up to be. Maybe little Michelle could kick your ass," Michelle prodded, brows furrowed. She wasn't in the mood to have her humanity deprecated. She had as much right to enter any building as anybody else. There weren't human-only bars. No, the supernaturals wouldn't allow that. It would be speciesist. It would be wrong.

"I have my rights too, buddy." She tapped her index fingers together—a gesture of profanity by good company standards.

There was a click, then the sound of rolling machinery as the door opened. Standing there was a large creature that Michelle had never seen before. He was big, and burly, and his veins were popping. Fists clenched and teeth locked, the guardian looked as if he was ready to beat the human into a pulp.

"Whoa, looks like someone has someone has human issues," Michelle quipped.

Ravin raised his hands in surrender. "There's no need to lose our heads." This was *just* what he needed right now. "How about we all take a deep breath and talk this through?"

"I think we could all stand to calm down," a familiar female voice sighed, "My dear sweet Golem, they are fine to enter. I think I know why they are here." Sin, in a blink, was standing beside the large thick man. Her caramel smooth voice floated like a sweet lullaby and made the creature take a docile breath. A sudden grave look appeared in her eyes. Sin turned and motioned all of them to follow with a flick of her tail.

Her hips swayed as she led the group into her bar and to a table where another man sat. She ran her fingers across the glossy surface until it met with a glass. With delicate fingers she took it and sipped furtively.

"My apologies, Zier, but I have to cut our time short," she said to the man. Her tail flicked gently. "But, of course, we can catch up soon. I can't wait to talk to you again." There was a subtle change in her tone. Her eyes looked back at the trail of people behind her. It was a rare occasion that she entertained humans. Or humans got the chance to entertain her.

The fact that Ravin had dragged two girls all the way out to her humble abode meant that something was wrong. She hadn't been expecting everything to go bad so quickly, but with Ravin, you could never tell. He liked to keep things fresh. That meant things were fun more often than not.

The dark man shrugged and stood. "Remember what I've said Sin." He spoke in a voice richer than the peal of a church bell. His eyes were an unnaturally brilliant yellow streaked with orange.

There was an air of power about him; every move he made was precise and meaningful. There were muscles packed on his tall frame, and tattoos on his exposed skin.

Everything about this 'Zier' made the hair on the back of Ravin's neck stand up. For a long moment, that disturbing gaze lingered on the younger demon's face, clearly sizing him up and taking stock of every flaw.

"Contact me when you know you will have more time so we can fully discuss this situation." With that, he walked from the building, attracting more than one set of gawkers.

Ravin suppressed a shudder and made sure that the strange man had departed. "Sin, we have some serious issues right now." He forced himself to speak in a calm voice. How did he explain to her that he had already lost the one girl he had needed to keep the closest eye on?

"This is about the Marked, isn't it?" Sin replied in a cool tone. "What happened?" Her dark eyes flared, showing her true demonic nature more so than her horns and tail ever could. Slowly, she took a seat and gestured for the others to do the same. No one in the room would have denied the beautifully dark creature. Not even Michelle could think of something witty to say. There was a strange look on Sin's face. It was one-part pure caramel goddess, the other part angry disappointment.

Ravin nodded. She was pissed at him, that much he already knew. Truly he felt like a failure of a demon; it would have been nice if he had lasted longer than a day. "She has disappeared." He raised a hand defensively before she could throw accusations at him. "No, it wasn't my fault. She was safe in her wards until some moronic elf broke them with an enchanted sword."

Right now, he didn't need Sin against him because of something that was out of his hands. How could he have known that an elf would get sword-happy? Sometimes, things happened. Hopefully, she wouldn't waste time getting mad and punishing him.

"Disappeared? As in spontaneously gone?" Sin adjusted herself as she sat upright. If the girl ceased to be, that would be fine. No harm no foul. But a dark angel in the wrong hands... She didn't let her imagination stray too far.

He considered it for a moment. "She was gone. However, I suspect she was taken by someone." He didn't know if he would be able to break it to Michelle if her sister was no longer in existence. Would her human mind be able to comprehend it? Could she handle losing her only sister to some mysterious force that had taken her from the very fabric of reality? He could honestly imagine that some unseen unbelievable force would remove the possibility of the only dark angel getting free.

Not many people still remembered the beings that were known as the 'Archaics.' Ancient legends told that they were all the children of some highest power, and that it had created this world for them. They alone would have the abilities to pull someone out of existence. A shudder rolled up his spine. One was said to be Death itself. Now, that made sense to him when it came to wiping out the existence of an innocent human girl.

Sin let out a sigh and asked in an annoyed tone, "Did you feel someone else's energy?"

"I did, briefly, but it faded in a second." He was hesitant to admit exactly how strong he was in front of the humans.

Sin pinched the bridge of her nose and she closed her eyes. "Ravin, I hope you can comprehend the severity of what you have done." Dark power bubbled in her words. "I gave you *one* job. Watch the squishy human. And not even a *day* later. You have *lost her.*" Sin's fist struck the fine wood of the table, leaving a hundred credit dent.

"Now, you are telling me that you have no idea if someone took her or if she was wiped out of existence." Red creeped into her black glare, her generally obsidian eyes tinted with lava. "If I am going to clean up after your messes, you have to give me a mop—*something* to go on."

Ravin's shoulders slumped forward in a submissive display. "I have a potion that can help, back at my dorm," he informed her.

Sin clicked her finely manicured fingernails together. Her whip-tail flicked in aggravation. "Then why are you still sitting here?" She grabbed her drink and finished it. "You will meet me at the Marked One's dorm."

"I will be there," he guaranteed. With that, the demon grabbed Michelle and Jo, then transported them to his room. There was no time to waste. The sooner they knew Lian was safe, the sooner he could rest easy. No dark angels on the loose, no possibilities of irate older sisters coming to harass him for something out of his control.

It only took a few steps to get into his room. He squatted down and rifled through the contents of his fridge. Behind several energy drinks and half a dozen unlabeled philters, was the crystal vial he was searching for. A teal liquid was contained inside by a delicate stopper.

This was the little bugger that was going to get him out of the hot seat.

He became dimly aware that he couldn't remember seeing Kazun when he had arrived. Hesitantly, he walked out and looked around. The women were still there, unharmed. Yet, he couldn't sense Kazun. It was possible the boy had gone off somewhere, but unlikely. Kazun wasn't that stupid.

Fear bubbled inside of his stomach as he walked to the human's room, but he fought to keep it from showing on his face. He knocked on the door and awaited a response. Nothing.

The demon forced the door open and found it empty. Laying on the floor was an abandoned holophone with a familiar hockey charm attached. A series of loud curses left his lips.

Kazun was gone.

Seventeen

Furniture flew across the room at the demon's rage. The large objects gave the females a wide berth, but paid no heed to each other and to the walls. A stained and well-loved couch flipped over then slammed into a hapless ottoman which went flying into the wall. Tables flipped and the chairs spun away in fear.

"He's GONE!" Ravin roared. "How the hell is he GONE?"

This wasn't supposed to be possible. No one was supposed to know where Kazun was. This was the one place he was supposed to be safe. There was no psycho throwing swords around here, and the wards were intact.

There was going to be serious hell to pay. No one took his human and got away with it. Sin was going to have to help him get vengeance, and to return his friend.

"How do you know he's gone, gone? Couldn't he have gone to get some ice cream?" Michelle was bravely standing in front of Jo. Her hands rested on her hips.

"Oh, I don't know," Ravin sneered. "Maybe the demonic energy that's all over his room like stink on a warthog, maybe the fact that he always has his holophone on him, or maybe I felt like redecorating in an abstract manner. There's an energy in here that doesn't belong, and there are demons who want to drag Kazun's ass to Hell. Ice cream is probably the last thing he's thinking about."

Whoever it was, had left the energy here for Ravin to find, as a giant middle finger. Not that the little humans behind him would even understand the significance of that particular gesture. It was far before their time.

There was going to be blood for this.

"I'm giving this potion to Sin," he growled. "Then I'm going to find this demon to skin." Ravin stormed down to Michelle's dorm with the humans in tow. He didn't bother to make sure they were following, but they of course knew better by this point.

He flung open the door and thrust out his arm to his boss. "Someone stole Kazun," the demon grated with a forced grin.

Sin ran her finger along the bed skirt, ignoring Ravin.

"Whoever took Lian is quite the sneaky one, but not perfect. Try as they may, they have left subtle traces…" Sin closed her eyes and knelt on the ground. They were faint. It was like trying to smell a trail after a day's worth of rain. Even if she was a magical bloodhound, this wasn't going to be easy.

"Did you bring the potion?" She stood. "It would help to amplify this whisper of energy I'm feeling."

Silently Ravin seethed in what felt like an unending rage. "You aren't even listening to me, are you?" The demon crossed his arms. When she didn't respond, Ravin knew he was right. How the Hell could she be so nonchalant about this new problem?

"Do you feel anything yet?" he asked in a measured voice.

"Of course," Sin stated, as if it were a dumb question. "Don't insult me, big guy." She put her hands on her hips. It might take a day or two, but she would find this little mite who dared cross her path. She outstretched her hand. "Potion."

With a clenched jaw, Ravin passed the vial over to her.

Sin took the liquid and examined the teal contents. Not the best potion she had ever worked with, but it would do. With the broad pad of her thumb, she popped the stopper out and downed it like a cheap shot. As it trailed down her throat, the liquid became hot. Static rolled down her arms and legs. She felt power thrum through her horns. Closing her eyes, Sin felt the magic work within her.

The third eye of her mind opened wide and she began to see the room in a new light. It was as if she had put on night vision goggles—the only difference was instead of seeing through darkness, she saw through reality.

The once subtle traces turned into glowing specks. Sin leaned down and touched the floor. Her tail whipped about and she put her hand above the spec of energy.

"Gehennae ignibus mancipatur. Me replendo essence mortis ut tam captionem," Sin whispered, gathering a dark aura around her. She caressed the trace and pulled in into a tangible shape using her hellish words. A tiny purple tinted stone rested in her hand. It was small, barely the size of an ice cream sprinkle.

Her fiery red eyes on fixed Ravin. "And to answer your question, we will worry about Kazun later. No use saving him, if our entire plane of existence is dead. Am I correct?"

"I understand." Ravin's kept his response short, to prevent himself from digging himself into a hole with the woman he was indebted to for the next few decades.

"Good. I will prepare a spell to find whoever left this trace. If you have anything else that might be useful, fork it over. If not, I am going to go work. I suggest you and your little entourage be useful and pick up these items." Sin returned to a full standing position and straightened her shirt. With a flick of her wrist, a piece of paper appeared and she handed it to Ravin.

Ravin nodded curtly. "I'll bring everything I can to the bar as soon as possible." He needed a little while to get a grip on his turbulent emotions. "If you need anything else, all you have to do is ask."

A slight demonic smirk appeared on the attractive woman's face. A moment later, Sin was gone with a slight pop of energy.

Michelle walked up to Ravin and she placed her hand on his shoulder. Her eyes were determined. They would get Lian back, and in time, Kazun. They had to.

"It's going to be okay. Some way, somehow," she assured him. "I promise."

The male nodded. "Thanks." His voice was strained. As much as he wanted it to be true, part of him doubted that either of the kids would make it out in one piece.

Ravin shook his head and ran a hand through his shaggy hair.

"We need to start finding these things for Sin." It was all he could do to keep his voice even despite the turmoil inside. There was no time to waste on his emotions. They had to focus.

There were a few things that he knew that they needed for the spell, various essences, a few candles, and herbs. The quintessential locator spell item was the flower Sumsuneira, the national flower of the Summer Kingdom.

Determination flashed across his features. "Only then can we get them back." He would make sure that they would. So very much depended on them.

"Then what are we looking for?" Jo asked. "If it's something we can buy, my credit card is burning in my pocket." Now there were two people missing, and she couldn't have that happening. Not on her watch. The girl smiled with a resolute expression. They were both angry, and Jo could understand that, so if she had to, she would be the drive that boosted them forward.

"My father runs a multi-trillion credit corporation, so literally, I have bottomless pockets." Jo gave Ravin a thumbs up.

The demon arched a brow. Some obscenely rich girl had a job at a roller rink and didn't seem moneyed at all? He couldn't say this was the strangest thing he'd heard all day. "That's good. None of the ingredients are cheap," he sighed. He hated admitting his faults. "But, there are few shops in town that can accommodate us."

They needed to get what Sin required so they could save the humans.

"Let's get our asses in gear." He ran a hand through his hair. "Especially if we have no budget." That was convenient when one considered how pricey magical items could get. The demon looked sharply at the two humans. "Don't touch anything in the store."

One accidental bump could get him a deep fried human. At best.

"Then let's go." Michelle crossed her arms, ready for action.

Ravin nodded. "Hold onto your butts." He reached out and grabbed the two. Again he transported them out of the room.

This time he took them to the exterior of an interestingly decorated knickknack shop. It appeared to be a weird choice, considering their current mission. "Here we are." Ravin moved to the door.

It was a quaint looking place, painted a nice sky blue. Looking at it, the only word Michelle could think of was 'cute.' This place felt off, but she trusted the demon enough to know that he would know where a good place for magic was. Not that she had any clue. The group went into the building together, and as the door swung open, a soft chime of a bell sang out.

Inside was the soft smell of antiquity and resting dust. Almost like a beloved bookstore, but better. Happy looking collectibles sat proudly on shelves as they waited to be purchased, or at the very least, looked at. A gentle sound of a record player rolled through the shop. Singing along to the old tune that sounded from the equilibrium forties, was a teenage-appearing girl. She watched the group with curious cat eyes. The grin never left her face.

"Welcome to Nika's Nacks, how can I help you?" she purred happily.

"We need stuff for a spell," Michelle stated bluntly.

The girl behind the counter's eyes widened slightly.

"Well, no beating around the bush here, I see." Her tone was whimsical and lively like a rush of spring wind through a field of floating dandelion fluff. "I like that." She gave a casual wink to Ravin as she moved from behind the counter. Her every silky movement was in time with the whir of a rolling record. "What kinda spell are we thinkin'? Life? Death…?" Her feline eyes lingered over the two girls and the single male, "Love?"

Ravin did his best to repress an eye roll. "Search." As if he needed a love spell. "We need the items on this list." He passed over the piece of paper to her.

A silvery laugh of amusement slipped from the girl's mouth. "Search it is."

After a cute lazy stretch, she twirled her finger through a lock of red curling hair. She was a ginger who wore the fire well. Without another word, Nika went behind the counter, and all but disappeared into what Michelle could only guess was a cellar underneath the shop. This place was more than it appeared to be, that much was obvious. "So, she'll have what we need?" Michelle lifted a brow.

It was too easy. A nice one stop shop was always a good thing, it made things a lot simpler. If they could get things done that would be good. The fewer complications the better.

"Without a doubt, this is the best place to come for all your magic needs." Ravin's spell work was rusty; he didn't need that sort of magic for what he did. Most of the time.

He shrugged. "I wouldn't have wasted time and come here if she couldn't provide." The waiting was the absolute hardest part of the entire process. It was agonizing, every moment they spent without the ingredients was a moment that something terrible could happen to the others. Ravin knew for a fact that at the very least, Kazun's life was in danger. Lian was probably still alive, but he had no way of knowing that for sure.

Michelle nodded and leaned against the wall. When she heard the soft tired squeaking of wooden stairs, she turned her head to see that the girl had returned with a handful of various items in vials. There was a purple molasses thick substance in one, it was simply named 'Essence'. She set down a few other strangely shaped glass objects, all with labels as obscure as the last.

Mischa gave Ravin an uncertain look, but Nika seemed proud of what she had picked out.

"This everything that you need. Except for one teensy thing," Nika's words bounced in staccato. In a teasing manner she tapped her lips and sat on the counter amongst the things she had collected.

Before Michelle could ask what that was, the girl added, "I'm afraid I'm fresh out of Sumsuneira."

"I really hope that's a sneeze," Michelle commented coolly, which earned her a giggle from the girl.

"Sumsuneira means 'Summer's Blessing,'" she chimed happily "It is a white flower that blooms in the Summer Kingdom's Royal Garden. It is gifted to the nobility and to knights. It's a shame it's so rare. I mean, with such a beauty I'm sure you could find the man on the moon." The corners of her lips perked in a mischievous smile.

A frown touched Ravin's face. "So how are we supposed to get it?" He was pretty sure that they were fresh out of Elvan knights and he didn't exactly cavort with the royal types.

"Well if I had that answer, I would have that flower to sell, now wouldn't I?" The girl began to ring up the items she had collected. Her long nails clicked on the old register's keys and she examined each bottle and vial with care.

"Your total comes to—," Nika was silenced as Jo came forward and handed her credit card over. A smile came to the woman's lips and she nodded and placed the card on a transaction reader before returning it. She chirped, "You're all free to go. Hope to see you soon." She gave a wink.

"I know where we can look," Jo said as she gathered some of the purchases. "I so happen to have an elf's number in my pocket. If nothing else, he can lead us in the right direction." The girl had never been so happy to almost have been stabbed to death. The male owed her a favor; he had said so himself.

Her words struck the demon. "Marius," he said in an awed voice. "I knew he would come in handy eventually." The demon wanted to jump for joy. "Call that kid. He caused this, and he can help put it right." It was the least Marius could do.

Jo gave a thumbs up as she fumbled around for her phone and the number that rested safely in her pocket. After deciding she couldn't juggle everything in her hands as well as the task at hand, she shoved the items at Ravin. She was so glad she had kept the scrap of paper. It might be their lifesaver. Quickly, her fingers typed in the digits and she clicked the call button.

The dial tone sounded as the call went through. The happy chime rang once, twice, then halfway through the third, was interrupted by a click. A second passed before a confused, "Hello?" came through the other line.

"Marius?" Jo asked, then clarified, "This is Jo."

Michelle watched as Jo began her conversation. A subtle tickle of relief rolled through her veins. For a moment, she was worried that he would have given her the wrong number. Luckily, that didn't seem to be the case. Maybe things would start looking up for her and Ravin. They were in the same boat now.

A shudder passed through her spine. It had been terrifying seeing the demon using his powers to tear his dorm apart. The action had highlighted how demonic he truly was, and, at the same time, how human he could be. From what she had seen from Sin and other demons, most had a motive. Sin wanted to get paid, and she wanted to find Lian because she felt obligated. Ravin on the other hand, deeply cared about Kazun. He wanted to get the boy back not because Kaz was worth something in treasures, but because he was worth something in Ravin's heart.

They were going to get this stupid flower, and they were going to make the best damn finding spell in the world. Together, they would track down Lian, then eventually get to Kazun. If that meant going to the abyss of Hell and back, Michelle would do what was necessary.

Determination flared in her eyes and she reiterated, "We're going to find both of them, because I know neither of us will give up until we do."

Ravin looked over at Michelle. It was heartening to hear her confidence. "I won't give up. I won't rest until they're safe."

Nothing would stop him from doing everything he could. He

was going to make sure that all of them made it out in one piece. These squishy humans were going to see what demons were capable of.

"Alright," Jo said as she hung up the phone. "Marius said he thinks that Letvan has the flower in a small pot on his window frame. If he doesn't, Letvan has to send in a letter to the Queen for a replacement, which could take up to a week, but it's easier than going through customs and passports and that jazz." The tall girl looked mighty pleased with herself.

"Thanks Jo," Michelle said with a slight smile, which was returned tenfold by the other. She cocked her brow. "Why do you look so happy?"

Jo grinned and announced, "I have a date."

Eighteen

With what they had in tow, the ragtag band arrived back at Sinsation. Much to Ravin's relief, this time they were allowed in without incident. He made his way to the demoness' back room where she was starting to work the spell.

When he went to knock on the door, he spotted the man she had been talking to earlier. He was off to the side, observing the demon and two girls, watching them with dark unamused eyes. His black gaze was heavy and terrifying. Even though he showed no outward signs of an identifiable species, he was definitely not human. There was something foreboding about him. The strange tattoos on his left arm glowed darkly in the dim light.

Ravin couldn't help but wonder what he was and why he was still here.

In the back of his mind he could feel a prodding against his mental wards. He'd put them up to prevent his enemies from seeing into his thoughts and using what was there. Ravin dared to glare at the man, and the attempted intrusion stopped.

He rapped his knuckles on the door and called out. "Oy, Sin, we're back."

The caramel colored demoness swung the door open. Her hip rolled to one side as she adjusted her weight. Her dark smoldering eyes complemented her grin as she purred, "'bout time. You sure know how to make a lady wait."

With a laugh, she turned and gestured for the group to follow. As she moved from the doorway, they could see her office décor had changed. Instead of a desk, she had a large empty space with markings written in chalk on the floor.

The symbols all radiated a white glow. In the center was a series of concentric circles. A small bowl sat within the lines. A star was drawn around the container and at each point a candle waited.

"So let me see the presents you brought me," she said with a dark smile.

The humans came forth and produced the ingredients. With a long elegant finger, Sin perused the items. Her eyes sparked with interest. There was only one slight trace of disappointment on her face.

She looked up at Ravin and pouted. "You forgot something."

"The Sumsuneira." The male spoke in an even tone. "The seller was fresh out. It's not exactly an easy ingredient to obtain. But we have another source who should be able to get it to us soon."

Hopefully the elf had it. The last thing Ravin wanted was to wait another week. Leaving the humans in the wrong hands for a few hours was bad enough. He didn't dare imagine what a full week could lead to.

Ravin glanced back at the door. "Also, you care to explain who the beefcake out there with the stink eye is?"

The man rubbed him the wrong way. For all the demon knew, he had something to do with Lian's disappearance. And if he did, he could be spying on them or attempting to hinder their progress, and that did not sit well with Ravin.

The female demon sighed and rolled her eyes. "Don't worry about him. He is a close friend of mine. He isn't involved."

"Doesn't mean I have to like him," the demon muttered and cast a scathing glance at the doorway. There was no trusting anyone who wasn't in this room, or the two elves they had to rely on to secure the flower for them.

He was going to make Letvan pay if he didn't have that stupid flower. "I'll get the flower, then you can do the spell, right?"

"That is correct," Sin said as she carefully placed a few sprigs of herbs into a mortar. With dexterous hands, she began to grind them using the matching pestle. A soft mellow smell was forced out into the room. "I should only need the flower. I will keep you notified. Oh yes, please refrain from barging in on me. Call me when you get the flower and I will collect it. I need to focus." She gave him her signature smile, then shooed him away with the point of her tail.

The group did as they were told and left the old brick building. With a sigh, Ravin rested his hands behind his head, then pivoted and walked backwards to study the two girls. "So I'm guessing that our first stop should be to visit your pretty elf boyfriend." He only teased Jo to distract himself from the absolutely stressful situation that he'd found himself in.

Jo tapped her chin. "I only think we're going on a date, I don't think that counts as going steady. I wouldn't mind though," she giggled. "Then me, Michelle, and Lia could each have a cutie." She winked at Ravin.

Michelle shoved her friend, "Don't say it like that!" Her lips pulled into a frown. Michelle's arms crossed. "Like Hell I would ever date this guy."

The demon gasped and put a hand over his mouth. "You're so cruel, madam."

He didn't mention that he wasn't interested in dating her either. Ravin didn't like to make ties with others. That made one vulnerable. Attachment was one thing he attempted to avoid. However, he obviously hadn't done a good enough job; he was tied to Kazun, after all.

When Ravin's thoughts landed on Kazun, his eyes turned dark. There was a malicious glimmer in his sable gaze and his tail flicked in a clear sign of aggression. As much as he liked Letvan, the elf was going to pay if he didn't quickly provide. The male bristled with dark energy so strong that even the humans would be able to feel it. He let out a sigh and ran the palm of his hand over one horn, calming his mind.

He turned so his back faced the girls, his face twisting with a furious determination. Anyone who had been approaching the group down the street moved out of the way. A dark cloud hung over the demon, summoned by his black mood.

It wasn't long before the three of them reached the Elvan dorms. They were greeted by Marius, who was sitting at the entrance.

"Hey!" the elf called and waved. His grassy gaze landed on Jo and his eyes lit up like the sun. Marius offered her a broad heart melting smile. "It's good to see you again Jo, without the awkward presence of a sword."

Jo smiled and waved as she greeted the elf with cheer. "Yeah, the sword is kind of an awkward subject. Anyway, these guys are pretty antsy about that flower so if we could get it, that would be fantastic." Jo's dark green eyes glanced back at her friends. Michelle was rocking on her heels, and Ravin looked like someone had smacked him with a storm cloud. "Thanks so much for helping us."

Marius nodded. "Of course." He gestured at the door to the building. "I can show you up to Letvan's room." The elf looked at the other two. "I am really sorry, I didn't mean to cause this. I swear that I'll do anything in my power to make this right." Everything about his body language, as well as his demeanor, spoke of truth.

They were led up to the knight's room. Marius knocked on the door quietly as to not disturb the others on the floor. "Letvan, it's Marius."

The door swung open revealing the attractive knight, his hair a slight mess as if he had woken up from a short nap. Letvan yawned and surveyed the group. His emerald eyes shone with interest.

"Hello there." His voice was tinted with a touch of an Elvan accent. "Come on in."

It was a beautiful place, something fit for a prince. It was spacious, luxurious, and all around expensive.

Michelle was in awe as she stepped inside. It was like she was whisked away to a far off land filled with magic and mystery. Golden swords adorned the wall, and a few tapestries hung over the windows. The lighting in the room was dim. Before the only open window was a small shrine with an ink painting and a flower. Michelle grabbed Ravin's sleeve and tugged. She nodded over to the small plant that danced in the sparkling sun.

The demon followed Michelle's line of sight. "Bingo," he murmured under his breath. Ravin looked over at Kazun's teammate. "Letvan I'm sorry, but this is a time-critical situation." He was reluctant to elaborate on the details; the fewer people who knew about the dark angel the better. "Kazun's life is on the line, and so is her sister's," he gestured at Michelle. While it wasn't the whole truth, Ravin had a feeling that Letvan would be more eager to help his friend than a girl he might not know.

Letvan's brow cocked and he looked at Michelle, then back at Ravin. "Kazun was taken as well?" He closed his eyes and let out a sigh. "What can I help you with?"

Ravin lifted a finger and pointed at the flower. "It's the last ingredient for a spell to locate the two of them." From the appearance of the shrine that the flower was kept in, it was clearly something that was important to Letvan.

"Absolutely not," Letvan said and he crossed his arms. "I can send a note to Ani and get you one." His eyes hardened and his muscles twitched. There was a protective vibe rolling off of the knight.

It took a lot of energy to keep his anger tamped down, but Ravin managed. "That could take a week. Kazun could be dead by then, Letvan."

Marius looked between the two. "Ravin… I don't think pushing this is a good idea." There was sympathy in his tone. "Kazun's human, yes, but he could survive another week. This flower is important to Letvan. Please." He didn't want to see them fight, especially not in a place like this. This was a place that had a good energy, and this argument would ruin that, as well as a friendship.

"What's so important about it?" the demon demanded.

"It was my Mother's," Letvan responded. "She died when I was small. I was awarded her flower upon becoming a knight. It is the last token I have of her."

A sigh escaped Ravin's lips. He ran a hand through his hair and closed his eyes. "I'm sorry." The demon shook his head. "Is there any way I can get another flower quickly?"

Letvan let out a breath. He went over to the small plant and he studied it. Kneeling down, he touched the soft petals and his emerald eyes closed. For several long moments he was silent. Carefully, he picked up the plant's simple yet lovely pot.

"The flower is vital to the plant's survival. I think if I make a clipping it will be ok. It may take me the length of the afternoon since it's a delicate task. Will that work?" He fixed Ravin with an understanding look.

Ravin nodded. "Yes it will, thank you."

If their situations were reversed, Ravin couldn't be sure if he would be so generous. Nevertheless, he was glad that Letvan had agreed. Now would be better, but later in the afternoon would be bearable. Then he could get Sin what she needed and there'd be no threat of death by dark angel. "I guess we'll leave you to it then."

"See you later," Letvan said gently and looked back at his flower.

With that, Ravin gestured for the girls to leave. No doubt Letvan would want to be left alone for the delicate process. He felt a strange feeling in the back of his chest. Was it guilt? Did he know what that felt like?

And over a flower that he needed?

Taking the hint, the girls filed out of the room. Jo waved at Marius and gave him a sympathetic smile. It had been a very crazy day. And yet, it was nowhere near over. She was glad that the Elf Knight was willing to compromise. That would make both Michelle's and Ravin's life a lot easier. They sure needed a break after all that was happening.

"I think I need some fresh air. What about you?" Ravin asked Michelle and gazed outside the window. His body was still tense from talking with Letvan. He wanted to punch a hole in the moon, but he would hold it in, at least, for a while.

Going to the gardens sounded like a good plan. Anything but sitting in his room and waiting. He had to be passive and that killed him. At least if he waited outside, then he could pretend that he was doing something. He was rather good at pretending. It made things so much easier to deal with.

Michelle nodded. "Yeah sure." Her voice was muddled with emotion. Sure, she was glad they were going to get the flower, but it was going to take more time. Fresh air might help clear her head. While Jo was going out on a date with Marius, she would stay with Ravin. Together, they would have to try and get through the torturous postponement.

They went down into the beautiful gardens. It was serene and quiet. Not many students were out and about. The sweet smell of flowers danced in the evening air. The sky was a vivid painting above them. The human let out a sigh and looked at Ravin. There was no attempt to force a calm look.

"It's a nice day, all things considered." He leaned against a tree and watched the clouds above them. In his long, long life he'd experienced all sorts of days and nights. Most were the same, and very few stood out in his mind. This one probably would, but for all the wrong reasons. It would be marred by the fact that he had a looming apocalypse to worry about.

"Are you kidding me?" Michelle shot a glare at him, and stamped her foot down. Her emotions were bubbling to the surface. She had nothing to occupy her mind. She screamed and kicked the nearest tree. Pain shot up her leg as she felt the blow in her bones. What she was feeling needed to escape. She had to let out the pent up energy, or she would explode.

He had gotten the chance to tear up his apartment. She hadn't gotten a chance like that. Lian was gone and in danger. Their world could come crumbling down before their eyes. Michelle couldn't stand there and make small talk. Her fingers snaked through her hair and she pulled at the roots.

She was a human. How was she supposed to deal with everything on her shoulders? How was she supposed to face impossible odds to save not only her sister, but this entire plane of existence? This was a job for demons, vampires, elves, anything but her.

Ravin watched her, letting her get the energy out. "Feel any better?" He wondered how long this had been building up. "If not, I can think of a few ways to get it out. In a strictly platonic way." He didn't want her to get the wrong idea. After all, it was a stereotype that demons were more active sexually than other races. It wasn't entirely untrue though.

"Go to Hell." Michelle shoved him. No, it wasn't the demon she was really mad at, but he was the only thing around for her to take it out on.

"Come on," he urged. "You can let it all out, right at me, back at my dorm. I promise."

A soft vibration sounded in Michelle's pocket. She pulled out her phone and a text message from an unknown number lit up her screen. Her expression changed completely, cocking her brows as she opened the message. Bewilderment filled her eyes and she stuffed the phone in Ravin's hand. She looked up at him. "What the Hell does this mean?"

The male arched an eyebrow, looking down at the screen. "I honestly have no idea," he spoke as confusion filled him.

There were four words on the screen: "Corinthians One. Three Sixteen."

Nineteen

Michelle grimaced as rage flashed through her veins. Her eyes narrowed and her lips pursed. After a few more moments, she threw her controller to the ground, crossed her arms and snapped at the demon who was sitting in the bean bag next to her, "This isn't helping."

After the weird text, Ravin had convinced Michelle to attempt to get their frustrations out by playing some video games. The two were neck and neck. Michelle was good at games, and he was her even match.

The demon lounged back and caught the controller with his mind. "Maybe you're not trying hard enough." On the inside, he was still ready to burst as well.

The girl grabbed a pillow from the couch. She gripped it, nails digging into its plush fabric. Her face twisted. Something snapped, and she began to mercilessly beat Ravin with it.

"I'm. Trying. My. Hardest. You. Fucking. Asshole." She struck him between each word. When she was panting and out of breath, she stopped. Her sharp glare was a pointed cobalt dagger. "That's a bit better."

Ravin took each blow like a champ. The harmless hits fanned the flame burning inside him. He wanted to lash out right back at her. His muscles tensed and coiled, ready to spring and give her some well-deserved payback. Instead, he reined it in and stole her remaining life in the game, winning the decisive round for himself. "Looks like I win."

Michelle glanced back at the screen. She chucked the soft square across the room and she stood up, "I don't care, Ravin." Anxiously she paced. Her arms crossed her chest, holding herself together. This was pointless.

"I don't care," she screamed at him, reiterating her point. "This is wasting time. I can't stand it." She walked over to where the pillow rested and kicked it.

The worry was building in her chest, strangling her heart. The anxiety was a boa constrictor wrapping itself tighter and tighter. If it continued on, she would go mad. She bit her lip and turned away from him. It hurt, and Michelle hated showing pain. Her sister was in harm's way while she got to play some dumb games.

It should have been the other way around. Michelle could handle the thought of her own death. She could handle being alone. She could handle almost anything—except this. She knew her sister wasn't okay. Even if she wasn't hurt physically, Michelle knew mentally, Lian would be falling apart. It was a fate worse than death for the older sister.

Her teeth dug into her lip until she could taste salt. At first, she had thought it was blood.

It was a moment later she realized a tear had escaped.

Ravin rose to his feet and wiped a second tear from her cheek. He wrapped his arms around her and pulled her close against his chest. "I know," he breathed. "And I'm sorry. Let it out as best as you can, because we're going to need you at the top of your game once Letvan brings that flower in." His frustration had been vented a little bit, vicariously, through her.

It was quiet. Michelle leaned against the warmth around her. Since she was eight years old, she had been a fearless warrior. She had fought every monster in the closet and every creature under the bed. For thirteen years, she had been a comforting wall. Unmovable and unbreakable.

"I'm going to kick this bastard's ass so hard," she muttered into his shirt. Tears were escaping, and it was only fueling the fires inside. Whoever had taken Lian would regret it.

"You're going to make them wish they had never been born," Ravin agreed. "Then, we're going to save Kaz. It's too bad we have to wait, because he's got his huge crush on her, and he's going to be super embarrassed that he couldn't help save her." It felt cathartic to give away all of Kazun's dark secrets. It made him feel like somehow Kaz was right there. Like at any second, he would complain or break Ravin out of this very bad dream.

There was a knock on the door.

Michelle took a large step away from Ravin and rubbed her

arm. "Your place, your door."

"Don't worry, I've got it." In a smooth movement Ravin walked over to the door. He twisted the knob and jerked it open. "Hello?" Ravin asked lazily.

Letvan stood there and he held out the flower. "Here you are, Ravin. I'm glad I can help make up for my pupil's accident." He forced a smile. It was painful to hand over his prized flower, but a new one would grow soon.

"Thank you, Letvan. I promise to make this up to you at some point. I know it's worth more than making up for Marius' mistake." It was best not to antagonize a knight who was doing this out of the good of his heart.

"All life is Sacred. To save a life is to live my purpose, Ravin. I live these words, and I suppose this is the least I can do," Letvan said and he bowed his head, hand over his heart. "Good luck to you both." With a wave he turned and made his leave.

His work here was done.

Michelle wandered over to Ravin. Now that they had the flower, they could find where Lian was hidden. "Let's go poof, Rav." It was really nice having someone who could teleport.

The demon's eyes flared, "Damn straight, freckles."

Michelle blinked, "But I don't even have—"

He wrapped an arm around her and teleported them to Sin's bar. Ravin whipped out his phone and dialed the demoness' number. "I have the flower and I'm outside your office." Despite his baser urges, he was going to at least try to do as she asked and not barge in. He almost had, but had barely caught himself in time. The last thing he wanted was an angry Sin.

The door swung open with a satisfying squeal of the metal hinges. Sin looked up from her work as she hung up her phone. Her dark eyes landed on the two. How cute. She smirked and held out her hand. "'Bout time, Ravin," she purred, tail flicking.

"Elf had to make a clipping." Ravin handed over the flower. "Is the spell almost done?"

Sin took the flower and placed it in a circle. She simply said, "It's ready."

In a controlled motion, Sin placed her index finger to her lips, as if telling them to be absolutely quiet, and turned her attention back to the complex spell work on her floor.

Carefully, the demoness set her hand within the center circle. Her tail laid peacefully behind her. Pressure welled up in the room. Energy cracked and popped as if someone had poured milk into a bowl of puffed rice crisps. The hair on the back of the others' neck stood up as sparks of energy licked at their skin, as if someone was giving them a static shock.

Michelle looked around as all of the chalk circles began to glow like the stars in the night sky. A humming whirred in the room as a breeze began to circle around the female demon. The human didn't speak, primarily because she had been told not to. Mostly, because she wouldn't even know what to say. Her wide blue eyes looked up at Ravin.

The demon put a comforting hand on her shoulder. No matter how hard he strained, he couldn't get a hint of the tangible energy Sin had found. The circles contained it, and blocked him from getting even the faintest whiff.

There was a loud pop of energy and a spark broke through the light fixtures. Each snapped until the room went dark, except for the soft glittering light of the spell. Moments later, it too went out.

"Fuck," Sin cursed, then candles lit through the dark room. "The little shit who stole your squishy human is crafty. I need an amplifier." She looked down at the spell. It was perfect, save for one small problem. There was a shield of sorts protecting the location. She moved to her desk and took out a sheet of paper and began to write down information.

"You are going to be stealing from a very powerful man, Ravin. My word of advice for you." Sin stood and ripped the paper off her notebook and placed it in her minion's hand. "Don't get caught."

Ravin frowned as he looked at the information on the paper. "You can't be serious."

Sin couldn't honestly expect him to steal from someone this dangerous. No, oh no. This was insanity. Ravin knew that he had to get Lian back but… this was a terrible idea.

"This is a suicide mission." He was not onboard for this. On the paper, a name stood out. Vatali. This was a name that he recognized, and he didn't like it at all. "There has to be another way, Sin." Ravin raked his fingers through his strawberry blonde hair. "Stealing from Vatali could get us both killed." He cast a glance over at Michelle, "or worse."

He knew with definite certainty that there were far worse things than death that could happen to a human. Death, even when drawn out and torturous would result in Michelle going to Heaven. The demon could see her soul was more or less pure, some minor sins at most, nothing that would condemn her to be dragged to Hell for. No, death would be a welcome release compared to what a vampire mercenary could pull out of his sleeve, especially one as old as Vatali.

"Whoa, wait." Michelle held up her hands to stop the conversation that went on without her. "Who is this Vatali guy? Why should I be afraid of someone who sounds like he should have perfume named after him?" She hated that the demons acted like she wasn't there.

Ravin looked over at Michelle. "He has at least seven named after him. Right now Vatali owns a nightclub a few businesses away. It's exclusive and he's got security that could make us regret going in there and breathing wrong. The guy's an ex-mercenary whom even *I'm* wary of messing with." If Sin would change their destination... then they wouldn't have to risk life and limb.

"No," Sin insisted, her tail slashed back and forth. "Vatali is the only option. Unless you want me to … give up." Sin shrugged and sighed wistfully. She offered a look over at her audience. She knew they wouldn't give up on the kidnapped little ones.

"We are going," Michelle snapped. The human's harsh tone brought a smile to Sin's face. It was nice to have a reminder that these humans all had a bit of a devilish side. It was amusing to say the least. Ravin sure knew how to pick fun company.

Ravin sighed and put a hand on his forehead. "You're absolutely sure Michelle?" he asked in a calm, even voice. If she was serious, then he would go through with it… but he wouldn't like it. This would take all of the skill he had to make sure that they kept themselves in one piece. It wasn't going to be easy.

"I'm positive, Ravin," Michele said, her blue eyes flashing. What a stupid question. There were lives at stake, and she didn't even care about her own as long as it got someone close to saving Lian from whatever hell she had found herself in. It was her duty to do whatever she could. No exceptions. No giving up.

She couldn't take the easy way out.

Sin silenced him with a confident, "Oh, this lovely lady is sure." She waltzed over to the human girl and placed both of her caramel hands on the mortal's shoulders. Static thoughts tickled the demon's mind and a sly smirk appeared on her face.

"You both better dress up," she purred with a sweet tone. "I bet you'd look good in a sexy black dress." Sin's hand gently stroked the mortal's cheek. Michelle didn't flinch beneath her touch. Nay, only resilient eyes stared back.

With a silver laugh, Sin shooed them away. They had work to do.

Michelle turned, rubbing the skin the she-demon had touched. A tingling sensation lingered; the demon had left trails of hot lively energy dancing.

A sense of dread filled her. She didn't like the way Ravin had seemed so apprehensive. She had liked it better when he was overconfident. When he looked like he could take on the world, Michelle believed he truly could. Now, she was sure they were staring death in the face. It was frightening to say the absolute least. As her feet padded through the bar hall and out into the alley, Michelle's thoughts felt like a dark torrent looming overhead.

She wanted to believe everything was going to be okay, but… it was hard. Every difficult task they completed only led to another trial. It was in her to be optimistic. Always. Though, now nothing seemed to be going right.

Secretly, she wanted to curl up and cry. Instead, she put on a brave face, preparing for dangers unknown. Slowly she looked over to the demon. There was a pit in her chest. Michelle knew she would never give up fighting for Lian, but would he go to the same lengths?

An autumn breeze rolled through the alley, kicking up leaves and dust as it swept across the brick ground. Transports rolled solemnly down the boulevard and further down the street, a fanfare could be heard as a garishly lit building screamed for attention. A huge neon sign flashed, 'The Hot Spot' in bright blue letters. Nightlife started to gather as a gloomy overcast covered the last shred of daylight.

No stars were out watching them tonight. They were on their own. That was fine with her. No one was keeping an eye out for Lian but her. If she had to steal some artifact from some big wig, then so be it.

"You own a suit, big boy?" Michelle shot to her companion. "'Cause we got ourselves a date."

Twenty

"Are you sure it's supposed to look like this?" Ravin regarded his reflection in the mirror. He felt like an idiot. If this is what Sin meant by dressing up, then he definitely didn't like it.

Marius rolled his eyes. "Get your butt out here."

The demon groaned and carefully exited Jo's bathroom. He gestured at the suit hanging perfectly on his body. Despite the fact that it fit rather nicely, he did not enjoy the clothing. He felt like a trained animal dressed up to entertain the masses.

Deep down, actually, he kind of liked it. Maybe he would wear it again. The jacket was black silk, smooth and flowing. Beneath, his shirt was crisp white, pressed and starched. The pants matched his ensemble, and was made of the same material as his jacket. Really, he looked magnificent, but he felt ridiculous. The two inch heels didn't help. Dressing up wasn't his style.

"It's awful. Seriously, who made this thing?" he complained and gestured at himself. He hoped that all of his complaining would get him kicked out of their little band. However, it was certainly a suit that he could be buried in. He'd give it that.

Jo shouted from the next room over, "My mother."

From his position on the couch, the elf rolled his eyes. "You're insane." He sighed and crossed a leg. He was already completely dressed in a suit of his own, with a pale green shirt in contrast to the demon's white. "That thing was practically made for you, so calm down." Despite his somewhat serious tone, the elf's mossy eyes sparkled playfully.

"Your mother has amazing taste," Ravin yelled back, but still pouted and crossed his arms. He envied Marius' ignorance. The elf didn't know what was at stake tonight.

Marius rolled his eyes. "*They've* been ready for the past twenty minutes. They're waiting in the kitchen for your slow ass." He gestured with exasperation, though it was clear to the demon that he wasn't actually being cruel.

Though it would be better on his nerves if Marius was more solemn. This was a matter of life and death, not some simple night on the town. Lives were on the line, their own and that of Lian. If she was even still alive. He wouldn't bring that up in front of Michelle: that would send her spiraling into a relapse.

With a standoffish shrug, Ravin walked out into the kitchen. "Will you two tell me if I look like a suited monkey?"

Michelle looked over as she finished putting on a hint of red lipstick. Her bright blue eyes were accented with perfect makeup.

She put her hands on her hips and swayed a bit. Her black dress went to her mid-thigh and had light accents that rolled down to the dress tips. Her hair was gelled into spritely spikes, and when she smiled, it put stars to shame. She wasn't a sore sight on any given day, but when she was all cleaned up, Michelle was gorgeous.

"I think that's being cruel to the monkeys," Michelle quipped and looked over at Jo who was wearing a dress that complimented Marius's suit. With a long sigh, the girl continued, "But I guess you will have to do."

"You better look good," Jo giggled. "You spent twice as long getting ready as any of us."

She smiled and looked past the demon to the elf who was sitting in the other room. Despite the fact their mission was going to be stressful as all hell, she figured she might as well have some fun. She had always wanted to go on a double date before. Even if this wasn't official, she could still pretend.

Michelle walked over to Ravin and softly patted his for-once brushed hair. "It's okay, Monkey," she said. "The suit won't kill you."

Ravin snorted and rolled his eyes. "You say that now."

As the others spoke, Marius got to his feet and joined them. He gave them all a confident smile and offered his arm to Jo. "I'm guessing you're all ready to leave?" Every pore exuded confidence. "I'm kind of excited; my friend Nikki's said some great things about this place."

"Let's head out then," Jo led them outside where a limo was waiting. A trillion-credit grin appeared on her face as the driver opened the door for the group. All four of them climbed in and got comfortable.

Saying it was nice would be an understatement.

"If I didn't know how loaded you were Jo, I would seriously be shocked," Michelle laughed as she lounged comfortably on the luxurious dark upholstery. Michelle had never been in a limo before; it was so cool. For at least a moment, she could forget about the troubles of her life. For a moment, she could feel like everything was okay. Shooting a smile at Marius, Michelle teased, "You didn't know you almost killed a septillionaire, did you?" She was silenced by a swift shove from Jo.

Marius turned to face his radiant date. "Are you serious?" Despite the realization, he didn't sound all that shocked.

"Whoa, wait, really? You said multi-trillionaire, septillion is an entirely different story." Ravin leaned forward and gaped at the tall girl. Sure he knew that she wasn't exactly poor, especially with that unlimited magic supply budget. Septillion? He'd let her have some privacy in her mind and not invaded to learn what he could, but maybe he shouldn't have. That would have been useful knowledge.

Jo flushed and she had really wished that Michelle would have kept her mouth shut. With a sigh she said, "My father is Joseph Ferros, the owner of Holo Corp." It was one of the most well-known businesses in the world. Not only did they produce the holo-devices, and numerous amounts of medical equipment, there was probably at least one Ferros brand item in most every home.

The elf nodded. "Well, that doesn't mean I won't still buy your drinks tonight." He took her hand and gently kissed its back. "I mean, I've got to show you a good time." In his mind this still counted as a date, and he wouldn't let her down on their first time out. His mossy eyes glittered happily and he stroked her hand with his thumb.

Ravin pouted. "You're going to hook me up with free stuff, right?" He crossed his arms and slouched into the plush seat. There was still time for them to kick him out.

"You know what, Ravin?" a quirky smile appeared on Jo's face. "You got this suit, didn't you?" Her dark forest eyes looked over at her date. He was so sweet, and the fact that he still wanted to buy her drinks after hearing she was a 'septillionaire' brought rose petals to her cheeks.

"Even more reason we have to make it out alive," Michelle said, looking out the window. They weren't far away from their destination. It wouldn't be long until they were pulling up. With a flash of her father's name, Jo would get them all in, no questions asked. Then, the real fun started.

The limo came to a smooth stop as it pulled in front of The Hot Spot. Even from inside the vehicle, music could be heard. A line stood before the door and a large man waited sentry, making sure anyone who came in was on the list. His blonde hair was cropped and his jaw square, his thickly muscled arms were crossed in front of his bulging chest. The man's outfit was as black as his eyes. He looked frightening to say the least. When the driver opened the door, everyone piled out. Jo took in a deep breath and walked over to the guard.

"That's a nice Holo device you got up there." Jo pointed to a large screen that was displaying wild images of the fun nightlife that waited inside. "My father makes some pretty good stuff, doesn't he?"

She offered the guard a sweet smile that spoke volumes. And if showing up in a limo and being a Ferros wasn't enough, well, they would be shit out of luck.

The guard's gaze raked over her form and took in every detail. "You say that like we don't get that claim every day. There are three 'Ferros' kids at the back of the line already." His low gravelly voice came from deep within his chest.

Jo's looked back and let out a laugh. "And that's why they're at the back of the line, and I'm at the front." She and Clarence were the only Ferros kids. Her brother was a more well-known face of the company. Jo, on the other hand, was only really known by those who did some research. Maybe that was why three people even tried to pose as her.

From behind the large guardian a quiet voice piped up. "Uh, Creed, I'm pretty sure that's the real Josephine Ferros." A far smaller man poked his head around from the side of Creed, his eyes were wide as he beheld the human.

Creed appraised her once again and nodded. "I see. My apologies Miss Ferros." He bowed his head. "You and your entourage may enter." With one arm, he held open the heavy door for the four guests. "Enjoy yourselves." His eyes glimmered as he examined them again; they lingered mostly on Jo and her date.

Ravin didn't need to be told twice. He grabbed Michelle's hand and dragged her inside. They had passed the point of no return, so he decided to dive in head first. He also knew it wasn't wise to stay anywhere near Creed for long. That guy was as much of a mercenary as Vatali was. They must have had some kind of agreement, the demon reasoned; not only that, but he must get paid a pretty penny to stay here instead of go out and put those muscles to better use.

Once inside, he looked for a table through the sea of well-dressed bodies swaying to the pulsing beat of the music. The air was thick with the scent of booze and perfume. Ravin wanted to make sure they had a good vantage point on the huge stage that stood in the middle of the room.

"What's the stage for?" Marius shouted over the din of the music filling the air.

Instead of answering, Ravin made a gesture at a table towards the back of the club. He used a pinch of energy to transport himself and Michelle onto the plush seats before someone else could snatch it up. A few moments later, Jo and Marius arrived, sliding inside the booth.

"It's where they have performances. This place has quite the reputation for showmanship," Ravin finally explained.

"It looks fantastic," Michelle said in awe. Everything was so over the top with 'style' and theme. Overwhelming was an understatement. Above all, she was relieved that they had made it in. The first hurdle had been cleared. Now the real challenge waited. Her fingers trailed through a drink menu. When it came to this sort of place, she wasn't well versed. "And I have no idea what I want." Perhaps her Demon friend could help her.

"I think I'm going to go with the... ummmm ..." Jo pointed to a drink on the list. "An-re-is?" It was an Elvan drink. She had always heard wonders about the tastes of a fine summer wine. Pronunciation, however, was not her strong suit, especially such a complex and beautiful language like Elvan.

Marius nodded. "That one's delicious, though don't have too many, Elvan drinks are deceptively sweet and light. Most of the time only a few of them will knock you onto your butt."

Ravin pointed at a far tamer drink for Michelle. "I don't know how much you drink, but you know it's best not to have too much right now." He tried to be intentionally vague, knowing Michelle would understand.

"You're right Ravin, Sparkling grape juice looks delicious," Michelle sassed. It probably wasn't good to have much of anything, since she didn't partake in alcohol very much. Lian didn't care for it, and it wasn't worth the stress. "Then again, that lemon soda is looking pretty good too."

"Careful Michelle. Lemon soda is delicious, but they are deceptively sweet and light. Most the time only a few of them will knock you onto your butt," Jo teased with a wink. Despite the severity of the situation, Jo was pumped up and in a great mood. Maybe it was the rush of using her title to get into an exclusive place. She felt on top of the world and ready for anything. They could do this.

Marius laughed and poked Jo. "You're so mean to me!" He chuckled and nuzzled into her cheek. "I think virgin drinks are a good idea." A faint blush tinted his features.

The demon smirked. "I'm sure you wouldn't know anything about that, Marius," he teased and ordered them all a round of clear soda. Absently, he wrapped an arm around Michelle to create the image of a happy couple.

Fighting the urge to push him away, Michelle took in a breath and leaned on the demon, helping complete the picture of coupledom. Her gaze wandered from the table to the stage. Lights all around the club began to dim. The music quieted. A single spotlight flared, and standing on the stage was a man who exuded style. He was suave and when he smiled, not even the large fangs were frightening.

This man was attractive.

He took a microphone and smiled into it. As he looked up, he began to sing. The night club came to life as a band accompanied him. His voice was warm, delicious, tenor honey. It was sweet and smooth as it melted over the club. Michelle couldn't help but stare, mouth agape. Was this guy for real? His dark perfect hair was styled with a single curl at the very tip. He had smooth skin and he wore a button up shirt with the first two buttons undone, exposing his sculpted chest. Supernatural creatures weren't fair.

Ravin's eyes narrowed. "There he goes. This is our chance, while Vatali's busy."

A sound of surprise escaped Marius. "Wait, that's Vatali?" He couldn't take his eyes off of the magnificent man performing his heart out. It was an absolutely amazing sight to behold. The elf had never seen anything like this in his life.

"Yea, don't let the pretty face fool you." The demon stood and flicked his tail anxiously, "It's a distraction." His dark eyes landed on the door to the back, conveniently close to the seat he had chosen. A breath of determination left his lips and he glanced back at the others. "You coming or not?"

It didn't take much to get Michelle moving. Of course she was coming. What sort of question was that? She could fully believe that the vampire's flare was all a facade. Behind the chic mask was a monster Ravin feared. Michelle had seen it in his eyes. The human took her 'date's' hand and together they sidled to the back door.

Michelle inspected the obsidian barrier before them. She placed her hand on the handle and pulled at it. There was a soft click as the lock held strong. She should have known. How were they going to get past this? "You know how to pick locks?" the human asked.

"Of course I do." Ravin whipped out his tools and started controlling them with his mind. It was simple: he could keep his eye on the rest of the club. The fewer people who saw them leave the better. Within a few moments the lock popped open and the demon pulled Michelle inside before anyone could see them disappear. The hallways in the back were completely empty, which would make searching easier. "If I were a priceless artifact, where would I be?"

Sin had provided them with the description but hadn't bothered to tell them exactly where the item could be found.

He could sense the energy behind a few doors, but nothing too promising. There was one door that had a lot of activity behind it, but no magic. Another had no energy and no magic whatsoever. Now that was useless. Maybe there was something somewhere else.

That's when he felt it, that spark of power. He approached a door and looked back at Michelle. "This is it," he murmured before entering.

A bedroom with a huge four poster bed covered with cream

colored silken sheets, along with half a dozen matching fluffy pillows dominated the room. Everything was organized in a meticulous manner, with thought, and care. Not a single item was out of place.

Along one wall were rows of shelves covered in spoils of war. Various objects of all shapes and sizes were arranged in an order that made no sense to the demon.

He scanned the shelves for the source of energy, glancing at the page Sin had given him and rereading the description. They were looking for something small, no larger than his fist and covered in writing that was illegible and nonsensical. Among the thousands of random things, it wouldn't be easy to find. Even with Michelle's help to search it still wasn't a cinch. Though, she was quite efficient and would help speed up the process.

Every moment that they took to find the artifact was a moment they could be discovered. That made anxiety rise in Ravin's throat: this was all too easy. There hadn't been any kind of alarm. Nothing but a simple lock? Surely there couldn't only be an easily picked lock. That didn't feel like enough. Nobody as old as Vatali would have that kind of lax security.

"I think I got it!" Michelle held an artifact up for Ravin to see.

Hope filled his chest and he grinned. "That's it! Now, let's go get the others and get the Hell out of here." He grabbed her hand and felt the familiar hooks of dread lodge themselves in his heart.

"Do you care to explain what you're doing in my room?" Creed cracked his knuckles as he glared down at them.

Twenty-one

Ravin moved Michelle behind him. He scowled up at the hulking vampire and clenched one hand into a fist. "Grab on to me," the demon ordered and prepared to teleport them out of there. When he felt the girl's hand grab the back of his jacket he tensed.

He closed his eyes to teleport but nothing changed. They were both still in the room. His heart leaped into his throat as he tried again. Nothing. Somehow this vampire had sealed the room so that no one could escape through magical means. There was no visible mark that sealed his abilities, so Ravin couldn't destroy it. There were no windows, and only one door, which Creed blocked with his girth.

"Do you know what I do to people who try to steal from me?" the vampire growled and stood his ground, ensuring that they were imprisoned inside. "It's worse than what I do to the morons who break into my room."

For a moment, Ravin considered the possibility of trying to take down Creed. Yet, he knew better than to do that. This vampire was infinitely older than him; it would be suicide to get too close. Someone like Creed could drain a body dry in no time flat. It was no doubt that the vampire had powerful venom. If he made it out of this alive, he was never going to let Sin hear the end of it for getting them into this situation.

"Make one move, demon. I dare you," Creed growled. "See what happens to your little friends." There was a sadistic light in his eyes.

Michelle gripped tighter onto Ravin's jacket. She could be killed, and this time, it terrified her. Sure she had been up against death before, but this time she had a reason to live. Her generally laugh-at-death attitude was long gone when she needed it most. Her body trembled.

The vampire licked one long fang. "Summer is my favorite season," he smirked maliciously. "I'm also certain that Josephine will fetch a hefty price for ransom. I'm sure her parents would do anything to get their darling back." He cast a glance over his shoulder.

Michelle's eyes widened. Jo. He was going to do something bad to Jo. She couldn't let that happen, but she couldn't think of a way to stop it. Her mouth felt dry. This wasn't supposed to end like this. They were supposed to be able to get the artifact then make it out safe and sound. They were supposed to come out on top.

More than anything, Michelle wanted to scream at the man

and tell him to leave Jo out of this. But, that felt like a waste of what could be her last breath.

'Can't you do anything Ravin?' she mentally whispered to the demon.

Ravin took in a deep breath to calm and center his mind. "Look, feel free to punish me for this, but it's not like I didn't have a good reason." He hated that he had to tell the vampire that much. That was pretty damn close to giving it all away in his mind.

A disbelieving look crossed Creed's face. "Yeah, I bet you do. Why don't you tell me that little reason?"

"We need it to save her sister." The demon kept his voice calm as he danced around the subject. He wouldn't mention the dark angel. The fewer people who knew about that particular situation, the better. He took a slow step to the side, with the hope that Michelle would follow him. Maybe he could trick the muscle bound man. Rumor had it that Vatali was the brains and Creed was the brawn. Maybe it was true.

However, Ravin was disappointed when Creed shook his head. "That's not the whole truth, so what are you hiding little Hell-spawn?"

"Nothing." As soon as he said it, Ravin knew that he'd spoken too soon.

The smirk on Creed's face made Ravin's stomach churn. "Liar." He cracked the knuckles on his other hand. "I know how to get information out of people like you." The demon didn't need to read Creed's mind to know that pain was the only thing in his future.

One thought rose to the top of Ravin's mind. If Creed was torturing him, then Creed didn't have time to stop Michelle from escaping. "I'd like to see you try," Ravin sneered. "I'm oh-so terrified." He did his very best to try to set off his adversary and make him snap. The more Creed tried to get the information, the less focus he had for little Michelle.

The human watched in disbelief. Was the demon trying to get his ass thrown into next Tuesday?! If he wasn't careful, Ravin was going to get himself killed, or worse. Then it clicked and her hands clenched. She looked up at the demon. *'Ravin. Don't play the hero,'* she shot to him mentally, her thoughts sharp.

If he got killed right here and now, part of her would always feel that it was her fault.

"Puh-lease," Ravin rolled his eyes. "I bet this guy doesn't even know how to get a whore to spread their legs." While it wasn't the smartest insult, he didn't have to waste A-grade material on a meat head.

In a movement too fast for either of their eyes to follow, Creed closed the distance between himself and Ravin. His fist slammed into the demon's stomach. A gasp escaped Ravin's throat and he hung limply, the rib bones near the impact were shattered in an instant and their pieces flung into his organs. Blood trickled from his lips, and his brain struggled to cope with the agony.

The demon's fingers wrapped tightly around Creed's arm and held him in place. "That all you got?" he growled and glared defiantly up at his attacker.

"Ravin!" Terror locked Michelle's body in place. If that vampire could make the demon bleed, what kind of damage could it do to her? She might as well have been made out of spun sugar. Somehow she had to get out of there with the artifact. But if Creed got her, she was dead. The powerful creature only had to look at her funny and it would be over.

When Creed began another volley of blows, Michelle decided it was the best hope she had was to make a run for it. If she could get out and run to Sin's bar, she would be home free, right? As she made it to the doorway, she ran into a sturdy figure. She looked up and was staring into a pair of terrifyingly calm black eyes.

"Creed? You have house guests and you never told me?" The man's voice was smooth as silk, as soft as a cloud, and as whimsical as wind chimes. Michelle was stunned not only by the charisma that poured off his frame, but the power he exuded. It was a near rival for the burly Creed.

The muscular vampire growled and pounded one huge fist into the demon's back, which sent his body slamming into the floor. "House guests implies that I invited them, Vatali." Rage filled his sable eyes as he kicked Ravin. He turned his gaze to the other vampire. "Did you catch the other two?" The man asked in a low gravelly voice.

"Yes, well, I would rather say guests than admit that my fine establishment has been infested by rats." Vatali sneered and shoved in the tall girl and her date. He closed the door behind him and he took a gliding step into the room. With a simple motion, the door had been locked. A long sigh escaped his lips. "Such pests."

Michelle looked at Jo and Marius. So far they appeared okay, if shaken up. Things were getting worse by the second. Now all of them had been captured, and there were two ancient vampires instead of one.

"The demon keeps secrets." Creed picked Ravin up by the

front of his shirt.

The demon hung without fighting, though he was still breathing. Ravin placed his hands on Creed's wrist to enable himself to look into the eyes of his attacker.

"I intend to extract them." Sick delight sparkled in Creed's eyes.

A weak laugh came from Ravin. "Don't think it'll work," his voice was strained. "You hit like a puppy, Creed, a really, really weak puppy." He could feel his body mending itself slowly, his ribs were partially fragmented and his organs pushed the shards of bone out as they healed and fixed all imperfections. It wasn't that easy to take him out. A few punches wouldn't kill him, though they would hurt like Hell.

Vatali shook his head. "You know he has a point, Creed. You can beat him up all you want, but he won't say anything." The suave vampire looked down at the girl in front of him, and a sneer twisted his face. Like lightning, he lashed out and grabbed Michelle's arm.

The girl could feel the bone wrench, and sharp nails like bullets pierce her skin. She let out a cry.

"Tell Creed what he wants to know, or I will enjoy this snack." With his other hand Vatali stroked Michelle's face. "And then I will keep her as livestock and make her live out the rest of her life begging out for me to sap away the very blood that keeps her alive. Vampire venom is very addictive, though I don't think I have to remind anyone of that." Smoothly, he leaned over his prey and let out a warm breath on her soft flushed skin.

Unable to stop himself, Ravin lunged as well as he could at

Vatali. "Don't you fucking touch her," he shouted and kicked at Creed's chest. It was about as effective as kicking a bull elephant. The vampire wasn't going to budge. "I'll tell you, just let her go!"

"Go on," Vatali purred and he ran his tongue across Michelle's neck.

The girl shivered uncontrollably and looked over at Ravin with large terror-filled pleading eyes. The venom tickled as tears threatened to escape her eyes. Her heart was pounding out of her chest. She knew the beats of pumping blood would only entice the vampire's more, but she couldn't calm herself.

The demon let out a breath and slumped in Creed's grasp. "We need that artifact to find her sister who was kidnapped. She bears the Word of the Marked, but it's corrupted to connect with a dark angel. Whoever took her is trying to free the dark angel, and you both know what will happen if one of them is unleashed upon the world."

Creed's brows furrowed and his grip loosened on Ravin. There was confusion in his eyes as he looked over at Vatali to see what the brains thought of this development. "Do you believe him?"

Vatali's eyes locked onto the demon with utmost attention. His body tensed and he held up his hand. "Creed, release him."

The burly vampire wasn't sure what to think. Then again, Vatali had a good way of checking the legitimacy of the claim. He had contacts, and Creed knew a man who would be very interested to hear this.

With a graceful movement, Vatali pulled out his holophone and punched in a number. He waited a few long moments that felt like a lifetime before speaking. "I request your presence. It is very important, on a matter I believe is close to you." He paused. "I have a demon in my presence who is claiming someone is trying to free a dark angel."

A second later, the strange man from the bar appeared in the middle of the room. His eyes swept over the people. "What is this about a dark angel?" His voice was incredibly calm, but he emanated an energy that made the hair on the back of everyone's necks stand up. With a look, he made Creed drop Ravin, who collapsed and clutched his recovering organs.

The man from the bar knelt down in front of Ravin. In an even voice he instructed, "You are going to allow me inside of your mind so that I know you're not lying." It wasn't a request. The very serious look in his magenta colored eyes told the demon that there would be Hell to pay if he refused. "Don't make me ask you twice. I don't need your help to get into your mind. I can do it on my own. I'm being polite."

Ravin nodded and let his defenses drop. A pained look came over his face as he felt his mind being picked apart by this man. It wasn't the most pleasant experience in the universe, but certainly not as bad as Creed's treatment. He had to hide his disgust at this stranger rooting through his brain.

After a few moments the man put a hand on Ravin's head, and his wounds healed instantly. "Good." He stood and looked over at Vatali. "You may release that girl now." Once again, it wasn't a request.

Michelle was more than happy when the vampire let go of her arm and gave her a bit of distance. She looked over at Ravin, her eyes an ocean of worry. Silently she rubbed her wrist.

"I assume the demon was speaking the truth?" Vatali raised an eyebrow.

The man nodded. "Correct." He looked at the young ones in the room. "I will be taking them now."

"Can we at least keep the Ferros girl for ransom?" Creed's gaze landed on her with a hungry gleam in his eye.

Marius stepped in front of his date and shielded her with his body. "You'll have to go through me first," he declared and clenched his hands into fists. The elf took a fighting stance, though he knew he didn't stand much chance without a weapon.

The muscular vampire snorted, "Like that would be difficult to do."

"No." The mysterious man gestured for the humans and elf to come to his side. "I have much to discuss with them. All of them." There was no mistaking his intentions. He waited for them to gather around him and for the demon to get to his feet. He placed a hand on Michelle and healed the damage Vatali had done. Then he took the artifact from her. "You will be paid handsomely for this, gentlemen," the man assured the vampires.

In the blink of an eye the five of them disappeared, and rematerialized in Sin's office.

The man released his burdens and stalked up to Sin. "Do you care to explain what these children were doing trying to steal from Vatali and Creed? Oh, and the fact that they happen to be doing it to save someone who had been marked for a dark angel?"

Sin looked up at smiled at the man, as if she had been expecting him. Slowly her eyes drifted towards the clump of kiddos who looked spooked beyond belief, for good reason. Vatali could be such a wonderful host. It was a shame their personalities clashed. She sauntered over to her new guest. Back and forth her tail swished. "I figured you would find out sooner or later, my dear Zier. I didn't want to get you involved until I was absolutely certain of the situation. That time is now."

With a slight movement she stole the artifact from his hand and turned to walk back to her spell. The tip of her tail caressed his skin.

"You can be as involved as you wish," she told him. "It is more than your right, and I apologize sincerely for keeping it from you." With finesse, Sin bowed her head at the very powerful creature before her. He was one of the few beings out there that rivaled her in any way. It was her honor to keep him happy.

Her eyes darkened a bit, "If the Marked has been kidnapped, you can guess what that means."

"It means that she will soon be free." Zier crossed his arms and coldly regarded Sin. "You knew that I would want to be involved if there was even a whisper about her." His energy flared for a moment with intense emotion before fading again.

Michelle inched her way over to Ravin as the big guns talked. Carefully she put a hand on his torn suit and looked at him with concerned eyes. Streaks of dry blood caked the silky fabric. The girl was relieved to be out of that club. Above all, she was grateful that the demon had saved her life, even if it had brought him pain. The whole experience had been a disaster. She knew one thing for sure: it would not be hard to fall asleep. Feeling more than exhausted, Michelle wanted to curl up in her bed and pass out.

It had probably been the longest day of her life.

The demon looked down at Michelle and then wrapped an arm around her once again. "Do you still need us here? Some of us have had a pretty rough night. I did have my face beaten in after all." While this all sounded fascinating, he didn't have the energy to care. Whatever was going on would still be happening in the morning, of that he was sure.

Sin shot Ravin a nasty look, then she turned her attention back to Zier. Her fists clenched and she shook her head. "You don't understand, Zier. She wouldn't be free." She sat on her desk in the far corner of the room.

"I investigated Ravin's dorm and the same energy signature that took the Marked was there. They took Kazun, who is a purgatory soul, waiting to be collected." She cupped her chin. "Souls such as that are powerful for spell work. I have reason to believe that whoever is trying to free the dark angel… is trying to control her."

Darkness filled the air as pure rage rolled through Zier's eyes. The energy only spiked as tattered blood-stained wings flared from Zier's back. They stretched to their full length, each tip touching one wall. Chunks of feathers were missing as though someone had violently ripped them out. "Nobody controls Fenriel," he growled in a possessive tone.

Ravin's jaw fell open as he stared at the being in front of him. Horror pulsed through his veins as realization dawned upon him. This man, this… Zier… was a fallen angel.

Twenty-two

Lian sat on an old rusty swing. Back and forth she went, enjoying the gentle breeze. With every motion, the tired equipment groaned. Bright yellow rain boots covered her feet. Content, she admired the flowery dress she wore. Higher and higher she went. She thought she could almost touch the sky. Wind rushed through her hair. When the swing reached its apex, she hopped out. Like a dandelion puff, the girl was suspended in the air and floated down.

"Lian, dear," A motherly voice called from behind her.

The girl turned to see a tall woman. Her dark curls cascaded down her rounded frame. She was the most beautiful being Lian had ever seen. Her skin was pale and dappled in freckles. She wore a simple white sundress that danced in the breeze. Lian didn't know her, but the woman made her feel comfortable. The girl lifted her hands to her face, and she saw how small her fingers were. It was as if she were five years old again.

"Who are you?" Lian trotted a little closer, splashing through a puddle.

The woman leaned down to Lian when she was near. Lian stared into her star-like silver eyes. They were vast like the sky above. They were endless and enchanting.

"I am a friend." The woman cupped Lian's cheek, then kissed her forehead.

Lian stared up at the beautiful woman who felt so familiar. Yet, Lian couldn't recall ever seeing her before. She would have remembered such a woman.

"I will keep you safe." The words faded out as the world around them turned to black.

The cold surrounded Lian. It was the first thing she was aware of as her eyes opened. Then, she was aware of the stone cage that surrounded her. Her heart dropped and her stomach clenched. Bitter claws of fear gripped her. She tried to breathe, but the air caught in her throat.

Lian had awoken into a nightmare.

Panic struck her like a bolt. She pulled her hands to her face and curled into a tight ball. She could feel her heart pounding. The blood rushed through her ears. Her body shook and her mind went blank with fear. Her back struck the edge of the cage and she cowered into its frigid form.

Kazun was jolted awake by the sudden movement. His brown

eyes flashed around the thick bars. He couldn't bring himself to be surprised, or feel anything beyond the numbness that consumed him. So they'd finally caught up with him. Someone was going to cash in the bounty on his head, at last. Until that is, he spied Lian. "Lian?" he whispered as he scooted a bit closer to the cowering girl. "Is that you? Are you alright?" Why was she there?

From her corner, Lian continued to cower. The familiar voice did nothing to comfort her. The trepidation that lived inside her was an intractable monster. It overwhelmed and consumed her. She hid from it. Her eyes slammed shut, and her hands gripped at her ears so hard that her nails dug into the skin of her neck.

"Hey, hey." Kazun moved beside her and put a hand on her shoulder.

Lian let out a screech and recoiled from his touch. She lashed out and struck him out of reflex. Her meticulously manicured nails scraped across his face.

Kazun clutched the furrows in his cheek and sucked in a breath between his teeth. "Ow, okay, well at least this isn't a dream I guess." He sank back on his butt, and crossed his legs. "Sorry," he muttered.

The girl cried, rocking back and forth. For years, fear had dwelt within her; Lian had never become good at dealing with it.

Her face was flushed red with fever. A fit of coughs escaped her and she crumpled against the wall. She continued to shake and whimper, though exhaustion began to take its toll. For the first time, she noticed that Kazun was there. Her swollen eyes regarded him for only a moment before she hid away in her well-loved sweatshirt.

Kazun sighed and rested his back against the bars beside her. He glanced around at the world beyond the bars, but it was too opaque to make out. A single torch burned, making it bright enough so they could make each other out. Beyond their cage was a looming darkness. There was no hint as to who had brought them here, or why. He'd been so sure it was his bounty, but Lian too?

"I'm sure we can find a way out of this," he reassured the girl, though he didn't believe it himself. "I know that Ravin and your sister have got to be out there looking for us."

Lian replied with an unintelligible whimper into her sleeve.

Kazun shut his eyes and tried not to let his anxiety get the better of him. It gnawed at him like a werewolf on an animal bone. Ravin would find them. Ravin always found him. "I bet they'll show up, any minute," he reassured himself more than the girl. He wanted to join her in a ball of his own and let the fear consume him.

No, he felt compelled to at least try to be brave. If this wasn't about the bounty on his head, then maybe he could talk his way out of this with whomever had stolen them.

Or, maybe they'd be left to rot.

Looking up from her sleeve, Lian watched Kazun. Her gaze turned to the bars and she reached out to touch them. They felt good against her skin. She wanted to believe that Mischa would come out of nowhere and save her like she always did, but the cage dampened her hope.

"This stone," she coughed. "It's not from Eartha."

Kazun inspected the rock and felt his stomach sink. He'd taken several geology classes in the past. She was right. The texture was phaneritic: he could see the larger minerals that made up the stone, but there were bands of conchoidal fracture throughout the surface. The minerals absorbed the light from the torches instead of reflecting it. That only served to make identification harder for him.

He breathed and stroked his fingers along the surface. "I've never seen anything like it before."

"Me either." Lian wrapped her arms across her chest and held herself together. The mind numbing panic threatened to wash over her like a wave, but the wall of exhaustion held it back. She bit her lip and her arms pulled closer.

"That's because it's special." A cold voice echoed around the chamber beyond the bars.

Lian froze. Her eyes widened and her pupils contracted to needle points. Her feet madly began pushing her, so her back went as far against the bars as physically possible. Hysterical cries escaped her mouth. Her panic filled the cage and her breathing became choppy. It was the voice from her nightmares. It was *him*.

Her mind went blank as her primal instinct of flight filled her to the brim.

"I brought it with me from The Under," the voice continued, as though he hadn't been interrupted. "Something to make it feel more like home." Footsteps reverberated off the walls around the humans. Slow, and methodical, like a hunter stalking its prey.

Kazun gnashed his teeth as his gut told him to protect the terrified girl. His eyes darted around to find the source of the voice, to no avail.

"No," Lian whispered and covered her ears, hoping the phantom would disappear. There was nowhere to go, nowhere to hide. She was trapped and more vulnerable than ever. Her stomach heaved and if it had anything in it she would have purged. Sick coughs erupted and she cried out. "No."

"It's rude to interrupt." This time the voice came from right beside Lian's ear. The torch light gleamed off the obsidian points of his horns. His tail flicked out and stroked the skin of Lian's cheek. "That's no way to treat an old friend. We go way back, don't we, Lian?" The smirk on the demon's lips sent cold fingers of fear through Kazun's stomach.

Any color in Lian's face vanished as she stared in horror at the demon before her. Her throat locked in a scream. Frozen in place, she could hardly breathe. Tremors rolled through her body. She shook uncontrollably. Sweat covered her skin. Where his tail had touched her burned with an imaginary flame.

Her sole reply was a pathetic whimper.

"That's more like it." He rose to his feet again.

It took a few moments for Kazun to regain his ability to speak. He pushed down the lump in his throat and took on what he hoped would be a brave tone. "Who are you? What do you want with us?" the boy demanded.

The demon strode away as though he hadn't heard Kazun's questions. This time, his feet made no sound as they passed over the smooth floor. He waved a hand. At the motion, torches lit up around the area, illuminating the circular room. There were five stone spires jutting from the ground. They, too, were made of the hellish stone. In the very center was a large black stone tablet.

"You already know why you're here, Kazun," the demon replied. "You've been anticipating this moment for quite some time now. I thought you'd recognize it when the time came."

Kazun felt his heart go still. His mouth was too dry to for words.

"There's the response that I expected," the demon smirked. "If you have to call me anything, you can call me Ira." He ran his fingers over the surface of the tablet. The quiet rasping of his finger pads filled the air, where the silence should have been.

Kazun fought to find his response. "How did you find me?" he asked at last.

"Did you really think that he had you hidden so well?" Ira sneered. "I've known where Ravin's been keeping you for some time. But, you weren't of any use until now. I knew I would eventually need your purgatory soul."

"M-My what?" Kazun found himself taken aback.

Ira rolled his icy grey eyes. "What are they teaching you children nowadays?" He pressed his palms into the tablet. "When you sold your soul to Ravin, your soul was marked. A small sliver is sent to Purgatory in case you get the brilliant idea to hide, or run." He lifted one hand up and ran it along one of his horns. "I suppose it's still possible to hide away when you have a powerful arch demon like Sin on the job, but it was only a matter of time."

"I-I," Kaz stared down at the floor of their cage. "I wanted my dad back." The quiet, broken words were nothing more than a whisper.

"We all want something Kazun." Ira gripped the tip of his horn and tested the point with his thumb. "It so happens that your childhood mistake will help me get everything that I desire, along with that lovely young lady." His gaze landed on Lian.

The girl let out a sound as she covered her face with her sweatshirt. Her heart was pounding like a drum. There was one thing she wanted more than anything: to be able to go home and be in bed.

She coughed again and red stained the cloth of her sweater. Her tired, puffy eyes sagged. At any moment, she felt she could pass out. A single red line ran down the corner of her mouth as she stared at Ira in frozen dread.

Ira appeared in front of Lian inside the cage. He wiped away the blood from her face with a cloth. "Don't worry," he murmured. "You're the most important piece." The smirk returned to his lips.

Kazun threw himself at Ira as the instinct to protect Lian took over. Before he could even get close, an invisible force flung him to the other side of the cage. A million hands held him up against the bars, and kept his jaw forced shut. His nostrils flared as he let out a frustrated breath.

"What did I say earlier about interruptions?" Ira cast a sideways glare at the boy. "Next time, I won't be so polite."

The girl stared forward in abject horror. Her trembling ceased. Her thoughts flashed. Why was she here? What did he want with her? Lian wouldn't dare ask. No, she wouldn't speak to the man of her nightmares. She couldn't.

He was everything she feared. To be in his presence was a piercing dagger into her stomach. Lightning flashes of her memory crystalized. It was like she was five years old again. His smile was unchanged, his eyes the same.

"I knew I had picked well when I chose you." Ira stroked her cheek with his thumb. "I knew that you would become the perfect key when your mark became corrupted."

Lian stared, her mouth agape. A single tear ran from her eye and coated Ira's finger. She shook beneath his touch. She had no idea what he was talking about. What mark? A prickling sensation tickled across her back, making her spine arch. Coughs exploded once again, making a small spray of blood that streaked the demon's face.

Dread washed over her. "I-I'm sorry, I didn't mean to." She flinched and tried to cower away from retaliation.

"Don't be sorry," Ira soothed. "You've done exactly what you needed to." He rose to his feet and dragged the girl along with him. The demon teleported the two of them outside of the cage. With a delicate touch, he laid her down on the tablet. "Now be a good girl, and stay still."

She quivered, but stayed perfectly in place. She dared not move more than the involuntary shudders. For a moment, her heart stopped and she couldn't breathe. The sharp feeling like needles in her back soothed as she lay on the cold stone slab. A numb feeling tickled across her skin. A haze slid across her mind and she became motionless.

With deft fingers Ira pulled the sweatshirt off of Lian's body. As he did that, chains came to life and wrapped around the girl's extremities. Within seconds, she was bound to the tablet.

Ira leaned over Lian and placed his lips against hers. "Now my dear, the real fun begins."

Twenty-three

Michelle woke with a start. Beads of sweat rolled down her forehead and dripped off the tip of her nose. A vivid nightmare replayed itself in her mind, and she couldn't shake it off. Panic pounded in her chest like a timpani drum. Quickly her head twisted over to the bed next to her. Lian was still absent from its plush pink folds.

Michelle wiped away the moisture from her head and from her eyes. She was tough, but honestly, she had no right to cry. A lot of things had happened since Lian had been taken. Not many humans could say they had taken on two ancient vampires and lived to tell the tale. There was also the delightful fact that she had met a very cheery fallen angel. She had taken a mental note to stay out of Zier's way. He was very interested in the dark angel. Actually, not interested, but emotionally attached.

The memory of Zier flaring his wings out replayed in the girl's mind. He had called the dark angel Fenriel. Was that her name? It was strange to Michelle. So far she hadn't really thought of the dark angel as anything more than an idea. Now that she had a name, Fenriel was a trapped creature. A very powerful trapped creature. Everyone was frightened at the idea of her return. What would happen if she did come back?

A sudden vibration shocked Michelle out of her thoughts. She grabbed her holophone from her nightstand. Another strange message appeared on the screen. Her eyes scanned it and confusion filled her. "Let your light shine before men." As she looked, this was the number that had sent her the strange '1 Corinth 3:16' or whatever it was.

Great, now she had a cryptic stalker on top of everything else.

Frustration filled her. She did not need this kind of shit right now. Deleting the message, she hopped out of her bed and trudged to her closet to try and find something to wear. She really needed to do laundry; her dirty clothes were starting to spill out. With a sigh she kicked a pair of jeans. Lian was the one who did their laundry. Michelle would always throw her stuff in the washer, but that had made Lian angry. Apparently sorting the clothes by color could make or break the whole operation.

Hopefully, she would have Lian back before it truly needed to be done.

As annoying as was had been to have Lian nitpick about stuff like that, Michelle bit her lip and forced back another round of tears. She had already filled her crying quota for the day. To quell the pain in her heart, she punched her pillow.

Would Lian be okay?

Michelle grabbed her last pair of clean jeans, a shirt with a super hero cat on it, and some fresh undergarments before trudging into the bathroom. She twisted the knobs on the shower and closed the curtains. As she waited for the water to warm, she stared into the mirror. Dark circles crouched below her tired blue eyes. This last twenty-four hour period was taking a lot out of her. Not that anyone could blame her for it.

As steam began to fill the room, Michelle took off her night clothes. She glanced back in the mirror and let out a shriek. A tall figure stood behind her. As she whipped around, ready to kick some ass, he was gone. Eyes wide, the girl tried to calm herself.

"Okay Mischa," she reasoned. "You're imagining things because you're stressed out." She put her hand over her chest and waited for her heart to slow. Once she could breathe again, she continued to get undressed. Most likely, the steam had made a shape and she had let her eyes get the better of her.

There hadn't been some man standing behind her. The bathroom was nice and big, but she would have noticed another person.

As she stepped into the shower, she began to wash herself off. The hot water rolled over her skin. For one moment, she allowed herself to relax. Michelle needed that. Her body was tense and apparently she was starting to hallucinate tall muscular men with honey colored curls. The mental trick reminded her of the statue of David from pre-equilibrium Renaissance. Like he had been crafted, or something.

She forced it from her mind. It had only been an illusion. Nothing more. Certainly not something worth giving attention to. With everything she had to worry about, she didn't need to add anything to the list.

Once Michelle was clean, she stepped out onto the plush bath mat. She looked into the mirror and her eyes widened again. This time, for a different reason. In the reflection of her shower door, she could see a dark tattoo. Okay, she knew for sure she hadn't gotten that drunk last night. The scrolling black ink looked fancy, like lettering she couldn't read. It almost looked like Lian's tattoo... but different. She couldn't place it.

Panic thundered in her chest. What did this mean? Well, she only knew one person she could ask. The girl continued to get dressed. She was going to talk to a demon. Ravin to be exact.

A sound like static played in her mind. She had to hold her head to keep from falling over. After a few moments, the loud noise faded away. The girl pulled on fresh clothes and stormed out. As she walked to the front door, she grabbed her car keys from the bowl where Lian insisted she keep them. That way they never got lost.

She hooked a left and went up the first flight of stairs she came across. The hallway felt never ending as she marched. Her bee-line lead her straight to the demon's door. She knocked. No reply. Her fist pounded again. Nothing. The fires of aggravation lit and she began to take it out on the dark wood barrier.

"Fucking answer me, you piece of shit," she growled and continued to beat at the door.

"Hey Michelle," a voice said from behind her. Michelle turned to see one of her classmates. He tussled his hair, and took a swig of coffee. "You looking for Ravin? I saw him leaving about an hour ago."

Michelle turned and leaned on the door. Perfect.

"Thanks." She stuffed her hands in her pocket, "See ya around." Time for plan B.

Michelle didn't waste time. She stormed down the stairs and went to her transport, determined to get some answers. The moment she hopped into her vehicle, she had it started. Then she drove away.

It wasn't a long trip downtown. At this time of day, not much traffic clogged the street. There was a straight shot to the parking meters in front of the old red-brick building housing Sin's bar. Michelle looked up and saw the Hot Spot down the street. She would never go there again if she could help it. Then again, most likely she wouldn't be let in. So, it didn't really matter.

She went from her car and walked to the back of the building. The alley was getting strangely familiar. This place where monsters hid was now cozy to the human. She hadn't ever come alone, but she figured Sin would let her in. They had been working together on the whole dark angel ordeal.

The slat opened and two beady eyes peered through. An annoyed grunt passed through the guardian's thick throat.

"Hey Mac," she said. "Nice seeing you again." The response was another irritated snort, and then the door opened. What a gentleman. Michelle walked right in. After that first day, they seemed to have worked out an understanding. Somehow. She walked into the bar and looked around for the boss.

Sin was not hard to spot. She was sitting in a booth with a man in front of her. She seemed to be disappointed with how the conversation was going. Michelle was reluctant to interrupt. Generally, it was her style but, messing with Sin could be dangerous. If the demon decided to stop helping them, that would be a disaster.

Michelle did the only thing she could do. She sat at the bar and ordered a drink.

The bartender offered her a smile. If this had been under any other circumstance, she would have found it charming. She returned the gesture.

"There, was that so hard?" the man asked, his voice thick with an accent Michelle couldn't place.

"Really hard." Michelle twisted in her chair back and forth. The sturdy man with a warm laugh leaned on the counter. His eyes were like freshly fallen snow. He placed her drink on the bar and grinned.

"This one is on Viktor," he said. "Do enjoy."

The human nodded and took a sip. It was a flavorful drink. Mischa didn't even know lemonade could be so delicious. It was sweet and sour and had a slight tang that gave it a good amount of depth. This was the pick me up she needed. Best of all, it was free. She was certainly going to give the lovely Viktor a tip. He had earned it.

Michelle quietly sipped and continued to look back at Sin. Whoever she was talking to didn't appear to be complying with what she wanted. It was strange to see the generally very charismatic demon out of her element. Something was not going well between the two of them. Michelle could tell that much by the sour expression clouding Sin's exotic facial features. The woman looked ticked; yet she was forcing herself to stay somewhat pleasant. It wasn't working too well.

Eventually the man stood and he shook his head. From what Michelle could tell, he even apologized, then he vanished into thin air. It was different then when a demon would teleport. Demons almost always made a soft crackling sound and left a trace of dust. This man… faded away.

There was a pop of energy beside Michelle. "That was someone I was really hoping would help us out," Sin's voice came from beside the human. Michelle's head twisted to see the demon sitting lazily in the stool beside her. She was slouched over the bar, certainly not ladylike.

"How could he help?" Michelle asked

Sin let out a sigh and replied, "He is a Cambian. They are powerful creatures who can bend reality to their beliefs."

Michelle's eyes widened. If a creature like that simply believed that Lian was returned safe and sound, she would be? No wonder Sin was trying to enlist his help. Apparently it hadn't worked.

"Even he was afraid," the demon continued. "He didn't want to get in the middle of something so dire. His hands were tied." She paused for a moment as her dark eyes scanned the bar. "We are all in over our heads." The air settled between the two women.

Michelle looked down at her shoes. The demon was 120% right. If their problems were water, they would be drowning in them. She couldn't deny that much. She sat up straight. "Maybe we are, but I know I couldn't sit idly by."

A silvery sarcastic laugh escaped the demon's throat.

Michelle shot her a confused look.

"I think it's strange. With all the powers we possess, the most determined and headstrong is a human. A weak, breakable human." Sin's fist slammed on the table. Her smile looked tired, Sin's tail twitched. "So, what can I help you with?"

"Something weird is happening to me," Michelle blurted out. "And it's not puberty."

Michelle hated showing weakness of any sort. She was covered in it simply by being human. Humor was her shield to try and lighten a situation. Especially with demonic strangers.

Sin let out a choking laugh. If she had been drinking anything, it would have surely shot out her nose. Silky smooth amusement rolled out into the air. It was like bell chimes, beautiful as it rose on delighted notes. The demon wiped at her eyes and panted for breath once her laughter slowed, "Go on."

"I keep getting these weird texts, and hearing static in my head. Lastly um..." Michelle paused and looked around. The bar was all but deserted. It was an off hour in the early day. Lunch would start soon, but as of now, it certainly wasn't a popular hour for drinking. Once she was sure that no one would be looking, Michelle stood and pulled up her shirt a little show off her new tattoo.

"How much did you drink last night?" The look in Sin's gaze was intense as she looked upon the thick black tattoo. Before Michelle could even complain about her answer, Sin stood and said, "Come to my office."

Michelle nodded and together, the human and demon walked into the back room. They went into the dimly lit office that had once been home to the crazy spell, but now everything was back in order. Confused as to where all the incantation material was, the human shot a questioning look at the demon. Had Sin seriously gotten rid of everything? Where was it all?

"I took it all home with me," the demon said, either reading the young woman's mind or making an educated guess. "I couldn't have any patrons of my bar poking into it. That's bad for business."

Sin moved to the far side of the desk and sat down. She gestured for Michelle to sit in one of the chairs before her. The human obliged her and took a seat. They were comfortable. If Sin was good at one thing, it was knowing the fine intricacies of life. The soft, form-fitting foam welcomed Michelle and as she leaned back, she entered a new kind of heaven. It had really nice lumbar support.

The demon sighed and asked, "Do you want me to get straight to the point, or dance around it?"

Michelle rolled her eyes. "Lay it on me, Sin."

A smile appeared on the caramel beauty's face and she nodded. She was taking a liking to this spunky little human. If it were legal and good practice, she would keep this one as a cute pet. Unfortunately, laws against human ownership were very strict. The poor cuties liked to keep themselves safe after Equilibrium. Probably a smart move. At least the law was on their side.

"Alright then." Sin nodded and leaned back in her chair. Her tail twitched and her dark obsidian horns glinted in the soft light. "You, like your sister, have been marked for an angel."

Michelle could only stare at Sin. Another bout of panic rolled through the human's chest. There were so many fears attached to those words. Yes, she had heard many wonderful things about the feathered guardians of the Beyond. With everything that had happened to Lian, she had the right to be a bit afraid.

"Calm yourself." Sin sat up and leaned on the desk. "Your mark has not been tampered with, unlike your sister's. An Angel of Light watches over you. If I wasn't culturally obligated to hate them, I would even tell you that you were quite lucky." The demon stuck her tongue out. Sin had an unpopular opinion about angels. The high and mighties were just doing their job. Sure, she didn't want some feather butt coming in here and inciting divine wrath, but it was better they keep order than one of her brethren. Not many demons were as sociable and pleasant as she and Ravin.

"Your angel friend is probably trying to communicate with you," Sin continued. "The static in your head is like static on a radio. They are having a hard time finding the right channel. What were the texts that you received?"

Michelle recalled them from memory, "1 Corinth 3:16, and Let your light shine before men." This was all a bit much for Michelle. She had never really been the religious type. No, it wasn't hard to believe that there were stronger powers out there. Hell, there were even gods and goddesses. Did she believe that a singular powerful god could decide their fate? It wasn't a stretch after all the weird things she saw, but that didn't make her a Bible thumper. Then again, it didn't really have to make sense, did it?

Lian had been marked by a dark angel, and Lian was probably the purest soul Michelle knew.

"'Let your light shine before men in such a way that they may see your good works, and glorify your Father who is in heaven.'

Matthew 5:16., Sin recited, "and 1st Corinthian 3:16, 'Do you not know that you are God's temple and that God's Spirit dwells in you?'" A smirk appeared on the demon's face. "Isn't it sad that a demon knows the Bible better than a Chosen of God?"

"Thanks for the info." Michelle stood up. She had heard all that she had needed to, and she wasn't going to stick around to be made fun of. Some angel was watching her from above. She had been chosen by it. Michele reached into her pocket and asked. "So, how much do I owe you?"

Sin purred and her tail lazily swayed from side to side. "You know all this holy stuff is going to cost you extra."

Michelle tossed a pre-equilibrium quarter coin at Sin.

The demon looked over it, then back up at the human with questioning dark eyes.

A grin appeared on Michelle's face and she replied, "Keep the change."

Without giving Sin a chance to respond, the human walked away. She was sure she could hear the demon laughing that same beautiful laugh. It was scary how perfect-appearing a creature of the Underworld could be. That made Michelle wonder something.

What did an angel look like?

Twenty-four

The more Michelle thought about it, the more apprehensive she became. Being marked for an angel of light was supposed to be a good thing. Maybe it was a lot to take in at a bad time. It could have been worse, she guessed, but that didn't make the situation any easier.

Silently she swayed back and forth on the playground swing. She and Lian used to come to the park all the time. Not many kids came there during the fall. It was starting to be too cool. Michelle nuzzled into her hoodie as she surveyed the park. The trees danced with the colors of fall. Orange and red leaves stood out amongst the last greens that clung desperately to the branches. Soon the trees would be skeletons.

Seneal Park was a beautiful vista of winding pathways that

encircled a vibrant blue lake. The sun sparkled on the gentle tide. Everything was peaceful. Serene winds sang a silent lullaby that whisked Michelle away into a feeling of simplicity. This paradise was one of the last few places that made her feel like a kid again. A pain in her chest started to bubble up. Ignoring it, Michelle stared at the glittering water.

Everything was quiet as Michelle sat alone in the park, her mind blue with melancholy.

"I thought I'd find you here." Ravin gripped the chain of the swing beside her. "Is this seat taken?" Trees swayed in the light breeze, it was almost too nice out given how terrible the past few days had been. He half expected to find the trees actually on fire instead of bearing the vibrant colors that fall brought. Every gust made the branches wave as though they burned with an uncontrollable blaze, really it almost made him feel like he was back 'home.' Flaming trees were a staple of Hell.

He'd come to find her when he found out she'd been trying to get in touch with him. At first, he was unsure if he would be able to find her.

Michelle looked up and shook her head. There was worse company out there. She sighed and looked back down at her feet, shuffling them in the dirt as her swing swayed.

The demon slumped into the seat; the chains creaked in protest, but he didn't spare them much thought. He sighed and slowly swung back and forth. His toes dragged in the hard dirt. He didn't really know what to say in this situation. How did one comfort a sad soul when everything was looking down? His normal brand of 'comfort' wouldn't work in this situation.

She wasn't really his type. Humans were too fragile; one wrong move and he could seriously hurt her. Hell, Vatali had only grabbed her arm and he'd managed to tear her skin and almost broken her bones. Though, he had to admit that her spirit was quite… interesting.

Finally, after a long period of silence he asked, "What's on your mind?"

"I'm on an emotional roller coaster." She didn't look his way when she spoke. "One minute I'm punching something, the next I'm laughing. Every time I smile, I feel guilty."

Ravin couldn't hold back his smirk. "It's perfectly normal to be erratic. If you weren't, I'd be afraid, because there would be something wrong with you."

"I guess that's one thing off the list."

The human looked over at him, but she couldn't figure out a good way to tell him that she was an Angel Marked. Would he understand? If she was connected with a sworn enemy, would he want to be her ally anymore? Sin had been okay with it. That didn't mean they wouldn't have differing opinions.

Deciding to get it out and into the cool fall air, Michelle got up from her swing. She stood in front of Ravin, her back to him. Carefully she pulled up her shirt and hoodie, exposing the small of her back.

"I'm having an off day," she explained and pulled her clothes back over her skin. The air was a bit nippy. There were so many unknowns about the whole situation. Would she get sick like Lian had? How did this whole 'marked' thing work? There were so many unanswered questions and one too many things to worry about. Her voice cracked a bit. "It's supposed to be some sort of honor right? I think they made a mistake."

Angels were perfect. They were holy beings depicted as beautiful warriors with kind hearts for the pure. Michelle was far from pure. She was flawed. What if she had to live a different life? Not like anything would ever be the same since Lian was taken. Pressure gripped her heart and all she wanted to do was scream.

Why couldn't life be the carefree playground it once was? Not even a year ago, she could remember playing in the spring when flowers danced in the air of fresh life. Now all the beauties were going to fade and fall.

Ravin blinked in shock. He didn't know what to say. He should have seen this coming.

"I had a feeling that you would get one too," he sighed and rested his head on the chain. "Though I will admit I was hoping you wouldn't." His strawberry blonde hair fell over his face as he thought about what this would mean for them.

There was one thing that he knew for certain. "I'm sure they can help us get Lian back. An angel is a powerful ally to have." He sure wasn't going to be messing with them willingly. "Not that I would know what that would be like." He had a pit in his stomach: the idea of Michelle getting attached to an angel made him uneasy.

Michelle slumped back into her swing and slowly let it carry her back and forth. She watched the ground. He did have a point. They would have an angel on their side, though. She wasn't quite sure how any of it worked.

"I guess," she admitted. As she drifted, she felt a soft autumn breath against her cheek. Maybe it wasn't as bad as it felt. Mostly, she was afraid that she was going to have to change for some destiny that she didn't ask for. Michelle was wild. Angels were controlled and pious. She wasn't.

Then again, she really didn't know how or why she had been chosen to be marked by an Angel of Light. What made a sinner like her acceptable? She glanced over at the male.

"You don't have to have all of the answers, you know. Sometimes you need to have faith. I don't understand their selection process, I couldn't even begin to understand how they work." That was something that Ravin never had the opportunity to comprehend.

"Thanks." She studied him quietly. It had been a few days since the Vatali incident. Since then, she decided that Ravin wasn't the bad guy. He had risked his life to get the artifact as much as she had. He had taken the punches and tried to let her get away. The memory replayed itself in her head. At least she could have a bit of confidence that he was on her side. She wasn't used to trusting demons.

Her feet dug into the ground and gave a kick start push. Her swing swished up and down. As it did, she leaned, keeping the slow pace rolling. She didn't allow herself to get too high. That way, they could still continue their conversation.

"Don't mention it." Ravin shrugged.

"Have you ever met an angel before?" Her gaze kept skyward. The grey clouds rolled across the horizon. Cold nipped at the tip of Michelle's nose. "I've only heard stories."

Ravin thought long and hard. "Only in passing." He dug his

heels into the hard-packed dirt. "I didn't stick around for long. I've heard that there's a few different groups up there. I had the misfortune of coming close to the particular sect that likes to make friends by stabbing them with swords."

Images of angel tapestries flooded Michelle's mind. Her parents had once taken her to one of the oldest standing cathedrals in Europa. It was a massive place with depictions of the Beyond. Stern faced angels lined the ceiling, their swords ready for battle. Their eyes were blank, mechanical, and Michelle hoped that hers wasn't like that.

"Do you know what the others are like?" She leaned more into the downswing, causing her to go a bit further and faster.

"From what I can tell," Ravin leaned back and looked up at the sky. "The second group focuses on defending their realm from invaders, and the like. The last is all about balance. I think they're the most magical out of the lot."

She glided through the air effortlessly. For a moment, she let her thoughts wander. Swings, though very, very old in design, never went out of style. No matter how complex the holosystems could get, swings were always such a delightful classic. For a few moments, Michelle could feel like she was flying. She felt a breath of freedom away from the prison of her worry.

The girl waited till she reached the peak before jumping out of the swing and landing semi-gracefully. Pain shot through her legs and she bit her lip. After a breath, she turned and placed her hands on her hips. "So what you're saying it's a gamble on whether it will be okay or not."

Ravin paused. She'd played it off, and he'd almost missed it, but she'd hurt herself somehow. Still, he fixed her with an exasperated look. "You're asking a member of the single most biased species when it comes to your feathered friends." He shook out his blonde locks. "What kind of response did you think you were going to get? My personal experience is limited to one close call, and my race's legacy involves millennia of hate."

"As a demon," she started heading down the hill towards the lake. "I expected you to lie." The truth that awaited her was overwhelming. She had wanted him to butter it up for her. Tell her it would be fine. That's what a friend would have done. Then again, they weren't really friends. They were working towards an end point. A goal. He wanted Kazun back, and she wanted her sister. Sure, he was willing to jump through the hoops, but that didn't mean much.

"Guess I learned my lesson." She leaned down by the water's edge and picked up a smooth stone. With an aggressive chuck, the rock went spinning out over the lake surface. As it skipped, she counted. Seven. Not bad.

Ravin appeared beside Michelle. He'd watched her move away. Her limp hadn't been too pronounced but he'd seen it. Just how badly had jumping off the swing hurt her? "You need the truth more than you need pretty words." He scooped a rock off the ground and ran his thumb along the flat surface. "At this point, anyone who lies to you is trying to get something from you. We're past the point of no return. You already know the harsh reality that waits if we fail."

He was past the point of lying. There was nothing to gain from it anymore.

"I feel like I'm being crushed." She stared out at the still lake, "There is so much hanging over my head. The fate of the world, my sister's life. I've spent my entire life fighting against it, but stars above." Her voice cracked as if the weight of the world truly rested on her shoulders, "I'm only human."

Did she see herself making it out alive? Not really.

Ravin frowned and took a moment to consider exactly what her humanity meant. She was fragile for one, and she was also going to live for a very short time. Her time was but a blink in his already long life. Any friendship they had would be a distant memory soon.

"You didn't say that when you went up against the dragons," he countered.

She didn't give him a response.

His mind shifted and he thought about Kazun. The fact that someone had gone through so much effort to disguise the location of the two kids gave him hope that they were safe. When the two of them found out where the humans were being held, they would bust in and kick some ass. He eyed Michelle as she walked; he noted a slight limp.

There was one big problem with his master plan. Could a squishy human like Michelle even defend herself in a fight against a being that could expertly cloak their location? No, she couldn't. He knew that she would want to be there to bust in and save her sister like a good heroine should, but that would get her killed. The girl needed a confidence boost.

"Michelle, we need to make sure you can kick ass when it comes time to save Lian and Kaz." He sighed and threw his final rock. The demon caught up and placed a hand on her shoulder. "And I think we know a few people who can help us out with that."

"Do you honestly think a little training will be enough?" She crossed her arms.

It was probably wise that she had a bit of know how—so she wasn't useless when she busted in the bad guy's door. More than anything, she didn't want to hold the rescue party back. Michelle had a wild and strong spirit, but that didn't mean she had any skill when it came to keeping safe or as Ravin had put it 'kicking ass.'

The demon rolled his eyes. "It's better than you wallowing around in your pity party." He liked it when her spirit was full of fire; it was refreshing.

He pulled out his phone and sent a message to Marius.

A few moments later, he got a reply telling him that Marius would be more than willing to help them out. Ravin couldn't wait for Sin to find the location of Kazun and Lian. The sooner the better. He didn't know when Sin would have finished locating them. It could be two minutes or another few days.

"It looks like you're going to get a lesson from Marius, I hope you're a fast learner." Ravin winked and put his phone away. The more she knew about protecting herself the better. It would be pointless to lose her while trying to save her sister. "You ready?"

"Ready as I will ever be," Michelle shrugged and looked up at him. "Thanks. For being honest. Even if it wasn't what I wanted, I needed it." Her hand clenched and a blue fire ignited in her gaze. It was time to put everything behind her. If she was going to be of any use, she would have to be at her A-game.

Maybe it was another mood spike, but Michelle was going to

try and hit home with the upswing. Determination flooded her veins.

Ravin grinned and put a hand on Michelle's head. "Go run and find Marius. Helping you was the least I could do," the demon chuckled. "The more time you spend learning to kick ass, the better." In the meantime, he would go back to his apartment and see if he could find some useful spells.

Ravin waved at her before he winked and disappeared. Back home, he grabbed a drink from the fridge and laid on his couch. There was too much crap wrapped up in one tight shit burrito. If he hadn't pursued Michelle a few days ago, none of this would have happened. He couldn't tell if he regretted it, but he definitely wasn't liking the results. The situation was insane. He didn't have the time to deal with dark or fallen angels.

He summoned a tome with a wave of his hand and started flipping through it. There wasn't much in this spell book that would be of any use so he tossed it to the side. He gripped his head with a sigh of desperation.

Unable to lay there, the demon sat up and rubbed one horn. Ravin took another swig of his drink and stared at the floor. Nothing went well with him. If he had his way, neither he nor Michelle would be part of the rescue team that saved Lian. At the moment he couldn't pinpoint exactly what would go wrong, but it would, and nobody would be happy.

The taste of the drink on his tongue made him recall something he'd pushed from his mind.

The demon stood and trotted into his room. He rooted through the dirty clothes strewn about his floor and partially hanging out of his hamper. After a few moments of searching, he found the slip of paper in a pair of pants.

That other demon... what was his name? It was something simple, a pseudonym... Ira? Yes, that was it. There was a number on the paper.

It had been him who had started all this. He'd been the one who took Kazun, and therefore Lian as well. He'd been the one who he'd felt at the roller rink, of that he had no doubts. This was something that could help Sin. Hopefully.

One last drink strengthened his resolve as he used his energy to transport himself to the bar. He strode up to the door and waltzed inside quickly, without paying the doorman any mind. It took no effort to sweep the bar for the unique energy Ira had possessed.

There was nothing.

Confident in his knowledge, he headed over to the door of Sin's office and knocked.

"She's not in," Zier informed him. The fallen angel leaned upon the wall with his arms crossed. If he looked any more unconcerned, Ravin might have worried. He was a completely different person from the enraged man the few nights prior.

Ravin mimicked the man's body language and folded his arms. "Well, I need to talk to her. It's important." He held the paper tightly in his fist.

The man smiled pleasantly. Now his eyes were a soft yellow. It caught Ravin by surprise. So he was changing his eye color.

"What have you got there? Why not let Uncle Zier take a look? I happen to have a vested interest in this particular venture and I'd like to know any information, seeing as I was so rudely kept out of the loop before I saved your ass." He grinned smugly.

Ravin held out the slip of paper. "This is his number," he hissed. "He gave it to me before everything started. It sort of slipped my mind when the chaos erupted."

Zier snatched the scrap and examined the numbers. "I'm sure Sin would be able to get some information from this. You know, I'm sure that it'll be useful, and it would have been a few days ago." While it seemed like he was being friendly, there was a dark undertone to his voice that definitely wasn't so nice. It felt more like a thinly veiled threat. "Why didn't you remember this sooner?" The fallen angel offered a disingenuous smile.

"Because this isn't the first time I've gotten that kind of offer," Ravin explained. "It was as cryptic and vague as the rest of them, so I didn't put stock in it at the time. Then all Hell broke loose, and I was a bit more focused on other things."

The fallen angel listened silently and nodded where it was needed. "So, did you at least get his name so we could track them down?"

Ravin shrugged. "It wasn't his real name so I didn't press it. Some people are too smart."

A scuffle broke out a few seats away from where they stood between two people who did not like each other's faces. Zier glanced over and smirked. With a wave of his hand they both disappeared, leaving nothing but silence behind. "Well, what did he call himself?" the unperturbed fallen angel asked.

The demon did not want to know what had happened to the poor creatures. "Ira, that's all he gave me."

The fallen angel sighed and shook his head. "It's enough to do a search off of the face you've got in your mind," Zier explained and stared into Ravin's eyes.

"Whoa!" Ravin took a step back and held up his hands. "Stay the Hell out of there, my thoughts are private." It was bad enough that Zier had gone in with permission once before. Was it possible that the fallen angel had found himself a permanent back door through his defenses?

"Well I don't see the point in letting you have any privacy. You forgot about something that could be vital to finding your friends and saving the woman I love." He closed the distance between them and poked the demon's chest with a single finger. "You don't deserve discretion if it could bring about destruction the likes of which you couldn't even imagine."

Before Ravin could start forming a response, the fallen angel disappeared. He was left with a sinking feeling in his stomach. This was either going to destroy him or make him stronger than he'd ever been.

Twenty-five

Michelle rolled for cover and hid behind a tree. Her heart raced. Panting, she was running out of breath. This wasn't good. What had she gotten herself into? Leaves crackled. The sound of her attackers grew near. She only had one chance. Failing was not an option. Her hand gripped the sword tighter. The steps grew closer. Closer.

Suddenly the elf landed in front of her and a blade was to her neck. Michelle's eyes widened. A simple curse rolled off her tongue.

Without wasting any time, she twisted back and narrowly escaped having her throat slit. Michelle's ungraceful and tired steps had her stumbling. From the corner of her eyes, she could see the other. She was trapped. With a quick motion, she turned to face her other attacker; both figures approached. She was dead.

"This isn't fair!" Michelle complained and dropped her sword in frustration. "You two are like vegetarian wolves!"

"Vegan," Letvan corrected, he leaned down and picked up the weapon. "And when you go to save your sister, you will be in real danger. Your enemy won't fight fair."

The Summer Knight's words made her cringe. He was right, but it didn't make her feel any better. She sucked at this. Fighting was not her thing. Of course she wanted to be great. She wanted to be able to go to Ravin and tell him that she could do this. That she wouldn't mess up the rescue operation.

But she couldn't. She had been fighting the two for hours, and the closest she could get to winning was hurting Marius's feelings with a snide comment. Not like that had done much for her. What if Ravin told her she had to stay for her own good? ...or worse, for Lian's own good.

"Look, why don't we go by the stream and meditate a while," the elf said. He had noticed the trembling of her lip. "Find your center. Then we will start from the beginning." He put a strong reassuring hand on her shoulder.

The girl nodded. Even if the whole swordplay thing wasn't her strong suit, it would be nice to take a breather. This much exercise was not on her daily agenda. Her bones were aching. Maybe she needed to take Lian's lead and jog every once in a while. There was a reason Michelle was curvier than her slender sister.

Letvan helped the human through the woods. After all of their 'training,' her muscles were screaming. Michelle used him as a crutch. She watched him walk gracefully on the tips of his toes.

Elves were long and lean, beautiful creatures. Michelle couldn't help but admire. Of course, Letvan wasn't really her type.

Letvan was diamond hard all throughout and he knew it. Every powerful step radiated with a charismatic confidence. Together, they walked to the stream and sat down. She was supposed to be training with Marius, but Letvan sort of took over. He was a knight; it was his job to train people. Marius had been placed as a helper.

"Now close your eyes, and relax," Letvan instructed. "Listen to the sound of the stream and let it carry you away."

Michelle nodded a little, but the elf's words drifted on a soft current. The girl's mind went blank. There was a stillness inside. In a sea of night and darkness was a bright light. The sensation of cool air tickled at her. It was a weird place. Honestly she couldn't tell if this was reality, or a trick of the mind. Maybe she was dreaming.

It was as if she were literally walking in a place of cool darkness. Yet, she was sure all of this was happening in her mind.

Her consciousness approached the light on soft toes. She was confused; meditation had never worked in the past. Had she finally succeeded or was this something else entirely? Then she heard a soft voice.

"I want to speak with you," he said. "Please listen." It felt so close and so familiar. The male's voice was soothing, like a mug of warm cocoa on a winter's day. It was sunshine and birdsong. Nothing in her human vocabulary could quite place it.

It was strangely perfect.

"Who are you?" she asked in awe, reaching out to touch the light. When she got near it only moved farther away. Michelle tried to move closer, but the light was always a fingertip out of her grasp. The voice spoke its name, but she couldn't understand. Static began to hiss loudly, drowning out his honey-sweet words. Michelle fought the noise and she struggled to get closer to the light.

"I am a friend." She could make out the words as the voice spoke. "And I will keep you safe. I will give you strength." What did it mean keep her safe? She wanted answers. She wanted to know what was going on.

Michelle's eyes flashed open and she looked around. A large amount of time seemed to have passed, but strangely, it had only felt like minutes. When she had closed her eyes, the sun had been shining, but now the touch of night cooled the air. She looked up to see Letvan sitting on a stump, shining one of his many prized swords. At her movement, he glanced at her. A perfect smile appeared on his face and he commented, "I hope you had a nice nap. I suppose you needed it."

She had been sleeping? Was that place really a figment of her dream world? It would make sense, but she couldn't shake the memory of that voice. He felt so close, yet so far away. Michelle rubbed at her eyes. Sleep crust had formed in the inside corners and she wiped the gunk out. Feeling rested and refreshed, Michelle hopped to her feet.

"I'm ready to train more," she declared and grabbed the sword she had been loaned. It was a decently dull blade. It wasn't fit for battle, but for practice, it was perfect. The student and teacher's eyes met. Ocean and forest clashed for less than a moment before the two began to spar. Silver danced in a display of grace and determination. Michelle was far weaker than Letvan.

Michelle could see that he was going easy on her. Frustration prickled through her veins. This felt like a waste of time. With a sudden rush of energy, Michelle felt her muscles kick into high gear. When their swords clashed, this time, the girl pushed the elf back, if even a step. A subtle shock filled the handsome man's gaze. This was her chance. The human pushed harder and she forced her body to work faster. If she couldn't take him down, what hope did she have against anything else?

Angry that everything was going wrong, Michelle could feel a power rush into her every strike. Letvan took another step back. It was clear he was surprised. Michelle couldn't read much beyond that. She was over losing. For once in her life, she wanted to come out on top. Sure this wasn't life or death. However, the thought of beating a well-trained Knight sounded appealing.

'Sweep,' the voice from her dream spoke into her mind. The human closed her eyes and let out a soft stilling breath. Her body did as it was told in an unbelievably fluid and smooth motion. With great power and precision, she almost knocked the elf over. Michelle's every fiber was fighting to come out on top. The duel between the two forces was great.

Dull swords met. With every loud clang that rang into the forest, Michelle could feel her energy ebbing. As their battled raged on, it was obvious. She was tiring out. It was only a matter of time before—

Michelle's body couldn't take the strain any longer and she stumbled back, falling on her ass. The girl panted for breath, but everything in her body burned for more oxygen. Despite her loss, the girl felt a strange sense of accomplishment. As she looked upon the elf, she could see he had a slight glistening on his forehead.

"You did fantastically," he praised.

Marius knelt beside Michelle and offered her some water. "You're much better than I expected." Anyone who could hold their own after such a short time was impressive. Sure, it wasn't going to do her much good against a big bad… whatever it was that had captured Lian, but every moment she bought was a moment that she added onto their survival. "But you really need to rest or you're going to damage yourself so badly that you'll have to be benched."

Michelle glanced away. She took the water and guzzled it down. The idea of being put on the side lines didn't sit well in her stomach. Michelle was a woman of action, and if being demon fodder helped her sister get home safe and sound, she knew in her heart that she would do whatever she could. It wasn't a choice. It was who she was.

"Thanks." Her voice trembled. "Guess I can take a breather."

"He doesn't just mean from training, Michelle," Letvan said. "Look, you and Ravin have to give yourselves a break. You both are doing everything you can. I know it sounds hard, but maybe a night of relaxation won't kill anyone." His emerald eyes were steadfast. Michelle tried to tell him otherwise, but the trained knight simply silenced her.

"One soldier doesn't win a war, Michelle," he continued, keeping her from speaking her mind. "Armies do."

Though it was hard, the human conceded defeat. It killed her to admit it, but if she didn't take a break, the stress would pick her apart piece by piece. Hard as it was, she decided that one night would be okay. Honestly, she could use a pick me up. She shoved Letvan lightly and sighed, "Fine, you win. Again."

Letvan flashed her one of his million credit smiles.

Michelle responded with another shove.

Laughing, Letvan gave her a thumbs-up. A spark of epiphany appeared in his Summer-sweet eyes and he rolled his thumb along his neck where a simple silver chain rested. The necklace receded and disappeared under his shirt. With a gentle tug, the jewelry easily loosed itself and he removed it with delicate finger.

"I want you to have it," he said and he placed the silver chain in her hand. Michelle held up the shining necklace to the light. The moon's silvery gaze made the stone in the center of the simple piece shine. Her eyes widened softly.

"What is this?" Michelle asked.

"This is called "Oolamir 'es." The Elvan words rolled off his tongue the same way music dances from an instrument. Of course, he must have noticed the confused look on Michelle's face because he clarified. "The Night Watcher. It is a powerful ward that keeps away ill intent."

The girl carefully fastened the necklace into place. It rested on her chest, before the dip into cleavage. Michelle was in awe. The only thing she could say was, "Thank you."

Letvan was doing so much to help, like Sin, Marius, and Ravin. It might have been small, but they did have an army.

Michelle pulled out her phone and keyed in Ravin's name.

"We should hang out," was all she typed before she sent the message to the demon.

He could say all he wanted, but Ravin was in this because of her. She had asked him to help her with keeping Lian safe. Because of that, she had gotten Kaz taken away. No, she didn't feel completely at fault, but she couldn't help but feel as if it wasn't for her, the hockey boy would still be around.

Michelle looked up at the elves and bowed her head with respect.

"If we can ever do anything for you, Michelle, do not hesitate to ask," Letvan said, his voice strong and unwavering.

"Thank you, Letvan." Michelle then looked over at the other elf, "and I will put in a good word with Jojo for you, Mari." A mischievous smile appeared on her face as she waved and started the journey back to her room. She glanced back down at her phone, but there wasn't a reply from Ravin. He was probably busy.

Ravin had become a strange form of comfort. He was an ass and a demon. But she had learned to trust him. Barely. It was weird to her. For as long as she could remember, she hated help. She wanted to be the hero. He had been a shoulder to lean on twice now. He was assisting her through this mess and maybe she was helping him in some way.

Probably not. He seemed to have his shit together.

The memory of him ripping his dorm apart played through her mind. Then again, maybe he was good at hiding what was on the inside. Maybe he was as torn up with everything as she was. At least he could put on a sarcastic brave face. Michelle had cried more in the last three or four days than she had in years.

It was driving her mad. What happened to the girl who would go up against dragons without blinking? Had she been taken along with Lian?

Michelle's hand clenched at her phone and she heaved a sigh. It wasn't a big deal. Whenever he was free, he would reply. Most likely he was with Sin and they were completing the spell. At least, that was what she was hoping. Then again, there were a many other things to do with that beautiful woman. The human wouldn't be surprised if he was getting some stress relief of his own.

Another sigh escaped. She didn't want to think about that right now. Ravin was barely her friend. It didn't matter to Michelle if he found women to spend time with. Not only that, it wasn't her business. The demon was a free man. He could do whatever he wanted. He was someone…someone who would probably fade away when the whole ordeal was over. People tended to do that.

Her muscles were stiff and sore from the training. They complained the whole way to the edge of the forest. She looked back at the foliage, then ran a hand over her tattoo. It was strange to her that her first tattoo wasn't even one she had picked out. Some angel had inked her up.

She got to the front of the school and sat down on the sidewalk curb. She curled her arms over her knees and rested her head on them. She felt lost, confused, and angry. She wanted to cry and punch something at the same time. Exhaustion wrapped itself around her like a blanket.

The training and stress gripped at her. As she laid her head down on her arms, she let her eyes drift shut. Maybe she didn't want to hang out with the demon anyway. It was a stupid idea. There had to be more she could do. She looked down at her phone again. It was blank.

A pop of energy rippled beside her.

"So, what's this about hanging out?" Ravin hummed with a smirk on his face.

Twenty-Six

It took only a short time for the two to arrive back at Ravin's dorm room. As much as he wanted a break, there was work to do. All worry and no play made him a very unhappy demon. In this case, he might make an exception. Things would go back to being fine after they got their kiddos back.

"It's alright if you want to relax on my couch," he offered. "I have some stuff I need to do."

"I'm pretty exhausted." She walked over to the sofa and sank into it. "Do you have anything to drink?" Michelle could feel tension throughout her entire body. It took a few moments to force her muscles to unwind. Everything was notably sore.

The demon strolled over and opened up his fridge. "I have soft drinks, hard drinks, or water." He pulled out a soft drink for himself. He knelt and retrieved a well-loved alchemy set and set it on the counter top.

"Something hard." Michelle sat sideways on the sofa. Her arm draped over the top, and her head rested on her arm.

Ravin opened the fridge with his mind, then floated over a few options. Among the bottles were Elvan wine, a Dwarven style ale, and Dryad grown hard apple cider. He always kept a broad variety in stock, for when he needed to wind down after a long day.

Michelle reached out and grabbed the bottle of cider. With a flick of her thumb, the top popped and landed on the floor. The place was still in disarray. At least the furniture was back where it belonged. There were dishes strewn about, and the trash overflowed. It made her glad to know she wasn't the only one who was having problems with keeping up after herself. Michelle tipped back the bottle. The liquid had a sweet crisp apple taste, as if she had bitten into the freshest of fruit. There was a bit of a bite, but nothing she couldn't handle.

"So what are you doing?" She took another drink.

The demon glanced over his shoulder as he looked through his cabinets. His tail wrapped around his drink and lifted it up for him to open. With a thought, the cap popped off, and he took a long drag. "I'm making a potion." He retrieved a container full of various herbs and other substances. He placed it next to his alchemy stand and then grabbed a round bottomed flask with a cork stopper. "One that will help you out while we're on the mission."

"That's good." Michelle sank forward so her elbows were resting on the arm of the seat. She propped her head in her hands. "Because I'm not sure sword training helped too much."

Ravin looked over at her and sighed. "You're human. There is absolutely no shame in being on the sideline in a fight between ageless beings." He didn't consider himself ageless by any means, but that Zier guy definitely fell into the category, as did whoever it was that they were up against. "Sometimes, old creatures are too strong. I know you remember what happened when Vatali grabbed your arm."

It wasn't something he had so easily forgotten, or how quickly that had gotten him to spill the beans on their mission. It was shameful. He wasn't supposed to have any visible weaknesses or to allow anyone to get to him. The strong image he had built over the centuries was beginning to show cracks and that was absolutely dangerous for someone in his position.

"My mortality will get me killed one day. It's just a matter of time," Michelle replied, a slight smile crooked the corner of her lips. There was a deeper look in her eyes, something that spoke louder than her words. Something sad rested below those endless overcast oceans. The human was well aware of how easy her life would pass. Vatali gripping her arm was nothing.

Someday, death would come knocking, and when it did, she would rather have it be more glamorous than the one that was planned for her. Destiny was a bitch, so Michelle tried to ignore her as much as possible. It didn't mean it was easy. She regarded him steadily. "Probably sooner rather than later."

The demon put down the herbs he was rifling through. He frowned and searched her face for some kind of clue as to what she meant. "If you're reckless, yea, that humanity won't do you much good." As he watched her, he dared to press forward. "But you're not talking about being a human. So what aren't you telling me?" Ravin pressed his palms into the counter.

"My bones are dissolving." Bitterness rolled off of Michelle's tongue. "It's a rare disease called Osteovitrum. It means glass bones, or something like that. I'm taking treatments to combat it, but it doesn't fix anything. It only prolongs the inevitable."

"So…" She sat up straight and rubbed her sore arm. "I have to wait for them to disintegrate. Which from my understanding, hurts like hell." This was something that Michelle had never told anyone. Not even Jo. If Jo had known, she would make a scene and try and pay doctors millions to 'fix' her. There was no cure, no solution. Michelle's mother had been studying it for years. Twenty-two years of medical research leading to dead ends and treatments that only worked some of the time.

The only thing Michelle had to look forward to was a life of pain and agony. Slowly, she would wilt away to having to spend every day in a hospital bed. She would wait until her body shut down. Above everything else, Michelle hated waiting. Not only that, Michelle hated destiny. Hers was shit. If she made it to thirty, the doctors would call it a miracle. Many people waited for getting married, having children, and buying their first house.

Michelle looked forward to death, and she prayed that it came on swift, merciful wings.

Any response Ravin could form died on his lips. He selected the ingredients he required, then packed the rest up. "Well, you know what?" he spoke at last. "You're going to make your mark on the world, regardless of how long you've got left."

"That's the plan." She set her first empty bottle down, and got up to get a second. "I'm not getting my hopes up again. I've spent too many years waiting for something to fix me, but—" Her voice trailed off into nothing and she poked through his fridge. Trying to hold on to false faith had become harder than accepting the fact that she was going to die. Her life was fragile. For now, she could pretend to be normal. She could walk the walk and talk the talk. Soon, the stress of everyday life would do her in.

"I'd rather make every moment I have count." She popped off the cap and returned to the sofa.

The demon admired her resolve, but questioned her sanity. "I suppose that's a good solution." He poured some water into the small brass cauldron and lit the flame underneath it. Another sip of his cold beverage helped take his mind off the topic of death. He'd caused plenty in the span of memory he currently possessed.

He waited until the water came to a simmer, and then added the first of the herbs in. The delicate leaves floated to the bottom. Ravin stirred the mixture counterclockwise three times, then counted to ten in his mind. Once he hit ten, he added in a piece of sambucus bark, and used it to stir the liquid clockwise five times. Then, he let the bark settle to the bottom. After it came to a rolling boil, he dropped in a spherical piece of agate and turned the flame down.

Dying. She'd sprung that on him. How the Hell was he supposed to respond? He knew humans were weak, but from the sound of it, the slightest breeze would snap her in half in a year or two. The thought made his stomach churn. No one deserved that, least of all Michelle.

"So how did you meet Kaz?" Michelle changed the subject. It

wasn't one she wanted to linger on.

A sigh escaped his lips. Now that wasn't a topic that he was all that eager to discuss. "Well, it happened a little over ten years ago." If this didn't change her opinion of him to seeing him as the scum of Eartha then, well that would be a miracle.

"This isn't a happy story," he warned her before continuing. "It was shortly after his dad died, a long distance transport accident. An engine malfunctioned and sent it crashing into a mountain, nobody survived.

"The first time I ever saw him, he had run away from home. His mom had become quite different after the loss of her husband, and it was too much for him to take. The only reason his dad had been on the transport was because Kazun had begged him to come home. So the poor kid blamed himself: that kind of vulnerability is something that my kind thrive on. I approached him and after a bit of conversation I told him that it would be possible to bring his dad home... for a price.

"Back then he didn't know the cost and begged me with tears streaming out of those big brown eyes. I held up my end of the bargain and told him that I was going to give him ten years. To a seven-year-old that's a life. What do they know of their immortal soul? Life is what they're living and death is a scary thing that's far away and only happens to old people. Not that he knew that I was asking for his soul.

"I don't know what possessed me back then but instead of leaving right after, he asked me to stay... and I did. Over time I grew attached, kind of like he was a lost puppy dog that I couldn't let go of and well, I guess you can say that we've been friends ever since." He focused his attention at the potion bubbling away. The liquid had turned a soft yellow, like the early morning sun. He didn't want to see the look of disgust that she had to be wearing.

"You really are the worst demon I've ever met," Michelle commented dryly. "They should probably fire you." She took another drink and settled into the sofa. The room was starting to fill with the potion's earthy scent. Something told her that wasn't the end of the story. She wasn't really sure how the soul exchange really worked. The whole process seemed like something that one didn't simply get a take-backsie on. Kazun was still alive, meaning Ravin hadn't collected Hell's due.

She got up, and her muscles protested. In a simple comforting gesture, she took his hand and held it. After a few moments she looked up at him. It was silent as she studied his face. Already she could feel a warm haze creeping into her mind.

Honestly, she hadn't been expecting him to be a saint. Ravin was a demon after all. It didn't surprise her that he and Kaz had met because of a deal. What surprised her was the fact he helped a little kid get his dad back. Then, after that, he befriended that boy. Kaz's soul still remained, and she didn't get how, but that didn't matter too much. She knew one thing; friends don't steal friend's souls.

That was a fact of life.

"So, how did you get past not taking his soul?" She shrugged. "Can't you get in trouble for handing out freebies?"

The demon sighed and rapped his fingers on the counter. "When the time came, I was supposed to drag him down into Hell kicking and screaming… but I couldn't. I had twenty-four hours to do so, but I refused. Since then, we've been in hiding. The college has been a decent bunker, mostly from other demons that would try to find him. They have a leg up because there's a sliver of his soul held in purgatory. After the first week, I heard the news that a bounty had been placed on Kazun's head.

"I don't know who placed it. The King of Hell has no interest in this sort of thing. He doesn't care about a single soul, so someone else had to set it up. But, whoever can deliver his soul will be gifted with more power." He gave the potion another few stirs. "Since then, I've paid Sin to help me keep him hidden. I've had to kill a lot of demons to keep him safe."

"Jeeze," Michelle whispered and closed her eyes. Weren't they the most fun people on the planet? Heavy burdens weighed on both their shoulders. Michelle was wearing thin from it. Death was a heavy load. She was starting to crack under the pressure. It was hard being tough when your body was as strong as glass. Michelle was tired in a lot of ways.

Her gaze followed the stirring rod. The boiling bubbles popped. From the edge of the counter, she could feel the warm fire working its magic.

Ravin tapped some of the liquid off of his rod and rested it on its holder. "We have to let it sit for a while, until it turns gold." He didn't know why he'd told her about killing the demons. Maybe it had been to make her feel better about the fight they were going to encounter in the near future.

He lifted his drink up with his tail and finished it off in several large gulps.

The concoction's color slowly deepened as it continued to

simmer. He couldn't figure out why it hadn't reached the desired color. His eyes widened as he snatched up the essence of stone and allowed a single drop to fall into his brew.

A warm scent filled his nose, like dirt after the rain. Little ripples began to form on the surface as the color started to change. With each tiny wave, it deepened, and became richer until a pool of reflective gold awaited him.

Ravin shut off the fire, and lifted the cauldron with his mind. He pulled the stopper from the bottle and gingerly poured the precious viscous liquid into the glass container.

Once it was full he plugged it up with the cork and swirled the potion around. Perfection. A smile came to his lips. He was quite proud that his brewing skills were still up to snuff. It had been a few months since he had needed to break out the kit, and he hadn't let himself down.

The demon turned to Michelle and offered it to her. "It's a potion of protection," he informed her. "If something happens, and you know you're going to get hurt, chug this down and then hightail it out of there. It'll last for a while, but it won't make you immortal."

She scooped up the potion and stared into it. The shining gold reflected like a mirror. Michelle hardly recognized herself. The warm bottle rested in her palms as she gazed into her own eyes. She could feel the tempest rising in her chest. It wasn't going to be long before they headed out into the unknown. Evil waited for them.

Carefully, she set her liquid shield down on the counter. Her eyes were distant, deep in thought. The circumstances were strange. Before everything that had happened, she couldn't stand to be around demons. And yet, here she was, standing in one's kitchen, drinking his cider and exchanging 'light' conversation.

Had their paths met any other way, she wouldn't have given him a second of her time. He wouldn't have been worth it. She would have hated him for the horns on his head.

"Life has a weird sense of humor." Her fingers rolled across the smooth granite countertop until it met his hand. It was warm and filled with the comfort she needed. He was the only one who knew what she was going through. Ravin was facing this storm with her, and it was strange to her. All of it. It was strange that she had told him about her bones. It was strange that he told her about Kazun.

She looked up at him. "I'd never thought I'd make friends with a demon."

Michelle shook her head and squeezed his hand. It was hard facing everything that laid before them. Death, destruction, you name it.

"Thank you for the potion, Ravin," she said, looking into his dark gaze. "Thanks for this." She gestured with her free hand at his apartment. It was good to not be alone. It was good to be with someone.

"Any time," Ravin responded. "That's what friends do, right?"

Twenty-Seven

Long before Lian woke up, preparations had begun. Her frail body was laid upon a table blacker than the deepest night and colder than the frozen poles of Eartha. The stone fed upon her body heat and hummed with a sinister energy that trickled out and filled the seemingly endless room.

Ira ran a single finger up the human girl's exposed belly. A snide smile twisted his face as he examined her almost naked form. Oh, how the shy girl was going to enjoy that.

If he had to be honest, her body wasn't much to look at. She wasn't nearly as developed as her sister. Her breasts were a B cup at best. Still, it took a lot of concentration to keep himself from acting on instinct. Even without Michelle's sweet curves, this girl was still scrumptious. How was it his fault that she was tempting?

If she hadn't been so foolishly trusting then she wouldn't be in this situation at all.

It disgusted him how blissfully ignorant she was. How could anything survive while being so absolutely stupid?

His finger lazily worked its way up her body to her arms. Her wrists were bound with thick unbreakable ties. She was not going to be leaving anytime soon, not that there was anywhere for her to run to.

He trailed his touch down her body to her ankles. They were bound as her wrists were.

The only clothing on her tiny form was a pair of underpants and a thin bra. Only one thing kept him truly in check. Her soul had to remain in a delicate balance between pure and corrupt; and he was known to debauch oh-so easily.

"It's time for you to wake up little Lian." Ira's face twisted into a cold smile as he reached the girl's head again. The back of his hand stroked her cheek lovingly before slowly drifting down to wrap tightly around her pale throat.

Lian's eyes shot open when her breathing became troubled. She struggled against his tight grip, but to no avail. Her body was weak. Strangled sounds escaped her and her blue oceanic eyes were full of terror. Lian tried to reach out and pull him off, but her hands were tied. The only thing fighting against her bonds did was cause her air supply to shrink. Panic filled her as her body struggled violently to save itself.

Once he was satisfied that his prey was fully at attention, Ira released her neck. "Good morning sleepy head." He ran a hand through her hair and pressed a kiss to her temple. "Here I thought

I was going to have to start the fun without you."

His eyes gleamed with a calculating light. "You wouldn't want to miss the show, would you?" He gestured at her almost completely bare form as well as the overwhelming darkness that surrounded them. The only light came from torches mounted on the wall.

He leaned over her with a wicked look in his eyes, his face hovered a few inches from hers. "Do you like the nether table? I picked it out especially for you. This is a special occasion after all; any old slab of ancient evil rock wouldn't do. I think it accentuates your fear perfectly, wouldn't you agree?"

The girl's eyes were wide as she looked around. She couldn't help but shiver as the cool rock drained away her feverish body heat. Instead of being red, her limbs were tinting blue as her blood went cold. She looked anywhere but his eyes and tried to flinch away. Of course, she couldn't get more than a fraction of an inch.

She was exposed. If she had any real heat in her body, she would blush. The look he gave her made her want to crawl away and hide, but she couldn't. Her biggest nightmare had her trapped. She whimpered quietly and shuddered, turning her head to the side to look away. A cough ravaged her insides and the pain burned like a hot flame.

"I think it's about time we get started."

A smirk crossed his face, as he let his eyes drift down her exposed form. He wanted to watch her squirm helplessly and let the fear take over. "Especially with you dressed like that. It's not fair, you naughty little minx." He caressed her stomach to increase her heart rate and wear her out further. He wanted her will shattered beyond repair. "How is a man supposed to resist something like this? It's almost like you're begging me to play with you all over again. It's a pity you didn't turn out as sexy as that sister of yours."

Ira shook his head. "How does it feel to know that you'll never be as much of a bombshell as her? To know that guys will always pass you up when they have a shot with someone like her? I'll bet she and Ravin have been at it like bunnies since we disappeared. When he's done with her, she won't even remember little ol' Lia who forced her to have so many lonely nights when she should be out enjoying what little life she has left."

For his final blow, he leaned in close and let his breath wash over her. The little bit of heat that it provided dissipated in seconds. "Do you think she'll curse your name when her time comes and the reapers finally ends her misery?" He hissed, with a dangerous look in his eye. "You held her back from experiencing the world with that pathetic fear of anything that even so much as looks your way. It must be hard existing when you fear what lurks around the next corner."

Lian felt tears breaching. It was impossible. Her stomach was tied up in knots. Of course she knew she wasn't as busty as her sister. Lian was lean, more akin to a pencil than a pear. She didn't have feminine hips. Her chest was flat in comparison to most girls her age… It was something she had been made fun of for in school.

She coughed more and refused to look at the monster.

Maybe he was right. Maybe her fears were holding Michelle back from living a full life. Lian wanted to find a cure, she wanted to save her sister. She had started taking pre-med classes for that very reason. Maybe she was messing everything up. What if Michelle was glad she was gone? For once, Michelle could live her life the way she wanted.

Lian's face twisted in pain. Her insides felt like lava. Her extremities felt like ice. Her emotional, pained thoughts were running rampant like a hurricane.

"Michelle is looking for me…" she whimpered, more for her own benefit than his. Her voice was barely audible.

"No, actually, she's not. She's in bed with a demon, the very species you fear with all your little heart, having her world rocked, if I know anything about Ravin, which I do. I know him better than he knows himself. So that's how I'm certain he hasn't let her out of his grasp once." He punctuated his statement with a smirk and leaned near, allowing his warm breath to wash over her. "And why shouldn't she? After countless nights unaccompanied, a girl deserves to have her needs fulfilled."

He teased the skin below her belly button. "You know, I bet you would do absolutely anything for a sip of water, you poor dehydrated thing, you." From under her line of sight he extracted a bottle dripping with condensation. The demon cracked it open and dipped a finger inside. He pulled it out then held his hand out over her and waited for the freezing drop to land on her stomach. "How does it feel to be so utterly helpless?"

Lian flinched as the droplet hit her lower abdomen. It was cold, even compared to the stone she was laying on. The smooth rock dug into her back. Lian wanted to cry. Michelle wouldn't have left her…would she? Pain pulsed in her heart and her teeth clenched and began to chatter.

"Numbing," she weakly admitted, her voice saturated with defeat. Her mind was swimming. This sickness had sapped away all of her strength, and this monster had stripped away all of her hope. Maybe it would be better if Michelle didn't waste her time fighting for a sister that only held her back. Lian had only ever wanted to keep Michelle as healthy as possible. The fear of seeing Michelle in a coffin had fueled her to study medicine. Though, what if that fuel was only burning down the happiness that Michelle had left?

What was the point of fighting back anymore?

Ira leaned forward and smiled as he watched the girl's spirit slowly collapse in upon itself until she was left with almost nothing. He smiled as he leaned into her ear and whispered tantalizingly in her ear. "What if I told you that the dark angel is the secret behind curing Michelle?" It was only when she lost the desire to fight him any longer that he would reveal the truths that he kept hidden. A dark angel could lead his poor girl to salvation, but only if she willingly accepted the creature's bond.

Lian finally looked at his face with wide eyes. Her mouth gaped in surprise.

Ira allowed some water to dribble into her open mouth to show that he could be a nice guy when he felt like it. When she had earned it. He smiled down at her pleasantly. "Oh yes," he purred. "They can do about anything really. They have more power than light angels and a much more manageable disposition." This almost felt too easy to him. "If you're a good little girl, the dark angel can do anything that you want. There are, of course, conditions." He sighed and placed a hand on her bare stomach.

The demon traced his fingers in intricate patterns and muttered words beneath his breath.

Wherever he touched, he left black marks that stood starkly against her pale skin. "But those are mine. Without me, poor Mischa will have to do without any kind of hope. You can't free the dark angel without my help, nor can you control it. Something so powerful will crush your will with a look and you will forever be at its mercy. You'll be dominated by it for the rest of eternity." He let the ambiguity of his words speak for themselves. The girl would think what she wanted because of them.

"If you do what I say, your wildest dreams will be fulfilled." He placed a dot of darkness on the center of her stomach. From there he branched out down her arms and legs, and was naturally sure to pay close attention to her inner thighs, making her squirm.

Lian writhed at Ira's touch. She didn't like anything about it, but didn't know what else to do. If there was even a chance that she could save Michelle, she would. Her sister deserved more days than she had. Michelle wouldn't waste her time in fear. If Lian had to trade it all away to see Michelle healthy, it was enough.

"What do you say?" He whispered in her ear when he was done marking her.

"I'll do it," Lian conceded. "W-what do I need to do?" Lian didn't trust him, how could she? The only reason she was going along with this was she didn't honestly see any other options. He wanted to free this dark angel; something told her that he would do it whether he had her 'permission' or not.

She might as well try to get something out of it.

"Good," he purred and took a step back. "The linking spell

will bind you two together once the angel is free. You will have complete control over it instead of the other way around. You will have power beyond your imagination; with it you could do almost anything you desired."

Almost anything, except of course possessing any free will whatsoever. He would keep that little detail to himself though.

"Currently there is a gate holding back the dark angel. It's something that has held her for more years than most can remember, the ones who can should truly be glad for that. They say there is a very good reason that the angels eliminated the rest of the dark angels. You will need my help so that the dark angel's will doesn't crush yours until you're solidified into a puddle of utter uselessness."

Lian didn't respond. She didn't even look at him. More coughs tore through her body and she felt on the verge of passing out again. She could only take so much.

"Of course, we'll need your dear friend Kazun's help." He turned his attention back to the cage, where the human was chained and unconscious. "He's not nearly as important as you, but he'll serve his purpose."

Ira held up his hand. In a blink, the human boy had appeared in his grasp.

Kazun's head hung forward; his dark locks covered his face. Quiet breathing escaped his lips. He didn't stir as Ira laid him down onto the tablet beside Lian.

With deft fingers, Ira removed Kazun's bindings, then his clothing. The shirt, pants, shoes and socks all disappeared when he tossed them over his shoulder. The demon used the same bonds he'd used for Lian on the boy. "Aren't you two adorable?" he asked aloud before he began to paint similar markings onto Kazun's skin, all the while muttering words of power.

"It's too bad though," he mused as he finished the final strokes. "He won't get to see the dark angel. I would say your goodbyes."

Static began playing in Lian's head. The loud sound filled her every thought. It was an angry sound. Rage screamed through her mind and she couldn't stop it. Was this part of the demon's spell? Lian tried to reach up to hold her pounding head, but her bonds stopped her from moving.

The sound got louder and louder. It made the girl feel like her eyes were going to pop out of their sockets. The pressure was building inside her head. An angry storm raged. For a moment, the black spell markings flickered like a lighter.

A smile passed over Ira's lips. "It looks like it's working already." He ran a finger along one of the dark symbols. "Can you hear her?" He had no doubt the dark angel had something rude to say about his actions, and she would have to get over it. She wasn't in charge.

Lian let out a whimper as the static reached a fever pitch. Then the noise flat lined. Silence filled her head. Sweet silence. Then, Lian's markings began to burn white light. Her eyes glared the same moon bright color. A voice like a church bell rang out into her mind and took over her tongue. "You will regret these actions, demon."

Lian began to cough wildly and the light died. Unconscious, the girl slumped against the nether stone.

A chuckle escaped Ira's lips that echoed around the chamber.

Regret? He highly doubted that. She had only made it easier by knocking little Lian out. Now that both of the humans had been prepared, the ritual could begin.

The path was set, there was no going back now.

Twenty-eight

Michelle opened her eyes and stretched out. Her body was a bit stiff from the night before. After they had finished with the potion, she and Ravin had enjoyed quite a few more drinks. More so than she probably should have had.

With the sun in her eyes, Michelle was ready for a new day. She sat up gingerly and looked around. A thick comforter fell from her shoulders as she tried to figure out where she was. The bed was unfamiliar. Confusion wormed its way into her pounding head. How much alcohol did she have? She rubbed her eyes and forced herself to stand on wobbly legs. They were sore from her training the day before. At least, that was what she hoped it was.

Fumbling, Michelle made her way into the bathroom attached to the room. She looked at herself in the mirror. Her rumpled clothes were still on, which meant she didn't have to worry too much. Nothing too intense had happened without her memory.

She splashed cool water on her face, and grabbed a towel to dry off. It smelled dully familiar. Her head hurt, and her throat burned. Maybe she would get some coffee. That sometimes helped.

Michelle shuffled out of the bathroom and looked down at the disheveled bed. The sheets had been uprooted. They only covered about half the bed. The white mattress pad below was holding down the fort. As she made her way to the door, she kicked some discarded laundry. A shirt here, a pair of boxers there.

So it was a guy's room. She had a feeling she knew who it belonged to.

When she opened the door, there was a sight to behold.

Wearing a pink apron over nothing else but a pair of sweatpants was her host. The girl couldn't help but feel a smile pull over her face. It was quite the show before her. The smell of bacon floated thickly in the air. It was amazing. Hungrily, her stomach cried out.

"Well look at this." She stepped carefully across the room and slid into a stool at the breakfast nook, massaging her temples. Michelle looked over the layout. Eggs, bacon and burnt toast, her absolute favorite. Especially on a hangover.

Ravin's tail darted out and slid a thin vial over to her. "You'll need this." He waved his hand as he finished washing the last utensil he'd used to cook. "Just don't smell it."

Michelle inspected the thin glass tube. It looked like tar had a freak love child with an ooze monster. She popped the top off and downed it. The thick taste of old socks coated the inside of her mouth. A gag clenched her throat and she grabbed a jug of juice sitting out for breakfast. She tore open the top and drank straight from the carton. She didn't have time to find a glass.

"Holy shit," she complained. "Whose shoe did you scrape that off of?" Michelle stuck out her tongue. Almost instantly, the painful haze subsided as the after effects of her night of drinking washed away.

The demon chuckled and flicked his tail. "I mixed it myself, Ms. I'm-going-to-drink-myself-stupid." He sank onto a stool. A sigh escaped his lips that he smothered with a crispy piece of bacon. "Sleep well?"

"Yeah, but I think I destroyed that bed." Michelle happily accepted her plate. "It was comfy, though. Thanks for letting me crash, I guess. I don't really remember what happened last night." Her back popped as she stretched out again.

"Glad you thought so." Ravin poured himself a glass of juice from the ruined container. "My bed is probably the better of the two of them, after all."

With her fork, Michelle destroyed the tender yolk and watched the liquid gold flow freely. She didn't look up at him for a long moment. After dipping her toast, Michelle finally glanced up. A knot was growing in her stomach

"Your bed?" She nibbled on the dark brown triangle, refusing to think anything awkward had happened between them. "Where did you sleep?"

Ravin nodded his head at the second door. "Kaz's. You were already out cold in mine by the time I crashed, so it was that or the couch." He piled eggs and bacon onto a piece of toast and wolfed it down.

Michelle changed the subject. "I have to say that the apron is a nice touch. Pink is absolutely your color."

The demon grinned. "You think so? I agree 120 percent. It was money well spent." It had been a gag gift that Kazun had gotten him a few years back for the holidays. Wearing it made him forget the terrible things that had been going on for the past few days.

Michelle guzzled down her breakfast. Her body needed the nourishment. The girl wiped her mouth free of yolk and she looked up at her host. "Any word from Sin yet?"

He shook his head. "So far I haven't heard anything. This has to be some seriously bad mojo that we're up against. Do you really want to come along to fight? I know you've got that whole heroic thing going on but this is probably going to kill you, Michelle. I mean it." The demon leaned forward and fixed her with a serious look. Hell, he'd be surprised if anyone made it out in one piece.

"I'm sure," Michelle said. "Like I said, if I can even buy you a moment to get my sister out of there, I will take it." She couldn't return his gaze. There was no better way to go. Dying for her sister would be better than letting her body become her prison. That didn't mean she wanted to die at all, but if she had to pick one or the other, a swifter death would be preferred.

"Make sure she is safe, and make sure someone takes care of her when I can't." Her voice wavered as she spoke. "Promise me, as my friend." Her eyes peered deep into his. They were serious and certain. Michelle was heading to her gallows and they both knew it. Marked by an angel or not, Michelle was just a human.

Death was an ending. Death was the only ending she could

see. As scared as she was to face it, Michelle knew she had no other option. Angels had let her be born with the sugar bones; she highly doubted that they would take it away from her. No science could prevent her death. So, the only option she saw was to head to war and wait for her bullet.

The demon reached out and took her hand. "I promise to protect her," he swore, his voice unwavering. The girl would suffer unspoken misery if her sister died, but Ravin would do his best to make sure that Lian made it through whatever happened.

For a brief moment, he could swear that he felt the lingering energy of a pact being formed. There was no going back, he realized. Lian was going to be his responsibility should Michelle die. He sighed and shook his head. Yet another human to watch over.

He was shaken from his thoughts by a knock on the door. At length he stood and stretched.

"Were you expecting company?" Michelle asked, head turning towards the door.

Ravin shook his head and pulled it open. In the hallway stood the very intimidating fallen angel. Their last encounter didn't lift his hopes about how this one would go.

"Zier," he said, taking a step back so that the being could enter. He had the feeling that it wouldn't have mattered whether or not he'd actually let Zier inside; he would have come in one way or another, anyway.

"Having fun?" Zier asked as he crossed the threshold and made his way to the living space. He slumped into an arm chair and propped one leg up on the other. His eyes were once again a different color, this time lime green. He observed them like they were animals in a zoo.

"If by fun, you mean waiting aimlessly for some direction on what to do, then sure, loads of it," Michelle grunted and rolled her eyes. She was glad the fallen angel had showed up. They could get some answers about what they were doing. That was a golden trophy in her book.

Zier still gave Michelle the spooks. He was a really powerful guy. Silently, she wondered if he could cure her. Probably not. Even if he could, the human highly doubted he would want to waste his energy on someone like her. He had some dark angel to keep safe… why would he ever waste a second thought on her? It didn't matter, there were other more pressing matters.

"What can we do for you, Mr. Smiles?" She went to sit on the couch. Zier made her nervous, but she tried not to let it show on her face or attitude.

The fallen chuckled, "Good." Then he leaned back and regarded them both. "Sin has used the spell. The artifact you obtained allowed us to discover the location of your missing ducklings," he explained in an even tone. "I hope you like pocket dimensions because that's exactly where we're headed. Whoever took her has their own domain guarded by powerful magic. It won't be easy to breach its defenses, but I am capable of doing so."

"So what's stopping you?" Ravin shot, a bit harsher than he had intended. The demon fell silent when Zier turned to face him.

"What's stopping me is that neither of you are ready. As cute as that apron is, it's not going to do you much good when it comes to fighting." His eyes sparkled for a moment. "Unless of course that's the enchanted apron of enhanced slaying, which I very seriously doubt."

"If that exists," Michelle chimed in, "I want it, along with the ultimate spatula of death." She grinned a little. Maybe this fallen angel wasn't as much of a stick in the mud as he appeared. The girl leaned forward and placed her elbows on her knees. She looked back and forth from both males. Her heart rate quickened. They had found where Lian was, which meant she was alive.

"Oh, it exists, or so we're lead to believe. Though scholars have yet to find it," Zier explained with a wink.

"So what do we do to get ready, Mr. Smiles?" she asked, standing. They had places to be and monsters to slay. There was going to be action, and Michelle needed to be ready. Lian was going to be safe soon, and that was all that mattered to her. "But seriously, why are you taking me? I know it's not for my sparkling personality. Don't get me wrong, I want to go, I just feel like I could be a liability."

"Without you, our link will be a fraction of its strength, and the spell could shatter before we finish. Your flesh and blood is already inside the dimension, and we can use you to ensure we can gain entrance. Ravin can come because he is a demon; this dimension is attuned to his kind. No one else that we can trust with this information is capable of making it through the process." The fallen angel leaned forward and watched her with an interested look in his eye.

"But to answer the other question, the spell to enter takes around eight hours to prepare," he explained in a matter of fact tone. "It has already been started, but I need to be there for the rest of it, once I'm done explaining it to you two. There's a catch to this whole rescue plan." The man paused for what Ravin could only guess was dramatic effect. "I can only take two with me to get there. Any more would alert him to our presence; stealth will be our greatest ally in this endeavor. So we cannot bring Sin."

Zier gravely continued, "There is a very slim chance that whoever this is could have already summoned Fenriel. If this is the case then I am going to send you two as far away as fast as I can. You won't even have time to think the word 'oops,' before she turns you into a pile of ash."

Michelle nodded in understanding. But, she couldn't help but shudder. Fenriel sounded pretty fearsome. Part of her was curious how she and Zier had met, without him getting turned to ash and all. She decided to keep her mouth shut. That probably wasn't a good topic to prod at.

"Where are we going exactly? I mean, my human mind can only comprehend a little bit of what 'pocket dimension' means." The human sighed dramatically. "Excuse my humanity. I know it's showing." It was hard to be the cute squishy thing amongst titans. Luckily in other aspects, Michelle's personality was big enough to make up for it.

The fallen angel nodded. "It's ok, I'll forgive you this once, puny mortal." He punctuated his insult with a playful wink. "Basically, it is a realm that this being rules either by creating it themselves or because it was gifted to them by an even more powerful creature. It is effectively a fortress of solitude. There is a single door on this planet to access this other plane. Generally, the ruler is smart enough to guard the portal with a massive defensive force. It's easier to force your way in through a temporary door, which is what we are going to do."

"Isn't there a chance that there will be an army inside waiting for us?" Ravin countered, finally daring to speak again.

Zier nodded. "That is another very real possibility, but we have to risk it to save your friends, and to protect Fenriel." He clenched one hand into a fist so tight the skin turned bone white. "I would rather see her sealed for another five thousand years than have her bent to the whim of one who would control her. I will never allow that to happen again."

"Again?" Michelle tilted her head. Something like this had happened in the past? Part of her felt bad for the fallen angel. He was in love with someone who had been sealed away for five thousand years. That wasn't fair. Michelle would be lucky if she got to live over thirty. Five thousand seemed unfathomable. Being a human was frustrating.

Soft static fizzed in her head like the sound of soda foaming over a glass. Her angel was trying to tune in to her head, but it wasn't doing a good job. At least Michelle knew it was trying. If it could help them when they went into the pocket dimension, then maybe they could have a bit of back up. Again, she wasn't going to put her faith on the table. That was asking for a letdown.

The sound was starting to hurt her head and she winced a bit. The painful noise got louder before silencing completely.

Zier frowned. "You know, you'd think my siblings would have a better sense of timing." He crossed his arms. "Ex-siblings I suppose. Still, it's common courtesy to not interrupt." Something dark shone in his eyes, something that easily reminded them that they were lucky that this guy was on their side. "They were the ones who controlled her for most of her life. She didn't deserve that."

"Whoever is trying to talk to me, has been keeping at it," Michelle explained. It only made sense Zier had heard her little mind visitor. Ravin was an okay mind reader, meaning the fallen angel could probably hear her thoughts like they were on the loudspeaker. It could have been awkward, but Michelle had nothing to hide; at least, she didn't think she did.

"Sorry though," she sighed, as she thought about the situation more. "I mean, getting Lian back might make it so you can't have Fenriel free. It seems like a conflict of interests you know?" It couldn't have been easy for Zier. Then again, if he got Lian safe and sound, there was no telling what he could do. Maybe he planned to free the dark angel himself. Michelle shuddered. If there was anyone she didn't want to be up against, it was Zier.

Would Lian ever truly be out of the woods?

The fallen angel nodded. "It's alright. While your logic would be correct under any normal circumstances, these aren't quite so simple," he explained. "The only way your sister will ever truly be safe would be if Fenriel is free. A bonded angel is the most useful ally that one can possess. It involves becoming attuned to a powerful creature that will do everything in their power to keep you safe."

He let out a sigh and slumped back in his seat. "She is a kind and caring woman. Dark angels being equated with evil was nothing more than propaganda. Even after all these years, I refuse to believe she would be anything but the same wonderful woman I knew. She would adore your sister. This, I know for a fact. Her maternal instincts were always strong. She's known as 'The Mother' among the angels." A smile passed over his lips. "She would destroy anyone who upset Lian, and ensure that no harm ever came to the girl again."

He locked gazes with Michelle and held her there. "Do not misunderstand my intentions. I will free Fenriel," the fallen angel told her in no uncertain terms. "Nothing will stop me, not you, not the demon, not even your guardian angel. However, I will allow Lian time to grow comfortable with the idea. Fenriel will be free when Lian is prepared to handle the bond."

Michelle held his gaze strongly and she nodded. "Thank you, Zier," she said simply. "I mean, I figured you weren't helping 'cause it was a Saturday night and you were bored. The fact you are willing to ease her into it proves a lot." Michelle looked up at him. "Knowing she has someone like you and Fenriel who will keep her safe makes me feel a lot better..." her voice trailed away. It didn't take a mind reader to know what she meant. When she had passed on, it was nice knowing Lian had her own guardian angels, even if they were dark, fallen, or light.

The human fought tears back like a champion. She bowed her head with respect then turned to Ravin. "We should let him get to work. We have eight hours to live and I don't plan on spending them here." Her eyes looked down at the ward Letvan had gifted her. She had two shields, which probably wouldn't do too much.

Michelle could count the hours left on her two hands.

Her bright eyes lit up with determination. She was going to face the Reaper with a smile on her face. She was doing the right thing. If she didn't go down with a boom, something wasn't right. Michelle kept reminding herself that dying in battle was better than dying in a hospital bed. There was going to be a time where she couldn't even stand enough to go to the bathroom on her own.

Was that even really living?

No. Michelle was determined to go down with some sort of dignity. Her life would mean something. Even if no one knew it, she was going to die saving the world. That was a destiny she was okay with.

Zier nodded, and with a pop of energy he disappeared.

Ravin walked over and put a hand on her shoulder. "It's alright to cry," he murmured. "Hell, I would be if I was in your situation." Tears weren't something that he'd used in the past few centuries of his life. There was nobody to spend them on anyway. Kazun was the closest he had to family and in a few short years, he would be only a fading memory gathering dust in the back of his mind.

He offered his arms to the girl for a hug. Some comfort was better than none, he supposed.

Michelle looked up at Ravin, and a single tear escaped slowly and silently. She rose to her feet and hugged her friend tight. Her face rested on his chest and no more tears ran free.

"I guess I'm lucky," she said softly into the cloth of his shirt. "I get to spend my last few hours with a friend like you."

Twenty-nine

They spent the rest of the day eating, playing games, and preparing for the worst. When the alarm on his holophone went off, it was time. Ravin teleported Michelle and himself to the bar and they went in with no regrets.

Michelle clenched the demon's hand tightly. Of course it was hard not to be scared. Still, the girl wore a brave war mask as she stepped into the back room.

Sin greeted them with a melancholy flick of her tail. Exhaustion marred her otherwise lovely features. After spending a lot of energy fueling the spells, she had great reason to. Slowly, she walked over to Ravin and placed both of her hands on his shoulders.

"Don't die," she suggested. "You are no use to me dead." A soft grin appeared on her face as she tried to lighten the mood. She continued, "And if you guys make it back, drinks are on me."

Michelle was about to tell her not to pencil her in, but she decided against it. Sin was being kind, trying to get their spirits up. They were about to head into the ether, to some pocket universe ruled by a monster. Generally, this was the opportune time for joking. For the first time in her life, Michelle didn't feel like laughing.

The goal was simple: go into the death hole, then drag Lian and Kazun back.

"Zier, are you ready?" Sin asked the fallen angel. "When you are, I will open the portal and hold it open as long as I can. It will be your duty to open the way back here…" Her eyes fixed on him for a moment, telling him not to fail. There was a lot at stake, and everyone in the room could feel it. The atmosphere was thick.

After a few seconds the fallen angel nodded. "I am ready." He looked at the two he would be bringing with him. Zier did not say it, but he fully expected to only have one when he returned.

Ravin pulled Michelle over to Zier and looked into her eyes. For a moment, all he did was search them. He knew where her thoughts were. There was no doubt that she was thinking about her death and that wouldn't do. He pulled her close and gave her a warm, delicate kiss, something that neither of them would forget.

"When we get back I'll give you more," he whispered into her lips, the promise glimmering in his dark eyes.

Warmth flushed over Michelle's cheeks and her stomach swam with butterflies. A thick lump sat her in throat and she couldn't find the words to speak. All she could do was nod and think about that single moment. She had kissed quite a few guys before, but none of them had made her want to live so badly. The demon had somehow wormed his way into her heart. Michelle's hand clenched his tightly.

"You better promise," she said, focusing her mind away from death and on what had been a perfect kiss. He did not disappoint.

"Alright, cuties," Sin interrupted. "It's show time. Keep your hands and feet in in the vehicle at all times. Tails and wings must be tucked as close as possible to your body. Have a good day." With her last words, the female demon's eyes lit like cold blue fires. Markings that stretched across the room illuminated. Energy popped loudly and the air snapped. Electricity danced in a tight circle around the door hinge. Sin held her hands up and the door swung open. Light poured from the opening and she nodded to the group.

It was go time.

The three heroes piled through the door and they were sucked into the other side. A rough landing awaited them and they were thrown onto coarse pale gray stone. Surrounding them was a dead wood forest. Carrion birds cried demonically in the distance. A dark purple sky hung overhead where a red moon shone.

Shakily, Michelle got to her aching legs. This whole place was a perfect setting for a horror movie. Spider webs covered the trees and the smell of death filled the air. Michelle gripped her nose and tried to keep the awful week-old rot smell out. Unfortunately, it was no use. A gag clenched her throat as she tried to hold back vomit.

She turned and looked down the rocky hills and her eyes met

a large spire that rose into the air towards the sunless sky. The blood moon hung lazily, adding a nice finishing touch. "I have this sinking feeling," Michelle stated, trying to force her stomach to settle. "Please tell me scary door number one is not where we are heading."

Zier snorted. "Sorry, but that's exactly where we're going. The spell indicated that they were at the very top," he explained calmly.

"That's going to be a very long climb," Ravin remarked. The idea of climbing up there with a human was not going to be easy. "How are we supposed to do this?" he asked and gave the spire an appraising glance.

The fallen angel rolled his eyes. "Exactly how you'd think." He closed his eyes to teleport the three of them… but when he opened them again, they were still in the same place. A low stream of curses left his lips as he tried another time. "Or the old fashioned way, walking." Anger was clear in the undertones of his voice.

Michelle felt his pain; at least his legs weren't still very sore from a day of training like hers were. A least, she hoped that was the case. She placed her hand to her forehead and stared out in the distance. It looked like a day's walk if they kept a reasonable pace. Though, a thought occurred to her.

"If you guys can't teleport…what else can't you do?" she asked, hoping teleporting was the most of their worries. These two were supposed to be the main line of defense and if they couldn't defend… The girl tried to keep her face blank.

Things could get really bad really quickly.

Ravin reached inside of himself to tap into his stores of energy. He tossed a fairly decently sized boulder with more effort than he expected. "Well, I can still do that, kind of." He could feel that it had taken more out of him than usual, but at least he could. "I can carry you if you want," he offered. While he lacked some of his more attack-based skills he still felt as physically strong as he always did.

Meanwhile the fallen angel had closed his eyes. Absently he reached out and put a hand on Michelle's head; his touch eased her aches and pains in a blink. "This dimension blocks darker powers that do not belong to the ruler, and teleporting. I could perhaps fly us a short distance but my wings aren't known for their long travel anymore."

The demon kicked a dead looking tree. "So we're already screwed." He let out an angry breath to calm himself. There was no point in freaking out, yet.

"Save the wings for when you need to get out of there," Michelle said to the angel. She then took Ravin's hand. "We'll figure this out. Walking isn't so bad. I do it all the time." She slowly turned her head and looked into the distance. Clouds shuddered with lightning near the spire. It was like an ominous sign of 'look, bad shit happens here'. Their gracious host sure knew how to decorate his pocket universe. Michelle would have used more couches and throw pillows, but to each their own.

The girl started walking. There was no time to be wasted on pouting over disappearing powers. Luckily, she wasn't any weaker than normal. Nope, she was one hundred percent her. With the fallen angel's help of relieving her pain, the girl felt like she could walk for hours.

Silently they marched. Time was warped in this strange place.

The blood red moon never dipped below the horizon. The unmoving sentry satellite watched them. The horrid smell of death faded as they became accustomed to it, but the carrion birds' screeching never softened. Cold fingers of apprehension tickled up Michelle's spine. This place was almost what she would have pictured Hell to be like, except for there was no fire. On the contrary, it was pretty cold.

She shivered and walked closer to Ravin. He was warm. Not only that, but he was the only bit of comfort she had in this place. As they walked quietly, her mind would drift off to their kiss. Did that mean anything? A part of her felt stupid for thinking so. It was probably to calm her the fuck down. It had worked. Sort of.

"Hey," she chimed in after what felt like forever. "I think the tower might be getting closer." Then again, she could have been imagining things.

Ravin gave the spire an appraising look. "I'd say, probably," he half agreed. The demon felt at home here, almost. Hell had never been the most inviting destinations, and this place did its best to mirror that terrible feeling. It was missing the blood curdling screams and the presence of other beings.

"Be prepared in the event of a surprise encounter," Zier called back from his place in front of the two. "You never know what to expect," he explained, his eyes scanning every tree and rock in sight.

The demon did his best to do likewise, but he couldn't shake the feeling that they were all being watched. That alone messed with his ability to pinpoint other life. The eyes seemed to be watching from every angle, above, below, every possible position around them. Either they were utterly surrounded or the paranoid feeling came with being in this dimension.

"Aye, Aye, Captain!" Michelle's voice was still enthusiastic. One of her perfected skills was putting on an energetic front for the crowd. She looked around, seeing if she could spot anything, though all she could see were weird red-eyed ravens in the tree.

"Should I alert you to the birds, captain?" she asked, knowing the males could probably see the hundreds of carrion birds who were calling out to each other and watching them. "Or is that a bit too obvious?" From kittens to screaming flesh eating zombies, these birds hit a nice Creepy McCreeperton on the fear scale. Their eyes stared like the huge moon that floated above. Michelle suppressed a shiver rolling down her spine. Their gaze was unwavering.

Ravin glanced about, then looked over at Michelle. "What birds?" he asked in as calm a tone as he could manage. The demon had no idea what she was talking about. There were no birds that he could see.

"So what you are telling me, is your special demon eyes can't see the fact that there are hundreds of demonic ravens watching us?" she questioned. "Please tell me you are joking." Her hand clenched. How could he not see them? Another bird let out a scream in the distance. Michelle was on the edge of panic.

He shook his head. "I can't, Michelle." The demon looked around, to every angle, but saw absolutely nothing but dead looking foliage. That would explain why he felt like there were millions of eyes watching him.

"Perhaps they cannot be seen by impure eyes," Zier reasoned.

"Our host must have assumed that most of their adversaries would be of a demonic nature."

"So you can see them?" Michelle asked, hopeful.

For a moment Zier did not respond, he simply kept walking. After a long pause he finally spoke. "I cannot," he admitted. "Though, I know the location of every single one of them. Until you said something about birds I had no idea exactly what was up there. I suspect your necklace is the reason that they haven't done more than watch us."

Michelle sighed with soft relief. Her eyes darted around, but except for the birds all was still. That was good, right? She wrapped her fingers around the necklace Letvan had given her. The thin silver chain gave her confidence. She didn't want to imagine what the creatures would be doing otherwise. The men wouldn't even see it coming.

"Well I'll tell you if I see anything then," she said with a dutiful nod as they marched onward through the cold and eerie pass. Rocks stretched for as far as the eye could see. Mountains of black stone rose into the air and surrounded them and the bleached bone forest. Every towering tree seemed to be made of ivory. Creepy was an understatement. As they continued down the winding road, nothing changed much. The scenery was set.

Michelle leaned on Ravin a bit. Despite the healing spell Zier had done on her, she was starting to feel the trek in her legs. They didn't hurt, no; they were beginning to feel like they were made of gelatin.

"When I get back," she stated. "I'm going to get a cup of cocoa and wrap myself in blankets and sleep for days." Her eyes looked up to the demon. Though she didn't expect to find her way home, it was a simple conversation that didn't take much thought. A soft smile tugged at the corner of her lips and she asked her travel mates. "What will you guys do when you get back?"

The demon gave Michelle a cocky grin. "When I get back I'm going to kick your ass some more at video games," he declared. Ravin was going to make it happen; she had to make it back so that he could taunt her more. Nobody was going to take away his new squishy friend.

"Beating me would be too easy if I'm asleep, Ravin," she pointed out.

"I'll go back to selecting random places to stand still and look fine for hours," Zier informed them with a completely straight face.

Laughter sputtered out of Ravin as he tried to picture the reaction of anyone watching the fallen angel. It felt like a completely natural thing to do.

"We'll open you a nice museum. Then we can make a profit from your fine body," Michelle declared. "I've changed my answer! I'm going to open a man museum." Her eyes sparkled with excitement. She looked up at Ravin and appraised him for a long moment before declaring. "I think you could be an exhibit. Just don't try to outdo our star!"

The girl started to laugh, which earned her a few shrieks from the carrion birds. Maybe the sound of joy was like nails on a chalkboard to them. Michelle was all kinds of unconventional, so she could live with that.

"Sound good, Zier?" she asked.

Zier turned around to face them as he walked backwards. The fallen contemplated his answer before he struck a pose, both arms up, crisscrossed behind his head and his hands gripping the opposite sides of his face. "As long as I am the headliner," he declared as he started carefully choosing his steps to make himself look as sexy as possible.

A sound of complaint left Ravin. "How am I supposed to compete with that?" He threw up his arms in exasperation.

Michelle clapped for the fallen angel. He was some sort of fabulous. It was strange to see him acting so silly. Most of the time, Zier had been dead serious. There was something comforting about seeing him loosen up. The walk would have been maddening if they didn't lighten up the atmosphere. Michelle was glad the men were helping keep her anxiety at a manageable level. It wouldn't do any good to have them be sullen and panicked the entirety of the walk.

As she took a step forward, excruciating pain shot through the girl's leg. Michelle fell and landed roughly on the cool stone ground. A curse escaped her lips and she tried to force herself to stand back up. No matter how hard she tried, it was no good.

"Fuck!" she cried and smacked the ground. This wasn't fair. She was stuck in a kneeling position on legs that were burning like fire. Despite the healing Zier had done, they had been walking for hours. After stepping on a loose stone, she had twisted her ankle. She bit her lip to keep herself stable on the inside.

Ravin knelt beside her and rubbed her back. "We can take a break," he murmured soothingly. "I'm getting pretty exhausted myself," the demon lied blatantly. There was no need to make the human feel too self-conscious.

He glanced up at Zier who had stopped walking. "We're stopping for a while," he informed he fallen angel flatly. This was not up for discussion. As much as Michelle may have been fodder compared to them, they would stick to the pace of the slowest member. If not for her taking the initiative when she saw the Mark on Lian, then they probably would have no idea what had happened until doom rained down on them in the form of a dark angel's wrath.

"Thanks," she whispered. Her heart sunk a little. She was slowing them down. They were so close to finding Lian and Kazun, but she was so weak. Any human would have been exhausted by this point. That didn't make it any easier. The fact was, Michelle hated facing the reality that she wasn't bulletproof.

After a long silence, she sighed and looked up at Ravin with defeat in her eyes. "Is it still possible to take you up on that piggy back ride?"

A smile appeared on Ravin's lips. "It's never too late for a piggy back ride." He scooped her up and hiked her onto his back. "Let's go. We have some ass to kick," he declared and started off again. Absently, his tail wrapped around her waist to ensure that she didn't slip off.

Michelle latched on tightly with her arms around Ravin's neck. It was going to be a long embarrassing ride, but it was better than sitting around and making no headway. Even if she felt ridiculous for this, it was getting them somewhere.

The fallen angel tapped the top of Michelle's head. "In time, that should replace the energy you have lost. Let it rejuvenate you." Their little human was quite the trooper. Soon they would reach their destination and the truly taxing portion of the journey would begin.

This was only the beginning of the end.

Thirty

"I think it's time we start the festivities. It's so convenient, wouldn't you say Lia?" Ira sighed theatrically. The demon didn't give the girl a chance to respond. "I would say so."

"Do you think he'll be scared when he wakes up?" the man wondered aloud. "Or do you think he'll try to defend you?" He shot her a creepy look.

After a few moments, Kazun blinked awake. He struggled against his bonds, even though he knew that there would be no escape. "I'm going to kill you!" Kaz growled.

Ira ran his hand through the boy's shaggy hair. "Oh, I bet you will little one," he mocked quietly. "Your pure soul tells me otherwise. You don't even want to kill the man who utterly ruined your life. Yes, he brought that papa of yours back, but ten years is such a small amount to give a child. He could have made the deal last until they day you died on your own, but instead selfish, Ravin chose to put your head on the chopping block."

Every word was a dagger in Kazun's heart. It was all true, and while he'd try to pretend that it had been the only deal available back then, he knew it was a lie. Ravin had tried to steal his soul and send him to Hell to bolster the ranks of the damned.

"Even after you realized it on your own, you still call that man friend. Now tell me more about how you're going to end my existence." Ira propped his chin up on his hand and with his other hand gestured enthusiastically for the boy to continue.

The words were stuck in Kazun's throat and he slumped back against the stone that was leaching all of his body heat and energy.

"That's what I thought," Ira spat and turned his attention to Lian once again.

Ira touched her skin and lazily hovered above the table. He stroked her belly with his thin tail. "So, Lia, just thought I'd warn you: you probably won't make it out the other side of this in one piece. See," he flipped over so that he was looking down on his prey. "I'm going to take over that tiny brain of yours so that I can control the dark angel. She won't be happy about it, but it's going to happen. I've been perfecting this spell for the past century. I planted dozens of seeds like the one I put in you when you were a child. In all of the years that I've been trying, you're the only one who will ever achieve the glory that I hoped for."

Lian looked away from him. She couldn't even let her gaze fall upon Kazun. It was hard to comprehend death. It was never on her mind like it was on her sister's. Having her soul torn to shreds by some dark angel was terrifying.

"I don't care what happens to me," Lian whimpered, "Just please help my sister."

Kazun looked at her with brave brown eyes. They clearly said, 'I'm going to get us out of this.' Lian knew there was no way that he could. The two of them were trapped, and would be until this man let them go.

A dark smile spread on the demon's face. "I said the dark angel *could* help your sister," he clarified. "Not that I would allow her to." With that last cruel statement, he shifted so that he was upright above them and began the words of his spell. The strange language crawled over their skin and tickled their ears, though they could not begin to comprehend what he was saying.

Every syllable and sound was specifically paced and carefully uttered.

Nothing was going to break his concentration. Not even getting stabbed in the lung could prevent him from finishing the spell he had longed to utter for lifetimes. As he spoke, his words grew louder and more frenzied. Wind whipped from an unseen source and enveloped them like a blanket.

Lian let out a scream as everything went dark and she was pulled into a place in her conscious mind she had never seen before. There was no escape as dark hands pulled at her.

Before the human was a beautiful being who was wrapped in chains. Dark doll-curled hair cascaded all around her plump womanly figure. Suddenly, their eyes locked and Lian saw deep into the other. Lian could feel a deep painful stab into her heart. She let out a silent cry.

In her mind, a voice rang out like a church bell, "Lian, you are a brave child."

"Please!" Lian cried out, "Don't kill me! I have to save my sister!"

"If it were my choice," the woman replied, "I would do anything for you, my sweet child." There were tears in the woman's sad voice.

Everything became loud and Lian could feel her soul being constricted. Pain like she had never experienced flashed through her body. Her entire soul was pinned in a sea of dark. She cried out, but the darkness devoured the sound.

When Lian's eyes opened, instead of their natural ocean blue color, her irises were snow white. She looked up and tugged at the restraints violently. A loud inhuman hiss escaped her mouth.

"Demon, you will release me," she ordered, her strong voice reverberating against the smooth stone. There was something very different about the girl. She was wild and had an aura of power to her. Her eyes locked onto Ira and they thinned. Dark words escaped her mouth.

"You have linked me to a child," she accused, as she fought against the tethers. Anger flared in her white eyes. They fixed onto Ira. The dark angel was tired of being in chains. Only the first part of the spell had been completed. She had no power; her body was still locked away.

Kazun's heart sunk. "Lia?" he murmured brokenly and watched.

"Dear Lian is locked within these walls," the woman responded, without looking at Kazun. Instead she continued to glare at their captor. "I am the Angel of Night, Fenriel."

The boy fell silent and closed his eyes. A quiet whimper escaped his lips, but it died out as immeasurable pain filled his entire body. His throat constricted, trapping all sound behind the lump.

Ira paused his spell when he could, for now the dark angel could survive in her current state. "I'm sorry dark one," the man sighed disingenuously. "It is the best I could do; unfortunately every other recent subject failed. I could have waited a few more years, but I find I'm too impatient." He sank down to stand next to the tablet.

"About the whole releasing thing," he continued. "I'm going to have to say no, and considering I'm the only one with a vote, the results are unanimous." The demon gave his horn a very long stroke and let out a hissing breath between his teeth. "I have some goals I wish to accomplish, and I can't without you."

The dark angel thrashed against her bonds, trying to get loose. It was no use. She was caught in a weak girl's body with little power. Anger pulsed in her eyes as she struggled futilely. When she tired, her body stilled. She locked gazes with the demon.

"You will regret this," she warned. "Those who play with fire get burned."

"There's an important difference between those people and me." Ira bent over Fenriel, his face only centimeters from the dark angel's. "I like the burn." With that, he leaned back and carefully continued his spell. Tangled in the words were specific phrases to bind her will to his. He had tested it numerous times on angels, so it would work on a dark angel. He knew it would.

The demon's voice rose to a fever pitch as he chanted with all of his might.

Fenriel closed her eyes, she sent out a mental call loud and clear. She would make this insolent man pay. No one would imprison her. No one would tether her inside a body and force her to do anything against her will.

"Nineteen bottles of beer on the wall, nineteen bottles of beer," Michelle sang as she held tightly onto Ravin. "Take one down, pass it around, eighteen bottles of beer on the wall." It had been her sole duty to come up with entertainment since she was such a slow little human. The girl thought she was doing well.

That was until she saw the spire tip start to glow like a light house. Lightning cracked and struck the zenith.

"What the—?" she gasped.

Zier tensed and stared up at the peak with eyes filled with a mix of awe and pure unbridled rage. His hands clenched into fists and his entire body tensed.

"Holy shit, did you feel that energy?" Ravin whispered in pure wonderment. He shuddered and rubbed his arms. "There's a huge amount pouring out of that thing. I think Ira has started the summoning."

Without warning, the fallen angel began to run wildly towards the spire. It was almost impossible for Ravin to keep up, but he did his best to try. They wove between trees, and even though the spire loomed nearer it felt like they weren't getting any closer, no matter how hard they tried. The scenery sped by and was replaced by even more of the same.

"Wait up!" Ravin cried and struggled to keep pace. He could feel his muscles starting to protest at the insane velocity.

"Fenriel," was the only response Zier gave. He looked as though he was being drawn to the spire like a moth to the flame. It was as if it was pulling him by invisible strings.

Michelle held on tightly to Ravin. Her heart dropped in her stomach as they zoomed down the path. Silently, she prayed to whoever would listen that they weren't too late. Could they be so close, yet so far? Lian could be in grave trouble. Hell, the world could be on the brink of an apocalypse.

She was scared of what was to come. Was Fenriel so close to returning to this world, straight into the wrong hands? As much as Michelle respected Zier's love for the woman, she couldn't help but be terrified. Ravin and Sin had showed nothing but fear for her return. They had used phrases like 'do you know what this means?' Michelle knew this was a general translation for some really bad shit.

Life as they know it could have been hanging in the balance.

After everything, could they fail? Was that even a real option? Lian had to still be alive. She had to still be safe. Michelle wouldn't believe otherwise until she knew for certain.

"Please tell me we aren't too late," Michelle called out, though her voice was muffled by Ravin's shirt.

"Fenriel's consciousness is free but not her body," the fallen angel explained and ducked beneath a low hanging branch. Nothing but their destination mattered. Nothing would stop him from saving the woman he loved. "Lian is sealed away in her own body. When Fenriel is fully free... the girl will be no more."

Ravin did his best to speed up. "Then let's kick this into high gear," he yelled and pushed himself to the limit. Running wouldn't kill him, but Michelle would if Lian died and she lived.

Angry curses rang from Zier's mouth. Only half were in languages that were recognizable to the demon's ears, and he was fairly sure he did not want to understand the ones that sounded like gibberish. Some of the phrases he caught included, "feed him his own entrails," "torment his soul for eternity," and, "destroy everything he holds dear." Ravin could only imagine what the rest were like.

Michelle wanted to shriek, but she kept herself quiet. Zier was saying enough for the three of them. Not that she understood a word of it. Then again, she didn't have to. The inflection was enough. It didn't take a scholar to figure out he was cursing like a sailor. Actually, he made sailors look like cute little grannies who fed cookies to orphans.

What a man.

Every moment, the spire loomed closer. Its eerie shape was brought into tight focus. The inhuman speed the two males were maintaining was making their journey go swiftly. It wouldn't take too long before they were inside and ready to fight some crazy final battle to save Eartha from certain destruction. That was an ending Michelle found fitting. Dying with a purpose like saving the world was perfect. The only way it could be better was if there were literal fireworks.

As long as Zier could get out with Lian, good would have won this battle. No static screeched in her ear to tell her that someone was listening. In this battlefield, Michelle was alone. The moments felt longer and longer as the trio swiftly moved down the trail. Fear pounded in the girl's chest.

"Godspeed," she whispered as they neared the spire. It was then the static began to fizzle.

Thirty-one

It wasn't long before they arrived at their destination. The swift-moving males got them there in a little under an hour. Up close, the spire was even more terrifying. It was an intricate building. Carved into it were depictions of death. It looked like it was constructed from bones composed of black stone. There was a large decaying wood bridge that passed over a moat of brackish water.

The human tried to put on a brave face, but it was hard given the local decorations. It was nice, if you were a reaper or something she supposed. The smell of death poured off the walls like sour perfume.

If they had a choice, Michelle would have turned around and left long ago. Unfortunately, her sister was in there. If Michelle was scared, she could only imagine what Lian was feeling. If she was still alive. There was a distinct possibility that the dark angel had already ripped her soul to shreds.

Being optimistic was pretty difficult in the pessimist capital of the pocket universes.

"Well, I think this looks like a beautiful summer cottage," she commented, looking around for any signs of would-be danger. The coast looked clear, but they weren't out of the dead woods yet. At any moment, something could jump out and try to eat them. Michelle didn't think she would taste that good, but she wouldn't try and convince a monster of that. Everything was edible with enough ketchup. Lian had proved that when trying to eat Michelle's homemade fish sticks.

"I mean, it may be too early to book," Michelle continued. "But I think I would love to throw my birthday party here. I mean, the smell of death goes great with cake."

Ravin snorted. "You have fun with that, I'm going to avoid this place like the plague." He suppressed a shudder. As much as he wanted to go along with her joking, he was going to focus on the task at hand.

The fallen angel scanned their surroundings. "Our destination is the peak of the spire," Zier explained, gazing upwards. "We will need to start the ascent from the inside…" Again he paused and crossed his arms. "Naturally, we will need to find our way inside first." That was more than completely obvious to the rest of them.

"I vote we blow a huge hole in it." Ravin shifted from foot to foot anxiously and stared at the wall in front of him.

Zier rolled his eyes. "That would be a good idea if you actually could. Try to access your powers and do it right now, then," He crossed his arms and challenged the demon. Stupid suggestions would not get them anywhere but further from their goal. Every moment the demon wasted, was one that they could use to find an actual solution that could get them inside.

The male frowned up at the much more powerful being. "Yea, fine, okay. I can't." He kicked the ground and stared hard at the outer wall. His energy was out of his reach, which made him feel useless and defenseless. Such a state could cost him his life, as well as the life of his friends.

A chill ran down Ravin's spine as an unholy howl came from the forest they had left. They needed to be inside.

Now.

"Maybe there's a door along the side!" the demon shouted and started to bolt around the base of the spire. Zier was right on his heels as they sped away from the creature that would surely be their end. If their pace slowed, their organs would soon be dinner.

Michelle's arms tightened around Ravin as the males rushed on swift feet. The tension held thick in the stagnant air. The trees whispered songs of death as wild barking grew nearer. The human didn't know what was on their horizon. Fear could not even come remotely close to describing the ball of emotion welling in her gut.

Another blood-curdling howl rose into the crimson air.

"What is that?!" Michelle yelled, her voice full of panic.

Ravin shook his head. "You don't want to know. You don't want to see it. Start praying that we get inside before they reach us." His voice was strained as he held the girl tighter. Anxiously, he cast a glance about as they continued their charge. He turned the corner and skidded to a stop, panting, wide-eyed. The demon stared straight into a pair of eyes the color of rotten blood.

A huge creature a size of a horse stood in front of them, and behind it were dozens more. Their breath smelled of putrid corpses that had baked out in in a sun soaked swamp. Dozens of dagger-like teeth protruded from their canine-esque muzzles. Their bodies were torn, scarred, and mangled. The biggest of the monsters stood before them, obviously their alpha.

"Hellhounds?" Michelle whispered.

In a movement quicker than the eye could see, Zier burst forth and slammed a dagger into the tall creature's brain. Blood shot out of the wound and the hound let out an angry cry. "Run you fools!" the fallen angel screamed and Ravin took off, not wasting a second of the hard-bought time.

The pack rushed to help their wounded alpha, and for a few golden seconds, the path was clear. Ravin pushed his body to the limit as he bolted away. Not far from where he stood, he could see a large pool of water surrounding what appeared to be a cave of some sort that could serve as an entrance. The only issue was the fifty-foot plummet to reach it.

"We have to go back!" Michelle cried out, "We can't leave him!"

"Like Hell we can't!" Ravin retorted. Zier would be okay. The fallen angel was no lightweight. Even without his magic, he was a strong able-bodied being. Even if he didn't make it out, there were more pressing issues. They had to free Lian, and they had to keep the dark angel from being controlled.

"How are we going to get home?" the human demanded, but

Ravin didn't listen.

They would figure that out when they had their friends safe and sound. Right now, the only thing the demon was concerned with was not being hellhound chow.

Another scream of a beast cried out behind them. They didn't look back.

Ravin ran up to the ledge that overlooked the pool of water. It was the only way in. Michelle held tightly onto him. In her current state, she wasn't sure if she could swim all that well. The last thing she wanted was to drown in the murky depths.

"We'll find a way, Mischa," he declared, his voice strong. "Sometimes you have to take a leap of faith." With his final word, the demon leapt. He kept himself between the girl and the water while in mid-air. If anyone was going to hit the water first, it wouldn't be the breakable one.

The cold water shocked her body as it surrounded her. Michelle let out an involuntary gasp and water came rushing into her gaping throat. For a moment, Michelle simply floated. A sparkling silver chain caught the light as it disappeared into the depths. Ravin was torn from her, lost in the dank pool. His figure too far away to see. Pain splintered into her arm and Michelle turned to see a pair of angry dark eyes. A beast ripped her out of the water and threw her weak body to shore. Blood poured out of her arm from the sharp bite. Drooling with hatred, the hellhound stood over her.

Animals killed for food. They didn't hunt for pleasure, but in the monster's deathly dark eyes, Michelle could see pride. The hound stood over her, jaws gaping, and she could see its vile lips pulling back into a smile. A low growl rumbled through its throat, "Humans are a delicacy. So fatty and full of flavor," it chortled, voice rugged with the sound of bark and mucus. Its large leathery nose took in a great breath of air, enjoying the smell of her fresh blood.

The hellhound's tongue lolled from its mouth as it closed the gap between it and Michelle.

This is what real death looked like, and it wasn't pretty or heroic. It was a dark monster that smelled of rot and blood. Death was scary, and it was looming. Michelle closed her eyes. She couldn't watch. All she could do was feel her life slowly trickle from her mangled arm.

Michelle hated it. She felt so *useless* and she had spent her life trying to be one of those women people looked up to. Now she felt like a child waiting for someone to save her. More than anything, she hated that. Every second that passed, she cursed her bones and her humanity. If she had been anything else, she would be kicking ass right now. No, instead she got to wait as death brought its gross mangy face up to her.

Michelle scrambled in her pocket, fumbling to get at the potion. Glass bit into her finger tips. The vial had shattered in the water. Her protection washed down the river along with the small dagger she had brought with her.

With the force of a torpedo, Ravin shot from the water and slammed into the solid body of the hellhound. His fists pounded into its disgusting hide with the fury inherent in his race. Each strike produced horrible crunching and squelching sounds. The hellhound tried to fight back. Its razor sharp claws raked across the demon's skin but he didn't feel it. "Don't." Ravin struck the beast. "You." He punched again. "Dare." Punch. "Touch." Punch.

"MICHELLE!" He raised both hands above his head and brought them down onto the monstrosity's skull.

The hellhound let a cry before it let out a final breath and slumped to the ground.

Slowly, the demon straightened and looked down at Michelle. His breath came in short bursts as he flicked the blood from his fingers. "Can you walk?" Somehow he kept his voice calm, despite the fact that he was soaked in blood, most of which was not his own.

Michelle held her arm and looked up at her savior, the demon. It took her a few seconds to get her mind settled enough to process what had happened. Ravin had kicked that beast's ass. He had saved her. She was a bit in awe, but mostly because of the bloodloss. Her bones were sore, but she wasn't going to let that stop her. She nodded and forced herself to climb to her feet. It was difficult, but she was determined.

Once up, the girl felt shaky. "Y-you saved me," she stuttered.

A cocky smile appeared on Ravin's face. "You bet your sweet ass I saved you."

In response, the human smiled tiredly. She was starting to feel light-headed.

The demon took her hand and then inspected her wounds. "We need to get you some place safe so that we can take care of this injury." It was bad, especially for a human. If they weren't careful, she could bleed out. "Think you can make it?"

"I can try," Michelle responded and began to limp towards

the water. The opening was on the other side. Swimming might be hard, but it almost sounded easier than walking. At least in the water, there wouldn't be so much weight on her bones. She was worried about the blood, though. She looked at him. "I can do it." There was no way she was going to let pain stop her. Not after they had come so far.

Michelle waded into the water and began to doggy paddle with all her might to the other side. The gross hellhound bite was throbbing, but the cool water soothed it ever so slightly. It leached away the burning sensation she had felt, numbing her skin.

As he crossed, Ravin kept a close eye on Michelle. He easily glided through the water beside her, keeping pace to ensure she stayed afloat. "Almost there," he encouraged. His eyes scanned every angle to ensure more of the hounds didn't attack.

"I got it," the human insisted as she slowly swam to the other bank. Once there, she pulled herself on her hands and knees out of the water. She forced herself onto her feet and limped until she was inside the cave-like opening. Panting, tired, and out of breath, Michelle gripped her shredded arm. As the chill wore off, it began to sting again.

"I got it," she repeated, leaning against the wall. It was refreshing to the touch. It was nice against her skin. Her eyes were clouded with pain. "Do you think Zier is okay?"

"I'm sure he's knee deep in dead hellhounds," Ravin remarked, watching the human carefully. He frowned and reached out a hand to touch her injured arm. "Michelle this is really bad." The man could almost feel the pain radiating off of her. "We have to do something about it."

Michelle nodded and winced as he touched near her wound. "Help me," was all she could say.

At her plea, Ravin set into action. He ripped off his shirt and tore off a long thin length. He tied it above the first wound and knotted it above the major blood vessels to lessen the blood flow. Then he neatly wrapped the rest of his torn-up shirt around the wounds. "Just breathe deeply and hold your arm above your heart," the demon advised in a soothing voice.

To help the girl, he lifted her arm up and rested it on his shoulder. "See, you're going to be fine." Ravin would not tell her how much blood she had lost. Her death seemed inevitable. Her face was pale with a greyish tint. The normally rosy blush that graced her cheeks had vanished. His human's normally cheerful face was full of gloom. Where her eyes had once sparkled, a tired gleam remained. A sad flutter filled Ravin's stomach. Everything he had ever seen in his life screamed at him. Of all the death and misery, he had lived through, why did he feel her death would be the hardest?

"Of course I will be," Michelle replied, her voice weighed down with exhaustion. Her more than fragile human body had reached its end. The hellhound had done wonders. The blood was stopped by the makeshift bandage, but it wouldn't hold it forever.

Gently, the demon swayed their hips in time with music he heard in his mind. He would distract her for as long as it took Zier to get there. This girl would cling to life for as long as possible; he would make sure that she did. "Can you imagine the look on Lia's face when we tell her that we saved the world? I bet it will be priceless."

The girl leaned on him as their bodies swayed in a tired dance. More than anything, the demon was a delightful crutch. Her wounds burned with a hell-fire of pain. Honestly, she wasn't sure if she could stand on her own. Luckily, Ravin held her weight. His warm skin clung to the girl's damp clothes.

"Especially since I'm such a wreck." A smile appeared on her face as she spoke. It was worn down and tired, but it was genuine. Drawing in a ragged breath, she continued, "It's because I have a great cast of sidekicks." A laugh tried to escape, but when it came to the surface, a cough took its place. As if the motion was filled with daggers, more pain splintered through her weak body. A near silent curse followed the spasms.

With great care the demon rubbed her back. "Just breathe," he whispered and squeezed his eyes shut. Despite the many skills he possessed, healing was not one he excelled at. "I like to think I'm a great sidekick. We should have more adventures."

Carefully, he cupped the back of her head so she couldn't look up and see the pain on his face. "There are so many things to see, there are the four Elvan Courts, the Vampire kingdoms, so many more places that you can't even imagine, Michelle. I can take you to see them all." His journeys had taken him to all those places and more. It would be his gift to this human to let her see all of them as well. "You like traveling, right?"

"I never really had the chance," she responded into his chest. "I bet it would be fun though." Anything sounded fun in comparison to their current situation. Being close like this was nice. It didn't quite make her forget about the fact her arm had been made into ground beef, but it helped dull the pain. She knew once all of the adrenaline was out of her system, she wouldn't be able to bear the agony.

Ravin gently eased them onto the floor to sit. He placed her on his lap and held her carefully. With supple fingers, he stroked her hair in a comforting gesture. "Well then I'll show you absolutely everything that I can. No matter how much time it takes." He looked into her blue eyes and offered a confident smile in the hopes that she wouldn't see through it.

The girl was tired and leaned on him as they sat. He was a nice warm chair. Her body was losing heat. Michelle cuddled close and shivered.

Soft, warm energy pulsed around them. Again he rubbed her skin. "That was some cold water. You're doing so well," he murmured.

"I'm surprised I'm not d-dying from hypothermia," she said, jaw jittering from the chill. "Bet you've never seen such a resilient human." It was almost scary to think how fast her life could have been over. It was easier to laugh about it, or try to. Blood loss, hypothermia, becoming doggy dinner: all were excellent ways of biting the dust. Michelle prided herself on not kicking the bucket in any of those ways. As shitty as she was feeling, at least she still had the ability to experience it. The alternative was death.

He shook his head. "You're probably the most resilient human I will ever know," he chuckled quietly. For a moment he stared into her eyes. Unable to help himself, the demon pressed his lips against Michelle's.

For one peaceful moment, the worlds and the problems in them could be forgotten. Ravin worked his magic to ease her mind and bring them even closer. He did not want her to ever forget this, no matter how long she had left. Her soft lips yielded to his and sparked their own unique touch that ignited between them.

"Are you serious?" Zier's voice echoed around them, breaking the magic. "I've been fighting off a horde of evil demon dogs, and you're sitting here making out? Seriously?" he demanded and strode over to them. There wasn't a single mark on his body, nor was there a hair out of place on his head.

"To be fair," Michelle shot, looking up, a weak smile appearing on her face. She was glad to see him alive and well. "I totally got my ass handed to me." She gestured to her wrapped up arm. Already, blood was starting to seep through her demon-made bandage. It hurt to move it too much. Despite the chill that was biting into her skin, she felt warm inside.

Ravin smiled up at Zier. "I was helping her with the healing process," he explained and gently helped Michelle to her feet. "Everyone knows that kissing is a cure-all."

The fallen angel rolled his eyes. "Well whatever you were doing, you need to stop." Zier crossed his arms. "We need to go, you're wasting time." Impatience flashed in his dark eyes.

"Just waiting for you, pretty boy," Michelle stated and turned to look down the dark tunnel ahead of them.

Zier put a hand on her shoulder. Cool, healing energy trickled along her skin, and accelerated the healing of her wounds. He could feel the plane had begun to sap his angelic abilities as well.

A look of determination appeared on Michelle's face and she began to limp off towards their destiny. Body aching and spirit high, she was ready to face anything. Or maybe it was the adrenaline. Whatever it was, she held her head high and her arm a little higher.

Before them, death awaited, and the only fate worse than dying was failing.

Thirty-two

Darkness thicker than the blackest night swallowed the trio. They were greeted by corridors winding like the twisting intestines of a massive beast. Zier lead the way. His fingertips brushed the textured wall to ensure he had some sense of whether or not they were about to charge into one of the unyielding barriers.

"Can't you do something about this Zier?" Ravin shot as he tripped over his fifth rock. "I'm sick of flying blind." He was less worried about himself and more concerned with the human who was in a much worse state than himself. He shifted and made sure his grip on the girl was still holding strong. His fingers twined with hers and he offered a smile in her general direction, despite the fact that she couldn't see it.

A faint light appeared in Zier's palm; he lifted the sphere above his head and let the white orb illuminate their path. "That good enough for you?" he returned over his shoulder. For a moment, he looked back at them. During that briefest of seconds he seemed to age several decades. However, the mirage was gone in a blink and he turned the other way.

"It'll work," Ravin shrugged. "I thought someone like you could do so much better." The quip came out unbidden, but he decided to own it.

The fallen angel rolled his eyes. "You know as well as I that it's still more than you can do given the circumstances." Zier led them down another passageway that would have gone unnoticed if not for the light.

"Hey, I can make things kind of warm!" The demon snapped proudly and sped up a tiny bit; at least, as much as his human anchor would allow him to. Their speed increased for about ten seconds before it slowed back down. He bit back a curse and continued at a pace Michelle could handle.

"Oh yes, that's going to do so very much for our cause," Zier chuckled. "I'll let you know if it gets too nippy for me."

Under his breath Ravin muttered, "I'll nip you and you won't like it." That brought a weak giggle from his anchor.

"How do you even know we're going the right way?" Michelle questioned, more curious than anything. From what she could tell, they were moving randomly through the maze. She was feeling exhausted now that her steam was running low; she wanted to be sure they were going the right direction.

"I can feel her calling me. She is not fully free yet, but I can feel her more strongly than I have in more years than you could begin to comprehend." The frown was clear in his tone. Frantic energy poured through the halls, most of it originating from their leader. "She's still so far." The strain was clear, as he gripped the wall tightly and looked back at his companions. Fierce determination burned in his visage.

"We're doing what we can Zier." The demon did the best he could to sound sympathetic to Michelle's cause. Yes, she was resilient, but this was so much bigger than any of them individually.

He couldn't look down at the blood soaked bandage that covered Michelle's arm. If this situation wasn't so dire, then he would have demanded they go back immediately. Saving the world had priority, no matter how hard it was. More than this human would perish should they fail.

"You don't understand what this means." Zier slowed his pace, but his sense of urgency did not fade. "You couldn't possibly."

Ravin scowled. "You've talked about her a lot, and to be honest, you've been nothing but vague. Sure you told us that she was controlled, but who is she? What is your connection? I can tell she means a lot to you." He would do anything to distract their leader, Zier walked slower when he was talking. If perhaps he was diverted by conversation, then maybe they could keep moving forward at a pace that Michelle could handle.

At once, Zier's shoulders went back and his posture grew rigid. "She is everything to me." There was so much pain in his voice. "You couldn't possibly comprehend. Neither of you have ever experienced love as I have. You care for your families, for your friends, but you have never done anything close to what I have for love." His whole body sagged almost imperceptibly, yet Ravin's keen eyes caught it.

"So wait, is she the reason you..." The demon was cut off by the fallen angel's raised hand.

"Stay," Zier ordered and left the ball of light behind with the others. The fallen angel eased forward and around a previously unnoticed bend.

"What do you make of this guy Michelle?" Ravin asked in a low whisper. "I know it's too late to be asking, but he's giving me some mixed signals. Do you really think he's going to let Lian ease into the whole dark angel thing?"

"Don't really have a choice…" Michelle sighed. "I really hope he's on our side, or even Lian's." She looked down but couldn't even see the floor in the darkness, despite the light. While they waited, the human took the opportunity to rest. Her bones were aching; her mauled arm was screaming. It felt better after Zier had patched it up, but the pain wasn't erased. If she didn't absolutely have to go on, she would have stopped by now. She shifted her weight as she leaned against the cool stone wall. "Sorry I'm so slow. I know it's driving you two crazy," her voice trailed off.

Ravin shook his head. "Don't be sorry, it's not your fault," he soothed and helped her hold up her arm. "We're not going to play the blame game. We could spend the whole day doing that, and my name would be on the top of the list. For now, we have to figure out how to make sure that we save the world, and hope that our guide doesn't turn on us."

"Yeah…" the girl sagged against the wall. "I think we'll be okay." Or at least that's what she hoped. More than anything.

"You both talk too loud," Zier hissed from over Ravin's right shoulder.

The demon almost jumped out of his skin. He was at a loss for words. It took all of his energy to hold in a sound of surprise. The hairs on the back of his neck stood up.

"That's my bad," he whispered and did his best to slow his suddenly racing heart.

"If it makes you feel better," Michelle spoke up quietly, "I only said nice things."

Zier rolled his eyes, and in a hushed voice sighed, "I don't care what you two think of me. I know my intentions are pure and that's all that matters." The angel looked back the same way he had come. "There's also the small matter of the demonic patrols that we've managed to dodge so far. They will not be nice when they catch us."

"We can't sneak around when one of us is injured like this." Ravin's heart raced again; they could be caught at any moment if they weren't careful enough. There was no way Michelle would survive that. All she needed was more brutal wounds to add to her collection.

"So what do we do?" Michelle asked the fallen angel. "I'm pretty useless." She shrugged. Useless and mortal. Her life was turning out to be lots of fun.

The fallen angel closed his eyes and thought for a moment. He looked like he was about to say something but held it back. With a shake of his head he turned away. "I don't know." The admission was clearly difficult for him.

"How about you kill anything we run into?" Ravin offered and held out a hand out to Michelle so they could begin moving again.

It didn't take long for his companion reach out and take it.

"And if I get eaten alive," Michelle commented, "It will be a casualty of war." She sighed theatrically, more trying to lighten their spirits than anything. The girl offered up a smile. The tension was so thick, she could have drowned in it. Despite the intense pain she was in, she was a firm believer that laughter was the best medicine. Tiredly, Michelle leaned on her man-crutch for support. He was nicely warm. It was in all a win-win for her. Then again, maybe the loss of blood was starting to get to her head. "But having the big scary fallen angel blitzkrieging into the enemy lines sounds like fun."

Zier nodded. "I will do what I can, but you have to stay close." He eased through the hall again.

As they wandered down the path, cool air surrounded them. The silence was nearly deafening. Michelle could feel her thoughts growing loud with anxiety. She looked around, knowing that in a place like this, her thoughts could prove to be dangerous. With a long breath, the girl tried to distract herself. She looked up at the Fallen. In a very quiet voice, Michelle asked him, "What happened with the dark angels? I want to know more about her."

"You know already," Zier muttered back, his free hand clenched into a tight fist at his side. His strange eyes scanned for other paths, or for any of the creatures that could swoop in at any moment.

"Tell me more," Michelle urged.

Their guide remained silent for a long moment before sighing. "Honestly, she is the single most beautiful creature I have ever laid eyes upon." He lifted a hand to his heart as he continued, "She is grace and perfection, but also the last of her kind. The angels couldn't control the dark angels so they exterminated them. Dark angel isn't even their true name, they changed it to vilify them."

"What was their original name?" Michelle wondered aloud, letting her thoughts roll from her tongue in a quiet controlled manner. It seemed like a better option than having them flying out randomly. Her mind wasn't protected from others like her male companions were.

"They were the Angels of Night." Sorrow clouded Zier's tone. "There was nothing to do to stop the genocide."

Michelle shifted uneasily. The thought of an angel-brought massacre didn't sit well in her stomach. Carefully she touched the mark on her back. What if her angel was…? The girl's tired blue eyes looked down at the ground she couldn't see. "So, they really aren't all sunshine and rainbows?" This scared her a bit.

"Angels of the Light are as varied in personality as any other species. They're capable of hate, betrayal, and prejudice as much as any other." In that moment, the ball of light flared blindingly. It slowly faded back to its normal brilliance. There was something undeniably dark in the fallen angel's eye. "And they have a habit of letting everyone know," he added through clenched teeth.

"Their extreme dislike of demons is a prime example." Ravin's tail twitched. There was a distinct smirk on his lips.

"You don't even know the half of it." Zier clearly was restraining himself. However, he froze and turned his head, scanning slowly for sound. "Silence, I feel something." The light winked out.

The group fell quiet; heavy breathing filled the tunnel. However, it was almost impossible to discern which direction it was coming from. Heavy, thumping footsteps made the floor shake below them. None dared breathe. The tunnels trembled, but then fell still again. "What the Hell was that?!" Ravin hissed under his breath.

"I have a feeling we're about to find out." Michelle whimpered with dread as they continued moving forward.

Around them, the tunnel widened for the first time in ages. The ceiling expanded and the walls broadened. In the dim light, they could barely make out three massive beings that stood in the middle of the cavern. Each one had milky eyes that did not focus on the intruders. Giant gnarled hands clutched knobbed clubs.

Zier held out his hand to stop Ravin from advancing. "I will take care of this." He left the renewed light behind with the demon and human then strode towards the giants.

Sound caught the monster's attention; they began lumbering towards Zier.

With very little effort, Zier jumped into the air and landed a heavy kick into the closest creature's chest. It flew back and slammed into the wall. A series of sickening sounds filled the air that made even the demon's stomach turn.

Ravin moved Michelle so she couldn't see. "This is going to get ugly," he whispered and knelt down so she wouldn't have to support herself too much.

A horrid bellow of agony caught the demon's attention and before his eyes, another creature went flying across the cavern. However, it was missing an arm. The third already lay in a heap on the very edge of the light's reach. The coppery tang of blood filled the air.

In a matter of moments, the barriers blocking them were gone. "Come on," Zier called from across the cave.

Gingerly, Ravin assisted Michelle to her feet again. He tried to hide the pain in his eyes. Her skin was ashen. It took a great deal of effort to keep his gaze from the wounds that littered her arm. Michelle's ragged breaths told him she didn't have much more in her.

A fire burned inside the Fallen's peculiar lime green eyes. Something about that scorching was muted, like it was only a glimpse into the rage that lived inside this being. If those mangled corpses were a taste of ire, then Ravin did not want to see him truly angry.

Once they were within a few feet of Zier, he took off at a breakneck speed again. It only took a seconds for Michelle to run out of steam. Her feet tangled and she would have sprawled on the ground if not for her demonic crutch.

"Zier we need to stop," Ravin called, all concern about volume level thrown to the winds.

Michelle collapsed against the wall. Her fingers grasped at the rough stone. Her entire body trembled against its cool surface. As much as her spirit wanted to go on, her flesh was weak. So for a long moment, she enjoyed the refreshing coolness. It didn't relieve the exhaustion, but it did force the pain to ebb ever so slightly. Michelle was at her limit. Bones crying out, she couldn't pick herself up from the wall's surface. There was no way she could keep up with fallen angel and his swift feet.

"Damnit," she cursed and leaned her head on the wall.

"You should have stayed home. We could have found a way

here without you," Ravin whispered in a wounded tone. He couldn't fully process the difficult fact that he was watching her die. There was a pain in his heart that he had never felt before. It was as though what was left of his soul was being ripped to shreds. He had no word for what this emotion was, but he knew he hated it. "Why couldn't you stay back in your dorm?" Ravin's voice broke as he squeezed his eyes shut.

"You know I'm a glutton for punishment." She coughed, and looked over at the demon. "Plus, I didn't want to miss out on all this fun." Her hand rubbed against the rugged figure of the wall, but she paused as the texture changed. A smooth groove twisted and turned as her touch traced it. What was this? The girl couldn't see it, even with the small light. The cave's wall was dark, darker than night. It absorbed the light. She blinked.

"Also," Michelle breathed, a bit of energy returning to her voice. "I found something. Score one for the human." The girl reached out and grabbed Ravin's hand. Weakly, she pulled him to touch the strange, unnaturally smooth grooves in the wall.

Ravin indulged Michelle and felt what she was trying to show him. Shock shot through him. "You're right!" He felt each indent delicately. "This... this could be huge. Zier!"

In a blink, Zier was beside them. He looked over at the human. "That's why I brought you." The angel winked and closed his eyes. He felt out the divots and placed his fingers inside. Tense breathless moments passed, but nothing happened. "I don't understand," the fallen angel frowned.

"Let me try. It could need a demon's touch." Ravin pushed Zier's hand out of the way and slid his palm along the grooves.

He took a deep breath in and released a spark of energy. When the air left his lungs, the panel rumbled. Soft light cascaded inside the furrows. Like water, brightness rolled across the surface. Long scrawling swirls danced across the indents of the cave wall, illuminating the cavern. They were every color of the auroras in the night sky. A portion of the wall beside Michelle dropped away.

Like a playful spirit, the light swirled for a moment then arched down the newly opened passage, illuminating the floor. In the world of darkness, it was a pathway of hope. Despite this miracle, Zier glanced down at the demon. "How did you know to do that?" Dubious energy rolled off of him in waves.

The man's question went unanswered, as Ravin's face went blank. He released his anchor and started moving slowly down the path, without looking back.

"So close," the demon murmured in a voice not his own, blindly following the light.

Silently, Michelle stared at Ravin as he moved away from her. Utterly exhausted, her only crutch was the wall. What was up with that? He was a husk of his former self. Something felt off and she matched Zier's gaze with her own confused eyes. What was going on? Whatever it was it wasn't right.

"Ravin?" she questioned, breaths escaping in patchy bursts.

"I think he's leaving us behind." Zier wrapped an arm under her shoulder on her injured side. "Something isn't right, but I don't think we have a choice in the matter." He did his best to be a good crutch.

Led by the light and their suddenly possessed demon, the journey was less agonizing. Michelle was thankful for the slight reduction in stress that the light granted.

Again the tunnel began widening, and the light started dwindling. Crackling energy greeted them. Static raised the small hairs on their bodies. Acrid scents filled the air. While the light below them disappeared a new, harsh light appeared at the end of the tunnel.

Another solid wall blocked their way, but the light swirled around it as though trying to communicate. Ravin's fingers danced upon the surface, searching for the way to open the portal. He felt around until they slipped inside an almost unnoticeable crack. The panel groaned before coming to life; it shuddered and sunk into the floor.

Before them was a very small room. Ravin moved inside it and started feeling around.

Zier pulled Michelle along into the room. When Ravin found what he was looking for, the room illuminated—then the floor shot straight up as if they were in an elevator made of stone. When they reached the top of the shaft, they halted in a large room.

The sight before them made Michelle's blood run cold.

Lian and Kazun lay side by side, almost naked on a sacrificial tablet. Marks covered their skin that were indecipherable from a distance. A single man stood watching over them, pale grey eyes glittering in sadistic glee. The demon looked up and ran a hand over the thick horns that arched back over his head.

"It's so nice of you all to finally join us," Ira purred.

Thirty-Three

Michelle stared at her sister on the slab, eyes wide and mouth agape. If Michelle's body was any more than a painful husk, she would have charged forward to Lian. Well, that and the fallen angel's grasped her arm. More than anything, Mischa wanted to break from his hand and run to Lian. The girl was all but naked, as was the boy. Were they okay? From where she stood, the human couldn't tell if either Lia and Kaz were breathing. She couldn't force herself to think they were dead. They couldn't be.

"Lian!" Michelle cried out and she looked up at Zier. "Are they okay?" Her voice was a pathetic plea, but she had run out of pride. All that mattered was whether or not her baby sister was alive.

The fallen angel nodded. "I can feel their heart beats."

Ira's eyes shone with a dark inner glow. "For now," he added.

"I was wondering when you would finally arrive. However, you're not necessary, I already have all the sacrifices I need." His fingers drifted over Kazun's bared chest.

In that moment, Ravin joined them again, shaking his head to clear it. "Don't you touch him," he snapped and lurched forward threateningly. "Why the Hell are you doing this?!" The demand echoed around the room until it faded into nothing. Each reverberation made the demon sound weaker and more pathetic.

A smirk touched their enemy's lips. "You think you have any right to make demands, Ravin?" He leaned forward and continued, "The fool who has no idea who I am despite absolutely everything that we went through together?" He slammed a fist into the dark stone that held the two humans. "No, you have no right to even speak in front of me, not after what you did."

"What are you talking about?" Ravin demanded, his expression baffled. "I don't even know who you are!" What did this other demon know about himself that he did not? There was nothing in his mind before Equilibrium. The first memory he had was Sin finding him in a field. Before that? Not a shred.

Ira snorted. "Of course you don't know. It's not as if we fought beside each other for years during our brief stint of humanity. We never risked our lives to defend the other whom we considered a brother. It isn't like I took care of you after the worst moment in your life." His lip raised in a snarl then snapped, "Oh wait, that did happen."

The soul crushing sadness inside of Ravin was quickly replaced by a hollow fear. "You're lying. The bar was the first time I'd ever seen you."

"Stop listening to him, he's trying to buy time," Zier growled and shifted Michelle. Every muscle in his body was tense and ready to leap at a moment's notice. "You must keep fighting him, Fenriel," he shouted above the other men's voices.

A violent jerk of Ira's wrist sent the fallen angel flying across the room. "Don't interrupt, angel." His voice was the deadly calm before the storm. "I thought they taught you better manners in Heaven." He all but spat the words. "Speak out again and I may have to end your existence myself." The gleam in his eye gave no doubt that he would absolutely do his best to keep that particular promise.

While Ira was distracted, Ravin made a dive for his human friends. His feet flew over the inky black floor. One of his hands reached to grab onto Kazun, to shake him awake, anything. A powerful grip wrapped around his tail and pulled violently. It was impossible to prevent the scream of agony that tore from his throat. White hot pain seared through his spine, but was quickly replaced by the widespread ache resulting from a full force impact with the unforgiving ground.

"Nobody said you could move Ravin." The heel of Ira's boot pressed into his diaphragm. "I wasn't done talking, you bastard."

The weaker demon struggled to think through the burning wall of pain. "W-Why are you doing all of this?" he demanded before a ragged cough tore through his chest. He glared up at his enemy with hatred in his eyes.

"I suppose her gift to you was not remembering," Ira half snarled.

Confusion scraped at the edges of his mind, where it could

break through the enveloping agony. "What the Hell are you talking about?" The words tore painfully from his throat.

"She took the memories from you as you ripped out her still-beating heart. In hindsight, it's more of a gift to me." He ground his foot into Ravin's chest. "I know exactly what happened, I know what you've done, and it's given me the time to finally realize her vision after so many years."

"Who is *she?*" Ravin demanded with the strongest voice he could muster.

"Nara. Our creator, the woman who made us. She who gifted us with this demonic nature and freed us from the bonds of mortality."

Ravin felt his heart thump painfully in his chest. Instinctive fear and rage took hold in his heart at the mention of this woman he couldn't recall. "You're lying," he snapped. "We would have some kind of bond. You could have found me and killed me at any moment if this was true at all."

"Our bond was severed when you killed her. You waited like the coward you truly are until she had sent me half way across the world for our mission, then you murdered the woman who had never asked *anything* of you." Burning energy swept over the weaker demon's body. "When I felt you again at the roller rink I knew that fate had given me the greatest gift. My precious corrupted Marked, and my most hated enemy in the same place: it was too good to be true. To make things even better, you're the fool who angered the reigning King of Hell. You really are the worst demon," Ira sneered; triumph snuck into his tone.

"Shut your fucking mouth." Ravin tried to access the energy

repressed within him, but it was no use. He was utterly defenseless.

"You were once attuned to this place, Ravin," Ira smirked. With a flick of his head, Ravin flew across the room to the wall opposite the fallen angel. "You never learn, that's why she left this place to me."

The wind rushed from Ravin's lungs as he slammed into the wall. Once he regained his wits, he snarled, "What is the point of all of this?" His body throbbed agonizingly, but he kept himself from crying out by thinking about what Michelle must have been going through.

"Control, power, the utter destruction of Heaven, and anything that could be imagined. All things will be attainable through Fenriel's freedom." Ira's eyes focused on some distant point beyond anyone else's vision. "As she always dreamed," he added in a quiet, reverent voice.

"You can't do this," Ravin cried.

"Actually, I already am." This time, Ira turned his devilish gaze over to Michelle. "It's a shame you can't move. If you were actually as useful as I was telling Lian, you would have been able to do something helpful by now. Too bad, it seems you have made me a liar."

Michelle trembled where she stood, without a crutch. It was a miracle her legs hadn't already given out. Her bones were screaming and she knew it wouldn't be long. Her eyes cast a wary glance at Ravin. She muttered beneath her breath, "Shame on me."

"Shame on you, indeed." In a few quick steps, Ira was behind the tablet again with his hand on Lian's stomach. "Your pain will end soon, if Fenriel is feeling merciful... if I allow her to feel mercy." That elicited a snarl from Zier, but Ira paid him no mind. "Perhaps begging might do the trick, human."

As if her legs were feeling the dramatic irony, Michelle fell forward, her bones unable to carry her weight any longer. She was stuck in a bowing position. Cheeks burning hot with frustration and anger, the girl twisted her glare towards the monster. Her dull blue eyes were smoldering dark pits. She gritted her teeth and refrained from speaking. Michelle was determined to not give him any more satisfaction. She tried to force herself back into a standing position.

Despite the pain that burned in her every movement, Michelle managed her best. She stood, but not tall or proud. She felt crippled and weak. A puff of air could probably knock her over, and before her was the big bad wolf. The girl had no doubt that he would huff and puff and rip her spleen out. He seemed like that kind of a guy. Wordlessly, Michelle tapped her two index fingers together in a cross like motion. The rude gesture was all she could muster. Her breaths were short, ragged, and betrayed her weakness.

A smirk came to Ira's lips. "If only you had the energy." He laughed darkly. "I'm afraid you'd likely die if I took you up on that." The man opened his mouth to speak again, but was cut off abruptly by Ravin.

"Don't you dare talk to Michelle like that," he bellowed while fighting against the powerful, invisible force that held him pinned without escape. Rage burned in his eyes like an unquenchable fire.

"Don't interrupt, Ravin." Absently Ira sent a bolt of energy straight at his captive. It struck the man in the head and slammed it against the hard stone wall.

Something about the combination of head trauma and Ira's energy dislodged a piece of something inside of Ravin's brain. A spark lit up in his mind, and a name came to his lips, "Iraldin?"

Where it had come from he did not know. However, the name itself conjured vivid images of another lifetime that flashed in his mind, one after another, but nothing could quite stick. All that was left was the impression that this man had left on him in a time long past. "We were… friends?"

Iraldin stopped what he was doing and looked up at Ravin. "Yes, we were. Until you betrayed me." He turned his attention completely away from the humans and started muttering under his breath. Slowly he stalked up to Ravin and placed a hand on the center of Ravin's chest. Hot energy scalded Ravin's body for a brief moment before everything became a hazy blur. It felt as though his mind was shrouded in a dense fog that he could not shake. He could feel his muscles move, but could not begin to fully comprehend what he was doing.

"Try and fight me now," Iraldin whispered in a low tone.

At once, the demon's body dropped to the ground. Trying to get back to his feet was an impossible struggle. No matter how hard Ravin focused on an action, it felt unmanageable.

'We were once inseparable, yet you chose to throw it all away. You can be forgiven if you join me.' Each seductive word was etched into Ravin's foggy mind. *'Anything you want would be within your reach. All you have to do is follow my instructions.'*

He knew this was wrong. Ira was… bad, yes. That was it. Not

good. Evil. Trying to ruin everything. Each word floundered in an ocean of thick impenetrable pudding that wrapped around his brain and held all but Ira's voice back.

'Anything I want?' That thought alone was allowed to escape from his own mind, because it was what the other wanted to hear.

'Anything, Ravin. Would I lie to you?' Iraldin pushed inside Ravin's mind. The demon was unable to respond. He couldn't fathom an answer. However, one was given to him. *'Of course I wouldn't.'*

'How?' The question bobbed on top of the murky ocean waves in Ravin's mind.

'To free Fenriel, you must eliminate the one thing that stands in your path,' Ira coaxed suavely. Every moment, he could feel Ravin drawn further and further into his web of control.

'I will do anything.' The mental declaration did not feel like his own words, but he was incapable of fighting the urges. Infinite possibilities were beyond his grasp, and there was only one thing he had to do. This was *necessary.* He felt his head rise, as though he was experiencing it from some place other than his own body.

One of Ira's arms was outstretched, a single finger pointed to the girl standing on shaking legs. Ravin's eyes couldn't process her features. However, he knew what he had to do.

Ravin's fingers curled; he felt something in his palm. A knife? Where had it come from? It wasn't important. It had to strike home. He was standing, though he had never given his legs the order. Energy pulsed through his body in ways he couldn't begin to remember.

In a blink, Ravin was behind this girl. He wrapped an arm

around her waist. She didn't fight. The demon leaned over and whispered in her ear, "Everything is going to be okay."

As the last word left his mouth, he felt the dagger slip into her spine and hot blood spill out over his hands. The girl let out a gurgling choke as her last breath was wrenched from her lungs. In less than a minute, the light went out in her eyes. With a twist of his arm, the weapon pulled free. The grinding of steel against bone sliced through the fog.

Everything became clear as Michelle's body fell limp against his chest. Her warm blood gushed out onto him. Terror filled his heart.

"No!" he cried desperately. The blade clattered to the ground as he threw his arms around her lifeless body. "No, Michelle I didn't—!! I didn't mean to!"

He knew she could no longer hear him though. Despite every effort the demon had made, Michelle had met her death by his hand.

Thirty-Four

The fires of Hell were torn away from her and Michelle felt peace. There was no pain. Anywhere. Missing were the familiar ache of her bones, the new-found burning of her spine, and the injury on her arm. All she remembered from before was the white-hot pain of the dagger. Everything had happened so fast…. She had been quite literally and figuratively stabbed in the back. When she opened her eyes, it all made sense.

"Of course," she sighed and tipped her head back, looking around.

She was in a very large, very old chapel. Huge stones formed the walls, and each window was lined with glass that came in every color. Light filtered in serenely. The benches were white and they seemed to go on forever in front of her on either side of an aisle that was covered by a pristine red carpet. She gazed upon the sanctuary. Where she had expected a crucifix and an altar, a grand pipe organ sat. Its old styled, yet perfectly maintained body stood proudly. She looked up, following its skeleton as it stretched into eternity.

Carefully, Michelle approached the grand instrument. Her fingers touched the keys gently, too softly for them to produce any sound. The white bones of the organ were highly ornamented. Inscribed on them were symbols she could not even begin to understand. However, as she looked over them, a soft song played in her mind. It was as old and serene as the chapel that surrounded her.

Was this really what Heaven was like?

Michelle tried to feel sad; she had left her friends and family. The emotion simply wouldn't come to her. In this place of quite literal perfection, was there even such a thing as sorrow? Peace filled her heart and soul. There was no pain nor anguish. Simply light.

"Welcome to the Hall of Echoes." A transcendent beautiful voice reverberated through the chapel. Michelle turned to see a figure standing far, far away down the endless rows of church benches. Soft light surrounded him; around his head it shone the brightest. Suddenly, the human understood from where the symbolic halo originated.

"So this is Heaven?" Michelle asked, "And I'm dead? Aren't I?"

Her company chuckled warmly. His steps were slow and full of grace as he approached. When he was closer, Michelle couldn't help but stare. She probably looked like a slack-jawed idiot, but she couldn't help herself. No one could blame her for admiring the Angel's quite literal perfection. He was built like a Greek statue. Honey colored hair curled in handsome ringlets on top of his head. There were no faults on any part of his visible body. This man, no, angel, easily shamed a photoshopped super model.

"This is a part of Heaven. And no, you are not quite dead," he responded in his glorious melodious sweet voice as he approached. Michelle had to tilt her head up to look him in his soft swirling honey eyes as he stood before her. Michelle felt like a little high school student, gawking at the pretty boy. Not that it was her fault. The guy was an Angel: the beige dove wings and the bright halo around his head explained that much. He was gorgeous and it wasn't fair. His words should have left some impact on her and yet, she couldn't even feel scared about it. How could she? If the afterlife was filled with men like him, maybe being dead wasn't a bad thing.

Her back began to burn in the spot where her tattoo sat… the place where the demon had stabbed her. It took a moment, and then the pain ebbed away into nothingness.

"You're my angel?" Michelle questioned.

The male replied with a warm loving smile. He nodded his head and took the girl's hand carefully in his own. With petal soft lips, he kissed her skin. A velvety feeling washed over her body. Whatever worries had been there trickled away. Slowly, he tilted his head up in the most graceful and controlled manner.

"My name is Loviel," he explained, his voice tender. "I watch over the Hall of Echoes, where all song is made. You are my partner, and I am ever so gladdened to meet you, Michelle Neilson. I have long awaited this moment. I am sorry it had to come at such a cost."

Michelle carefully pulled her hand away and rubbed at the skin he had kissed. So that was one question answered, though there were many more left. How had she gotten here? Could she go back? Was Lian going to be okay? The final question was the most important. The last thing she remembered was the pain. She remembered being so scared of the one person in all the world she had come to trust. Michelle hadn't even seen it coming. Her 'death' had taken but only a moment. Quietly, and uncharacteristically shyly, Michelle asked, "You're going to help me, right?"

It was hard to have a lot of confidence after everything that had happened. The fact was, Loviel was her only chance to get back into the fight. Without him, she would be dead in a pool of her own blood. She would never know if Lian or Kazun made it out safely. What would happen to Zier… and Ravin? Michelle needed Loviel's help; she couldn't go back on her own.

"I am here to aid you however necessary," Loviel said, his words a song unto themselves. Michelle felt herself smiling. The angel spread out his strong yet soft looking wings, and he continued to speak. "But, there are matters to take care of first, Michelle." His tone was like that of an older brother, authoritative yet loving.

"Go on?" Michelle questioned looking up at the beautiful male before her. So far there was none of the genocide Zier had mentioned. That was a distinct plus. Ravin had mentioned there were different sects of heaven. So far, her angel didn't appear to come from the dickish variety.

The male gestured down the endless aisle and then began to walk down the infinite red carpet. His every step was fluid with an unfathomable smoothness. Michelle watched him walk for a long moment. Slowly, he turned and observed her with questioning eyes

Feeling compelled, Michelle began to follow him. Their steps rolled in unison and a strangely serene silence surrounded them. For once, the girl didn't mind the quiet. She didn't feel obliged to fill it with talk. Together they walked and walked. Time was strange where they were. Moments passed that felt like hours and yet like seconds. Then again, what could be expected of a place such as Heaven? It didn't have to follow the same rules that Eartha did.

Michelle closed her eyes for a long moment, and when she opened them, the cathedral had disappeared and all around them was a garden. Bright flowers danced in a soft wind of serenity. It was a bright clearing of vivid colors Michelle wasn't even sure she had seen before. In the very center of the garden was a fountain where crystal clear water spouted up and glittered in the light. If Michelle had been the breathing type, her breath would have been taken away.

"Eden," Loviel answered before Michelle could even form the question in her mind. Slowly he moved over to the fountain and sat on its stone ledge.

Michelle followed suit and placed herself beside him. Together they listened to the sound of the fountain. Together they sat in silence.

Again, the angel broke the reverie. "Michelle, I know your people look to angels as miracle workers, and some of us are. I will help you however I can, but I cannot do everything. On Eartha, with no link, I am weak. Without you, I am no more than a mere mortal." He sighed. "I cannot promise you I can heal the wound that originates in your deepest being, but…"

"Wait, what?" Michelle piped up, feeling a bit less on edge now that he had shown her a bit of his own imperfection. Wait, did she even have extreme emotions up here? Now was probably not the best time to wonder. She had to keep focused. Well, as focused as she could, all things considered. Basically, from what she had gathered, Loviel couldn't fix her bones.

"I'm going to die because I'm made of glass," she stated, her tone bitter. "What does it matter if you bring me back?"

Loviel gave her a confused look, as if, he had never expected such words to come from her mouth.

"Michelle," he spoke, his voice stern, "There is a real danger, one only you and I can face. Perhaps I cannot grant you eternal life, but I can give you a while. I can give you the time you need to tie up loose ends. So you can see your sister smile. Time so you can say goodbye. You have been so scared of the nightmare of dying, you haven't given yourself the chance to dream."

"If you can't heal me, how can we stop Iraldin? Ravin sort of severed my spine," Michelle accused. "How can you beat him?"

The angel sighed and closed his eyes. "Together, we have a great deal of power. Together, we can defeat this demon, and together, I will bring you back to life, for as long as I am able. I promise this to you, Mischa, but you have to trust me."

Michelle looked up and stared into his eyes. "What about… Ravin?" The last word barely shuddered out of her lips. She was having a hard time remembering all that had happened before he had stabbed her. What they had shared had meant so much. At least, she had thought it had. Michelle didn't give her trust so easily. Through the trials they faced, through what they shared, she had let her guard down.

Pain tried to fight its way through the perfection around it. It wanted to pierce the veil. A warm hand rested on Michelle's shoulder, the same one the hellhound had torn apart. In this place, her skin had no mark.

"He did not do this to you of his own will. He is not a bad man," the angel said, reassuring her. "I can feel that despite being here, you mourn for what he did. We both know it wasn't the Ravin you knew." The angel shook his head side to side, his gaze far off in the clouds. He was right, of course. Michelle knew deep down, that it hadn't been Ravin's choice. It was all Iraldin's fault. It was his fault for everything. Knowing this still didn't stop the hurt.

In all honesty, Michelle was scared.

Carefully, she leaned her head onto Loviel's shoulder and sought comfort. His hand brought her closer as her tears began to erupt. More than anything, Michelle didn't want to appear weak, but how could she be strong? At the moment, she was in a limbo between life and death. She had to rely on someone to bring her back. She had to rely on someone to save her sister. She had given her trust to the demon. She had let him be her crutch. Never before had she allowed that of anyone. If she was going to stand, it was going to have to be of her own doing.

Because of everything that had been happening, Michelle had lost her self-sufficiency. Maybe it was when Iraldin stole her sister.

Or, perhaps it had been washed away when her bones gave her that painful reminder of her imminent death. Then again, it was possible that the hellhound had ripped apart more than her flesh.

Maybe it was the act of betrayal.

Michelle didn't trust the Light in her life. Everything good ended, so why shouldn't her life? Why did she have to be the one to save the world when she couldn't even save herself? Hers was a painful existence. Every moment, she was reminded how useless her attempts had been. Death was at her door, knocking loudly. Why didn't she let herself fade away? Hadn't she earned it?

What if she failed Lian for a third time? Her body trembled as the tears flowed harder.

"It is okay, Michelle," Loviel soothed. "Together, we will make this right. I need you and I cannot save your sister on my own. I cannot stop this demon from harming her, or Kazun. I cannot stop him from summoning Fenriel, or from killing Ravin and Zier." He turned and faced her, eyes serious yet still with the same gentle glow.

"Don't think because your body isn't powerful that you aren't," He continued. "The life you have still in you…" He paused as if he was composing his thoughts. A simple yet striking smile appeared on his heavenly perfect face. Softly, he took her hand in his own. He looked down at her for a long moment. "Michelle, strength comes from where you least expect it. One day, you will be surprised by what others can do for you, and what you can do for others. Allow your heart to open, and allow us to be partners in the purest sense."

Her hand gripped his in silent reply. He continued on, spreading out his beautiful beige wings.

"Be the hero of your own story Michelle," he said. "Today, together, let's give victory to the good guys." His honey eyes lightened with love. Something switched on inside the girl, something she hadn't felt for a while. Maybe she did have a reason to go on. No, it wasn't the world, and it wasn't for her sister.

The human wanted to live so she could truly have a life. No more fears and no more suffering. It was time she wrote her own destiny.

Michelle looked up at the angel; fierce determination burned brightly in her blue eyes. Loviel was right. He may not be able to do everything, but he didn't have to. They were in this together. Neither of them had to carry the burden by themselves.

"Loviel," she grated past her drying tears, a grin appearing on her face. "Let's kick some ass."

Light turned into darkness, and there was the sound of the saddest song in all of the worlds. Michelle could feel it all return in a fraction of a second. She could feel the pain she had lived with her whole life. More than anything though, she could feel the warmth of skin touching her own. Soft tears landed on her skin, and reaching up, she touched silky hair.

Her gaze was met a pair of very familiar eyes. They were twisted in pain and red with sorrow. She had caused so much pain by leaving. No, Michelle wouldn't be doing that again. At least, not today. The girl sat up and her eyes began to thrum with power and energy. White fires burned in her soul and hot energy rolled off her skin like smoke.

She could hear a soft gasp from the body next to her. Other

sounds flooded in from all around the cave: there was anger and surprise, a scream of pure hatred, and a muted sound of amazement.

"It's okay Ravin," she spoke, reaching up to wipe the tears from his eyes. "Everything is going to be okay."

Thirty-five

Michelle stood with ease. Reaching up, she ripped the bandages off her arm and no brutal bite wound remained. Color had returned to her skin, as did the proud look in her eyes. A determined smirk appeared on her face. She felt better than she had in a long time. Ignoring Iraldin, she leaned down and kissed Ravin on his cheek.

She offered her hand to help him to his feet. It felt good being able to do that simple action. Ravin gripped onto her hand and she pulled him up. Their eyes locked for a moment, and hers spoke of soft forgiveness before she twisted around to finally give Ira her attention.

"Surprise, mother fucker," she sneered, suddenly feeling livelier than ever. "Can't kill me that easily."

A cold look filled their enemy's eyes. "I barely even tried."

Around him, darkness came alive. "You haven't even seen me start to exert myself." His shadow loomed above them, like a massive serpent ready to strike.

Michelle stood her ground as if she were facing a horde of dragons. She didn't back down and she didn't waver. Her spirit was strong and renewed. Bright lights trailed down her arms and her starry white eyes flared.

"You know..." The words rolled from her tongue, they were full of strange inhuman power. "I could say the same thing about myself." The white lights extended from her fingers and onto the ground. Spirals rolled into glowing white intricate patterns.

Illumination filled the room. It was as if a light bulb brighter than the sun had been flipped on in the air. Sweet soft music danced like a gentle breeze. Peace filled the space where fear once resided. The star that burned through the darkest night landed onto the ground. When the pure luminosity faded, all that was left was his figure. Loviel.

"Oh, I hope you don't mind I invited a friend to the party," Michelle added. "It's okay, I promise he won't finish all the cookies and punch." She looked over at Loviel, who was assessing the situation with his warm, light-filled golden eyes. His gaze landed on Iraldin. Power thrummed in the air like a lingering piano note. It didn't dissipate. The angel stood strong, wings outstretched.

This seemed to finally evoke an emotional response from Iraldin. "How?!" he demanded. In a blink, he was standing on top of the tablet between the humans. "How did you summon him?! Magic is sealed in this place!" Something dangerous glowed in his eyes.

"If you had sealed a human's innate magic, though very small…" Loviel said gently, explaining as if it were a child before him. "How would Lian be able to call Fenriel to her? A small loophole in your world to fulfill your needs has worked against you. Then again…" Loviel's voice trailed off and he looked back at his fallen brother, then to Michelle. His gaze met Iraldin's obsidian glare, "You probably didn't calculate that a human could come here without your express permission either."

Loviel tilted his head in the way a curious puppy would have. "Is that why you spared no time in removing her from the picture? Did you not know she shared a bond with an angel? You do know when our partner is in danger, we will come to them. I would assume you do. That is why you chose her sister? Because of their family line?" He sighed. "Were you so assured of your abilities that your hubris allowed me here?"

"Pride is a sin. Perhaps you will understand why," Loviel continued. His honey-sweet voice was strong and still thrumming with the power of trumpets. He commanded attention. "Because it shall soon be your undoing. My people can accept demons, though not when they threaten the balance such as this. I wish it could be another way—but I must remove you from this life."

The air settled as Loviel fell silent. Michelle couldn't help but shiver. Her angel was a total badass. Okay, she could get behind this 137 percent.

"This is my domain," the demon growled and stepped forward off of his tablet. "You have exactly twenty seconds to leave before I kill you both." There was not a glimmer of fear in his eyes. His rage seemed to pull the air from the room.

Loviel shook his head side to side, "Perhaps it is your little world, but that does not mean you hold all the power." As if to prove his point, Loviel twisted his head back and looked to where the fallen angel was bound to the wall. At the same time, the angel and Michelle's eyes flashed bright. Zier fell forward, and he was free.

"My Fallen brother," Loviel spoke, soft and gentle; his words were full of love, "are you well?"

With the grace of a cat, Zier landed on his feet. "I'm peachy," he replied coldly and brushed off his shoulders. Then he turned from Loviel and paid him no more mind. "I am going to rip out your intestines," he hissed at Iraldin.

"I would love to see you try, Fallen," Iraldin sibilated. "None of you will make it out of here." He took in a breath and sent a wave of powerful energy straight at Zier.

At the last moment the fallen angel rolled out of the way. The attack punched a dent in the floor where Zier had been standing seconds before. He tried to retaliate, but the power would not come to him. A curse left his lips as he glanced back over at Loviel. "What's your brilliant plan now?"

"Get Lian and the boy out of here," Loviel instructed. It was not so much of a command, but a strong suggestion. "It would be wise to get her to safety." He began to approach the demon at a slow, intimidating pace. Lights began to shine in both of his hands. Eyes locked on eyes. He was ready to strike.

For the first time in his life, Ravin was useless. He stood behind the human he had almost killed and put a hand on her shoulder.

"Kick his ass Michelle," Ravin urged, though he was sure to keep his gaze from Loviel. "Do you want me to stay with you?" he asked quietly, otherwise he would have to find some other way to help.

"Stay with me," she said, reaching out and taking his hand into hers.

Iraldin faced off with Loviel. "Bring it on you pathetic winged bastard," he growled and stepped towards him. The demon would not be intimidated.

A whirring sound exploded, and the first blow was struck. Loviel snapped into action and he threw a great ball of energy at their enemy. It missed, but barely. White hot energy sizzled in the air. More power welled in his hands and the angel charged forth.

While their enemy was distracted, Zier stalked slowly around the outside of the room. He sprinted when he saw his chance and put his hands on the bindings holding the humans. He snapped the fastenings on both of them.

"Up and at 'em," he grunted as he pulled them to him. Zier slung their limp bodies over his shoulders.

Lian weakly shifted and held onto the new shape. As her eyes opened, a strange sense of comfort came from being near him. Her voice could barely be heard over the sounds of blasts and energy popping. Quietly, she whispered to him, "Zier?"

"Shh," the fallen angel soothed. "You'll be safe soon."

"She wants...me to tell you," Lian continued, her voice weak and dry, "That… she loves you… and she's glad you are here… she m-misses you…" Her next words were drowned out by an explosion of power.

Zier took in a deep breath. "I miss her too," he murmured, though it was impossible to hear. "I love her more than anything." The angel quickly made his way to the passage they had come through and rested the humans on the floor to ensure that they were safe.

Loviel was doing all he could. He was very powerful, but so was Iraldin. They were mighty titans battling for the fate of all. Michelle stood with Ravin and together they could only watch as it all unfolded before them. Zier had Kaz and Lian, and Loviel had Ira. They had each other.

An unholy blast struck Loviel's beige wing, and he let out a cry of pain. Hot burning rage roared in his once serene hazel eyes. Too much was at stake for him to fail. Gritting his teeth, the angel flared his wings and a huge gust of wind tore past the demon. The gale roared through the room.

Iraldin focused his energy and split the winds in front of him. He dove through the gap and fired two blasts of pure darkness at Loviel. From a strap on his belt he pulled twin daggers and sent them flying behind the energy, but in another direction. Both flew straight at the angel's weak spot, Michelle.

Dodging to his best ability, Loviel felt the blasts on the tip of his wings. The feathers burned. He only had a moment. No, he didn't even have that. With a breath his eyes flared white and so did Michelle's. She lifted her hands. Dagger one hit an invisible barrier that gleamed at the contact. Crack. Dagger two came flying in behind it, and it shattered the defense.

Sharp pain filled her shoulder, but it would have been far worse had both hit her.

Loviel let out a cry and he grabbed his shoulder. They were linked.

"Ravin," Michelle breathed "I need you, to..." The pain made it hard to think straight. "I need you to... protect me." She looked up at him.

Loviel placed his hand on his own wound. As Michelle pulled the dagger out, the tear closed itself. Blood stained what little of her sleeve was left. The shreds left behind by the hellhound had a nice new coat of blood.

Ravin nodded and moved in front of Michelle. There was only so much he could do with his energy sealed.

A dark chuckle filled the air. Iraldin had used their momentary distraction to teleport behind the angel. He gripped onto Loviel's wings and pulled with great force. Not enough to rip them clean from his body, but the angel knew he was there.

"Your death will bring on a new era," Ira hissed and pressed a large knife into his captive's back.

Both Michelle and Loviel let out a scream.

"Brother!" Loviel cried out. Feedback rang through his words, loudly. The painful sound reverberated against the cave walls. Michelle fell into Ravin and she held onto him tight. White searing pain nearly blinded her.

In a movement that was almost too fast to see, Zier burst back into the room. His leg shot out and landed a blow into Iraldin's spine that would have broken a lesser man's back. With one hand, he grabbed the demon's skull and wrenched his head back as hard as he could. A chunk of hair came out in his hand as Iraldin disappeared.

Ira appeared across the room, his breath labored. Blood ran down the side of his face, below a ragged bald spot. There was a frenzied look in his eye as he stared at the angels.

Loviel healed the wound on his back as he pulled the knife from it. Wordlessly, he thanked Zier and panted. The Angel of Light lifted the dagger, and the blood that soaked the blade began to glow pure white. An angel's blood was a holy thing. It had the power to heal and the power to cleanse. Loviel's eyes went deadly. His once warm gold gaze was full of heavenly fury.

"This has gone on long enough," Loviel growled as he offered the blade to the fallen angel. Starry light gleamed around it. The angel put his hands together and began to chant quietly in the tongue of his people.

He figured Zier knew what to do from there.

Zier lunged one direction and then sprung forward in the other. He shot straight up to Iraldin and plunged the weapon inside of his stomach. In an act of rage, he twisted the dagger inside of his body.

Not more than two seconds later, Loviel appeared behind the demon and he placed both hands on Ira's head. He whispered quietly, and yet his words were still as powerful as a trumpet choir. Each angelic syllable he uttered tore into the darkness that was Iraldin. A bright halo formed around them, and it expanded like a lightning flash.

Blinding light filled the room.

There were two options for the demon: fight or flight. He could die, or he could flee. Whichever he chose, all that was known was that he was no longer there. Iraldin was gone.

Loviel fell forward panting and he looked up at Zier. "Get Lian and the boy out of here; bring them home. I will get the others." Though his body was worn out from the fight, Loviel still had energy. His source was the human who was laying weakly against Ravin. The angel knew he would have to take a bit more from her, but it was nearly over. After this, she could rest.

"Go," he urged Zier. "I will meet you on the other side." Loviel felt immense gratitude towards his brother, Zier. Fallen or not, Loviel would always honor him as family.

The fallen angel nodded and returned to the unconscious humans. In a blink, they were gone.

Once they had disappeared, Loviel walked up to Ravin. He placed a hand on the demon's shoulder and a kind look returned to his face. He looked back at Michelle who was holding onto Ravin, her body worn from the battle. The angel felt guilty; their connection had harmed her, but it was because of her he had been able to do anything.

"It's a pleasure to finally meet you Ravin. I've heard all about you," he said gently. "Let's head home."

Sin lounged in her office. The days had been long since the others had left. She hoped everything was okay, but since nothing had had destroyed their world, the demoness was forced to assume all was still well.

Pop!

Suddenly, there was a tall man and two humans in her office. She was relieved to see Zier, but where were the two he had left with? Sin stood and moved over to inspect her new crowd. One was Kazun. She knew him well, and the other she could only guess was Lian. Her resemblance to Michelle was striking.

"What of Ravin and Michelle?" she questioned, though she was soon answered with another pop of energy. There were now two other men in her office. It was starting to feel a bit cramped. The other was tall and very handsome, and Sin didn't like him at all. He was an Angel of Light. In his arms rested the weak frame of a human—Michelle, and beside him was Ravin.

Loviel held Michelle as if she were a child.

"Well boys," Sin sighed and looked around at all the faces in her packed office. All of them were covered with dirt, blood, and grit. "I guess I owe everyone a free drink." A grin spread across the demoness' face. It was a relief to know that everything should go back to the way it was.

"It would probably be wise to take them to a medical facility," Loviel said, his voice tired from battle.

"Proooobably," Sin mocked and tossed her holophone to Ravin. "Do you need the number for 911? Sorry, but that may cost you." She winked.

"Ha, ha, Sin," Ravin shot as he caught the phone. "I think you'll have to scam me out of my money some other way." He dialed the numbers and felt relief wash over him in a wave. For the first moment in what felt like a lifetime, he felt as though he could finally breathe.

Perhaps everything would be okay.

Epilogue

Michelle sat on the swing and watched as Lian played in the park. The sun shone brightly and the birds chirped in happy choir. It was a beautiful crisp early winter day, if she had ever seen one. Lian was starting to come out of her shell; weeks had passed since everything that had happened. Maybe the cause was the fact that Iraldin couldn't hurt her anymore, or maybe it was because she had her own guardian angel. Whatever the case, Michelle was relieved.

Things were peaceful now, despite everything that had happened. Sure, Michelle had failed all of her classes because of it, but the break was nice. Honestly, even if her teachers had believed she had helped save the world from a dark angel, she wouldn't want to go back. Right now, all she needed was rest. Her body had been used as a pin cushion. This was a hard-earned break from life.

Suddenly her sunshine was gone and a shadow cast itself over her. Slowly, she looked up and smiled, "You're blocking the sun, Ravin."

"My bad," Ravin chuckled and plopped into the seat beside her. "Is that better?" he asked, and pushed himself back bit to sway like a pendulum.

The girl thought about it for a long moment. She put her finger to her chin and tapped it lazily, building dramatic effect. She sighed, "I gueeessss." Her voice were warm. Michelle held out her hand to the demon, and he reached out and took it in his own.

"So, everything goes back to normal?" she asked him. "We get to be crazy college students?"

He nodded and stroked the back of her hand with his thumb. "We get to be the craziest college students. Everything is how it should be," he confirmed. "Though, it's less normal now, because you can say that you've saved the world, even if no one believes you."

Happy laughter escaped her lips and she nodded.

"Yeah, I'm pretty important," she declared. It was nice to not have any real worries. Sure, the fallen angel would want to free Fenriel at some point, but they'd cross that bridge when they came to it. For now, Michelle could be happy; she could focus on living. It was nice not having to stress about Lian's safety. Not that she had ever minded, but the fact was, her sister looked a lot happier as she played on the merry-go-round with the human boy and her fallen angel.

"Were you surprised by how badass Loviel was?" She swayed;

it was nice that her angel didn't mind the demon who had swiftly become one of her best friends.

"I was." It was hard for the demon to admit that. Loviel had turned out to be a surprisingly great guy too. "He's not at all what I expected an angel to be. He's lent me a bunch of music and all of it is perfect." He gave Michelle a broad grin.

The girl giggled, "He sings in the shower, and I think I should sell tickets, 'cause I could make a fortune." Amusement sparkled in her bright blue eyes. More than anything, she liked being able to sit here in the sun with Ravin, hold hands and chatting about nothing really important.

A smirk touched his features. "We would make so much money." He chuckled. "We should start right away." The demon leaned over and kissed her cheek gently. As he did, he could feel the warmth of a blush against his lips.

"This is so weird," he murmured and rested his head against the chain that held up his seat.

"What is?" Michelle questioned, looking over at him.

"This." He gestured at the two of them. "I've never actually felt like this before." Ravin shrugged. "It wasn't particularly encouraged in the life I've lived the last few centuries."

"We've been through a lot together over a pretty short period of time," she responded, feeling rational about the whole situation. It would be nearly impossible to go through what they had and not feel close... right? Right. She bobbed her head in a matter-of-fact way.

Ravin nodded in agreement. "Yes, but it feels different, I don't know how to explain it." He ran his free hand through his blonde hair.

Michelle shrugged her shoulders and squeezed his hand softly. Maybe it was a mystery, but she would enjoy it while she could. Staring blankly into the distance, her thoughts wandered away. Loviel had given her more time, but eventually her bones would erode away again. He couldn't stop it forever and only she and the angel knew that. More than anything, she wanted to enjoy what time she had left.

"Well, whatever the reason, I am glad for it." Her blue eyes glowed in the winter sun. "It's nice having someone fun to spend my time with." Michelle winked and returned the kiss to his cheek, she enjoyed the rough feeling of stubble against her skin. The girl felt drawn to him, and she was happy he seemed to feel the same about her.

The demon looked over at the younger humans and their peculiar companion as they frolicked. "Lian seems to have taken to Zier well," he remarked.

"I know. I'm surprised. I would have thought tall, dark, and intimidating would have scared her," Michelle agreed as she watched Lian hide behind Zier as they played their game. It was like she was using him as a protective base so Kazun couldn't tag her. It was sort of heart-warming, like puppies frolicking.

"It's too sweet, I think I'm going to implode." Ravin clutched jokingly at his heart. "We're going to see a lot more of him in the future, I think. So, I'm glad he's playing nice with all of us."

"Me too," Michelle nodded. "Especially with Lian... I mean... he could be forcing her to try and free Fenriel, but... he seems to be giving her a bit of space about it. For the moment anyway." She watched as Lian fell and scraped her knee on the ground. Both of the males were at her side immediately. Michelle couldn't help but beam.

At least she knew that once she was gone, Lian was going to have people taking care of her. That relieved a lot of tension. Michelle stood up and pulled on Ravin's hand until he got up with her. She looked up at him, and her eyes shining in the sunlight.

"Everything isn't okay," she said and kissed the back of his hand. "Everything is perfect."

About the Authors

The Eden R. Souther duo, Brennan and Nicholas, have been writing together since 2007. They've perfected a synchronistic style and have collaborated on many projects together.

Angel Syndrome is their first novel, but they also have many more in the works. This team cherishes the art of storytelling, and bringing magic to life.

Made in the USA
Columbia, SC
29 March 2018